Also by Robert Andrews

The Village War
Center Game
Last Spy Out
To Kill the Hangman
   (a screenplay, with Victor Gold)

DEATH
IN A
PROMISED
LAND

ROBERT ANDREWS

POCKET BOOKS

New York   London   Toronto   Sydney   Tokyo   Singapore

This book is a work of fiction. Names, characters, places, and incidents are either products of the author's imagination or are used fictitiously. Any resemblance to actual events or locales or persons, living or dead, is entirely coincidental.

 POCKET BOOKS, a division of Simon & Schuster Inc.
1230 Avenue of the Americas, New York, NY 10020

ISBN: 0-671-86648-6

First Pocket Books hardcover printing May 1993

10 9 8 7 6 5 4 3 2 1

Printed in the U.S.A.

This is for

Private William Barnes
Sergeant Powathan Beaty
First Sergeant James Bronson
Sergeant Major Christian Fleetwood
Private James Gardiner
Sergeant James Harris
Sergeant Major Thomas Hawkins
Sergeant Alfred Hilton
Sergeant Major Milton Holland
Corporal Miles James
First Sergeant Alexander Kelly
First Sergeant Robert Pinn
First Sergeant Edward Ratcliff
Private Charles Veal

3d Division, U.S. Colored Troops

who won the Medal of Honor
at the battle of New Market Heights, Virginia,
29 September 1864.

Acknowledgments

This book owes much to many others. First and above all, there is B.J., who kept the book and me moving along. She was there during the exciting months as the two of us tracked the footsteps of real and imaginary characters through coffee shops in Vienna, snowstorms in Toronto, and the last Communist days of Prague and East Berlin. But she was also there in my darker times, keeping her faith in the book when I had lost mine.

I'm reserving a special place in the writers' pantheon for my daughter Elizabeth, who patiently read one rewrite after another, gently commented, and buckled down to read again. She is joined by Marci Robinson, Kathy Hill, Sally Squires and John Wilhelm, and Michelle Van Cleave, who listened, read, and enriched the story. And a place too for my extraordinary agent, Lila Karpf, and for Vic Gold, who took the sting out of the word *rewrite*.

Elizabeth Bancroft, keeper of the National Intelligence Book Center, guarded many of her secrets but nonetheless shared a special few, and revealed a hidden talent for editing as well.

The detailed research owes much to Paul Joyal, now in the international security business, who dug deep to come up with such exotica as the King autopsy reports, ballistics tests, and Dan Rather's interview with James Earl Ray. And a special thanks to Judy Edelhof, who steered me through the National Archives and the King files, and to Marilyn and Gerry Moon, ex-LAPD, and Detective George Ward, District of Columbia Metropolitan Police, who patiently instructed me on police procedures.

Gulfstream Aerospace's chief pilot, Howard Hackney, introduced me to the wonders of the Gulfstream IV, without question the world's most erotic flying machine. Jack Keliher kept me straight on my military history and the U.S. Army regimental system.

Josh Muravchik said at the very beginning something was there.

Carl Watt worked valiantly to keep my Russia, Russian, and Russians straight. The successes are his; any failures are mine. George Weigel's and John Kester's regular applications of wit and wisdom helped see this through.

And a special access thanks to _____, _____, and _____, who are still at CIA and the FBI.

Author's Note

Secrets remain about the assassination of Dr. Martin Luther King, Jr. These secrets have frustrated many, including Taylor Branch, a noted authority on the King years. In his Pulitzer Prize-winning book, *Parting the Waters*, Branch recounts that

> Since 1984, I have sought the original FBI documents pertaining to the Bureau's steadfast contention that King's closest white friend was a top-level Communist agent. On this charge rested the FBI's King wiretaps and many collateral harassments against the civil rights movement. In opposing my request, the U.S. Department of Justice has argued in federal court that the release of thirty- to thirty-five-year-old informant reports . . . would damage the national security even now.
>
> Almost certainly, there is bureaucratic defensiveness at work here . . . *and also, I suspect, some petty spy rivalry with the CIA—but so far the logic of secrecy has been allowed to reach levels of royalist absurdity.* [Emphasis added.]

Branch has learned that governments have secrets they wish to keep forever buried. But he is wrong as to why this is so. Rivalries and sensitivities about sources and methods obviously play a role.

What Branch misses is that there are secrets that, if revealed, would inescapably alter the world in which we live.

This is a story about such secrets. It is, of course, fiction.

Robert Andrews
Washington, D.C.

Let me not die ingloriously and without struggle,
but let me first do some great things
that shall be told among men thereafter.

Homer
The Iliad

DEATH
IN A
PROMISED
LAND

———

Memphis, Tennessee
Thursday, April 4, 1968

The barrel slipped neatly into the fiberglass bed of the wooden stock. He tightened the two bolts; one, then the other, meticulously checking the torque dial on the small stainless-steel wrench. Next came the Unertl scope, a long black tube that hovered above the barrel of the Winchester.

Crossing the room, he carefully slid a large cardboard box from the closet. He laid the contents onto a cheap bedspread on the floor. From a pocket, he took a small notebook, searched for a page, and went over the list. There was the rifle, a Gamemaster, he noted with contempt. Then the other things—the binoculars, cartridges, transistor radio, and toilet articles.

Humming quietly under his breath, he gathered the corners of the bedspread and tied them securely. He jerked the bundle vigorously up and down. Satisfied, he placed it next to the door to the hallway.

The room's single window framed the motel balcony beyond. The man stared at it as he went quickly through the shooter's calculus. Distance: 207 feet. Light: good. Wind: six knots right to left.

He checked his watch, consulted the notebook, then looked again at the watch. They were scheduled to leave for dinner at six. Fifteen minutes. He fished in his pocket and came up with an old stick of gum, unwrapped it, and slipped it into his mouth. It was brittle and cracked as he bit into it. He worked it around in his mouth until it softened. He carefully rolled the wrapper into a tight ball and jammed it deep into his trousers pocket, then stood motionless, chewing the gum, occasionally stretching his shoulders in a rolling shrugging motion.

Ten minutes later, he lifted a heavy sandbag from the floor and positioned it in the middle of the table. He pulled over the chair from the desk, and sat down. He leaned forward, elbows on the table, and nested the butt of the Winchester stock into his shoulder. With small sawing motions, he worked the front handrest of the rifle into the sandbag, giving himself a solid rest. The wind had dropped slightly.

He began his slow-breathing ritual. As he did so, he conjured up the image of his nerves as rubber bands, loosening, loosening.

He watched through the window as two men across the way came out of a room together, one putting final adjustments to his tie. They stood on the balcony, finishing a conversation. Then one went down the stairs.

His heartbeat caused the scope crosshairs to rise, then fall. He let out a breath, deliberately took another, and slowly let half that out.

The man in the scope stood at the railing, looking down into the courtyard. He was talking to someone, making a gesture. Smiling.

The crosshairs steadied.

At 6:01 P.M. Ralph Abernathy heard the sharp report. Rushing onto the balcony, he saw the sprawled body and the awful blood. "Oh my God," he shouted. "Martin's been shot!"

1

Washington, D.C.
Friday, December 27, 1991

The conspiracies that killed Martin Luther King started unraveling two days after the Soviet Union ceased to exist.

It began among ill-tempered knots of commuters packing the Foggy Bottom Metro station. In their post-Christmas letdown, most Washingtonians had taken a disappearing Soviet Union in stride and were now absorbed with the more immediate issue of next week's playoffs between the Redskins and the Falcons.

Suddenly, protests rippled through the crowd as a slender middle-aged man frantically elbowed his way onto a departing train. Seconds later, and laboring for breath, his ears popped as the subway passed beneath the Potomac. Another minute, and the train slowed, coming to a stop at Rosslyn. The doors opened and he waited, coiled and tense, for the sound of the door chimes signaling last call. Springing from his seat, he charged the closing doors, stumbling through them, landing on the platform as the train pulled away.

He scanned the crowd, sweeping his head in the quick nervousness of the frightened. He abruptly stiffened—he saw one of the followers, the short, powerfully built red-haired man.

A cramping pain in his leg fueled his desperation as he ran to the base of the escalators. The moving stairs ceaselessly fed upward into a concrete tube, conveyors into a dark gray gullet. For a moment, the man considered turning back. He could surrender to them and have it all over and done with. There was an attraction to it. Up the escalators lay the unknown.

He shook the temptation; it was the lure of suicide, and he wasn't ready for that. He hesitated for perhaps a second more, then began

3

bounding up the escalator two steps at a time. Soon his heart was at the bursting point.

Near the top, two navy officers stood shoulder to shoulder talking, blocking the way. Muttering an apology, he pushed roughly by them, leaving them cursing and following him angrily with their eyes.

He stabbed his fare card at the turnstile slot, but it bent and refused to go in. Over his shoulder he saw the red-haired man brushing by the navy officers. He vaulted the turnstile. Behind him, his follower soon cleared the turnstiles. To his right, a Metro security guard, some fifty feet away, shouted and started making his way toward the two of them.

The fear of communal involvement caused the crowd to part. To his front, only two figures stood between him and the street exit: a tall, athletic black male and a cowering Latin charwoman. He cut toward the woman, hearing the follower's footsteps coming closer.

Sims had been waiting as planned, just inside the exit. He first heard the Metro guard's shout. Then he saw the man run past him. The face matched the photographs, profile and full front. No doubt. None at all. Close behind, Sims saw a red-haired man, obviously in pursuit, claw inside his overcoat.

Sims twisted violently to his right and wrenched the wet mop from the charwoman's pail. Planting his right foot, he swung with all his strength. The mop caught the red-haired man in the jaw, snapping his head back. A heavy blue automatic flew from the man's hand and clattered across the concrete floor. The charwoman began a high-pitched scream.

Sims threw the mop to the floor and ran out to the sidewalk. Pausing only a second to get his bearings, he dashed into the busy street, barely dodging a speeding delivery van. Across, he lunged and pinned the running man against the wall of an office building. He grappled for the man's wrist, found it, and brought it up behind his back, lifting the man to his toes.

"Miloslav Valek?"

The man—Valek—breathless, his face bathed in sweat, turned wide-eyed to Sims. It was the black from the subway! He nodded fearfully, unable to talk.

"CIA," Sims said in Czech. "I'm your friend. Come with me or they'll kill you."

Sims pushed the man back toward the nearby intersection. Just as the light turned green, Sims wrenched open the door of a taxi. The driver and his passenger, both startled, started to protest.

"Shut up!" Sims shoved Valek into the backseat, then threw himself into the front seat with the driver.

"Fort Myer," he ordered. Sims looked out the rear window. Behind him, two men stood on the sidewalk outside the Metro entrance, searching the street. One pointed, then both started running toward Sims and the cab.

"Go!" Sims shouted.

"Fella, you in some kinda trouble?" whined the cabby.

Sims's left hand found the cabby's neck. "No trouble at all if you move this thing." For emphasis, he squeezed the cabby's carotid artery between thumb and forefinger.

Tires screeching, the cab made the corners through Rosslyn, then labored up the slope of Arlington Ridge.

"Right here." The cabby made the turn and started to stop at a military police gatehouse.

"Go through!"

"But . . ."

Sims squeezed the cabby's neck again. The cab accelerated. As they careened by the gatehouse, a startled sergeant blew his whistle and simultaneously began fumbling for his pistol.

"OK, mister, *now* stop," Sims ordered. The cab was inside the gate. Sims got out. From a nearby ready-room, military police in battle dress sprinted toward Sims and the car.

Outside the gate, another cab screeched to a stop. The MPs apparently were enough to cause second thoughts. The cab wheeled a U-turn and was gone.

Sims slowly raised his hands. Six rifle muzzles eyed him. He gave a smile of relief and gestured into the cab with a casualness he didn't feel. "I'd appreciate it if you'd call your duty officer," he told the sergeant from the gatehouse. "We've got a visitor from Moscow here."

Bradford Sims finished shaving and leaned into the mirror. Women had said it was a strong face; a few had gone so far as to describe it as handsome. A thick black mustache framed his generous mouth. The family nose had taken a beating in thirty-five years, he mused, pinching the spreading nostrils together. The football dings—dueling scars above the eyes and along the cheekbones—only showed on closer inspection: darker ridges against an otherwise smooth milk chocolate skin.

Sims touched the half-moon on his right cheek with a grin of proprietary satisfaction. That was from a particularly nasty Delaware defensive end. Four plays later, he had run over that son of a bitch, throwing an especially satisfying elbow that had rearranged some dental work.

His eyes dropped to more serious scars, like the puckered mass of tissue at his left shoulder. That had come on an entirely different playing field.

It had been a year of upheavals. Less than seven months ago, he had been in Prague station, feeding headquarters the first reports of high-level dissatisfaction with Gorbachev and whispers of growing unrest in the western Ukraine. His reports had gotten all the way to the president, who used them to warn an unbelieving Gorbachev. Then came the August coup, and rumors that Gorbachev's enemies had made a deal with the Ukrainian nationalists.

Headquarters had then wanted everything, anything. Janik was his opposite number in Czechoslovakia's new, democratic, thoroughly incompetent intelligence service. They could meet with the Ukrainian resistance, Janik had promised with confidence; he could arrange a meeting on the Czech side of the river.

Headquarters had said no border crossings. But he and Janik had gotten to the Uzh and there had been no choice. Janik's contacts weren't coming across. Stay in Czechoslovakia and get nothing or take your chances in the USSR. Sims still remembered pulling on the oars against the swift current, hiding the rowboat, and making the fearsome trek through the tangled underbrush.

Everything that could go wrong did. Botched recognition signals with the Ukrainians, sloppy radio procedures, zero light discipline, no perimeter security. The MVD border guards had been on to them almost from the beginning.

Janik took the first bullet in the gut. The second shot had hit Sims's shoulder. Sims had lifted the Czech into a fireman's carry and made it back to the rowboat. Just ahead of the Russians—he had thought. Not far enough ahead. He now slowly raised his left arm. No pain, just a slight grinding.

He had thought it was a colossal fuck-up. Headquarters had chosen to see it differently. The after-action report cited the documents Sims had swept up as the MVD closed in. The Ukrainian resistance held the plotters in even higher contempt than they did Gorbachev. More-over, from his captivity in the Crimea, Gorbachev had managed to get out a secret—and sweeter—offer to the Ukrainians: indepen-dence. Because of Sims, the Agency had been able to beat out DIA and NSA in warning the White House and Congress of the coup plotters' weakness. The White House, originally disposed to recognize the coup, trimmed its sails, hedged a bit, then came out against the coup. Now *that* accounted for something on the seventh floor, particularly when it came time to justify next year's budget.

They had patched him up and flown him directly back to Washington. The orthopods at Bethesda Naval Hospital had fixed the shoulder as well as it would ever be fixed, which was good enough unless he wanted to go back into serious football.

Two days after his operation, there was a small ceremony in Sims's guarded room. The director of Central Intelligence—the Judge—promoted him. Then while the Judge and Riddle stood at an uneasy semblance of military attention, Cantwell read the citations for the medals. There was the Intelligence Star ("for acts of courage performed under hazardous conditions") and the Exceptional Service Medallion ("for injury resulting from service in an area of hazard").

Cantwell read well, his voice burring with emotion at just the right break points. The citations were a smooth flow of devotions to duty, bravery above and beyond, and reflections of great honor on the intelligence service.

Sims felt tempted to interrupt, to tell them that it had been none of that: It had been a night that began in foolishness and ended in fear. But of course he said nothing.

The Judge didn't pin the medals on; he clumsily laid them on Sims's pajama top. The medals had to go back to Langley, back to a vault with other medals for other secret acts. Riddle, the Judge, and Cantwell were the only witnesses to the presentation. But something like the ceremony couldn't remain secret for long in a building filled with fifteen thousand spies. Upon his return to Langley, Sims was treated with a new deference. Colin Powell had been the first black to be Chairman of the Joint Chiefs. The current Langley line had it that if a black man could make it to director of Central Intelligence, it would be Bradford Sims.

He looked at himself for a long moment. The grinding shoulder reminded him of the thinness of life. After the Uzh, it seemed to Sims that he would sometimes catch himself moving more cautiously, as if once damaged, he could be more easily damaged the next time. As he thought about it, he unconsciously clenched his fist to stop his hand from trembling.

"Miloslav Valek," he said to his reflection, getting his mind off the fear. He was now Valek's case officer. Responsibility for Valek's interrogation and debrief—fine. That was part of basic counterintelligence. But he wasn't happy with the rest of it.

After being wrung out, Valek would need hand holding and resettlement. Sims dreaded the prospect, seeing to the logistics involved. New identities meant not only driver's license, voter registration, and Social Security account; he would also have to attend to such touches as fabricating a credit history. Even more difficult, he would have to find something in America for a former KGB spy to do for the rest of his life.

The tar baby principle at work—he grimaced—the first person to touch an unpopular job gets stuck with seeing it through. He had been the only Czech-speaking officer on watch when Valek had dialed one of Langley's better-known trouble numbers and announced he was coming over. Valek had been in a hurry. He had blurted his name, the Rosslyn subway station, and the approximate time, and then hung up. The watch officer had beckoned to Sims. There had been no time to work out even the most rudimentary recognition scheme—Valek was on his way.

"Bradford Sims"—he gave himself a highball salute—"baby-sitter." He made a mental note to think about some way to shift Valek's resettling onto the shoulders of some unsuspecting junior officer.

Minutes later, Sims left his apartment building. The air was crisp and tingled deep in his lungs. Not for the first time, he savored a gratifying sense of arrival. After all, upper Connecticut Avenue was the refuge of Old Washington establishment, the home of the aristocratic white cave dwellers, a canyon of baroque and carefully tended apartment buildings built before World War II. He had managed the down payment through his mother's insurance and the sale of her small house over in Southeast. Now, with a glow of well-being, he started for the underground garage.

Someone was behind him. He turned and gave a perfunctory nod. It was a well-dressed white man of about fifty. Sims had often seen him in the building but had never learned his name. Just someone you always seemed to catch in the act of going somewhere.

"Sir? Pardon me, sir." It was a tentative, uncertain voice.

Sims turned toward the street, toward the voice.

The car had Iowa plates. The man driving was leaning across a woman to call through the window. Sims stepped across the sidewalk to the curb. A few feet from the car, he saw the woman shift her widening eyes to him. He felt his face flush as he realized they had been calling to the white man who had been standing near him. The woman began cranking up the window.

Sims walked more slowly, putting on a smile. He stopped at what he judged to be a reassuring distance from the car and, hands on knees, bent forward toward the small opening the woman had left in the window. After their question, he politely gave directions, then stood watching as they left.

Minutes later, driving to Langley, Sims summoned back the woman's vacuous face as a target for his anger. But he couldn't hold the face together; it kept dissolving. There was nothing special about the Iowa couple. In all likelihood, they were dull people trapped in dull lives. Even so, he would have done almost anything for the woman to have left the window down.

A cold realization slithered into his consciousness: He wasn't angry at the tourists. He was angry at himself, for having wanted their acceptance. The wanting gave whites a power over him. They went away stronger while he was sapped by the corrosive poisons of failure and inferiority.

"You make yourself," his father had drummed into him. His father the Korean War vet and D.C. cop. "Nobody will push you harder than you can yourself. And if you don't push, nobody else'll give a damn." Then, like fathers do, he contradicted himself and pushed. Country came first, then family, then school and sports. After his father's death, his mother, his uncle, and the good sisters took over. The streets never had a chance.

He began writing for his school newspaper. He still had the articles his mother had proudly clipped and framed to hang in her living room. His English teacher aimed him toward Georgetown and his coach saw to a small scholarship. His uncle had wanted him to go into the ministry; his mother, medicine. He had chosen neither.

His journey to the Agency had begun, unknown to him at the time, in his junior year. Zuckerman, his faculty advisor in European studies, had asked him to drop by. There was a part-time job available, Zuckerman had explained, one passed to him by an old friend. It was in an obscure government agency, one that's not political. Zuckerman said *political* with palpable distaste.

He had done nothing until Zuckerman later asked about it. More to please him than anything else, Sims decided to apply. A brass plaque on an old Massachusetts Avenue mansion said Media Analysis Service. Inside, he met a large round man named Riddle and learned that the work, which involved cataloging foreign broadcast transcripts, paid well enough. And so he spent several hours a day in a stuffy office filled with old ladies who scissored and photocopied, clipped and filed.

Riddle came by occasionally to check on Sims's work. Gradually, his visits grew more frequent and his questions more pointed. "Your résumé says you play chess," Riddle commented one afternoon. Sims was startled and overcompensated by nodding too vigorously. "Come," Riddle commanded, walking toward his office. Riddle, of course, won.

Riddle resembled a great unmade bed. His fair-complexioned face ran to chins and jowls, with unmanageable tangles of gray hair springing like barbed wire from his pink scalp. His suits were stretched shapeless by his lumpy body and his constant rummaging through overstuffed pockets for pale blue index cards on which he was forever making notes.

However rumpled, Riddle still struck an unmistakable note of fastidiousness. He was always immaculately shaved, his skin a taut, almost bristling, ruddiness. Only the slightest web of wrinkles made its way about his hazel eyes. And while a shambles, his clothing was impeccably clean. A discreet peek at a label would reveal they had been expensively tailored during one of Riddle's many passages through London. The nails of his oddly delicate hands were carefully manicured, and his shoes showed the burnishing care of Meltonian cream and a soft horsehair brush.

The following year, a senior and facing graduation, Sims began his job search. By this time, he had begun to win at chess. Not often, but enough to keep Riddle on guard. They still played in Riddle's office, but there were also games on park benches over the lunch hour or at a coffee shop near Eastern Market on Thursday evenings. On one such evening, Riddle looked up and somewhat vaguely recommended an interview with "a government board."

Sims had been mildly surprised to see Zuckerman on the board. With, of course, Riddle.

For weeks thereafter, a blur of nameless people poked and prodded him. There were psychological batteries in Georgetown town houses, physicals in sterile offices across the river in Rosslyn, and finally, hours in the coils of the polygraph—disembodied voices asking questions while a machine assayed his skin, breath, and heart for truthfulness.

Then, for weeks, nothing. No calls, no official letters. Arriving home after classes one afternoon, he found in the mail a small square envelope. The address was scripted in a tiny, meticulous copperplate hand, as was the invitation to dinner on the stiff white card inside.

La Brasserie was in an old brick town house on Capitol Hill. The restaurant's neighbors were a seedy law office that was never open and a convenience store in front of which police cars always double-parked. Riddle's Sunday dinner table was tucked away in a small room near the bar and just off the kitchen.

After the grilled salmon, Riddle sighed, touched the napkin delicately to his lips, and dropped his hand into a coat pocket. Among his many blue index cards, he found a plain envelope.

"An offer," he had said, handing the envelope to Sims. "Read the terms and conditions. You may accept or not, but in any case, you must return that to me."

Riddle's—the Agency's—offer was one among many. He should have turned it down. A New York investment firm and several *Fortune* 500 companies held out the prospects of a helluva lot more money. But there was a tug to the Agency that wasn't there with the others.

It was an ill-defined restlessness that finally nudged Sims toward CIA. Whenever he pictured himself in banking or business, alarms rang. He didn't want to spend a lifetime with people who went to the same office every day; men and women who got turned on fantasizing about the next quarter's increase in return on equity. CIA promised nearly nothing, yet between the lines of their bland brochures, he read a secret invitation to those to whom winning still meant something, to those who thought there was something special about running along the edge.

At the Farm for career training, his aptitude tests pointed to Eastern European languages. Prague followed, then CI—counterintelligence, spying in order to catch other spies. Czechoslovakia ended with the operation on the Uzh and that led to the medals, the stiff grinding shoulder, and the reception for Miloslav Valek in the Rosslyn Metro. All of which came around to today, his driving to work like hundreds of thousands of Washington's commuters.

Twenty minutes after walking away from the Iowa tourists, he drove into Virginia over the Chain Bridge. On his left, the Potomac rushed through a granite gorge. Morning mists clouded the river, creating the illusion of an ancient wilderness. Whipping his vintage Mercedes through the turns on Chain Bridge Road, past the homes of senators, ambassadors, and real estate speculators, he crossed over the George Washington Parkway before turning onto the road leading to CIA headquarters.

At the first gate, Sims slipped his plastic badge through a scanner, waved to the policeman on duty, and drove through. Ten miles downriver, the crumbling gray heap of the Pentagon suffered under the flight path from National Airport and the noise and fumes of the Shirley Highway, but here pristine glass and alabaster buildings shared a wooded park neatly defined by quiet tree-lined drives.

Through two more checkpoints and finally at his desk, he opened his work file on Miloslav Valek. The defector was still in prelim phase: medical and psychiatric exams. Next, Valek would write his personal history. That could take a week. During that time, Valek would be in the hands of the security goons, the baby-sitters. Meanwhile, Sims had his work cut out for him, getting ready for the big event: the first in-depth interrogation.

First interrogation sets the pace for everything that follows. Let a defector get a run on you, set the agenda, and you'd be chasing him forever. Success depends on an apparent contradiction: going into the first interrogation smarter than the defector.

He did not have the luxury of working at his desk, as did the analysts in the geographical divisions. CI's computers were linked into the core of the Agency's deepest and most sensitive files. And because the newest of the Agency's growth industries was spying on other people's computers, CI was careful to guard its own.

The computer was one of four in a tiny windowless room. Entering the room was like going into a freezer locker. Its single thick door, the walls, ceiling, and floors were insulated with nonconducting felt and then sheathed in a thin copper foil that was randomly charged with a veritable tempest of darting electrons.

He logged on, called up the files search program, entered Valek's name, and leaned against the high back of the chair to watch the monitor. Within seconds, the screen flashed a short menu. There were two files on Miloslav Valek—201 and 303; 201 meant personnel and 303, operations. That the Agency already had biographical information on Valek meant the defector had figured in earlier Agency activities.

Sims highlighted the 201 offering and clicked the mouse. The screen popped up the first section, general personal data. Miloslav NMN (no middle name) Valek: born 23 November 1933. Place of birth: Tisovec.

A town in Slovakia, Sims bet himself. He clicked the mouse in rapid succession, and a map of Czechoslovakia replaced the 201. A bright arrow pointed to Tisovec—in Slovakia. "OK," he whispered in victory.

He clicked the mouse again and went back to the 201. Blocks for Valek's physical data, citizenship, education, languages, foreign travel—all the bits and pieces intelligence agencies found useful to know about their opponents as well as their own officers and agents. There also would be many pages behind the one on the screen. He uncapped a fountain pen and began making notes.

An hour later, he glanced through his notes, scrolled through the computer pages of the 201, and pushed away from the console. He stood, groaning in the pleasure of stretching his cramped back. He noticed an alphanumeric reference at the bottom of the 201's last page. Still standing, he keyed in the letters and numbers of the reference. The screen flickered and came up with a name. He wrote it on the legal pad: Edward C. Houghton.

Settling back into the chair, he called up the 303 operations file. Here was message traffic between headquarters and the field about Valek. He noted from the summary that all the field reporting was from Prague station. The first report was a station recruiting recommendation. Someone in Prague had wanted to make a run at Valek. Sims flashed through the subsequent messages, a dialogue between Langley and Prague. Apparently both headquarters and the station had wanted the Czech, but nothing had come of it. Sims was not surprised to see that the Prague officer was Houghton, the chief of station, the one who had built Valek's 201.

Sims ate a quick lunch alone in South cafeteria. He sat for a moment over his tray. Outside the window, a slow rain was sifting through the pines. The gray skies turned the grass a Day-Glo green. He felt a familiar sense of loss; he often thought of his father's death, which had occurred when he was just twelve years old. Even then he had beat his fists against the iron irreversibility of time. The first night after, he had cried himself to sleep, trying to make sense of a present and future without a father when only the day before his father had been beside him. It had seemed impossible that a man so strong and invincible—so *good*—could suddenly just not be. He often fantasized that he could turn the corner in the twisting corridor behind him— *just* behind him—and find that time when his father was still alive.

It had never left him, the reflex to search the past to understand the present. History didn't interest him so much as human motives. That's what was bothering him now, he decided. The lifeless files had given him little insight into Valek, no grit or sense of texture.

He left the cafeteria toying with a half-formed thought. What about Houghton, the Prague chief of station? Where is he now? Instead of taking the elevator to his fifth-floor office, he took the stairs to the second floor. He found a door marked DA/P, the personnel division of the administration directorate.

A receptionist steered him to a files clerk. He explained to her that he wanted to know the status of Edward C. Houghton. She entered the name on her console and after a few moments looked up at Sims and shook her head. "Try retired," Sims urged. She made another entry, then shook her head again. "Deceased?" Another entry: negative.

"Check 1967," Sims told her, thinking that Houghton had certainly been in the Agency throughout that year. Wrong.

"Perhaps I've entered it incorrectly," the clerk suggested. She spelled out the name and raised her eyebrows inquisitively at Sims.

She had it right. He gestured toward her computer. "You have them all?"

"Why, yes," she said resolutely. Then, thinking about it, she narrowed her eyes. "Well—I suppose so," she said with less conviction.

Sims knew what she was thinking. The Agency kept all information separated in compartments, like the watertight compartments of a ship. And for the same reason. If one compartment was breached, the result might be serious, but the other compartments could keep it from being fatal. But the ship analogy wasn't a perfect one; all hands on a ship knew the ship's compartments. At the Agency, you never could be sure you knew everything. Quite the opposite. You could only be sure you *didn't* know everything. And, of course, you never knew what you didn't know.

The clerk pointed toward a glassed-in cubicle, one among many in the large bull pen office suite. "You could check there," she suggested.

In the cubicle, her chair tilted back and her feet on the desk, a tall, attractive woman had a phone at her ear and an impatient frown on her face. Her plastic nameplate identified her as Walker. She waved Sims in, at the same time swinging her feet to the floor.

Walker nodded at Sims over the mouthpiece of the phone.

Sims introduced himself. "I'm looking for an Agency officer," he explained. "Probably retired. Houghton, Edward C." He motioned toward the clerk outside. "We didn't have any luck."

Walker held the phone away from her ear and her frown deepened.

"I spend my life on hold." She tossed the offending instrument into its cradle, picked up a pencil, and looked up at Sims. "Spell it, the name."

Sims did, and Walker jotted it down. She swiveled her chair around to a keyboard and monitor, and tapped in the name. After several tries, she looked at Sims. "I need your badge number."

"Badge number?" asked Sims, exasperated. She nodded and waited. Sims gave in. He watched her as she tapped in the number. Late twenties, early thirties, Sims guessed. Sleek, smooth, and *very* nice.

"You're CI?" She looked at Sims for confirmation. "Date of birth and Social Security?" She waited.

Stealing a look at her legs, it took Sims a moment to realize she was talking to him, then, flushing, he answered. Walker seemed not to notice. She checked the screen, then nodded as his access was approved. She gave Sims a sizing-up look. "Marital status?"

Without thinking, Sims turned and answered, "Single." Then, catching on: "What's that for?"

Walker smiled. "For me."

Sims tried to catch her eyes and smile back, but she was already back at the keyboard, intent on the computer screen before her. Finally she turned to him.

"Houghton. Edward Cameron. He was one of ours."

"Why the problem outside?"

"Outside"—Walker pointed to the clerk—"they just list active, retired, and former."

"Well?"

"Well, your friend Houghton was fired."

Sims took that in. Walker had made it sound as if Sims had been hanging out with bad company. "What for?"

"For the convenience of the service." Walker shook her head. "That's all it says." She paused and eyed Sims. "That's all it is necessary to say."

She was right, Sims knew. Unlike every other American government agency, CIA could let you go on a moment's notice. No appeal, no civil service board, nothing. For the convenience of the service.

Sims stopped on his way out. "By the way, when did they fire him?"

Walker punched the computer. "Sixty-eight. June '68."

He nodded. She turned back to her telephone, thinking he had gone. Looking up, she was surprised to see him still standing there. "Marital status?" he asked her.

She smiled. "See you around?" Her voice was smoky; burgundy.

He returned the smile. "Hope so."

For the next hour, Sims noodled around at his desk, unsuccessfully trying to draft a strategy for the Valek interrogation. He couldn't get started. The Houghton matter kept coming back to him, begging for completion, like a book missing its last pages. "Damn," he muttered to himself, and capped his fountain pen.

"Be gone long?" asked his secretary, Jo, as he left.

"Back to the computer room. Something I didn't finish."

Minutes later, the computer screen cast a graveyard glow in the small room. A highlighted box now centered Houghton's name at the top of the screen. Beneath was a chronological listing of documents that the search program unearthed. By each date was a short title, a files designator, and the geographic origin of the document.

Sims moved the highlight bar down the list to the first entry and clicked the mouse. The first page of the document flashed onto the monitor. It was a surveillance report, signed Edward Houghton, Budapest station, March 1951. Probably his first assignment, Sims guessed, just after finishing the Farm and advanced training. He clicked the mouse and moved back to the main menu. The screen showed only the early fifties. He scrolled down and the years flew by. Houghton's reports were an electronic blur. In parts of seconds, the Korean War, the Hungarian uprising, the Berlin Wall, and lesser milestones of the cold war flashed by. Finally, the computer reached the end of the menu and the screen blinked rapidly in protest.

The last Houghton document was dated 13 June 1968. Sims clicked the mouse. He was startled when he didn't get the document's first page. Instead, a notice flashed across the center of the screen:

TRF MURKIN REPOS

He dropped back one document, to 12 June.

TRF MURKIN REPOS

Frustrated, he rapped the enter key three times in succession, working back down the list, repeatedly getting the same message: TRF MURKIN REPOS.

"Shit, shit, shit," he echoed. He retreated to the index of all Houghton documents. Before mid-April 1968, the documents originated in Prague. He highlighted the last Prague document. Its first page duly showed up on his screen. Thereafter, and through the first half of June, the documents originated in Langley.

He went back to the first Langley document, dated 15 April 1968.

TRF MURKIN REPOS

He stared at the screen and chewed on his lower lip. All right, he reasoned, TRF is short for transferred. REPOS is repository. All Houghton's Langley documents had been transferred to a repository. But where? What the hell was MURKIN? He keyed the letters into the files search. Nothing. For a moment, he absentmindedly tapped his fountain pen against the edge of his teeth. Then, with a Hail Mary shrug, he turned to another computer, one not connected to the Agency's internal system, and logged into Nexis. He queried with MURKIN. The screen flashed a PLEASE WAIT.

In a few seconds, the message disappeared. The public subscription information network had searched its vast files and had found a paragraph from the *Washington Post.* The *Post* quoted a document written in turgid government prose, laden with split infinitives and passive voice.

> In view of the numerous communications in connection with the case involving the murder of Martin Luther King, Jr., in Memphis, Tennessee, on 4/4/68, it is felt that the code name MURKIN should be utilized to more efficiently handle the mail. This code name has been checked through the indices and there is no prior record of it having been utilized as a code name.

Sims scrolled to the bottom. Dated 1978, the story covered the hearings of the Select Committee on Assassinations of the House of Representatives. The quoted document was an internal FBI memorandum the *Post* had gotten through the Freedom of Information Act.

So that's where the Houghton information went. The Agency had turned it over to the Bureau. He stared at Houghton's name. You knew Valek, he told the name on the screen. Your last job was mixed up with Martin Luther King, and the Agency fired you. There's more, he thought, not really wanting to think about it. The FBI, unlike the CIA, made up its code names from words bearing on the case at hand. MURKIN, he said to himself: murder King.

2

Sims locked his car and sprinted through the evening rain across
K Street to a glass and stainless-steel office building. It was one of
many along Washington's power corridor where mighty law firms
sheltered those just out of, or about to be back in, government.

On the sixth floor, Sims pushed through a glossy black-enameled
hallway door and entered a closet-size anteroom. Above him, a television camera swiveled, making the slightest of mewing sounds. The
small brass plaque on the door read TABARD BOOKS. He pushed a
buzzer. The rattle of an electric lock release answered him, then
Riddle swung the door wide.

"Happy New Year, Riddle."

"And to you, Mr. Sims."

It had never been anything but Riddle. And from the beginning, it
had been Mister Sims. Or "young man." There was a comforting
timelessness about Riddle. Sims thought that if he lived to a hundred,
an ageless Riddle would still be around, calling him young man.

Entering Tabard Books was like stepping into nineteenth-century
London. Rolling ladders traversed towering mahogany bookcases.
Green glass shades topped brass reading lamps. And through it all
were the rich spicy smells of leather, Latakia tobacco, and Turkish
coffee. Sims heard the muted sounds of a brass quintet.

"Figaro, young man. Do you like it?"

"Good French horn, Riddle," Sims answered, shouldering out of
his coat, "but isn't it *The Magic Flute?"*

Riddle gave him a small approving smile and turned to walk into
the depths of the shop. Above, his office overlooked the shop from

18

a loft. Riddle moved with ponderous grace to a kitchen alcove and returned with two Limoges cups of syrupy *turska kava.*

Standing, Sims took his first sip of the pungent coffee. Riddle's taste for Turkish coffee, like the bookstore, had been inherited from a man named Bazdarkian, with whom he had served in the OSS during World War II. Together they had set up a bogus trading company shuttling between Stockholm and Geneva under Swedish cover, stopping along the way to build networks within Hitler's Germany. After the war Bazdarkian retired from the Agency and bought out the shop's previous owner, himself a former Agency officer. In October 1991, Bazdarkian reportedly was killed in a plane crash during a visit to his home village in eastern Turkey. A few weeks later, Riddle applied for his Agency pension and took over the shop.

It was a bookshop that dealt only in espionage. Books on shadowing and surveillance shared shelves with treatises on Bayesian analysis and data bases of international terrorism. There was fiction: McCarry and Le Carré to be sure, but Poe and Conrad as well and, of course, Chaucer, who had been in secret service to his king.

Sims took his seat at an antique Pembroke gaming table, where the board had already been set up. Riddle opened: pawn to e4. Sims studied the board. The Thursday evening game, begun when Sims was an undergraduate, slipped into suspended animation whenever Sims was away from Washington. Upon his return, it picked up as if never interrupted. When a game was finished, Riddle would dissect the moves, the ploys, the gambits. From there, talk inevitably turned to intelligence.

Three moves, and Sims sacrificed a pawn. Two moves later, he sacrificed a bishop attempting to draw out Riddle's king. Riddle's king was too well defended, and in minutes, Sims saw he was in deep trouble.

In three more moves, Riddle took Sims's king. "You started boldly enough. But you lost your concentration." Riddle waited, and getting no answer, cleared the board. He looked up at Sims. "You are distracted."

Sims put his cup down.

"We've had a defector."

Riddle read the seriousness in Sims's face. He held up a hand in a delaying motion and gathered their cups. Seconds later, he put a fresh cup before Sims and settled himself in his chair. "Now," he said over the top of his cup, "your defector."

For the next half hour, Riddle listened, making notes on his blue index cards. When Sims finished, Riddle pushed the last card across the table. He had printed across it in block letters:

VALEK   HOUGHTON   MURKIN

The card lay between them, and Sims knew Riddle was not yet done with it.

"The first commandment of counterintelligence?"

Sims looked at the card, then at Riddle. "Find the connection."

"And we build connections . . ."

"From chronologies." Sims ticked off a point on a finger. "First there was Valek." He stopped and thought. "No. *First* there was Houghton," he corrected himself. "Houghton in Prague, trying to recruit Valek."

"Anything in the 303's to show why he failed?"

Sims shook his head. "No." He raised a second finger. "Then there's Houghton at Langley, working on the King case. And finally there's Houghton, fired. All within months."

"Why does that bother you?"

"It's too choppy."

Riddle reached across to the card with the names on it. He drew one arrow from Valek to Houghton and a second from Houghton to MURKIN. "Is there a connection?"

"You knew Houghton?"

Riddle pursed his lips in thought. "Edward Cameron Houghton. Yale, I believe. Our paths crossed, but we never worked together. He was Angleton's understudy. Reputation for operational brilliance. Not as cerebral as Angleton, but more tenacious. A curious mix of a man, Ivy League breeding and waterfront instincts. Cultured and profane. An unlikely sacrificial lamb."

"They dumped him?"

"That was the talk, what little there was."

"Houghton's files on King were shipped to the Bureau."

"Not surprising. There wasn't a great hue and cry within the Agency to get in on it."

"The King case? That's hard to believe."

"Cultural bias of the seventh floor." Riddle shrugged. "You see, American intelligence grew up under the influence of the Atlanticists. Those that ran the Agency in the early days—the Brahmins—saw Europe and North America as the natural masters of the world, the appointed shapers of events. They only grudgingly devoted any attention to Asia, and it took Mao and the Korean War to make them do that. The rest of the world was inconsequential."

"Spearchuckers."

Riddle frowned at the indelicacy, but nevertheless nodded. "The Brahmins never considered black Africa worth targeting. They rewarded Soviet specialists, even some of the China hands, and an Arabist or two. But those who showed an interest in Africa withered on the vine. I think that bias explains why the seventh floor shrugged off involvement in the King matter." He found an offending ground in his coffee cup. Capturing it on the tip of his finger, he pursed his lips in disapproval and wiped his hands with a napkin. "The Bureau was just the opposite: Badgering King was their meal ticket."

Wiretaps, bugging, anonymous threatening letters, salacious bedroom stories—J. Edgar Hoover had been at the center of it all, carrying tapes and rumors to his nominal boss, Robert Kennedy, and into the White House itself. Sims tasted the bitterness of revulsion and he realized it mattered very much to him that the Agency—*his* Agency—not be wrapped up in that shit.

And there was King. King had been a special adult of Sims's childhood. His uncle, Calvin Harris, had marched with King. On a wall in Sims's apartment, a photograph captured a solemn four-year-old Bradford Sims looking into the camera. Behind him are two smiling, playful adults: Calvin Harris and Dr. King. Like all adults first seen through a child's eyes, Sims's memory had retained a heroic aura around the image. His King wasn't supposed to be on computer screens at CIA or in ominously named files down at Ninth and Pennsylvania. Martin Luther King belonged where Sims first learned of him, slaying the dragons of segregated schools, white-only lunch counters, and seats at the back of the bus.

"What?" He was startled from his memories.

"I said"—Riddle leaned forward to catch Sims's attention—"your problem now is Valek, not King." He reached across the chessboard, picking up Sims's king and holding it up. "Concentration. Start boldly, young man. But keep your concentration."

Sims nodded gravely. "There's a lot of domestic content to this."

"I should imagine."

"I mean, there's a lot that I don't have access to."

"You're leading to something."

"There's a story—"

"A bar story, no doubt." Riddle sniffed. "One of those Agency fables that begin 'Once upon a time.' "

"Like that," Sims agreed. "It starts with an assumption: that in almost fifty years, the Agency's come across a lot of sensitive information about Americans. It's accidental. You tap an embassy phone to find a spy and you end up learning that a network anchorman is hooked on coke. Or that a senator is gay. Volatile stuff the Agency wasn't looking for. You find out who was embezzling, cheating." Sims paused a beat. "Even murdering."

Riddle's face was an expressionless pink mask. "The Agency is prohibited from keeping that kind of information." He shook a finger at Sims. "It is illegal."

"Exactly." Sims sipped his coffee, enjoying himself. "But it might be of value sometime. You never can tell. It's too dangerous to keep, but too good to dump."

"So?"

"So a long time ago, the Agency set up a safe place for that kind of information. A place outside the Agency. A place that didn't rely on government funding. A place the congressional committees would never learn about."

"And?"

"And this place was run by someone trusted by the Agency, but at the same time not of the Agency."

"Not *of* the Agency?"

"No access, no badge. All ties broken. Nothing that can be traced back to Langley—plausible denial. Someone like a retiree. They even have a name for that person. They call him The Keeper."

"Ridiculous."

Sims looked steadily at Riddle. "The talk used to be that Bazdarkian was The Keeper."

"See here, young man." Riddle made a show of exasperation. "You always were impetuous."

"You recruited me."

"Because, young man, I thought you had talent." Riddle came down heavily on *talent*. "You had an ability to put things together. But rationally. This—this is—" Riddle paused, seeking the ultimate pejorative. "This is *silly*." He leaned in his chair toward Sims. "A *good* intelligence officer builds his case on facts, Mister Sims."

Sims looked at him seriously. "I *am* a good intelligence officer, Riddle. You know that."

There was a long silence. Sims heard the creaking sounds of Riddle's leather chair. His mentor's solemn hazel eyes measured him.

From the alcove came the hydraulic whispers of the coffee machine. Finally, Riddle gave the trace of a nod.

"Yes, young man," Riddle sighed heavily. "You are a good intelligence officer."

Riddle paused and seemed to settle more comfortably into the chair. "They taught you a term in your first days at the Farm—'denied area.' "

Sims nodded. The seminar had begun.

"When I came into intelligence, 'denied area' meant German-occupied Europe, Japan, and the Pacific islands. After the war, my denied area spread from East Germany to the Pacific; to China, Korea, Laos, Vietnam, Cuba.

"Penetrating the denied areas—that was our reason for being, for the huge budgets and the catalogue of dirty tricks. We were the only game in town. Only we had the satellites, the listening stations, the human agents.

"Then the Wall came down and the people sent the Communists packing. The residents of the White House—our only customers—came to rely more on television than on us. CNN took over the situation rooms around Washington. The Judge, Cantwell, most of Langley still don't realize how the Agency's currency has been devalued. That's why I left to come here." Riddle gestured to encompass the bookshop, but Sims sensed he was including more than just the shop.

"Now, young man, the only denied area is the past." He rose from his chair, motioning for Sims to stay seated. "I'll fetch more coffee. We must talk more about this defector."

The next morning, Jo ambushed him when he walked in. "Morris just called. Wants you up there." She frowned and rolled her eyes at the ceiling. CI head office was right above them. "He's called twice." Sims saw from his secretary's expression that once was too often.

Sims nodded without comment. "Nice dress," he said to her, smiling, and continued on into his office. He hung his coat, opened his safe, and found the Valek file. Killing time, he flipped through the file for just over five minutes. Long enough, he decided, and walked out to see what Cantwell wanted.

Several minutes later, Sims watched as Morris Cantwell's plump white hands busied themselves first at the center of the desk, shifting, adjusting, making minute alignments of the telephone, blotter, and lamp. Sims had come to think of them as Cantwell's sentinels. Vigilant, the hands then patroled the desk's front—the outer battlements—and inspected the row of sharp yellow pencils laid points out—a picket fortification.

The Agency's first-generation officers—the OSS veterans—carried themselves with a casual, cruelly cynical self-assurance forged by the successes of World War II. Most had died, retired, or been killed long before Cantwell.

Cantwell was the progeny of decades of Agency failures, a dismal string that ran from the Bay of Pigs through Vietnam and Iran-contra. A doddering and befuddled Agency shaped Cantwell; an Agency that cowered under the threat of Congressional probes and the ever-present fear of special prosecutors and inspectors general. And Morris Cantwell was that Agency's chief of counterintelligence.

"Good morning." Morris smiled widely, as if he had not made the phone calls and as if Sims had dropped in on his own. He touched a stainless-steel mug and then asked Sims if he wanted coffee. With Sims's head shake, Morris paused a second longer. "The defector— Valek? yes, Valek—how are things going?"

The phone calls, the overdone hospitality: warning flags. Sims knew to be careful. "OM is doing the physicals this week. Morse and her shrinks have him this afternoon." Sims was guarded, noncommittal.

Cantwell waited for more. His eyebrows inched toward each other when he realized Sims was waiting.

"Your—ah—initial. When do you plan that?"

"I want to get Morse's report on Valek." Sims knew for certain that Cantwell was uncomfortable about something.

"I have—" Cantwell paused to choose a safer formulation. "Ah, registry has—um, sent a report." Satisfied that he had pinned liability for the meeting on registry, he moved on, cautiously keeping to his elliptical path. "As you know, registry gets a monthly printout of file queries. It seems—"

"I didn't know." Sims gave in to the temptation to needle Cantwell.

Thrown off stride, Cantwell looked crossly at Sims, then quickly dropped his eyes back to the paper in front of him. "Well, they do," he declared primly. "They got a printout. And they think it odd that you've been into the King files."

"If they 'think it odd' "—Sims faintly mimicked Cantwell's pinched Back Bay accent—"why doesn't registry talk to me about it?"

Cantwell floundered. Leaning slightly back from the desk, shadow masked his face. "It can be put this way," he tried. "Registry took note that you were going into the King files. It was reported." He

24

waited. When Sims said nothing, Cantwell added: "And a copy of the registry report was also sent to the director himself. If he asks me—"

The director? Sims didn't believe it for a second. The Judge didn't have time to read that kind of crap. What did Cantwell take him for? *All right, Morris. The story you can tell the director* . . . "Valek—we've dealt with him before. I ran him through the computer. A former Agency officer had worked him. The same Agency officer was in on the King investigation—Edward Houghton." As he said it, he could tell that Cantwell knew the name.

"Now, Sims"—Cantwell bobbed his head, working up a let's-be-reasonable tone—"I—your thoroughness is appreciated. Commendable even. But this man Valek—he isn't one of our priorities."

What are your priorities, Morris? Sims asked behind his eyes. "I was curious," Sims said aloud.

"Curious?" Cantwell rolled the word suspiciously.

"Curious," Sims repeated. "We were in on the investigation, then dropped. Quite suddenly."

"Yes," conceded Cantwell, carefully dodging any expression of interest.

"You were around. Was there talk of it?" Sims pushed.

Cantwell didn't like it. His hands darted around the desk. They nudged the parallel pencils ever so slightly, swinging their sharp ends toward Sims. Drawing on his last reserves, Cantwell loudly cleared his throat and at the same time interlaced his fingers, locking his hands on the desk. "Stay out of those files, Sims."

"But—"

Cantwell tried to be friendly. "Brad," he began, unaware that no one called Bradford Sims Brad, "you're on a fast track here. You've gotten a number of very good tickets punched. You have a very promising career ahead of you." Cantwell summoned up an ounce of daring. "I was brand-new here during Houghton's tenure. Like yourself, he thought he had the world by the scruff of the neck." He paused to let the implication sink in. "The King case is closed." Cantwell gave a prissy schoolmaster's emphasis to each word. "Proper authorities have closed it. It is enough for me and should be enough for you."

"What do you want?"

The battered metal door had been painted too long ago with a cheap green industrial enamel. Sulfurous yellow hallway walls bore sour witness to decades of grilled sausage, cheap-cut roasts, and boiled vegetables.

"Edward Houghton?"

"What do you want?"

Sims registered on the slurred voice, the washed-out blue eyes that dissolved into veined jaundiced whites.

"I want to talk to Edward Houghton."

The door, only narrowly opened, began to close.

"I got the address from personnel."

"Personnel?"

Almost closed, the door stopped. One watery eye now surveyed Sims.

"At headquarters. You weren't in the phone book." Sims offered a contact card: the Agency crest and an open-line phone number, but no name. A hand took the card and disappeared behind the door.

The door opened wider. Houghton had a thick shock of salt-and-pepper hair. A spray of broken veins blushed his nose and cheeks. Behind the damage of years and alcohol was a thin and not unhandsome face. It was the kind of face, Sims later reflected, that you saw looking out at you from Ivy League yearbook photographs. White faces clustered in boathouses and on squash courts. Confident, assured faces that knew partnerships in the best firms and top-rung government positions were theirs for the asking, simply because of where they went to school and who their forebears had been.

"Headquarters? What are you talking about?"

Sims ignored the question. "You—left on 14 June 1968. Your badge number was HX-685."

Houghton searched the hall past Sims, then stood aside. "Might as well."

Sims stepped in. A glance was all it took. The living room painted the same dusty yellow as the outside hall. A grimy wide-slat venetian blind covering the solitary window. The portable television within arm's reach of a cheap sofa on the long wall. The place was too warm and the hallway's odor mixed with the marshlike smell of leaked cooking gas.

Houghton pointed to the sofa and, after Sims was seated, took a seat opposite in an upholstered reading chair. Moving an ashtray nearer, he lit a cigarette with a cheap plastic lighter. Putting the lighter on top of the cigarette pack, he inhaled deeply as he examined Sims.

Having wrung all he could from that, he asked: "You in operations? Security? What?"

It was the first question inside the Agency—the rooting out of pedigree. Tightly knit clans brawled among themselves behind the round blue crest with its shield and brave eagle.

"D-O." The Directorate of Operations.

Houghton noticed how Sims said it with a trace of arrogance. That in itself rang true. The Directorate of Operations had, over the years, convinced itself and others of its primacy, its eliteness. It was the DO that did the real spying, the recruiting and handling of human agents. It was the DO that did the coups, the special operations, the nasty jobs. The rest of the Agency were drab desk-bound drones: scientists, clerks, and academicians.

"What division?"

"I'm in CI."

Another period of silent, mutual scrutiny. Sims heard footsteps in the apartment overhead, and from somewhere came the incongruous sound of a violin.

"Someone recruited you?"

"Riddle."

Houghton's face softened. "He still around?"

"Just retired."

"When were you at the Farm?"

"Thirteen years ago."

"What was your basic curricula?"

Sims felt a flush on his neck. Ah, yes, exam time. "Reporting, communications, surveillance, and operational security."

"Specialty training?"

"Locks and picks, unarmed combat, weapons."

"The cabins—how're they named?"

"After trees," Sims replied with growing impatience. "Mine was Birch."

Houghton took a last drag, then concentrated on stubbing the cigarette in the ashtray. Satisfied, he looked up at Sims with resignation. "What do they want now?"

"I need help."

"From me?" There was as much derision as surprise in Houghton's voice.

"I was searching the files. Your name came up."

Houghton's eyes narrowed.

27

It's still not too late, Sims reminded himself. He was bypassing procedures for outside help. He didn't know what Houghton had been doing. He had been fired, and KGB's recruiting rule number one had been to look for pissed-off spies.

Those were the arguments against. But why would the Russians bother? Like the Agency, they looked for access. Houghton had access to nothing. Except his memories.

Sims again surveyed the seedy apartment. Get out, he told himself. This wreck of a man, this awful place dismayed him. He could work Valek without Houghton. King? He wasn't getting paid for that. And it was more than apparent that Cantwell wanted it left alone.

Houghton sensed Sims's internal debate. "Why you? Why do you care?"

Sims decided on one last try. "You were in CI. You know how one thing leads to another." Sims plunged in. "A defector's come over. Miloslav Valek." Houghton's surprise gratified him.

"You've interrogated him?" Houghton asked it in a distant voice, as if more and more of him were drifting away to work on the meaning of Miloslav Valek.

"Not yet. Initial is coming up. We're working through his bio, establishing his *bona fides*. You know the drill."

Houghton didn't answer, lost as he was in long-ago Prague: the cold attic wiretap stations, watching the glow of the monitors while straining against the silence to hear the dreaded footfalls on the stairs below. Dodging StB surveillance for frightening meetings with sources whose gibberish might carry only the tiniest nugget. Still, it was a great game. The highs, the suspense. The goddamn high-wire thrills you could get nowhere else, skirting danger, the triumph of nailing another scalp to the wall. They took all that away from him, and more. And now this nigger was sitting here, treating him, Edward Houghton, as if he were a backward child.

Sims took in Houghton's preoccupation. As he watched him, the Valek-Houghton-MURKIN connection tugged at Sims. Why not just ask?

Houghton started, as if seeing Sims in his living room for the first time. "What?"

"I said, there were other files. After Prague. Files on Martin Luther King."

"The King files?" A startled look. "You got into them?"

"No. Just the index. The files themselves were transferred to the Bureau."

"So?"

Sims saw that Houghton was working to keep his voice even, his face expressionless. Here were unsuspected depths and currents. "So in June, two months after the killing, the Agency suddenly dropped out of the investigation and the next day you left."

"Meaning?"

"I don't know." It was an honest statement.

Houghton laughed scornfully. "You can root around till hell freezes over. You're not gonna find anything. All you'll get is what they want you to know. How—"

"How you were blamed for it?" Sims guessed.

Houghton jumped to his feet, unsteady with sheer fury. "I don't need that. I didn't ask you here." He fumbled with the door, then flung it open. "Get out. Get out, now!"

Sims pushed off the sofa, angry at Houghton's belligerence. "Look, damnit, I—"

Houghton was almost shouting, his face red. "It's all over. They've got the answers they want! Leave me alone. I don't need *you people* digging in my life."

Sims, now in the hallway, spun around, fists clenched. "You people?"

Houghton eyed Sims for a moment, the well-dressed black who thought he was such a hot-ass CI officer. A vicious smile crossed his face.

"You think I might get back in CI?" Houghton taunted, not really looking for an answer. "Maybe," he said, in a drunk-sly way, "maybe they've got a quota for me. You know, needed: one over-the-hill white male drunk. You think they might have a quota like that?" Sims maintained control, but Houghton knew he had scored. "Well"—Houghton put on a mock innocent air, closing the door—"I thought you might know. About quotas, I mean."

Houghton leaned stiff-armed against the door, head down, chin on his chest. The footsteps receded in the hall outside while he remained motionless. Finally, slowly, he pushed away and walked into the kitchen.

He opened the refrigerator door. He stood, rocking slightly in indecision. Then, with a rapid motion, he thrust his hand into the coolness of the ice-encrusted freezer and came up with the bottle.

The vodka poured thickly. Putting the bottle back, he watched as the humidity slowly frosted the glass, advancing toward his fingertips clutching the rim.

He'd been good, goddamnit! Many had said the best. He had savored the talk and the speculation. In the Agency halls and in the dark cheap bars around Langley they had whispered his name and called him the golden boy, the Agency's premier spy-catcher. Only thirty-nine, he had already been number two to the legendary Angleton.

"Hoover's panicked," Angleton had said in his hoarse whisper. "Lyndon Johnson's on a tear. The Negroes and the newspapers are all over him to find the killer."

Houghton remembered how Angleton, a tall knife of a man, had peered through the thick horn-rimmed glasses that made his eyes look like peeled grapes, how Angleton had pursed his wide, sensuous lips. "Hoover wants us in. Not to find anything. But as insurance."

Houghton saw that the frost now covered the glass up to his fingertips. He had taken it on as Angleton had asked. Angleton had been right: Hoover—someone—didn't want the Agency to find anything. His mind wandered. They could have tucked him away somewhere; let him cool off in a slag heap station somewhere at the back of beyond. Brought him back a couple of years later in a new administration.

Instead, they threw him out. His office mementoes came to him through the mail—through the fucking *mail!*—in a battered cardboard box with no return address. Doors slammed, telephone numbers changed. A check drawn on a Chicago bank showed up each month for nearly two years, long enough to carry him through his divorce and into a job seeing to the security concerns of a small commuter airline.

He looked at the clear vodka. First would come the heavy numbing coldness, then the fire in the throat and stomach and, last, the wonderful flush and tingle of the nerve ends of his face and arms. The second wouldn't be quite as good. But good enough. The same for the third and the rest that it would take to float him down the dark river. He rocked his wrist gently, and the vodka offered itself seductively to him, rising to the rim and bulging ever so slightly over.

With an abrupt, savage motion, Houghton threw the glass into the sink. It bounced once, then shattered, spraying the vodka around. Clutching the sink's edge, staring into the rusted drain, he cried.

3

Sims felt as if he were being fire hosed with a torrent of phrases that sounded like various combinations of "levels of rationalization" and "cross-deviational maturity." In her office, Sims glumly regarded Jane Morse, the Agency's senior psychologist, thinking that ahead lay the even denser thickets of Valek's Wechsler and Rorschach results. It was too much for a Friday afternoon. Next week, before the interrogation, he would come back and try for a layman's explanation. He thought about dropping by personnel, seeing if Walker—what *was* her first name?—was doing anything this weekend.

Morse's telephone intercom buzzed. She answered it, then frowned and handed it to Sims. It was Houghton. He had called the contact number and operations had forwarded the call. He wanted to meet and suggested a time and place. Sims agreed and hung up. Walker would have to wait.

For now, anyway.

Sims knew Georgetown from his undergraduate days. Its bars, saloons, and restaurants put it in a class with Dodge City and Gomorrah for drinking, fighting, and general fucking around. On weekends, the whole town went on a binge. Saturday's hangovers were milder than Sunday's. But Saturdays were worse in some ways because on Saturdays, Georgetown can't sleep in. Sky King and his band of homeless buddies have to be rousted from their sleeping bags in M Street doorways and Friday night dinners have to be hosed off the sidewalks so Saturday's safaris of suburban shoppers and drinkers can get a fresh, early start at Ralph Lauren, Clyde's, and Banana Republic.

Georgetown's cleanup was under way when Sims took his ticket from the attendant and found a parking space in the garage below Georgetown Park, their designated meeting place. He checked his watch. He was ten minutes early. That is, if Houghton were on time. Or if he even remembered calling. *Bastard.* Quotas, Houghton had flung at him. Six-letter word meaning teacher's pet, or move to the head of the line. He sat in the car, waiting.

It angered him, having to make his skin his first concern. He had other priorities: like how to get ahead without getting cross-threaded with pricks like Cantwell; or finding a woman who could put up with him. But Houghton had come up with that race shit. He didn't want to care about it anymore. But Houghton had made him care, and the caring about it when he didn't want to flat-ass wore him out.

"Hello."

The grating voice snapped Sims upright against the steering wheel.

"It's just me. Open the other door."

Sims caught Houghton's image in the rearview mirror as the man crossed behind the car. Then, before Sims could lean across to raise the lock, Houghton was standing impatiently at the door, jiggling the handle.

Houghton levered himself into the car, slamming the door behind him. He motioned toward the ramp. "Let's go. It's not good to talk here."

Sims caught a whiff of day-old alcohol. "I don't know if I want to talk to you anywhere."

Ignoring him, Houghton motioned again. "You can drop me later."

Sims wheeled out of the garage, turned right on Wisconsin. Soon they were passing the Watergate, then the overhang of the Kennedy Center.

Houghton sat with his back partially toward the door, turning occasionally to survey the roadway behind them. "Left here. Go down to Hains Point." He gestured to the drive that would take them to the riverside park south of the Lincoln Memorial.

"The other night . . . I . . ." Houghton began a clumsy apology.

"You were an asshole," Sims finished.

They drove in silence. Sims pulled onto the looping park road. The weather was unseasonably warm and the park was filling up with cars, bicyclists, and runners. Half a mile later, he found a parking space and shut off the engine. Across the Potomac, a passenger jet screamed skyward from National Airport. On the expanse of grass nearby, two young boys were passing a football, throwing in high, spiraling trajectories. Sims watched them for a moment, envying the joking, the teasing, and most of all, the innocence. But there was Houghton.

Dressing that morning, Sims had included the recording rig: a German Grundig voice-activated device the size of a cigarette lighter. Driven by lithium batteries and recording into a bubble memory, the gizmo could go forever. It fit into a harness under his right armpit. "You didn't want to talk before. Why now?"

Houghton shifted uneasily, not sure how to answer. "You . . . you're the first person in . . . since . . . that I can talk to. Nobody else gives a shit. I tried to put it behind me, to get on with my life, but . . ." He remembered the vodka, how it had looked in the glass, his desire for it. "It keeps coming back."

Sims saw Houghton struggling and for a moment felt a tug of sympathy until he remembered the exchange in the hallway. "How'd the Agency get involved in the King investigation?"

"Hoover. For years, Hoover was telling everybody that King's outfit was riddled with Commies." Houghton noticed Sims's wince. "Used them as an excuse for Bureau surveillance. With the uproar over King's killing, I guess he wanted to pin it on them. To do that, he had to prove a foreign connection. And that's why Hoover wanted the Agency in.

"We formed a joint FBI-CIA task force. I was in charge of the Agency side, which was supposed to look into foreign involvement. The Bureau was going after Ray, King's killer, and his domestic connections."

"And what did you find?"

"Didn't have time to find anything. We were just getting started when the Bureau suddenly wanted it dropped."

"Hoover wanted the Agency in, then wanted it out?"

"Yeah. I fought it. Too hard. Hoover went to the White House and talked to LBJ about me. I was history."

"The Agency didn't back you? They folded?"

"When the White House wants something, it usually gets it."

Sims couldn't believe it. "You were thrown out and the Agency taken off the investigation? Just like that?"

"Yeah, yeah. I always thought Hoover found a hair in his mashed potatoes." Houghton fished in a pocket, came up with an antacid tablet, and cursed under his breath as he struggled with the foil wrapper.

Sims saw Houghton's growing agitation and switched courses. "You were in Prague when King was killed, weren't you?"

Houghton nodded, chewing on the tablet.

"Why did Angleton bring you back for the investigation?"

"We thought there might be a Prague connection," Houghton explained. "We'd been tracing money coming into the antiwar movement."

Sims laughed derisively. "Vietnam paranoia."

"Paranoia my goddamn ass," Houghton snarled. "Of course Moscow was helping all those Hollywood cunts and their Viet Cong fan clubs. Wouldn't you have done it if you were on their side? You think we didn't help Yeltsin in Russia, or those ragheads in Afghanistan?"

"But there was never any proof—"

"None that ever came out, you mean. Dig back in those files of yours. Dig long enough and you'll find it. Johnson and Nixon decided to keep the stuff on ice. Not that any of the Beverly Hills goof-balls knew where the money was coming from. And that suited Moscow fine. The Russians weren't looking for publicity. They just wanted results."

"So you—"

"I was in Prague. KGB had put together one of those united fronts to work the American antiwar movement—the Afro-Asian Solidarity Committee. Used a lot of people from the 'fraternal countries': Cubans, the East Germans and Czechs, of course, and a bunch of Vietnamese. AASC set up shop in Prague. Made it more palatable to the Third Worlders. Angleton organized a counterintelligence group in Prague station to watch the AASC. I was in charge."

"The American antiwar movement. Did that include the Southern Christian Leadership Conference?" Houghton nodded. Sims felt a tight knot of apprehension: SCLC was not only Martin Luther King, it was Sims's uncle, Calvin Harris, as well. He had to struggle with the question, fearing Houghton's answer. "Did you make any connection between the AASC and King?"

The next second seemed to last forever. Then, Houghton shook his head. "I *knew* there was a link somewhere," he said in frustration, "but we never proved it." He could tell that Sims was relieved.

"Valek. How did you come to know him?"

"We met at one of those national-day receptions at one of the embassies. It must have been the fall of '66. No, '67. We made small talk. Nothing about the racket, of course. We met again. A number of times."

34

Houghton took in Sims's inquiring look. "I was trying to recruit him and he was trying to recruit me," Houghton said in the nonchalant way of the field man. "Nothing ever came of it. Finally, we decided to lay off. After—we'd run into each other in Prague—once in a while we'd even have a drink or two."

"What made you think you could turn him?"

"He was greedy. Conversations sooner or later always got down to something he'd managed to promote—a new stereo from West Germany, some French wines. I thought a money approach might work." Houghton thought about Valek a moment more, retouching old images. Then: "Why'd he come in?"

"Says he's gotten fed up with the system."

"Took him long enough."

"You sound like you don't buy it."

Houghton grinned cynically. "Let's just say I don't see Miloslav Valek getting worked up over the rights of man."

"We won't be holding him long."

"Oh?"

Sims shook his head. "We don't think he's star quality."

Houghton gave Sims a puzzled look. "Not star quality? Hell, Valek was up to his ears in the AASC. He was the guy who was pumping the money into the antiwar groups. If we'd kept up the investigation, he would have been a prime target."

"I don't think that would put him on Cantwell's top ten." Inside, Sims felt a growing excitement. The pieces *did* fit together. Valek playing games with the antiwar movement. Houghton watching Valek. And finally, CIA coming in to pin King's murder on Hoover's convenient Communists. "Did you develop anything?"

"Nothing direct. Not on Valek anyway."

"Then why did you push so hard?"

Houghton twisted an earlobe, searching back over the years. "Oh, intuition, I guess. Valek and his merry band had the motive, the means, and the access. Mostly, though, it was Ray himself."

"Ray?"

Houghton nodded, recalling the gnawing strength of the old doubts. "James Earl Ray—something was never right about him. The guy was a loser. High school dropout. Army boarded him for unsuitability. Not much of a burglar—got caught lifting a typewriter out of a restaurant. Arrested for armed robbery—holding up a taxi driver for ten bucks. Made the big time—got twenty years for sticking up a grocery store for a hundred and twenty bucks."

"So he was a punk," Sims said. "All he had to do was pull a trigger once."

"It was more than that." Houghton stared through the windshield, looking out into infinity. "It was the aliases."

Sims thought for a minute, then remembered: "They looked for Ray by another name, didn't they? At the start?" He searched for the name.

"Galt. Eric Starvo Galt." Houghton paused before adding, "There was a real Eric Galt. Did you know that?"

Sims looked at him blankly.

"Toronto," Houghton went on, his memory picking up speed. "Eric Galt was a warehouse supervisor in Toronto. Ray used three other names, all of men living in Toronto." Houghton paused, summoning up the names. "Willard. Yes. John Willard. Ray used that one in Memphis to rent the room near King's motel. Then there was a Bridgeman. Schoolteacher, I think. And Sneyd—Ramon Sneyd. Hell, Sneyd was a Toronto cop!"

Sims still couldn't make sense of it. "So Ray used aliases of real men in Toronto. Why'd you think that was unusual?"

Houghton went over it patiently. "The Bureau said Ray acted alone. They said he was a dumb shit. They never could explain to me how this dumb shit, acting alone, could have come up with those aliases, since he'd never been in Toronto."

Sims was astonished. "Never in Toronto?"

"Not before the killing. You know where he went after?"

Sims didn't really know, but he was certain where it would be. "Toronto," he whispered. A chill puckered the back of his neck.

"Yeah." Houghton belched silently and a gust of the day-old-booze breath assailed Sims. "Toronto, where he got a passport using the Sneyd cover."

"Did you find out where he got the names?"

"No." Houghton shrugged. "Nobody ever asked. Another thing: Ray claims he didn't kill King."

"They found him guilty."

Houghton shook his head. "He *pleaded* guilty. There was never a jury trial. There was never any evidence presented."

"Ray *was* in Memphis."

"He said he was there with a buddy, a man named Raoul."

"And Raoul did the killing?"

"That's what Ray claimed. Nobody ever found Raoul."

Sims watched wheeling gulls fight over a scrap of garbage in the river. From Houghton he had caught the crawly feeling that something was circling out there in the darkness. Faint, troubling hints that there was more to it than James Earl Ray doing a singleton job. *Alias* was a word police used. Good aliases and the use of them was also called something else—cover. *Cover* was a word spies used.

"You think somebody was running Ray?"

"I'm saying three things. One"—Houghton ticked off his fingers—"Valek and his friends had targeted King's organization. Two: Ray was too dumb *before* the killing and too smart *after.* Three: Hoover kept me from asking any questions about it."

"Let's go back to Hoover. Why would he have shut you down?"

Houghton cocked his head toward Sims like a schoolteacher. "Think about it. It wasn't until years after King's death that everybody found out that the Bureau had been trying to fuck over King."

"The wiretaps . . ."

"Sure, the bugs. Suppose after the killing Hoover found out there was more than just the bugging and taps?"

"And so Hoover suddenly wants the Agency out of it."

Sims studied Houghton, imagining him twenty-five years before. Black hair. Clearer eyes. None of the facial blotches. Thirty pounds lighter. Lighter on the booze, too. Twenty-five years ago, he would have been looking forward to something, never suspecting he would end up like this.

"You want help on the initial?"

"Yes." Sims waited a beat. "What do *you* want?"

"Want?" He tilted his head, as if trying to see Sims from a slightly different angle. "You *are* a CI officer." He grinned for a moment, then thrust his chin defiantly. "I'd like to have those years back they took from me." His eyes narrowed and he coughed to clear his throat. "But I'd settle for my rehabilitation."

Rehabilitation? To Sims, it sounded like physical therapy.

Seeing Sims's perplexity, Houghton explained: "Like the Commies used to do. You know, they would have all those purge trials. Find all their heroes guilty of crimes against the state and shoot them or send them to the Gulag. Then, twenty years later or so, they'd make a speech at a Party congress. 'Mistakes have been made!' they shout. Everybody would shake a fist at Stalin or Brezhnev, who were safely dead, then they would restore the good name of the asshole they shot."

Sims thought it was a joke, then saw Houghton wasn't smiling.

"This doesn't have the Agency's blessing, does it?" the older man asked.

Sims thought of Cantwell and his disembodied hands. He shook his head and watched the disappointment flash across Houghton's face.

"So it all comes down to how far you'd be willing to go. How much you'd risk." Disappointment settled and hardened around Houghton's mouth.

Sims gripped the steering wheel as hard as he could, recalling the night he had decided to cross the Uzh. He felt his knuckles grind painfully. "How much? Nobody ever knows how much they'd risk until it comes time."

"*I* know." Houghton pointed a thumb toward his chest. "I'm willing to risk it all—everything—to find out what happened to me and why." Houghton took in Sims's Mercedes, his clothes, the gold Rolex, and above it all, Sims himself: the strength, the unsagging flesh, the confidence that the best lay yet ahead. "Then again, I haven't much to lose."

"I can't give you any guarantees."

"I'm not looking for guarantees. I just want a commitment."

"Commitment for what? A kamikaze mission?"

"*You* came to *me*, Sims. I didn't invite you. I was getting along—"

"Getting along?"

"I was getting *along*," Houghton said quietly with unexpected dignity. "I was managing my devils in my own way."

Contrite, Sims turned his eyes away. For a moment, he watched the boys passing the football. Warmed up, they were now throwing harder, the ball slapping into their hands with a stinging sound. He turned to Houghton. "I'm sorry." He felt it and meant it. He started the car, then turned to Houghton again. "I owe you an answer."

Sims dropped Houghton off in south Arlington, then, several blocks later, found a telephone booth and called his uncle. Minutes later, Sims was back on the road driving south out of town. Finally clearing the clotted traffic at the Springfield interchange, he picked up speed on U.S. 95 toward Richmond.

By the time he reached Quantico, he had settled into the welcome tedium of driving. The sounds of the tires on the road and the car smells of upholstery and hot oil reminded him of trips with his father and mother, of a snug backseat cocoon filled with coloring books, cookies, and a thermos of lemonade. Calvin Harris had always been the mythic relative, the fire-breathing minister, the mother's brother who had marched with King long before King had leapt into national prominence. King was no longer of this world, but Calvin Harris was just ahead, an hour down the road.

Sandston, Virginia, is a hardscrabble farming village southeast of Richmond and bound forever to the South of another and darker era. Calvin Harris was AME, African Methodist Episcopal. His home was a small white frame house separated from the church by a thick stand of rhododendrons and mountain laurel. A large holly wreath hung on the door, and a big evergreen in front of the church had been draped in Christmas lights.

Harris had come here fifteen years ago, leaving a larger and far wealthier congregation in Washington. Harris had never explained why, and Sims, only intermittently curious, had never found just the right time to ask.

Seconds after his knock, he heard footsteps inside, then the door swung wide. Calvin Harris was a huge man who moved with the sure grace of a stevedore. He filled the doorway, and Sims marveled, not for the first time, that such a big man lived in such a small house. His size was emphasized by a bulky lumberjack's shirt, canvas work pants, and sturdy walking shoes.

"Bradford." Sims was moved by a rush of affection and security. Calvin Harris had always meant warmth and shelter. The voice was a majestic Niagara of rich, rolling bass, the voice of a man who could speak to the multitudes. Harris was obviously pleased, then as obviously curious. "Dora's down to Raleigh visiting. She won't be happy that she missed you."

"It was sudden. I realized I wanted to see you." Sims felt the need to explain. "Something subconscious." He gave it a light touch.

Harris pushed the screen door open with one hand and with the other pulled Sims inside. "It's the Lord who guides our feet, Bradford, not Sigmund Freud."

He turned and led the way back into the house. The largest room in the small house, the warm kitchen smelled of baking and yeast and heating oil. A corner served as a study, with an old Smith-Corona typewriter crouching on a battered metal rolling stand. Tracts, clippings, and stacks of books covered an unpainted wood desk and spilled over to take up half of a worn sofa. Two pictures hung on a wall: Jesus and Martin Luther King.

Harris made a pile of papers into a neat stack and set them off to one side on the large table. "Notes for tomorrow's sermon." He smiled broadly, wrinkling around the eyes, anticipating the service the next day. "It's cold enough to preach about adultery. Too hot for it in the summer—that's the season for sloth." He motioned Sims to a chair, then went to the refrigerator. "Iced tea?" He held a large frost-covered pitcher. Without waiting for an answer, he poured two massive glasses and dumped in a handful of cubes.

Sims took a long sip of the iced tea, then began, telling the story without identifying Valek. Leaning on his elbows, hands clutching his glass of tea, Harris listened intently, his eyes never leaving his nephew.

Something had come up, was the way Sims started it. He had just talked with a man who had been in on the assassination investigation in 1968. The man told him how Hoover had suddenly stopped the investigation. And the man thought then and thinks now that James Earl Ray didn't act alone. That if Ray did it, he had to have had some help.

There was a long silence after he finished. Harris had a reflective, faraway look on his face. Sims tried to imagine how it would have been; to have been a living part of the events that he knew only from the files.

"Ray had help?" Harris asked himself the question. "Your man might have it the wrong way around."

"How?"

"Could be that Ray didn't *have* help." Harris squinted skeptically. "Could be that Ray *was* the help."

Sims thought about it for a moment. "You mean he was just the triggerman?"

Harris got the faraway look again. "The FBI, the police—they were supposed to be protecting us, but they were a shadow army against us. We were afraid to use our telephones. They made us distrust one another. They even went through our garbage. Sent anonymous letters to Martin. Threatening letters. No doubt about Mr. Hoover. His role in it." Harris's face tightened thinking about it. "Then they named that building for him. Right there on Pennsylvania Avenue. Halfway between Congress and the White House." He shook his head, still unable to understand it, even after all the years.

Sims pointed to Harris. "What do *you* believe?"

Harris tried to dodge Sims's intensity. "I try not to think about it anymore, Bradford. When I do, I swing back and forth. Sometimes Ray's at the center of it. Other times, he's almost a nobody."

Sims leaned across the table, put out a hand, and captured Harris's wrist. The older man's eyes opened wider in surprise at the strength of the grip. "Do you think the government did it?"

Harris sat still, listening to the long-ago voices. They whispered wisdom paid for in blood and denied hope. It seemed to Sims as if his uncle were praying. Finally: "Where does it put me, Bradford, if I say yes? And then go about the rest of my life as if I hadn't said anything at all? If I say yes, then I have to do something. I don't want to take on that battle."

"I think I see." Sims was disappointed.

"Do you, Bradford?" Harris looked at him, certain the younger man didn't understand.

"No, I really do." Sims thought of Cantwell. "The Agency doesn't want to get into it, either." As he said it, he knew it had been the wrong thing to say.

Mention of the Agency set Harris off. "You got a good education, Bradford." He nonetheless said it gently because it was an old argument between them, the kind of argument that holds two people together as long as neither of them ever wins. "You could have—"

"Gone into the ministry?" Sims asked, knowing how Harris would have finished it. "Instead of CIA?"

"We were a mighty force." Harris's chin went up and his shoulders squared with a parade-ground pride. "We led our people out of slavery."

"You did that, uncle," Sims said huskily. "But you've got to realize, the Agency's done right by me."

Harris let it go. "Not only the CIA doesn't want you messing with those times, Bradford."

"Who?"

"Just about everybody." A thought struck Harris and he leaned forward, intent that Sims understand. "History is a story of people struggling. People carrying impossible burdens, bearing insufferable pain. They get through one trial and they don't want to go back through it again, because they're already into another."

"Even if the world's wrong?"

"Even if the world's wrong, Bradford."

Harris turned toward the picture of King on the wall. The civil rights leader sat in a white short-sleeved shirt at a table covered with notes and books, obviously deep in thought. Behind him, also in a white shirt, was Calvin Harris coming out of the cell they were sharing. Sims had examined the photograph hundreds of times before. It was a wire-service photo of King and Harris jailed in St. Augustine, Florida. Sims had long ago memorized King's inscription, written in black ink in a bold hand: "Under a government which imprisons any unjustly,

41

the true place for a just man is also a prison." And then King closed with, "I only wish my cell mate wouldn't snore."

Harris sighed and looked at Sims. "You see, people think they know the story of Martin's death. You change that and you'd be ripping open a healed wound. They didn't want to know then and they won't want to know now."

"I want to know for *me*."

"And that's important?"

"I'm beginning to realize it is." Sims took a deep breath, trying to push away the sharp probing fingers of old agony and bewilderment. "My father died that night, too."

"He died because he was a policeman." Harris said it compassionately, as he had when he had first told Sims. "Because a looter shot him."

Sims remembered the sirens the night King died. Sirens everywhere. Throughout the night and into the day. Washington was in convulsions. What wasn't burning was being carried away. His mother had dragged him off the sidewalk into their small row house. There he had watched the shattered images on television, waiting for a father who never came home.

"He died," Sims said, "because of what happened in Memphis."

"Memphis." Harris got a gone-west stare. "And all the places before that. Albany and Birmingham and—oh yes, Lord"—his voice thickened—"and Selma! Bloody Selma." Harris remembered the brutal face of Sheriff Jim Clark, the burning crosses, the bombed churches, John Lewis and Bernard Lafayette beaten so badly he couldn't recognize them. "And there was Martin—" Harris got a smile and it grew until he laughed. It was a rich, warm laugh. "Martin preached a mock funeral service over Abernathy. Asked the Lord to forgive all Abernathy's sins. Abernathy's eyes bulged as Martin went on. Then he laughed. We all laughed, holding on to each other, laughing until we cried."

Sims waited, and his uncle finally turned to him. "I'm not telling you to walk away from it, Bradford." He paused to think about his next words. "I *am* telling you it's a decision you've got to make." Harris looked at the window, then the clock, and got up from the table. "Come on. We've got another hour of light."

"Where're we going?"

Harris took an old bird-hunting jacket off a peg and smiled the same mysterious smile as when he'd brought childhood surprises to Sims. "Come on. I'll drive."

Some minutes later, Harris pulled his battered sedan into a rest stop on a country road south of Sandston. Getting out of the car, Harris stood looking toward the crest of a low hill.

"What's this?" Sims asked, his curiosity rising.

"Calvary," Harris replied in his rich, sad bass. "Let's go." He motioned. "I'll show you from the top. You can see it from there."

Scant clumps of trees dotted the hill. Otherwise it was covered with brambles and frost-browned scrub grass. The sun was setting in an incandescent display of orange and purples, and from the Appalachians came a gathering evening breeze. Harris set a steady pace, familiar with the faint path that wound its way to the crest. Making the top, Harris led Sims to a slight depression. He stooped, and came up with a crooked stick several feet long.

"You don't know much about the Civil War, do you, Bradford?"

Sims made a dismissing shrug. "The usual—Fort Sumter, Sherman, Appomattox, Lee and Grant."

"September 29, 1864?" Harris held the crooked stick, looking like a conductor before a symphony. Eyebrows raised, he looked inquiringly at his nephew.

Sims shook his head.

"Where we're standing, the Confederates had a signal station. And down there"—Harris pointed with the long stick—"down there is where the Union Third Division came to fight."

Sims's eyes followed the stick. Three hundred yards away, down at the base of the hill, a narrow road ran right to left. From the road to where he stood, the ground rose evenly. Clear fields of fire—no friendly folds of earth to shelter a man. Every inch of the hillside could be raked by musket and cannon from the top. The Uzh had been bad; what would it have been like to come up this hill? He trembled at the thought of being with the Union troops that day.

"The Third Division?" he asked Harris, curious that his uncle would know such things.

"Under command of Brigadier Charles Paine," Harris answered. "The Third Division was made up of what was called USCT." Harris rolled the explanation slowly: "United States Colored Troops."

Harris pointed off to the right, where Four Mile Creek ran along the western slopes of the heights. "Earlier that morning, the division had been stopped by barricades of staked logs and fallen trees. The troops had to chop their way through with axes. The Confederate fire was deadly. Five hundred men died or were dying within minutes. Then Paine ordered the Second Brigade to attack.

"The black troops had never been in battle. They were facing veterans of Lee's Grenadier Guard. They came up the hill. Into a slaughter. Black sergeants took command of their companies when the white officers were shot down. Finally, a handful of blacks from the Second Brigade led the surge over the top and took this place." Harris swept the stick over the old killing ground.

"Fourteen blacks," Harris rumbled, "won the Medal of Honor on this hill. On this hill," he repeated in his throbbing pulpit cadence, "where we now stand."

Sims looked down the hill. It would have been warmer, that September morning. There would have been no wind and the gray clouds of gunsmoke would have hung in the still air with the cries of the dying. A somber awe struck him that this quiet hill had seen such a struggle, so much noise and pain, and that men's blood had drenched the earth where he now stood.

"I always thought—thought you were a—a pacifist."

"Pacifist?" Harris made a face like he had never heard the word. "No. We weren't pacifists. We *fought*. We—Martin—all of us around him—we weren't going to beg for our rights any longer. We demanded them and that meant a fight. And once you decide to fight, you pick your weapons and your tactics. Martin's weapons were fairness and equality. He chose nonviolence because he knew our enemies would sooner or later be overcome by their own consciences. But if he'd been here that day . . ." The wind was picking up—colder now—and making a sound through the trees like the passing of time.

"We've gone into battle for our freedom, Bradford. And we've gone to jail for it. There was a time for killing and there was a time for marching." Harris scratched at the earth with the stick, pushing away the grass and leaves, making a furrow in the red clay. He nudged the clay around, then looked up to Sims. "But those times are over. We can't keep blaming our problems on fat Southern sheriffs. Maybe now's the time to find out the truth. You've got *your* fight," Harris said with resignation tinged with pride. "You chose it. I don't know whether you're wise or foolish." Harris looked steadily at Sims, then put his hand out, fingertips touching Sims's forehead. "But God watch over you."

Harris turned to look out over the hillside. "Many who lay claim to Martin, they've lost that: the will to fight. Instead, they play the *vic*tim." He curled the word in contempt. "They demand that the whites *give* us victories." Harris's rage was that of the prophets, that of Moses come down from the mountain. "Can't they see?" he cried into the wind to the ghosts of New Market Heights, "no one can *give* us victory. Handouts won't do it. *We* must take it, fight for it."

Harris sailed the crooked stick out over the whispering, mournful battlements. Sims watched as it hung for a moment in the air, revolving slowly; then the wind took it and carried it far down the hill.

4

Two days later, Sims chose an empty bench on the Mall. To his left was the Capitol. On his right, the granite spike of the Washington Monument aimed at a crystal winter sky. Sims tugged his overcoat closer around himself and waited; the picture of a civil servant on his lunch hour getting a breath of fresh air. Clusters of tourists shuttled over the yellow gravel paths among the galleries and museums of the Smithsonian.

He waited ten, then fifteen minutes. With rising irritation, he pretended to read a sports magazine he had pulled from his coat pocket.

"Warm for January."

Startled, Sims swiveled around.

"You always come up on people from the rear?"

"Try to," Houghton rasped, settling on the bench. He wore a dark blue field jacket. Cheap sunglasses and a black baseball cap hid his face. From a crumpled pack, he pulled out a cigarette and lit it, cupping the lighter in his hands.

"I didn't know you were an Orioles fan."

Houghton gave a puzzled look over his cupped hands, then raised a hand and touched the cap in understanding. "I just bought it." He jerked a thumb over his shoulder toward the street vendors. He looked expectantly at Sims. "You said something about a decision."

"We do the initial on Valek. Look for a connection with King. The way you would have then."

"And if it's there?"

"We follow it."

"How far?"

Sims shrugged. "One step at a time. All we have is Valek."

"I want to talk to him."

This came at Sims from far out in left field. He was going to do the initial. It had to be that way, one person. It was too easy for a defector to play games and dodge when more than one person was asking the questions. "Not possible." Incredulous, Sims shook his head.

Houghton drew deeply on his cigarette. "Where're you keeping him?"

"Where he is doesn't have anything to do with it."

"You said you were running the interrogation." Insistent, demanding, Houghton turned to face Sims. "Are you?"

"What do you want with him?" Sims saw himself in the mirrors of Houghton's glasses. Here's where we set the rules, he thought.

The two men froze in an instant of confrontation. Sims saw the white man's jaw muscles tighten, the cruel mouth deepen into a menacing frown. "You want my help in this, you—"

"I want your help," Sims snapped, "but I'm not going to be your boy." He waited, but got no reaction from Houghton. "*You* tell me what you need him for. *I* decide about you seeing him."

Houghton's face hardened. Sims impassively returned Houghton's stare. I hold the cards, white man, and that's what's bugging you, isn't it? Footfalls ground the gravel of the path. A muttering bag lady approached, passed, then receded in the distance. As if the bag lady had been a cue, Houghton's mouth softened.

"I want to hear from him myself when he knew. It's important to know where he was at the time and who were the players involved."

"I can get that—"

"No you can't. Not as well. I can give you the questions to ask, but you wouldn't know how to work the follow-ups." Houghton paused to see if this got a rise. It didn't, and he continued: "You didn't live through that time. You don't know what's important and what's not. And you said yourself that Cantwell's scared of the King stuff, so you aren't going to get anybody else to help you."

Sims studied Houghton. A subtle difference about the man eluded him. For a moment, the incongruous baseball hat distracted him. Then he realized the liquor smell was absent. Houghton's speech was less mushy and there was a hint of a new vitality.

"There's something else, isn't there?"

Houghton's hand trembled slightly as he adjusted the baseball hat. He dropped the cigarette on the gravel and ground it out with his shoe. Still leaning forward, elbows on his knees, he looked at the brick towers of the Smithsonian castle for a long time, then finally turned to Sims. "I've got to see Valek for myself. I've got to find out what happened to me. He's the key. Stay in the game long enough and you learn there's a feeling about these things. I had it. I was good at it."

Sims felt a warm spill of sympathy, then reminded himself of the night in the hallway outside Houghton's apartment. "Give me a day or two," he replied. "I'll see what I can do."

Two days later, Sims stood under the canopy of a rundown apartment building in north Arlington. He nervously checked his watch, then scanned the parking lot. A chill afternoon rain and the north wind were stripping the last leaves off the poplars lining the lot. The leaves scuttled along the grass, stopping to rest against the curb, only to be flattened by the rain and plastered to the water-slicked pavement.

An ancient high-backed BMW 2002 turned off Lee Highway and found a parking place in the lot. The door opened and Sims saw the whiteness of Houghton's face as he surveyed the apartment building. Houghton wore a battered Irish walking hat and a cheap tan raincoat, the kind you ultimately forget and leave in a restaurant. He carried an umbrella that flapped in the wind like a monstrous black broken-backed bird.

Houghton soon stood under the streaming canopy, eyeing Sims and folding the wounded umbrella.

"How'd you work it?"

"Valek's regular sitter has a zipper problem. He wanted off for the day. I got a substitute from security."

"And me? What am I supposed to be?"

"You're an analyst. Here to talk to Valek about Czech political stuff."

Houghton pursed his lips questioningly.

"Nobody's interested in him except you and me. And there's nobody around who knows you."

"Yes." Houghton drew it out, as though thinking while he said it. "I suppose you're right. Nobody knows me." He lost the wistful look and made a jerky gesture into the apartment building. "You keep him here?"

"No. We only use this for interrogations. He stays out in the country. I've got to get him back before five."

Sims knocked on a door midway down the hallway on the second floor. There was a sound in the apartment, probably of someone eyeing them through the judas hole in the door. A pasty-faced man let them in. He was your standard security handler: cheap sport coat, tieless shirt, and thin greasy hair. Houghton could tell it was a safe house as surely as an old soldier would recognize a battlefield. There was the impersonal emptiness sketched by an ill-matched assortment of cheap furniture and the stale smell of cigarettes, burned coffee, and reheated canned food. And there was the usual safe-house litter: the bent-cover paperbacks, cups used for ashtrays, and the deck of cards strewn across a coffee table.

The interrogation room, once a bedroom, had been stripped bare. Like the living room, its furniture was castoffs: a battered wooden desk, two ragged upholstered chairs, and a drunkenly tilting floor lamp.

Houghton studied the room, noting the angles of sight of windows and doors. He peered into both closets and inspected the small bath.

"He ever been in here before?" Houghton asked, noisily adjusting the blinds to block a direct view of the outside but to let in the metallic winter light.

Sims frowned his answer, stung that Houghton would question something so basic.

Ignoring Sims's irritation, Houghton shifted the chairs, looked at the window, then made minor adjustments to the floor lamp. Satisfied, he stood still in the center of the room, head cocked as if listening, trying to sense some invisible tracery in the room's parched air. "Dead spots?"

Sims shook his head. The techs had wired the room from one end to the other. Everything ran into an adjacent bedroom, into two different recorders. There were two battery-driven backups as well. A fisheye in the overhead light fixture and a zoom behind the two-way mirror would focus on Valek and snare his every move and facial expression on videotape.

"You want to use the desk? Something to take notes on?"

Houghton shook his head. "No. Let's see his 201 again." He motioned to the folder in Sims's hand. The day before, Sims had sat nervously in Houghton's apartment as the older man had gone over the polygraph tapes, handwritten autobiography, and the reports from medical and psychology.

Houghton leafed through the contents for several minutes, then handed the file back to Sims. "That's enough."

Sims went into the adjoining bedroom. A tech was rewinding one of the recorders. Sims motioned for the sitter to fetch Valek, then sat down to watch through the two-way mirror.

In an oddly monochrome presentation, he saw the sitter bring Valek into the room next door, then leave. Houghton, his back to the door, was looking out the window. He heard the door close, then turned. Valek was unable to make Houghton out because of the light from the window. The defector stood blinking, an aura of vulnerability about him.

Houghton did a quick inventory. Valek still had his foppish-thin good looks. Hair grayed, but well styled. And still the dresser, Houghton noted sourly. French tennis shirt, English slacks, and shiny Italian tassel loafers—a regular walking United Nations.

"Hello, Miloslav," Houghton said quietly. "It's been a while since Prague."

Valek stiffened in surprise. Suspicion quickly replaced surprise, and wariness tightened across his face. His mouth worked soundlessly before he managed to speak. "Edward!" He stood in uncertainty, working off his shock. Then he put on a smile and extended his right hand.

Houghton pointed to the chair, ignoring Valek's hand. "Sit here," he commanded. The two chairs faced each other, Houghton's face in partial shadow from the window and the floor lamp.

"It *has* been a long time since Prague." Valek forced a hollow geniality. "I thought—I heard that—"

"That I was out of the racket?"

Valek nodded.

Houghton leaned forward, catching Valek's eyes with his own. "They've called me back to talk to you about a few things, Miloslav."

"About—"

Houghton let a small smile play on his lips. *It's for me to know.* He thought the message to Valek, knowing the smile would tell Valek just that. "About a few things, Miloslav," he repeated, with hints of darkness. "A few things that we'll get to in good time."

Valek patted his shirt nervously and with the other hand reached toward his trousers pocket.

Houghton jabbed, his voice stern, commanding. "No smoking."

Valek's hands stopped in place and he gave Houghton a controlled neutral look.

Houghton changed pace, smiling disarmingly. "I quit some years ago. Now the smell of smoke bothers me—you understand?"

Valek hesitated, then nodded, crossed his legs, folded his hands in his lap, and waited, brown eyes fixed steadily on Houghton. This was going to be harder than he'd thought. His mind raced, searching for everything he remembered about Houghton, hoping to find anything that would let him gain some mental handhold to narrow the odds against him. I give and they take, he told himself. I know nearly nothing about him. He knows everything I've told the others. And whatever else they have in their files. And whatever he remembers.

"Why did you come over?"

In the control room, Sims punched the buttons that began the audio recorders.

"I've written it out. Surely you've read it—"

"I want to hear it from you." Houghton arched an eyebrow. "Does it cause you difficulty?" he challenged.

Valek took a breath, then began.

Houghton listened and watched. He already knew the story—the *words* of the story. It was almost a casebook story of an ideological defection—the final failure to paper over the gradually deepening disillusionment. The escape attempts through sex, alcohol, even drugs. The coming to terms. The decision.

What he wanted now was Valek's telling of it. He wanted to feel the quality of Valek's expression, the balance and timber of his voice, to fit the intangibles against the 201 file's story written in such a neat, European cursive.

"So, here I am, again face-to-face with you." Valek finished it long minutes later.

Houghton crossed his arms across his chest and leaned back in his chair. "Well, Miloslav?" Houghton asked expectantly.

Valek was puzzled. "Well?" he echoed. "I've finished."

"I don't mean that," Houghton explained. "It's just that you seem to be—how to put it—waiting? Yes, waiting."

"Waiting?" Another echo.

"Yes. Maybe you're waiting for a grade from me?"

"Grade?" Valek's face pinched in a wounded expression. "What do you mean?"

"A grade on your performance," Houghton said innocently.

"Do you think I'm lying?" Valek asked indignantly. "Why do you think I'm lying?"

"Lying?" Houghton raised his eyebrows. "Why, I never said anything about you *lying*, Miloslav. Just that it seemed to me you were waiting for some signal from me that I bought your story. That's all."

Valek defiantly tilted his chin. "I passed the polygraph."

"Oh?" Houghton raised his eyes mockingly. "They told you? Just like that? 'Miloslav, congratulations, you've passed.' Is that how they do it these days?"

"No, no." Obviously backpedaling, Valek groped for an answer. "I meant that it seemed to me . . . it seemed they never acted as if—"

"As if they'd caught you lying, Miloslav?" Houghton asked it with a soft deadliness.

"You're twisting everything I say!" Valek cried, anger mixing with fear, his face flushing. "You can't do this to me!"

Houghton regarded him with an executioner's sad, dispassionate look. "Yes, Miloslav, I can." His eyes took on a hint of pity. "I can do this to you. I can do a lot more to you," Houghton finished in a hoarse whisper.

Valek's face lost its lean angular definition as fear puffed his features, making him suddenly much older. Far away, Houghton heard traffic noises and, closer, the whir of the heating system. *There's something you know,* he imagined saying to the Czech, *something that changed my life forever. You might not realize you know it. And I might not recognize it if you say it. But we're going to dig for it, Miloslav, we're going to dig for it in this goddamn room.*

Houghton leaned forward. Raising his eyebrows, he asked with evil innocence, "Why did you defect?"

Valek's face took on the look of a man mired in a quicksand nightmare, where one struggled with all his failing strength only to have his efforts bring him nothing but more desperation.

"My God! I've already told you—" His voice cracked with mounting desperation. The headache that had plagued him earlier now returned as an evil, pounding throbbing, a malicious devouring thing shooting spines of pain through his brain.

"Oh yes, your sudden disenchantment with the spy business." Houghton said it mockingly. "No. What I meant was, why did you have to defect? This isn't the bad old days, Miloslav. Democracy's all over the place. Why didn't you just walk out? Put in for your retirement and ask disbursing to send the check to Miami Beach or wherever? And why were those guys chasing you?"

Valek laughed. It was a braying insincere laugh, as if complimenting Houghton on a magnificent joke. It was an obvious attempt to slide by.

Houghton, face impassive, waited for Valek's answer.

Valek's strained smile vanished. He chose his words carefully. "There is freedom for others, but I transferred to the KGB. They

52

wouldn't have let me go. Because of what I know. What I do—what I did."

"The last irony of communism," Houghton taunted. "The jailers have to stay in the jail."

Through the two-way mirror, Sims saw Houghton get up and go to the desk. His back to Valek, he poured two cups of coffee from a large thermos. He offered a cup to Valek.

"The last Communist director of the *Statni bezpecnost* was Tomas. Tell me about him." Houghton used Czech for the StB, Prague's secret intelligence service.

Momentarily off balance, Valek hesitated. The interrogation was entering a new phase. No more probing for motives—now came the minefield: the trick questions, the testing of who knew what and who would tell what. Gingerly, he answered, "Tomas had nothing to do with StB. He was head of *Verejna bezpecnost,* the uniformed police."

Houghton acted as if he were weighing this. He surrendered the tight smile of a man reluctantly admitting error. "Yes—yes, of course," he corrected himself. "It's Broz who had StB. You were close to him, weren't you?"

"In the early years," Valek acknowledged. He related the StB chief's background. The American's face was a blank; his eyes dead and expressionless. This drove Valek to talk, if only to fill the uncomfortable void. He found too that he could evade the energy-sapping parrying with Houghton by talking, and so he continued for fifteen more minutes. He got to Broz's service in Washington as head of the StB *rezidentura* in the Czech embassy and purposely gave a wrong date.

Inwardly, Houghton smiled as he retrieved the date from the files Sims had brought him. "Broz wasn't here in '82," he interrupted in a cold laconic voice. "It was '84."

Pretending to think over the dates, Valek wrinkled his forehead.

Before he could continue, Houghton asked, "Your role in the Afro-Asian Solidarity Committee—tell me about it."

Valek recognized the change in course. Here it is, he thought. What he's really after. But why? What has it got to do with anything now?

"I asked about—"

"I was a delegate—"

"Delegate?" Houghton gave a small laugh. "You and Broz? Truly inspiring, two of StB's fast movers, donating their time to help their little friends of color."

Valek sat and waited for Houghton.

"Let me tell you how it looked from our side, Miloslav. The Afro-Asian Solidarity Committee was owned and operated by Service A." The face of Houghton's adversary came back with startling clarity. The KGB's Service A had been responsible for disinformation: the systematic deception of American intelligence. The Czech StB, with its own extensive windows into the West, had been one of Service A's most accomplished allies. "Service A used the committee to stir up American opposition to the Vietnam War."

"You give us too much credit." Valek smirked, dropping any pretense about the committee being anything other than a KGB front. "Your own generals and politicians did a better job than we could have."

Houghton went on without seeming to pay attention. "Broz ran the Service A cell that controlled the committee, didn't he?"

Valek nodded, his face expressionless.

Houghton recognized a trick of the trade: In a hostile interrogation, throw out just enough to answer a question. See how much the interrogator knows by forcing the follow-up questions.

"You were his deputy until late '67. He got promoted and you took over."

"Yes." Valek closed his eyes and pinched the bridge of his nose between thumb and forefinger. "It's been a long time—"

Enough of this shit, Valek. "Yes, it was a long time ago. Let me help you," Houghton offered in an obviously insincere air of friendship. "Your headquarters were on the third floor at number two Valdstejnske Square in Prague. After Broz left, you took over." He looked at Valek and waited for a confirming nod.

Valek's eyes glittered, as if hypnotized by Houghton's recital. He felt the need to urinate. "Yes. I took over." He breathed deeply, straining to get oxygen past the crushing pressure on his chest. Which could harm him more, a lie or the truth? What did the Americans know? What was in their files on him? What was the life of a lie? Could they catch him later? If they did, what would they do?

Sims saw Valek squirm. It had been a good performance. Houghton had made it all the more impressive by his casual, confident manner, as if it were but a small sample from a vast hidden lode.

Houghton delivered the stinger with exquisite timing. "The Afro-Asian Solidarity Committee, Miloslav, had many targets. One of them was Martin Luther King."

Valek fought the twisting coils of doubt and counterdoubt as the shout rang within himself, *How much does he really know?* Reflexively, he fumbled in his pocket and had the cigarette pack almost out before he caught Houghton looking at him. He dropped his hand back into his lap. "We had nothing to do with King."

"You operated against Martin Luther King's Southern Christian Leadership Conference, Miloslav."

Valek shook his head. "No. We had nothing to do with—"

"With what?" Houghton almost shouted. "With the killing?"

"We had nothing to do with it."

"You were running disinformation against us during the Vietnam War and you put King out of bounds? Come on, Miloslav. You guys weren't fools. Don't think I'm one, either."

"I don't." Valek's voice climbed. "We . . . we went after King. Targeted him. But—but nothing happened. We got nowhere."

"Why?"

"We tried to get inside his organization through—through some contacts."

"Party members?"

Valek nodded. "There were several."

"Did King ever learn about them?"

"I understand he was warned."

"What'd King do?"

"He did a housecleaning."

"Did they—the party members—know that you were trying to use them against King?"

Valek gave a cynical laugh. "Of course not. They were old-line members. Altruistic naïfs."

"Yes," Houghton said dryly, "expendables." Houghton then got up and walked around the room, stretching his back. He stopped at the window and looked through the slats of the blind. Dark was coming and some of the cars already had turned on their lights. The rain had stopped and the evening sky signaled more snow. He turned around. Valek's shoulders were slumped and his face drawn in a study of weariness and fatigue.

Houghton came back to his chair and sat down. "Tell me, Miloslav, about the AASC. I've always been curious. What happened in Prague after the King killing, after I left?"

"Andropov closed it down."

"When?"

"Oh, by the end of April—early May."

"Why?"

Valek shrugged. "He didn't consult me," he answered ironically.

"Perhaps he thought it had been compromised. Perhaps the King killing made Center nervous."

"But you said you didn't have anything to do with King."

"*I* didn't have anything to do with it. *I know nothing,*" Valek said quickly.

"And the Center?"

"You know the answer to that. If others did it, Center wasn't going to tell me."

"Now, Miloslav," Houghton began almost casually, "tell me when you first learned about Ray."

"Ray?"

"James Earl Ray. King's killer."

"When? You want a date? I don't remember if—"

"*Before* April fourth—before the killing?"

Valek hesitated. Houghton, sensing Valek's discomfort, repeated loudly, "Did you know of him *before* the killing?"

Behind the looking glass, Sims's breath caught. The two men were frozen figures suddenly shrunken, as if seen through the wrong end of a telescope. Only the slight whispering of the recorders told him time had not stopped.

Valek's eyes widened as he saw where Houghton was leading. "No." He held up a protesting hand. "I swear I didn't—"

Houghton studied him for long moments. "Did others know of him before?"

"We've been through this before, Edward. I know what *I* know. I don't know what the others knew."

"But isn't it possible that—" Houghton persisted.

"Anything's *possible,*" Valek answered, wearied by the continued attempts to drag him in.

"After, then. What did you find out about Ray after the killing?" Houghton tried to narrow Valek's running room, knowing the session was coming to a close.

"Nothing." Valek said it emphatically.

"Anything about a traveling companion, a man named Raoul?"

"Nothing," Valek repeated, "except what I could gather from the newspapers. I told you, they assigned me elsewhere. As I said, there was much disorder. Everything was in turmoil."

Behind the mirror, Sims again heard the sirens, smelled the smoke, and felt the terrible emptiness of a boy who had just learned his father would never come home again.

5

Sims took the stairs to the basement. Passing the gym and indoor running track, he cut through an underground corridor. He slipped his identification card into a slot by a bank of elevators, stepped inside, and punched a button. The pressure squeezed his chest and ears as the car plummeted into the granite ridge running along the Potomac.

The elevator opened onto a corridor that, right and left, curved gently out of sight. Eggshell white walls, bright indirect lighting, and pale blue carpeting further blurred any sense of dimension, creating an impression of infinity. The air had a sterile, oiled taste; a trace of ozone crackled in the nostrils.

He walked but a few paces to a door on which a small black plastic plaque read INFORMATION MANAGEMENT CENTER. It was one of those characteristic Agency titles that identified an office without saying anything about it.

Again the card-in-the-slot trick: the doors slid open with a hydraulic sigh and he felt a slight draft of air go by. He faced a massive room that seemed to extend forever, filled with row on row of computers.

"Come on up, Bradford." The odd quacking voice came from a loudspeaker just inside the door. Sims took the ramp leading to a glass balcony that jutted out over the computer room. Inside, banks of video displays created a surreal light show.

"How's it running?" Even without the loudspeaker, the voice kept its high, quacking quality. Sims turned to see a small block of a man in a motorized wheelchair. The drug thalidomide had ravaged Matthias Alberich before birth, leaving his genius to occupy a legless torso from which small, almost vestigial hands sprouted directly from the shoulders.

Alberich was another Riddle recruit. A near chess master at fourteen, Alberich had caught Riddle's attention at a pickup game in a New York ice cream parlor. Riddle had talked with an old friend in Boston, and by nineteen Alberich had earned a doctorate in engineering from MIT. He then disappeared into the bowels of Langley. Only Alberich's intellect and the Agency's budget could have created the computer room, an electronic alter ego that carried him into places barred to other men.

"I'm still getting some knocking."

"Shit." Alberich frowned. "What speeds?"

"Around three thousand rpm. High-end of second, low of third. Noticed it coming across the bridge this morning. And compression's still off in number two."

Alberich gave a disgusted look. "I thought the rings would do it."

Just after Czechoslovakia, Sims had discovered the 1959 Mercedes convertible on blocks in a barn on Maryland's Eastern Shore. The brakes were shot, the body badly rusted, and the engine and transmission needed overhauling. He had mentioned his restoration efforts one day to Alberich and was surprised at, then later grateful for, Alberich's passion for automobiles.

"Cars are freedom," Alberich had said, without the slightest trace of wistfulness or self-pity.

For the past months, he and Sims had worked together. Alberich designed a web of fiber-optic strands and sensors that monitored every function of the car. He made sense of the jackstraw heaps of numbers on computer printouts while Sims translated Alberich's analysis into specifics such as clearances, timing, and fuel-air mixtures.

"Maybe we can look at it this weekend."

Alberich nodded. Still engrossed with the number two cylinder, he reluctantly got to the business at hand. "The initial tape—we're done with it." Alberich touched a control, spun his chair around, and was off.

Walking quickly, Sims caught up with Alberich at a large conference table.

Alberich docked his chair, maneuvering smoothly into a slot in the table. On either side of the slot, banks of controls snugly encased him, their switches, buttons, and keypads positioned so that his flipper hands could reach them. The effect was of a hybrid being, part flesh, part electronics. But the face and the eyes left no doubt that the human was in control.

Alberich touched a keypad and studied a small flat-screen display. "We ran the tapes through the grinder." He pursed his lips. "Initial interrogation, KGB officer Miloslav Valek," he read from the display.

Like so much ore, the Agency processed and refined the tapes of Valek's interrogation. They were then sent to various Agency offices to be hammered and shaped. The written transcripts would be a check for inconsistencies in later interrogations and would support or refute testimony of other defectors and agents. Already, Morse's psych staff was nosing jackal-like into the audio- and videotapes, snarling and fighting over such leavings as the Jungian implications of Valek's body language. For his part, Alberich had computer-minced Valek's voice into minute particles, then fed them through the Crays. The raging supercomputers had been tamed by a software program that supposedly could measure the speaker's stress, hence an attempt to deceive.

"It's all mumbo jumbo." Alberich's eyes flicked across the screen. "The Agency's latest flyer in truth-finding technology." He touched the keypad again. Tap—again. "I don't trust this stuff worth a shit—"

"There's a 'but' in there," Sims guessed.

Alberich touched the keypad yet again. "If you concede that those adding machines out there"—he eyed the floor full of Crays—"can *sense* anything, there are some areas you ought to check into."

"Such as?"

"No specifics—not on the basis of a single interrogation. But there are strong indications of evasiveness. You've got a guy who's trying to bob and weave on you." Alberich gestured toward the computers. "They're only machines. I depend on them more than you do, so I know their limits."

Sims nodded, taking another look at the rows of computers. A white-robed tech was moving among them. Priest? Servant? It struck Sims as surreal that the tech was examining the large computers, then punching in the information into a small hand-held computer.

Sims made getting-up motions. "Anything else?"

Alberich undocked from the conference table and the banks of controls. Without the surrounding banks of controls, the face was quite human and almost handsome.

"I ran the *entire* interrogation."

Sims tried to puzzle out Alberich's meaning. He thought he heard a note of apology. "Yes?"

"Well"—Alberich hesitated—"the other voice. The interrogator. His voiceprint doesn't match anybody on our rolls."

Sims looked steadily at Alberich. "He's not. Used to be." He chopped up the words, not wanting to lie to Alberich.

Alberich considered this, then swiveled his wheelchair toward the ramp.

"I'd appreciate it," Sims began hesitantly, "if you didn't mention the voiceprint."

Alberich said nothing but continued his whirring progress toward the ramp.

"Cantwell would be pissed."

They reached the top of the ramp. Alberich stopped and spun his chair to face Sims. "Cantwell?"

"Yes," Sims answered. "He'd be *very* pissed."

Alberich gave him a conspiratorial grin. "Cantwell's a fuckwit."

Sims knocked and entered. Cantwell, behind his desk, didn't wave him to a chair, so Sims stood.

"HPSCI wants a briefing on your defector." Cantwell pronounced the initials HIP-see. The House Permanent Select Committee on Intelligence.

"Why?"

"Well, I suppose the obvious answer is that they asked for it. They get a routine report on all defectors."

Sims could tell from the snotty tone that Cantwell was unhappy. "But why Valek?"

"Who knows? Some goddamned fishing expedition."

"Who's fishing?"

Sims saw Cantwell's mouth tighten at the corners as he said the name. Donald Stanley. Sims's image of the Illinois congressman came from television news clips. Thin, handsome. Maybe mid-fifties. Café au lait complexion, neatly trimmed silver beard. Large, luminous eyes, index finger shaking menacingly into the camera.

"He's always after us," Cantwell said. In hearings, Stanley's style was a fearsome mix of a hellfire sermon and a rubber hose beating. Cantwell had been an Agency witness before Stanley several years ago. He still shuddered at the memory. "He's hell on defectors."

"He doesn't like defectors?"

"Not that. He uses them against us. How we handle them and all."

Remembering his own desire to dodge the tasks of settling Valek, Sims felt a flush of embarrassment. "You going?"

"No. I want to keep it low-key. Legislative counsel's sending someone with you."

Since the Agency's founding in 1947, the relationship between Langley and Congress had been one of distrust and suspicion spiked with
moments of mutual lust; an affair between a charming lecher and a
proud but aging whore.

In the beginning, the Agency found shelter and sustenance under
the wings of Congress's old guard. The Agency's first directors could
slip into Capitol Hill cloakrooms and hideaway offices, meet with
legends like Sam Rayburn and Richard Russell, and come away with
a sign-off on a new spy plane or a coup in Guatemala.

But in the mid-sixties, television and Vietnam ganged up and
mugged the rickety congressional seniority system. Washington was
beginning to respond to the demands and rewards of network news.
Cleverness increasingly came to be mistaken for intellect as the nation's leaders discovered the power of the sound bite. It was at this
time that the Agency, wounded in Southeast Asia, staggered onto the
scene, offering itself up as a victim. Junior congressmen and senators
shoved aside the old boys who had run Capitol Hill and competed
with one another for the chance to batter Langley on prime-time news.
Hearings became frenzied circuses in which blow-dried lawmakers
fed Agency witnesses to the lions of CBS, NBC, and ABC.

The good times rolled until adults got the asylum back under a
modicum of control. In 1976, Senate Majority Leader Robert Byrd set
up the Select Committee on Intelligence. A year later, Speaker Tip
O'Neill followed suit in the House of Representatives with a similar
committee, HPSCI, or House Permanent Select Committee on Intelligence.

Formal organization and accountability having restored a semblance of responsibility, the Agency and Congress entered a period
of wary reconciliation. To see to the proper care and feeding of the
intelligence committees that held its purse strings, the Agency quickly
set up its own legislative counsel's office. Agile officers like Frankie
Cole went to charm school, where, with all the cunning and enthusiasm they had previously devoted to penetrating the Politburo, they
learned to work Capitol Hill.

Cole swung open a wooden cabinet on the wall to expose a white
drawing board. Uncapping a bright red felt-tip marker, he sketched
a rudimentary organization chart. "HPSCI's divided into subcommit-
tees. Stanley's chairman of the subcommittee on oversight. He's been

in the House fourteen years. He came in as a radical." Cole held his hands out away from his bald head. "Bushy Afro and all that. Settled down over the years, but still doesn't pass up a chance to trash us." Cole snapped the cap back onto the marker and bounced it in the palm of his hand. "He's also dean of the congressional black caucus."

Sims looked back at Cole with an expression of disinterest.

"Appointment's tomorrow—ten-thirty. Come here at ten. I'll have a car to take us to the Hill."

Sims nodded. At the door, Cole called out to him.

"By the way, you *do* know we sent him a transcript of Valek's initial?"

"No."

Cole raised his eyebrows. "Funny. I thought Cantwell would've told you."

Stanley's office was in the Rayburn Building, a graceless stack of marble and granite slabs. Stanley's chief aide, a thin, taciturn man named Terrell, met them. The congressman, Terrell explained, was finishing up a committee meeting and would be here shortly. He showed Sims and Cole into Stanley's office, saw that they had coffee, and excused himself.

Stanley's desk was in front of the single large window. The window framed a Hollywood set's view of the Capitol, the dome a resplendent white against a cornflower sky. The office walls were a crowded gallery of framed photographs chronicling Stanley's fourteen years in the House of Representatives. Sims recognized most of the men and women with Stanley. World leaders, athletes, writers, actors. Sims came to a photograph of Stanley and Mandela. Standing together on a speaker's platform, both men were grinning happily into the crowd. Sims could almost hear the gale of shouts and applause. Behind them was the banner of the African National Congress. Stanley, both arms over his head, was giving a double thumbs-up gesture. Mandela's right arm circled Stanley's waist, his left raised in a clenched-fist salute.

"I should like to think that Nelson has a copy of that one on *his* wall, but I believe that is rather unlikely." It was a round baritone voice. The gliding elocution was precise and grandiose, almost to the point of foppishness.

Sims turned from the photograph. Stanley was in the doorway. The congressman was not as tall as Sims had imagined, but the face was leaner and younger-looking, set off by the high stiff collar of an obviously tailor-made shirt. Sims had read in the briefing book that Stanley still played a fast-breaking game of basketball in the House gym. The book also had a press photo of Stanley, his arm flung over the shoulder of a teammate, a notoriously conservative Ohio Republican. The smiles on both faces said that party labels were only jock-deep; love of the game transcended party and ideology.

Stanley carried a dark red portfolio under his left arm. There was a shaking of hands all around and Stanley graciously apologized for keeping them waiting while walking Sims and Cole toward a sofa. Stanley took a chair opposite them, holding the portfolio in his lap. Sims saw that the cover bore the cabalistic stamps and warnings from classified registry. Stanley pulled out a thick sheaf of legal-size paper bound at the top by a shiny metal clip. From a coat pocket, he produced a pair of horn-rimmed reading glasses with half-moon lenses. Folding back the bright green cover sheet, he leafed through the first several pages, reacquainting himself with the contents. Finally, he looked up at Sims.

"The transcript." Stanley tapped the papers in explanation. "You did the interrogation?"

Frankie Cole handed Sims a copy of the transcript. Sims was somehow reassured by the bulk of it. "I was in charge of it, Congressman."

"Make it Don. And they call you . . . ?" Sims told him, and Stanley paused to remember the name. Then, diving into the transcript, he found a page marked by a paper clip. "I want to go back to the defector's claim that"—Stanley consulted a copy of the interrogation transcript—"yes, here it is, Bradford—that Valek was an operative in the Afro-Asian Solidarity Committee."

Stanley sat back in his chair. He took off the reading glasses, twirled them by one stem.

Sims turned to the passage in the transcript. "Yes?" He looked up to Stanley.

"Are you saying that the AASC was an arm of the KGB? That Dr. King was being manipulated by the Soviet Union?"

"No, *I'm* not saying that at all," Sims answered. He started to use Stanley's first name, but feeling uncomfortable with it, didn't. "*Valek* said that he was working with the KGB's disinformation operation, that the AASC was a KGB front, and that Dr. King had been a target."

Stanley stared for a moment at Sims, weighing the statement, then put on his glasses and returned to the transcript, turning several pages. "There's another—yes." He stabbed an index finger at the paragraph. "You say here, quote, 'There were several party members in the King organization.' Unquote."

Stanley made a theatrical gesture of taking off his glasses and pointing them at Sims. "My question to you, Mr. Sims: Is CIA trying to drive this into the defector's testimony? That there were Communists pulling the strings?"

"Drive it in? It was just an interrogation question. And nobody said anything about pulling strings. The defector said the approach didn't work. Why would the Agency try to make more of it than it was?"

Stanley narrowed his eyes and pressed his lips together in a tight, determined line. "Bradford, I was one of Dr. King's closest confidants. I know the efforts the United States government made to smear Martin." He paused, then said as an afterthought, "I was with him throughout. I was there when he died."

"Yes," Sims said quietly. "I know about that."

Stanley stopped, thrown off balance in what was obviously an often-told story. "I suppose I'm in your files out at CIA."

"My uncle told me about you."

Stanley paused and a small smile softened his face. "Your uncle?"

"He was with Dr. King, too." Sims saw Stanley's smile become condescending and knew what the congressman was thinking: Every black who'd shaken King's hand at a rally or saw him from a crowd now claimed he'd "been with Dr. King."

"Calvin Harris."

Frankie Cole saw the cloud appear briefly on Stanley's face. Something there, he thought, and said a small prayer that it wouldn't be gotten into here.

"Calvin Harris?" Stanley put on a huge, glowing smile. "We shared many a cell together."

"Snore?"

It took a second to register, then Stanley laughed, clapping his hands at the same time. "Olympic class. I presume he is still down there in—"

"Sandston. Near Richmond."

"Too bad. A man like that"—Stanley shook his head—"exiling himself down there. He could be here in Congress. God knows, we could use him."

"He seems to think he's needed where he is."

"He's still preaching that bootstrap business?"

"What he talks about is self-help."

e caught by
Yassir Arafat
Everyone sat
of the room.
one sat with
he chairs—
he German
ater of anti-
se man with
file photo in
rseas station
looked again.
nted energy.
o know. "Ya-
n."
k to Stanley.

ggle for lib-
ood looking
ng out there

shoulder.
Nidal from

cross the El-
ned a store-
e fifties, the
lowed them,
s, then later
eviewing the
rish neon-lit

aiting at the
put them in
nd the meal

ack solidarity." Stanley said it with
back into the transcript, searching

ring its grandness to Harris's study

back on and he found the page he
n that Communists infiltrated Dr.

ral party members in the King or-
put it carefully.
ou any names?"

h anxiety. "We're not out to grind
ar anybody."
—Stanley gave Cole a hard look—
ole nodded enthusiastically. Stan-
cerned about the reputation of Dr.

those who could use something

eeing the rise of Mr. Duke down
emocrats as well as Republicans,
he black community. Divide us.
l. "Why do you think they served
eme Court?" He glared into the
w on Dr. King . . ." Stanley raised
mforting to me that you are han-
ntest hint of invitation in Stanley's
wait for a response.
msy thank you. A loud insistent
anley looked up at a wall clock.
hts burned.
into the portfolio. "Floor vote,"
f his chair.
way, Cole stepping out into the

receptionist's area. Sims stopped on the way out, his e
yet another of Stanley's photographs. Next to Stanley,
beamed his wet-lipped jackal's smile into the camera.
side by side in overstuffed chairs, facing into the center
The meeting room symbolized the Middle East—every
their backs to the wall. Sims recognized others in
the concerned Episcopal bishop, the Irish lawyer,
industrialist—ever-ready extras in Arafat's traveling the
Israeli agitation. Just to Stanley's right was a thin, inter
a drooping mustache. Sims matched the face against a
his memory, a photo the Agency had posted in every ove
and base. It was Abu Nidal, the gold-card terrorist. Sims
The terrorist's eyes seemed to gleam with a wired, deme

"Last year," Stanley explained, thinking Sims wanted
sir invited me. A conference on the Palestinian questio

Sims looked at Stanley, to the photograph, then bac
"Must have been interesting."

"Inspiring"—Stanley made it a correction—"the stre
eration." Stanley made no motion toward the door but s
at Sims, as if measuring him. Finally: "What're you do
—at Langley?"

"CI officer, I—"

"I don't mean that. I mean, why're you at CIA at all?'

"I like the work. I think it's important."

"Repression? Putting down liberation movements?"

"I haven't seen any of that."

"I have," Stanley said sadly, putting a hand on Sims'

Sims turned to leave, catching the killer stare of Ab
the photograph on the wall.

Sims turned onto Calvert Street and made his way a
lington Bridge. Adams-Morgan's ethnic restaurants for
front frieze of America's foreign policy disasters. In t
Hungarians came. The Vietnamese and Cambodians fo
and in turn were followed by the Afghans and Ethiopia
by the Salvadoreans. Now, ominously, food critics were
latest Russian and Ukrainian offerings along the g
streets.

Saigonnais, as usual, was crowded. Houghton was
bar, smoking and watching the crowd. Tin, the owner
a relatively quiet corner. Houghton did the ordering

went swiftly. The nearest table was taken by a couple whose conversation alternated between the seductive and the argumentative. They finally left with clutching haste during a swing back into the seductive. After the table was cleared, Houghton ordered another coffee, looked around, then leaned forward.

"You got Valek back all right?"

Sims nodded.

Houghton stirred the coffee with exaggerated care, taking the spoon out, tapping it delicately on the cup edge, aligning it just so on the table. He looked up at Sims. "He's a lying sack of shit, you know."

First Alberich and his Crays, now Houghton. Sims drained the last of his beer in a long, thirsty draft. Over the top of his glass he caught Houghton watching him. He put the glass down, moving it to the side, so it wouldn't be between them. "What makes you think so?"

"He didn't want to talk."

Sims had sensed it too. Valek hadn't run true to form. Defectors talked. And talked. They did it to unburden themselves. They did it to justify what they'd done. You didn't need to pry it out of them. You had to get them to shut up. "Big lie or little one?"

Houghton thought it over. "Probably both. But big ones for sure."

"Those are?"

"Why he defected, for starters."

"You're still on that?"

Houghton shook his head, a dog worrying a bone. "It's not right. All that failed dream crap is just that—crap. Ideology didn't make Valek sign up and it didn't make him leave."

"It's been a long time since you knew him in Prague," Sims suggested, playing the devil's advocate. "People change."

Houghton waved him off. "I know people," he maintained, making that an important point, one he didn't want Sims to doubt. "I know Valek. He's an opportunistic bastard. Everything he does he does for Miloslav Valek. He's here because it somehow suits him."

"Another big lie?"

"His operation," Houghton answered slowly, thinking about it. "About it folding up after King's death."

"Why not? We've shut down like that."

"It wasn't that kind of operation. You have to realize, we were at war, and it was too useful to them."

"Did you trace Valek after—after the killing?"

"Hell no, I was fired."

"But as far as you remember, he was inside the AASC until then?"

Houghton nodded.

"For at least two months after the killing? Until June '68?"

Houghton nodded again.

Doing what? Sims wondered. And why did Valek lie about it? Sims went on to summarize the meeting with the Illinois congressman. Houghton listened, lighting one cigarette after another. Sims finished and waited.

Houghton stubbed out his cigarette, took the napkin off his lap, and tossed it on the table. "They're both lying. Valek's fucking lying," he said with emphasis. "There *was* a connection between our friends in Prague and your Dr. King."

"How do you know?" As soon as he asked it, Sims saw Houghton's wolfish grin and knew the older man had been waiting for him.

"You know I tried to recruit Valek and that it didn't work. But I did get somebody else in the outfit. He's the one who reported on Valek."

"But I went through your files. There wasn't anything about a recruitment."

Houghton fiddled with his coffee spoon. "It was in my soft files. In Prague station. King got killed, Angleton called me back, and, well"—he shrugged—"it never got into the files at Langley."

They sat quietly while the table was cleared, Sims tracing lines in the tablecloth with a finger. Sims began a straight line, extended it several inches, then ended it in a spiral. He looked up at Houghton. "Your source?" he asked. "He told you about the connection?"

Houghton's eyebrows raised. "Just that there was one. I was going to go back to him for more but time ran out."

"He still alive?"

Houghton nodded without hesitation.

"How do you know? You've been in contact with him or something?"

"Or something." Houghton gave another wolfish grin. "Our friend Valek told me he was still around."

Sims tried to remember the interrogation, the names Valek had mentioned. One stood out because of its sheer unlikelihood. "You mean—"

Houghton's smile grew even larger. "Yeah," he said with pride. "Josef Broz."

Sims looked at Houghton in astonishment. "You had the head of Czech intelligence on the hook and you didn't turn him over to the Agency?"

"In '68 he wasn't running StB. He was just a guy."

"But when he moved up—"

"Yeah. When Broz moved up, I was out on my ass." Houghton mistook Sims's astonishment for accusation. His voice grew harsh and bitter. Sims had never known the long squalid days, days without meaning or direction, of drunkenness and morose self-pity.

"I should have gone back to the Agency and told them? 'Oh, dear sirs, I wish to make you a present,' " Houghton minced in a prissy falsetto. "That it?" he challenged belligerently. He waited for Sims's answer, which he knew wouldn't come.

Worried, Sims scanned the nearer tables. No one seemed to be paying attention. He grinned and tried to put a lid on it. "I'd say you have some strong feelings on that."

Houghton stared balefully at him for a moment, then laughed in a small shamefaced way.

"How'd you recruit him?"

"Money." Houghton's eyes darted, now worried himself about the nearby tables. "He was keeping an actress on the side. Like all of them, she got demanding," he answered, leaving it for Sims to fill in.

Sims called for the check. Paying, he sat for a moment, then put both hands on the table palms down, a decision made. "Well, now we know where we go next."

"Oh?"

Sims pushed back from the table and watched for Houghton's reaction. Smoothly, Sims pulled his rabbit out of the hat. "Yeah. Next we go talk with Broz."

6

Vienna, Austria
Sunday, January 26, 1992

A week later, in Vienna's Hotel Ambassador, Sims poured a cold beer from the minibar in his room. Taking the beer to a small writing desk, he inspected his passport, visa, and business papers through the fog of jet lag. He had done so countless times before. Now, as then, they *seemed* genuine enough. He locked them in his attaché case, undressed, and made himself do his push-ups, sit-ups, and leg lifts. Satisfied at having worked up a sweat, he stood for a long time in the shower, enjoying the hot water pounding his back. He got out and glanced at the clock. Two hours before meeting Houghton; time enough for an afternoon nap.

He stretched out on the huge feather bed. Fatigued as he was, sleep would not come. His eyes darted around the room. First, he traced the diamond pattern in the mustard-colored silk wall covering. Then a largish crack in the carved plaster ring around the chandelier caught his attention. In the corner of the high-ceiling room, a patch of flaking paint flagged the arthritis of aging plumbing.

He had—what?—shaded the truth to get Cantwell to approve the travel authorization. Getting Houghton's documentation—no way around it, *that* had bothered him a lot. All to talk with Broz, who might tell them nothing. And worse, Broz, whom Prague station could not find. High risks, low prospects. He had the feeling he sometimes got just before falling, a premonition of balance giving way.

He punched up his pillow and resettled himself in the bed. He would meet up with Houghton and tomorrow they would drive to Prague. Broz is probably still alive, Sims tried to reassure himself. It was not surprising that he was out of sight. Much of the Czech Communist *nomenklatura* had gone underground, aided by Prague's almost democratic government that didn't want to be embarrassed by its former spymasters parading around in public.

The clock's alarm startled him. He had drifted off without realizing it and it took a moment for him to place himself. After splashing water in his face, then hastily toweling off, he left the hotel at four. Vienna's coffeehouses were crowded for the customary afternoon tortes and ice cream. Still somewhat groggy, he walked the several blocks to the Stephansplatz, where he took an escalator to the subway station. He rode the red line to the end stop at Kagran, studied the passengers who got off with him, then walked around to the southbound platform. There he caught a train heading in the direction from which he'd just come, getting off at Alte Donau, the next station, a short walk to the amusement park. Houghton, huddled in his tan raincoat, sat on a bench reading a newspaper. The older man had flown into Vienna the day before and found a room in a small pension near the Hofburg.

"Haven't seen that in a long time." Houghton folded his newspaper and squinted up at a huge Ferris wheel, a monster outfitted with small cabins rather than seats.

Sitting down beside him on the bench, Sims followed his gaze to the Ferris wheel. It was one of Vienna's famous landmarks and figured in an Agency cult classic, *The Third Man,* a motion picture of intrigue and espionage in which Orson Welles met Joseph Cotten in one of the cabins. *"Der Riesenrad."* Sims remembered it in German.

"All we need is Harry Lime and a little zither music," Houghton mused. "What time do we leave?"

Sims turned from the Ferris wheel to Houghton. "Tomorrow morning, eight-thirty. I'll pick you up." He named a street corner on the Ring and described his rental car, giving the license plate number. "You'll need this." Sims looked around, then passed a small bundle closed with a stout rubber band.

Houghton slipped the documents into his newspaper. Behind the shield of his opened newspaper, he scanned the passport cover staff had prepared. Tomorrow morning he would become an Austrian, Franz Luckmann.

"And you?" He looked over at Sims.

"The legend's in there." He pointed to the rest of Houghton's package. "I'm on a Nigerian passport. You're a middleman. We're looking into exchanging oil for machine tools, if anybody asks. I don't think they will."

"You're casual about this."
"It's not like it used to be."

The old woman who pumped the gas gave Houghton a gap-toothed smile for the tip, and said, yes, the border crossing was just on the other side of the village. As they drove away, Sims turned and saw her through the rear window, one hand still on the gas pump, the other at her breast, as if frozen in the motion of crossing herself.

Half a mile later, the tidy Austrian farmland abruptly ended at a bare, packed ribbon of earth perhaps twenty feet wide that ran out of sight from the right and left of the road. This was all that was left of the death strip that had grown the guard towers and electrified barbed-wire fences and hidden the virulent seeds of land mines and electronic sensors. Houghton slowed the car and gawked at the border, not quite believing a man could now simply walk across. There had been arguments—an endless array of them—about the *why* of the Iron Curtain. But never any arguments about the existence of it. It was *there* and you shaped your life on the man-made geography of it.

"First time you've seen it like this?" Sims asked. "Everything down, I mean?"

Houghton was battling a mix of emotions. This couldn't be. It just couldn't! For as long as he could remember, this had been part of The Curtain. This had been the dividing line between two worlds. It had given birth to the vast espionage empires. It had nurtured the secret legions that waged shadow wars, often independently of the nations that created them. Along this line, Houghton had fought the defining struggles of his life. It had been a deadly comfort, a verity, something of unarguable substance in a slippery world.

Houghton should have felt victorious. After all, the vanishing act was the ultimate *fuck you* to the Marxists and their friends, who had claimed the future belonged to them. But instead of triumph, Houghton felt loss. Looking at it now, he realized why he missed the death strip. It had created a world he understood. He looked for another second. "Yeah," he answered, still looking in perplexity. "I used to think it would be forever."

Two border guards stood by an open pole gate and followed the silver Audi with glum stares. Their submachine guns and ill-fitting brown uniforms were leftovers from the old regime. Just ahead, two buildings connected by a tin roof straddled the road. In the approaching lane, a long line of trucks, cars, and buses waited to leave the country.

Houghton pulled in under the roof behind a car from Poland. The Polish car was stuffed to overflowing with bulky plastic bags. Two belly-heavy men in cheap nylon jackets, alike enough to be brothers, were unpacking the car, prodded by the two guards.

"They're probably taking stuff back to Poland to sell it," Sims said, feeling sorry for the harried Poles who by then had emptied their car and were standing by anxiously as the guards poked with their truncheons among the plastic bags lying beside the car.

Sims opened the map, spreading it over his half of the car and blocking out the Poles. "Hundred, hundred twenty miles," he estimated. "We ought to make Prague by—"

There was loud shouting outside the car.

"Shit!" Houghton swore.

Sims dropped the map in time to see the guard's second swing on one of the Poles. The first blow had opened a cut over an eye. The truncheon slammed into the man's kidneys. The guard stood back in satisfaction as the Pole doubled over in pain.

"What was it?"

Houghton pointed to the second guard. "That one asked a question about something. The Polack gave him some lip."

Trembling with anger and fear, the Poles reloaded their car. On the sidewalk, the grinning bright-eyed corporal watched them, softly slapping his truncheon into the palm of his open hand.

Unbidden, Sims recalled flickering black-and-white television images, scenes all the more terrible for having been seen through the uncomprehending eyes of a child. It was Selma, and men, women, and children were trapped in the choking approach to the Edmund Pettus Bridge. The state troopers urged their horses into the marchers. They cut out a woman, an old woman, pinning her to the walls of prancing, rearing horseflesh. The old woman turned in panic. She raised her hands in supplication to the riders. Battered against the horses' sides, she dropped down among the slashing hoofs.

And watching it all were white faces, idiotically wide-eyed with excitement and hate, white faces cheering the troopers and their horses.

For a moment, the border guard with the truncheon had the face of the Alabama trooper.

* * *

For over an hour after the border crossing, Sims and Houghton drove northwest over narrow high-crowned roads. Passing through drab villages, they saw only an occasional old woman or two trudging alongside the weed-grown roadway. Farmers were busy on the small privately owned plots, but there was no life, even cattle, in the massive fields still run by the state.

Just outside the medieval town of Jihlava, they turned west onto the divided highway to Prague. Half an hour later, they pulled into a rest stop. In the large parking area were only two other cars, several TIR long-distance cargo trucks, and a Bulgarian tour bus.

In the chilly latrine, Houghton whuffed explosively and zipped up his pants. The ammonia stench was overpowering. Standing beside him, Sims gave up on holding his breath. "God"—he inhaled—"they haven't cleaned this place since Hitler came through."

"Napoleon," Houghton corrected him. Perhaps ten paces away and fortunately upwind was a wooden shack. The two got in line behind several Bulgarian tourists and, when their time came at the large window, ordered hot spicy *klobàsa* and roasted potatoes. After paying, they took the paper plates to a nearby table.

At the next table, a knot of Bulgarians stared. The Bulgarians, bundled to their chins, whispered and nodded among themselves. Finally, one, a boy of fourteen or so, came over and stood smiling bashfully in front of Houghton. "American?" he asked in surprisingly good English.

Startled, Houghton was momentarily at a loss. In the half-second or so before he could answer, he felt his heartbeat race and the skin on his face tingle.

He gulped a breath. *"Nein,"* he stammered in German. *"Ich bin aus Österreich."*

The young boy openly studied Houghton, then Sims for a moment with innocent eyes, then nodded, smiled, and returned to his table to make his report. The older Bulgarians looked in unison at Houghton and Sims, still staring without expression, then dismissing them, returning to their conversation.

"Damn," murmured Houghton. Sweat oiled his hands. It was still thc sixties and the Curtain was still up and his cover had been challenged at a foul-smelling rest stop miles from any help.

Sims was unperturbed. "They were just curious," he said through a mouthful of sausage. "They're coming out of a longtime shell." He smiled at Houghton, as one might smile to reassure a frightened child or a punch-drunk fighter.

"That shit at the border got me, I guess." Houghton pushed away his sausage and lit a cigarette, his hands still weak and close to trembling.

"The border?" Sims said it warily.

"You know"—Houghton gestured with his cigarette—"crossing it. It bothered you, too."

The television images of the Edmund Pettus Bridge came back for an instant before Sims could banish them. "It was nothing." Sims took a long swig and finished his beer. "It was nothing," he said again, feeling that Houghton was watching him particularly closely. "Come on. It'll be late getting to Prague."

Sims took over the driving. Houghton filled a quarter hour with small talk, then, in the warmth of the car, slumped down in his seat and dozed off, his chin on his chest.

Houghton was still asleep two hours later when Sims reached the Vltava, then swung left along the embankment road paralleling the river. Turning south, he slowed, knowing what would come next, yet thrilling all the same at the prospect. Prague—*Praha*—*prah*, Czech for "threshold," an unfinished and thrilling word. Another turn and there across the river was Prague Castle, its solid bulwarks dominating the seven hills of the city. And within the castle, a thousand years in the building, St. Vitus Cathedral, its spires piercing the blue of the afternoon sky.

They drove slowly through a maze of narrow one-way streets to the Alcron, half a block from Wenceslas Square. The hotel clung to the old days, when Cedok, the state tourist bureau, had extravagantly rated the place deluxe without fear of contradiction. The surly registration clerk examined their passports and took only half an hour to check them in.

Czechoslovakia might have turned over a new political leaf, but old habits were hard to break. Remnants of the peoples' democracy littered Prague. Closed-circuit television cameras still scanned the Alcron's lobby, bar, and dining room, and Sims had few doubts that conversations in any of the rooms could be monitored at will.

Their small rooms were identical, having been done by a decorator whose taste ran to brown. Sims unpacked, pausing to snap on the television. There were but two grainy gray channels: one devoted to agricultural news and the other to obscure sporting events in places like Trieste and Kinshasa. By the time he'd finished, an athletic meet had given way to a documentary about the sidewalks of Prague, which apparently were in desperate need of repair.

*   *   *

At noon the following day, Sims walked through the Lesser Quarter and found a window table at one of his favorite restaurants. Across the rooftops, he could see the river and, beyond it, the Old Town. Along his left rose the sweeping cliff that was the ancient district of Hradčany, with its castle, palaces, and the grandeur of St. Vitus Cathedral. He ordered a coffee and sat back to wait for Janik.

He had gotten to the embassy early that morning, paid his respects to Harrington, the chief of station. In the tank, he had duly taken in the first round of briefings Harrington and his people reserved for visitors from headquarters. He had asked the usual questions, then, pleading jet lag, begged off lunch and the afternoon briefings, detecting, as he did so, Harrington's relief at being able to get back to real work.

He sipped the acrid coffee and scanned the small square. He had been gone just over four months and the Czech economy had continued digging out from under the dead hand of forty years of state planners. The menu was larger and a sprinkling of cars driving by were newer, brighter, and painted something other than pumpkin orange or tomato red. He watched as a small blue Fiat circled the square and found a parking place directly in front of the restaurant.

Janik got out of the Fiat and locked the door. He was a dark, compact man in his mid-thirties with the grave tentativeness of Eastern Europeans. With his streamlined face and brown hair combed straight back without a part, he resembled a sleek water animal. When he saw Sims, he tilted his head back and gave an almost laughing smile that showed a mouth full of small white teeth.

They shook hands and Sims motioned him to sit. "You look well, Felix," Sims said, slipping easily into Czech. He waited as Janik glanced casually around, placing the nearest ears and eyes.

Satisfied no one was listening or cared to, Janik nonetheless bent slightly across the table toward Sims. "They have taken me out of the field." He shared a conspiratorial grin with Sims. "They were unhappy with our river-crossing expedition."

The grin reassured Sims. He had not seen Janik after that night on the Uzh and didn't know how the Czech had taken it. "I made a lousy decision."

Janik dismissed it with a wave of his hand. "You got me into the shit, Bradford, but you also got me out. You're not a man of half measures." He nodded toward the blue Fiat. "One of the compensations to working in Prague. I have a scar that intrigues the women and now I have a government automobile to drive them around in."

Over potato dumplings and beer, they exchanged small talk: Czech and American politics, sports, and women. The waiter cleared the table and Sims gestured for two more pilsners.

Again Janik glanced around, then leaned forward, resting his elbows on the table. "It's a long way to come for lunch, Bradford."

"My first visit to the station." Sims didn't want to make it seem like a big deal. "But while I'm here, I'd like to talk with Josef Broz."

Janik's expression, except for a slight flattening of the eyes, didn't change. "Broz." He sounded it in his soft neutral voice, then sat back in his chair, and crossed his arms loosely over his chest.

Sims sat back, too, trying to show a nonchalance he didn't feel. Work the thread gently, and you can undo any knot, Riddle cautioned over and over. Pull hard and the thread would snap.

"Broz," Janik repeated, as if trying to make out some ill-defined immensity behind the name. Perhaps the Americans were after something big. "He has been, ah—*retired.* Since 1989." He waited to see if this pried something loose from Sims.

"It would be useful, Felix."

"I should think your station could arrange it."

"I can do that easily," Sims lied, "but I thought you might wish to be helpful."

Better to be part of a deal, Janik reasoned, than not to know of it at all. The new Czech intelligence service was ostensibly on good terms with CIA, but still, it paid to develop your own sources within American intelligence. Janik didn't want to miss that opportunity. He, too, held a very delicate thread.

"We do maintain certain contacts," Janik began with caution. "As you might suspect, the relationship between the old regime and our—ah—*democracy* is a delicate one." He paused to look meaningfully at Sims. Getting an understanding nod, he picked up the check. "I'll see what I can do."

"So—two Americans want to talk with me." Josef Broz frowned. His voice carried a rebuke.

Felix Janik made a helpless gesture. "That's all I could get." They were walking along the Vltava. Across the river, the cliff-top castle, floodlit in green bronze, floated eerily in the cold darkness. Though early evening, the riverside path was deserted. As they neared the Smetana Museum, they heard the occasional thin cries of the gulls on the pilings.

"That's all you could get." Broz repeated, making it a judgment. He watched as Janik hung his head. He slowed, then stopped. Janik faced him, waiting. "I will call you when I decide." He turned and walked away, leaving Janik standing on the path.

Alone, Broz picked up his pace to clear his head. He glanced to his right. There, on the sidewalk across the street, a dark figure limped, but kept up with him: faithful Schmar.

Broz made himself breathe deeply. Focus, he told himself. You accomplish nothing without focus. Still the panic fluttered in his chest. After all this time. *Houghton!* It had to be! For over twenty years, especially his years as chairman of the StB, he had lived in fear of the call. At first, he thought the Americans were playing a waiting game, leaving him inactive. The resentment grew and smoldered, at Houghton for trapping him, then at himself for his weakness, and finally, perversely, at the Americans for not making contact and ending the suspense.

Over the years, he had built a thesis. That, for some reason, Houghton had kept the recruitment of young Josef Broz a personal secret, that Houghton had not revealed it to Langley. He had followed Houghton's fall with curiosity and not a little anxiety. But still nothing. If Houghton were going to shake him down, the time would have been while he, Broz, was on the top.

Now? Broz felt a chill that matched the night. Now, in a way, there was even more to lose. He was older, with fewer choices before him. He had to cling to what he had in order to see himself through his last years. There was the retainer from the Russians, the modest funds Moscow paid him to keep a rump operation going in Czechoslovakia; enough for the major pleasures of life and to keep a few of the old boys like Schmar on the payroll. But there was more. Broz's stomach warmed as he undid the wrappings around his hidden prize, the Syrian connection. Damascus still needed *plastique* for its explosive political games, and Damascus paid handsomely for it. Broz's rainy day store was Semtex, the fireworks of choice in the better terrorist circles. Before the curse of democracy, Broz had tucked away enough to keep the Syrians supplied—and himself comfortable—for many years to come.

Focus, he scolded himself again. If it was an Agency initiative, he could make an accommodation. They might close an eye to his Moscow connection and perhaps even to the *plastique* trade as well. Langley had certainly danced with the devil before.

No, Broz decided, this wasn't the Agency. The Agency could get hold of him directly. They didn't have to go through Janik. It was Houghton's shakedown, and therefore, Houghton had to be discouraged. Broz felt his heart beating and he slowed his pace. His heart was betraying him, a clock running down within him. His chest tightened in panic. He would need everything he could get from the Syrians for his last years. He couldn't afford any self-invited partners.

He motioned to the dark figure across the street. Schmar, ever watchful, came limping over.

Sims was leaving his room to pick up Houghton for dinner when the call came. It was Janik asking in German for a Herr Gruber. Sims fumbled for a pen and scratch pad. This was not Herr Gruber's room, he replied. This is 23 59 41? Sims jotted the number down. Sorry, he said, wrong number. Janik hung up with a polite *auf Wiedersehen.* Sims looked at the number on the pad. He and Janik had used the convention before. It was January, and so to each digit pair he added one. He walked the half block to Wenceslas Square, and from a public telephone called the new number. Janik answered with a neutral hello.

An hour later in an evening mist, Sims and Houghton made their way up the hill toward Hradčany Square and the castle. "Goddamn," Houghton cursed, and clutched for the handrail. For the second time, he stumbled on the broken walkway. They had had to park their car in the public lot two blocks down the hill. "We could have met somewhere dry."

In spite of the weather, Sims was enjoying the walk, and he leaned into the hill to stretch his legs further. The protocol was that if you called the meeting, the other guy named where. Where he felt safe. Hradčany was a good place. There were always soldiers and police around because of the government buildings and museums. At the same time, the square was large enough that three or four people could meet in relative privacy.

Sims turned a corner, and the expanse of the square opened before him. It was as if he had stepped back in time. On his immediate right, a baroque seventeenth-century palace, its mustard stucco still bearing the coats of arms of the dukes of Tuscany. Then, farther around, the even older Schwarzenberg with its ornate facade and windows. And dead ahead, dark and rising from the cobblestones as if emerging from the sea, the castle.

The mist and the fading light had nearly emptied the square. To the left, perhaps fifty meters away, a sausage vendor was folding his tent, the wooden poles making a forlorn clacking noise.

Standing well back from the second-story window, Broz aimed the binoculars at Houghton and adjusted the focusing knob. It happens as you get older, Broz thought. Seeing a face again after twenty years is a shock. But only briefly, for seconds, then your brain reassembles the features. The once-young face melts into the face before you and you never again remember it with quite the same clarity you had held so long. With some regret, he turned to Schmar and offered him the binoculars. "It is him."

Schmar held the binoculars the way soldiers did, fingers wrapped around the double barrels, thumbs straight back, gripping his temples to get a steady picture.

"The black?"

"Our friend Janik's contact."

Schmar dropped the binoculars. He was a tall, long-boned man who moved with a coiled reptilian grace. "Both of them?"

Broz regarded Schmar: the black hair, the pale, luminescent face of an aging, fallen angel, the black raincoat. Then he turned away to look down again at the two Americans waiting. The emperor's palace has drawn the nomads here, he thought, and we must use Schmar to drive them away. And why not? Schmar enjoyed this kind of thing. He was made for it. He nodded to Schmar while keeping his eyes on the square. "Yes, both." He heard Schmar leave while still watching the two men in the square.

"A no-show," Houghton muttered, looking at his watch.

Sims stared past the gate into the castle's first courtyard. Two white-gloved sentries stood at attention, one on each side of the gate. On the huge gateposts, statues of giants crouched, dagger and club raised to dispatch fallen victims. He checked his watch. Four minutes. Houghton was right. They should have left two, three minutes ago. Again, the protocol: Spies, even retired ones, are on time. On time plus or minus two minutes or you scrub and go about the goddamn tedious process of rescheduling. You didn't hang around a meeting point. Someone *might* be late because of heavy traffic or a faulty alarm clock. Or just maybe they had been rolled up and were even now spilling their guts about the meeting they had been going to.

Sims searched the square a last time. The mist had abated and the electric lights were coming on. It was no longer a place out of time.

The buildings were merely old and tired and in need of attention. He shrugged out of his raincoat and threw it over his shoulder. "Let's go," he said to Houghton.

From the top of the hill, the walkway made Sims think of a tunnel. On his left, small shops with apartments above for the owners. Midway down to the car was the patio of a coffeehouse, with outdoor tables and chairs stacked and chained to its accordion-gated shutter doors. On the right, chestnut trees along the narrow street sent their branches over toward the buildings.

"You're going to call Janik when we get back?" Houghton asked as they made their way down the walkway.

Sims made a dispirited acknowledgment.

"Scrubs happen more often than not," Houghton tried without conviction. A taxi, its service light out, rattled by and was gone, leaving the street somehow even emptier. The sidewalk narrowed, squeezed by sawhorses, piles of paving blocks, and a portable concrete mixer.

The sound came tentatively, so much so that Sims wasn't sure he had heard it at all. Another couple of steps and he was sure. A third set of footsteps had joined Houghton's and his.

"Somebody—" he began in a warning whisper to Houghton.

Another sound. "Two. Behind us," Houghton said softly.

Sims made a slow quarter turn, as if taken by a shop window display. The men behind were closer than he had thought. Twenty, twenty-five feet at the most. One, a short, stocky man in a workman's cloth jacket and cap. The other, a tall, smooth-moving man in a black raincoat. Slight limp. They were making no pretense at talking with each other. Both were clearly fixed on Houghton and Sims.

"Let's move it," he said to Houghton.

"Oh shit," Houghton muttered.

Ten feet in front of them, two men had stepped from the shadows of the coffeehouse. The one closest to Sims held his hand out, as if returning something Sims had dropped. An oiled *flick,* a blurring flash of steel in the night. Sims gasped involuntarily. Not so much at the wicked blade as at the smile on the knife-man's face.

The knife-man's partner closed on Houghton with both hands in a karate attack posture, fingers locked and ready to jab, hook, or chop. Houghton backpedaled only to be brought up against a construction sawhorse. One foot jammed painfully into a loose pile of paving stones, nearly throwing him off balance.

Sims's body reacted instantly. His teeth clenched and nostrils flared. Pupils dilated to gather more light while breathing and heartbeat moved into high gear to carry more oxygen to his brain and muscles.

His mind almost got him killed. For the smallest part of a second, he fell prey to civilization's paralyzing reflex, the wishful notion that those who are about to do violence are somehow not really serious. Or that they are mistaken, that they should be going after someone else. Anybody but him.

Then other reflexes took over. Those shaped by his father, then the football coaches in college, then the instructors at the Farm: "Do something!"

Sims leaped toward the knife-man. Whipping the raincoat off his shoulder, he cast it like a net toward the knife-man's face. At the same time, he began a lifting, swinging kick up from the sidewalk while throwing himself to the left of the knife-man's thrust.

The karate-man was in the middle of a classic move, bringing the blade of his stiffened hand in a graceful, murderous arc toward Houghton's throat just as the veteran spy swung the pipe he had wrenched from the construction debris.

The point of Sims's shoe caught the knife-man squarely in the testicles with all the force of Sims's two hundred pounds. As if struck by lightning, the knife-man froze, mouth and eyes wide in a stunned grimace.

Houghton's heavy pipe first broke the karate-man's left shoulder, then, continuing its deadly arc, fractured his jaw. Houghton backed away from the falling man. He shifted his grip on the pipe. He had to be ready for the man behind him. *Turn around!* he screamed inside himself.

Schmar hit the American hard, hoping to make him drop the pipe. His momentum carried them upright against a huge chestnut tree. This one was older and weaker than the black. Schmar grunted in an almost sexual excitement as he wrestled the man, pinning him against the tree.

On the ground, Sims caught an electrifyingly painful kick to his left shoulder from behind. Rolling right, he dodged the next swinging kick meant for his head. He wrapped both his hands around the man's ankle and twisted it violently, putting his entire leverage behind it. He felt, and heard, a hip socket pop. The man gave a surprised coughing gasp and fell heavily to the sidewalk.

Houghton felt the man's weight against him, inexorable, overpowering, relentless. Wildly, he reached for Schmar's face, his fingers scrambling to get to the eyes, or to hook a nostril and lift. But the man was too strong.

Schmar rammed his left forearm against Houghton's throat and lifted the American's chin. With his right hand, he pulled the long skinning knife from the scabbard under his coat. The blade glinted in the dim light like an evil silver tongue. Schmar was at the height of his blood lust. Nothing mattered except slitting Houghton's throat, seeing the American's eyes as he realized he was dead and yet, for still a moment or two, alive.

On the ground, the knife-man was making mewing sounds, clutching his smashed testicles. The two others sprawled unconscious. Never quite getting his feet fully under him, Sims made a scrambling lunge for Schmar.

He hit the Czech in a waist-high diving tackle. At the same time, he locked onto Schmar's right wrist. The two crashed to the ground. Houghton staggered away from the tree bending over nearly double, massaging his throat, struggling to get his breath.

Wild with the fury and adrenaline of the fighting, it took Sims a moment to realize that Schmar was oddly still. Cautiously, he raised himself off the man. Schmar was huddled at the base of the chestnut tree, his back to Sims.

Sims stood up, then nudged Schmar with his foot. Schmar was conscious. He slowly rolled over. His eyes flicked at Sims with corrosive hatred. His left hand was pinned to the trunk of the chestnut tree with his own knife.

Sims was startled by a hand on his shoulder. "You do neat work," Houghton croaked, his voice raw and rough. Houghton knelt by Schmar. "When you get ready to leave, you carry a message to Broz." Houghton reached out and put his first two fingers on the handle of the long knife. Blood had now covered Schmar's hand. Houghton shook the knife ever so slightly and smiled as Schmar winced with the pain. "You tell Broz that you met Edward. Tell him I just want to talk. I can talk to him or I can talk to the Russians." Houghton shook the knife again. "Tell Broz that."

Sims forced himself to drive slowly, to pay attention to the sparse traffic. He made it over the Vltava and into the New Town quarter before the trembling started. He was suddenly feverish and sweat began to roll down his back and arms.

"Me too," Houghton said. It was the first time he had said anything since they had gotten in the car. "There's a park. Let's walk."

The park stretched toward the National Museum, and in the near distance, Sims could hear the metal sounds of work in the railyards. A stout woman, intent on walking her two small dogs, glanced at Sims and Houghton, then passed on.

They walked in wobbly silence for a minute or two. Sims felt his trembling and heartbeat gradually slowing, and with that, the coming on of a bone-weary fatigue.

Sims and Houghton both swore simultaneously as each realized how close it had been, how it could have been.

"This place was safer in the bad old days," said Houghton. And then, "Thanks. I thought—"

"He was strong," Sims croaked, his own throat dry. The struggle with Schmar was a blur of clumsy fumbling and grasping. Sims was still far from over it and not yet ready to talk.

"That was a nice touch, his hand to the tree and all."

Sims chilled at the thought, and a spasm of nausea swept up from his stomach. Then he remembered the hate in the man's eyes and felt better. "It just happened." He wondered if the man were still pinned there. "You think he was working for Broz." He made it a statement.

Houghton looked at him questioningly. "Your guy would have done that?" He waved vaguely in the direction of the river and the castle.

Sims thought about it, then shook his head. Janik wouldn't have planned it on his own. And the new Czech service wouldn't have dared to go up against Langley. "We'll see if Broz gets your message."

Walking back to the car, Sims stopped for a moment and listened, clutching to the sounds of life and work in the nearby railyard. There are people alive out here tonight, he thought. We all will have a tomorrow. He felt a needle-sharp awareness of his body, a tingling feeling, and he rejoiced in not being dead.

"That's him." From the backseat of the car, Houghton pointed to the lone figure walking toward them perhaps halfway across the vastness of the Old Town Square.

This morning, the desk clerk had called Houghton. Broz had sent a note.

In the driver's seat, Sims twisted around to peer out his side window. A battered bakery van was pulling up on the opposite side of the street. Broz was now perhaps ten paces away. Sims saw a man of medium height in a dark blue suit and rich camel-hair overcoat. Hatless, Broz's thick chestnut hair was only slightly streaked with silver. Large photo-gray glasses with heavy plastic frames partially covered his smooth jowly face.

At the car, Broz stopped, both hands deep in his coat pockets. Leaning across, Houghton opened the rear door, showing himself to Broz.

"Good afternoon, Josef." Then, leaning even farther across, Houghton reassured the man. "It *is* me."

Bending over, Broz peered into the car. "So it is, Edward." His eyes met Sims's. "And this gentleman?" A rich bass voice smoothed out the angular Czech consonants. For an instant, Sims thought of his uncle's resonant voice.

"We're together," Houghton said brusquely.

Broz scanned the car interior once again, straightened to look around the square, then turned to Houghton. "I'm not comfortable with meeting like this, Edward."

Houghton patted the empty seat beside him. "I don't think you have much choice, Josef."

Broz searched Houghton's face, then Sims's, shrugged, and swung himself into the cramped backseat. They soon left the maze of Prague's Old Town quarter behind them.

Broz caught Sims searching the rearview mirror, checking for back-up or a tail. "You are taking precautions."

"We should have taken a few last night," Houghton commented dryly.

Broz turned to Houghton and put on an embarrassed smile. "Ah yes. You have to understand, Edward. I have many enemies. I certainly didn't know it was you."

Sims glanced in the rearview mirror. Houghton saw him and rolled his eyes.

Sims and Houghton had planned the route in detail. Down the right bank of the Vltava to Zbraslav at Prague's outskirts, then across and back up the left bank back into Prague, with a drop at the Plzeňská subway stop. Sims mentally checked off the necessary safeguards. They could keep moving. There were double-backs to identify surveillance. And the drop was nowhere near the pickup.

"So." Broz exclaimed with a satisfaction that was too hearty. "A meeting on wheels. Better than safe houses that are never quite safe, eh?" When neither Sims nor Houghton answered, Broz turned to Houghton. "I wondered if you would ever turn up again, Edward. It is ironic, is it not? I am no longer in the business and you apparently have returned?"

Houghton didn't let it go by. "You're not in the business, Josef? You've got quite a stable for not being in the business."

"Edward"—Broz put on an earnest tone—"you know the word *lustrace?*" Without waiting for Houghton, he gave the answer. "It means 'purifying sacrifice.' All those who served the old regime"— Broz held his hands up in a gesture of self-pity—"they're hunting us down. The president of our new republic says to look forward, not back. But then his men—"

"Sure, Josef," Houghton interrupted, remembering the knife at his throat just the night before. "You're just an old worn-out spy trying to keep body and soul together."

A smile played around Broz's lips.

"We've got Valek," Sims said, wanting to keep things from getting worse.

"So I understand." Broz left it at that in his heavy voice.

"Does it surprise you?"

Broz opened his eyes wide, making them very round behind the thick lenses of his glasses. "Surprise me? Why, yes it did. Though I must tell you, I wasn't particularly shocked."

"No?" Houghton asked. "Why not?"

"I always thought Miloslav was an opportunist. Even more than I. You caught me and I always thought you could have caught him as well." Broz paused, then with a sly smile asked, "Or *did* you catch him, Edward? And were you playing us both?"

Houghton ignored Broz's probe. "He was working for the Russians. They treat their people well."

"Ah, Edward!" Broz exclaimed, enjoying the prospect of corruption in others. "There is a saying about greener grass. Like all of us, Miloslav was getting older. Perhaps the lights seemed brighter and the women prettier in America."

"Bright lights and women aren't much."

Broz thought. "There were other opportunities. Miloslav was the paymaster for much of your antiwar movement. He knew where the money went and who got it. Over the years, some of those people have prospered. Some have money, others political power. Who knows?" Broz asked mischievously. "A charming rascal like Miloslav might go into business for himself."

Houghton considered this, then asked, "When did you last see him?"

Broz stared momentarily past Houghton, then shrugged. "A week, perhaps two or three weeks before the change."

"The change of governments?"

Broz nodded. "Who'd ever have thought it could go so quickly? It was over, just like that." He snapped his fingers.

Sims and Houghton began their carefully charted interrogation. At times racing through the years, then seemingly drifting aimlessly, they traced Broz's career. He had taken over the Afro-Asian Solidarity Committee in February 1966 and turned it over to Valek in December 1967. Broz recalled the names of the party members—Poles, East Germans, even Vietnamese. The operation had been a veritable montage of Soviet bloc intelligence.

"How long did it stay active?" Sims asked, trying to keep the tension out of his voice.

Broz was silent for a long time. "It is difficult to remember. But I know we were still controlling the solidarity committee until spring 1969."

The road rose rapidly as they drove south, and they were soon passing the eleventh-century cliff-top fortress at Vyšehrad. Below was the Vltava River. Sims was checking his rearview mirror when Houghton began the next line of questioning.

"Valek told us about targeting Martin Luther King."

Broz threw his head back and smiled, a riddle answered. "King! So that's what you're after? Picking up where you left off, Edward?" Getting no answer, he leaned toward Houghton. "Why now? Why do you care?"

"Just wrapping up some loose ends, Josef. Why don't you tell us how it started? You were running the Afro-Asian Solidarity Committee. It was '66, maybe '67—"

Broz thought for a moment. "The objective was to create unrest on your home front during the war."

"And—"

"We thought it would be useful if the FBI came to suspect King of conspiring with Moscow."

"Go on." A trace of tension hardened Houghton's voice.

"The most effective disinformation is that which the target is conditioned to hear." Broz gave it by rote, remembering his Russian instructor decades ago. "In this case, the target was the FBI director. Hoover wanted so badly to believe the blacks were linked with Moscow that he eagerly took whatever we gave him."

"You couldn't work the FBI that way and get away with it," Houghton said suspiciously. "Even Hoover would have tumbled to a fabrication like that."

"It wasn't a fabrication," Broz said with obvious self-satisfaction. "We were making payments—contributions—to them."

"How?"

"Through our friends. There were several party members in the King organization."

"I thought King had gotten rid of them."

"He thought he had, too."

"So you fed these guys money and then you made certain Hoover found out."

Broz nodded. "We never controlled King or his organization, but we didn't have to. It was enough to make Hoover think we did."

"Names?"

Sims thought he detected a note of weariness, perhaps resignation.

Broz laughed reprovingly. "Edward, I'm surprised at you. All I knew were the cover names."

"Those then."

Broz laughed again. "You expect me to pluck out cover names of a specific operation nearly a quarter of a century ago?"

"Try, Josef."

Broz thought, then shook his head in frustration. "One, perhaps—Laura."

"A woman?"

"I don't know."

"You left the operation in December '67. It continued under Valek?"

"I assume so—it was a gold mine."

"The King killing didn't spoil things? Cause the Russians cold feet?"

Broz got a calculating look, his eyes narrowing. "Spoil things?" He pulled a handkerchief from a pocket and blew his nose loudly. "Not that I could see. Of course, I was out of the operation. It was highly compartmented, you understand—"

"Go on. Valek?"

Broz motioned to Houghton. "Let me have one of your cigarettes, Edward. I should quit, I suppose, but there are worse things than to die from one's indulgences." Broz leaned forward to let Houghton light his cigarette. He puffed several times, then turned to Houghton. "Valek. Where do you want me to start?"

"After he left the solidarity committee in 1969."

Broz thought. "He was on detached service with the Russians for a number of years. By the time he came back, I'd become director for North American affairs. I asked for him because of his experience working the Americans during the Vietnam War."

"This was . . . ?"

"1980."

"You got Valek in the North American directorate in '80," Houghton repeated. "How long did he work for you?"

"Four years."

"Until you went to the States?"

"I was four years in our *rezidentura* in Washington. When I got back to Prague in 1988, Miloslav was again working with the KGB. All very tightly held. He left Prague just before the change—as we were closing down the StB. He went on to Moscow, to a job in the Center registry, and I suppose from there to Washington."

Broz laughed with irony. "Miloslav had a good nose for the wind. He even missed my retirement party." There was the tumultuous day when the mobs had burst into the StB compound, a day of near riot and emotional pillaging, a day of settling accounts. He'd spent some hours in one of his own cells until the provisional security of the reform government had freed him.

"When Valek came to your directorate," Sims interrupted, "in—when was it?—'80?" In the rearview mirror, he saw Broz nod. "What was his assignment?"

"Assignment?" Broz needed no time. "Why, I made him head of our Canadian section."

"Canadian?" Sims asked. "I'd have thought you would have assigned him to the U.S."

"I would have," Broz said, "except that the U.S. section was full and we needed people to work Canada. And besides, Valek had operational experience there."

"When was that, Josef—the operational experience?" Houghton asked the question delicately, as if he were moving precious crystal.

Broz felt the car slow. The black's eyes were on him in the rearview mirror. He sensed the Americans' interest. They might have Miloslav, but they didn't have all his story, and this was a missing part of it.

"He didn't tell you?" Broz asked, knowing Valek hadn't.

"You know better, Josef—don't pull that shit with me," Houghton warned. "The operational experience—when was it?"

"It was 1968. He was sent to Toronto. He was there several weeks."

"Doing what?" asked Houghton. "What was he doing in Toronto?"

Broz was unusually slow in answering, then spoke hesitantly. "You understand, Edward, I don't really know this. That is, I only know it because Miloslav told me one night. There was nothing in the files. Just what he told me."

"What was that?" An edge of impatience sharpened Houghton's voice.

"We met just before Miloslav left for Moscow and Washington. It was a chance meeting in Prague. We had dinner that night and both drank a lot. He was quite proud the Russians had taken him on. He would always have a meal ticket with the Russians, he said. He boasted of the missions he'd done for them. I was always curious about the Toronto assignment."

"So?" Houghton asked.

"I asked him." Broz's voice dropped to a bass whisper. "He told me he'd been sent on orders from Yuri Andropov himself." Broz's instinct for accuracy made him cautious. "Again, Edward, this is only what he told me while he was drunk."

Houghton could barely restrain himself. "I understand. He was drunk, boastful." He cut the words into sharp bits: "What . . . did . . . he . . . say?"

"He said that Andropov sent him to Toronto to kill James Earl Ray."

7

Without a backward look, Broz disappeared down the escalator at the Plzeňská subway station.

"Son of a bitch," Houghton muttered, still stunned by the enormity of the man's revelations. They had thoroughly squeezed Broz, adding a half hour's driving to their plan. They had gotten a few details about time and place, but nothing more. The words stood as Broz had first said them, hard, irreducible, incapable of being twisted or misunderstood. Miloslav Valek had gone to Toronto to kill James Earl Ray.

Sims slipped the Audi into gear and checked the mirrors before pulling out into traffic.

"Now we squeeze Valek," Houghton said to himself and to Sims. They were now crossing the Svermuv Bridge. To his right, the castle poised itself on the purple green prow of Hradčany, and the rapidly moving clouds cast it in shadow and sun and shadow again so that it seemed to be plowing flicker-flick through light and time, leaving Houghton behind. Prague, once mystical and promising, now seemed frayed and corrupt. He sensed somehow that he would never come back, and he wondered why he didn't care.

At the same time in Washington, Valek stood, slightly lightheaded, looking around the plush men's store. Brooks Brothers!—*now* he was truly in America. Even though he knew the States, the *choices* in America always exerted an almost erotic effect on Valek. Along one wall—shirts. Hundreds of them: solids, stripes, English spread collars, button-downs, tab collars. And the suits and the sport coats; racks upon racks of them!

"We don't have all fuckin' day."

His baby-sitter, Mike, stood just behind him. Mike wasn't happy at having to drive Valek into town and fight the afternoon traffic back out to the safe house. But Valek had insisted. Two changes of clothes weren't enough, even for a defector. And the walls of the safe house had been closing in on him. Besides, wasn't this America? Wasn't the clothing store less than ten miles from CIA headquarters? Security finally gave in.

Twenty minutes later, Valek had made his detailed inspection circuit of the store, with two clerks in tow. Mike sat in an easy chair by the belts and accessories, working his way through an old *People* magazine. One of the clerks pointed Valek toward the changing rooms that lined either side of the hallway leading to the back of the store.

His clothes hanging on a single hook, Valek clumsily balanced on one foot while spearing the other into the leg of the strange trousers. The changing room was little more than a cubicle and he leaned his shoulder against one wall while wrestling with the trousers.

Suddenly, the door flew open, hitting him in the back and pushing him against the far wall.

Turning, his protest froze as he recognized the face. "Yazov," he managed in a strangled whisper, "what . . . ?"

Viktor Yazov smiled as he raised a handkerchief to cover his nose and mouth. "Good-bye, Miloslav." His other hand held a gray tube. With a soft coughing noise, a cottonlike mist shot from the tube. Valek took a breath to shout. As he did so, he felt a slight scorching numbness at the back of his throat, then nothing.

Two hours later, as Sims and Houghton were finishing dinner at the Pelikán, Jozef Broz was climbing the stairs of an exclusive apartment building several blocks away. He cradled a bottle of Moët '82 in the crook of his left arm, his hand securely wrapped around the foil-covered neck. He felt a sweaty eagerness. Gabriela waited, and Broz imagined he could already smell her musky perfume and feel her lush body.

On the landing below her flat, he paused to catch his breath. He was about to continue when he noticed a shadow passing across the bar of light coming from under the door to his front. At the same time, he heard a soft noise on the landing above, as if someone waiting had shifted slightly.

Broz spun and started down the stairs.

"Derzhi yevo!" Broz had taken several steps before he realized the

call to stop him had been in Russian. The landing abruptly brightened and darkened behind him as an apartment door opened and slammed shut.

In a stumbling fall, Broz barely kept his feet beneath him. Making the next landing below, he saw yet another door open, this one just in front of him. A tall man in a leather jacket charged toward him.

Without slowing his rush, Broz swung. The heavy bottle caught the man in the leather jacket along the side of the head. Broz felt the grinding crunch of bone. The bottle broke. Champagne and shards of green glass sprayed the wooden floor.

At street level, Broz shoved past the building concierge, a wizened old woman who was glaring up the stairs toward the gathering tumult. Throwing open the door to the street, he was blinded by the glare of a large battery lantern. His arms suddenly were pinioned roughly behind him. A blade of stiffened fingers drove into his solar plexus. Doubled over and beginning to retch, he barely noticed the pricking sting of a hypodermic needle in his biceps.

The following morning, Sims and Houghton flew out of Prague-Ruzyně. They would do the identity switch in Frankfurt and from there fly straight into Washington-Dulles.

Frankfurt was always crowded, though less so in January than in the summer tourist months. As Sims and Houghton made their way past coffee stands and sex shops toward the departure gates in the B concourse, a short pouter pigeon of a woman turned abruptly from a duty-free display and bumped squarely into Sims.

There were the requisite clumsy apologies, and Sims and Houghton continued down the long corridor.

"That it?"

Sims nodded, eyes busy on the overhead signs. "This way." He turned down a narrower hallway that opened onto the luggage lockers. Using the key the woman had passed to him, he opened a locker, Houghton standing casually by to shield him. He thrust the heavy envelope containing the new passports and tickets into his inner coat pocket.

Houghton scanned the locker room. "Clear," he muttered.

Moving to another locker, Sims deposited a cheap plastic portfolio, dropped two German marks in the slot, and took the key. This he put in a magnetic container that he would fasten to the underside of the third phone booth in the corridor just outside. Within a few minutes, pouter pigeon's partner would use the same booth, retrieve the key, and carry away the identities of the Nigerian oil man and the Austrian broker.

Clearing security, Sims and Houghton found seats in a far corner opposite their gate. Over Houghton's shoulder, white and blue Lufthansa jets slowly taxied by out on the tarmac. Soundless and sleek, Sims thought, like large fish through an aquarium window. He looked forward to the seven-hour flight home. No one expected you to do anything at 38,000 feet over the Atlantic. For seven hours, he had a shelter against what he knew he had to do once he got back to America. Part of him, the tired, pissed-off part, wished he had been on vacation when Valek had decided to jump.

"Looks like there's something in this for both of us."

"What do you mean?" Sims wasn't certain he had heard Houghton right. Outside, a huge 747 rolled into view. The heavy-nosed airplane seemed comically sinister, a killer whale on the prowl.

"Well, I might get to prove I was right and you get to raise white guilt another notch or two."

"That's what I want?"

"That's what you'll get. Your new friend, Congressman Stanley—what do you think he'll do if we tie the KGB to King's killing?" Houghton gave a cynical laugh. "You guys will cut a swath—'Donahue,' 'Oprah,' book deals—no stopping you—white establishment tries to silence promising black CIA officer."

Sims felt a dulling disappointment. He bent forward in his seat, reached out, and locked Houghton's forearm in a crushing grip.

"Let me ask you something." Sims's voice was low and earnest. He leaned close to Houghton. He cocked his head, a black inquisitor: "Have you ever thought about being white?"

"*Being* white?" Houghton was baffled. Sims might as well have asked if he had ever thought about being blue-eyed.

Sims saw the opening and pressed on. "Think about this. Of all the things that put you where you are, have you ever thought that one of them, maybe the biggest one, is that you're white?" As Houghton wrestled with that, Sims jabbed again. "But how often are you reminded you're white? When you look in a mirror, is your first reaction, 'Hey, I'm white'?"

Houghton knew where this was leading and he tried desperately to resist. Years ago, he thought he had settled all the questions of how the world was and why. He shook his head, almost hypnotized by Sims's eyes and voice.

"I don't need a mirror to know I'm black. I know from the way you whites react to me."

"You don't want me lumping all blacks together. Now you're doing the same with whites."

"No I'm not. Different whites act differently."

"Such as?"

"Start with the outright bigots." He watched Houghton drop his eyes. "They're easy enough to read. Then there're the sanctimonious ones. Ones who'd never admit it, even to themselves, but it comes through in the way they act." Sims thought of the lost Iowa tourists in front of his apartment building.

Houghton felt himself sinking, but he knew Sims wasn't finished.

Sims looked at Houghton for a moment, then bored in. "You know who's the worst?" He got a bitter smile. "The ones who ooh and ah over anybody with a black skin. They work a deal with us: We stay in our place, don't get uppity and challenge them, and they won't hold us to the same standards they have for themselves. They look at Willie Horton and see a black. I look at him and see a criminal."

"You bitching about a free ride?" Houghton made a feeble attempt to pick himself up.

"I don't know exactly when it happened, Houghton, but I don't believe the party line anymore. People who talk about a 'black view' of the world are nothing but fucking charlatans." Sims shook his head angrily. "There aren't any free rides. We pay for what's been done to us. We're not going back to the plantation. We won't be chained by excuses for us to fail: drugs, poverty, repression, the idea that nothing's ever our fault. Then test scores are rigged so we don't see how we're being robbed. I'd rather put up with your Archie Bunker garbage, Houghton. At least I know where you're coming from."

Houghton was taken aback. Not just at Sims's outburst, but at his own reaction to it. He felt washed out, defenseless. He looked for a long moment at Sims. "All blacks don't think like you, Sims."

Sims gave Houghton a lazy grin, breaking the tension between them. "If you can see that, maybe there's hope for you yet."

At this point Sims felt an insistent buzzing vibration from the pager disguised as a ballpoint pen. He got up from his seat.

"Where're you going?"

Sims shouldered a small bag. "Call in." He motioned toward the telephone booths.

Closing the door of the booth, Sims ran a credit card through the slot of the telephone and listened as the electronic winds whistled and bleeted. He fished in the bag, moving so his back would block the booth window. Fumbling with the scrambler's rubber boots, he fit the device over the telephone's handset, then flipped two switches. A liquid crystal display pulsed, then reeled out a long run of digits. Sims punched the numbers into the telephone and was soon in touch with a secure phone in Langley's operations center.

A few minutes later, Houghton watched as Sims walked somewhat uncertainly toward him.

"You make contact?"

Sims slumped into his chair and sat for a moment, saying nothing. Finally, looking up to Houghton, he nodded. "Yes. I made contact. They just missed us in Prague." Sims's brown eyes were almost an obsidian black. "Valek's dead."

8

Lips thrust outward in appraisal, Riddle contemplated the board. He was clearly unhappy.

"You told me to concentrate," Sims reminded him.

"You didn't have to take me so seriously," Riddle groused. He glanced at the board again, sighed, and put away the pieces. That done, he sat back in his chair, put his hands on his thighs, and looked expectantly at Sims.

For the next hour, Riddle listened, questioned, got up for more coffee, then sat down to listen and question more. On the small Queen Anne table by his chair, the stack of blue index cards grew. Then, satisfied with the facts, he began the probing, the hunt for motives, for unseen links.

Riddle pushed his lips outward again in appraisal, fixed on another quarry. "I'm intrigued by a second-order question." Riddle stopped and lost himself in thought for long seconds, occasionally nodding to himself as he laid another idea in place. "Yes," he said finally, wagging a blue card like a baton. "Why do you suppose that Valek, with all Center's resources behind him, couldn't find Ray?"

Sims thought about this, then shook his head.

Riddle shuffled the index cards from hand to hand, the cards making clean whispering sounds. "Think about Valek in Toronto," he began, setting the stage, "sent by Yuri Andropov, head of KGB, to find and kill King's assassin. Not finding him—"

"Desperation . . . ," Sims said picking it up, "really in a sweat . . ."

"Searching everywhere in Toronto . . . ," Riddle encouraged Sims.

"Careless . . ."

"Yes, careless," Riddle said approvingly, pouncing on the word. "And careless men leave trails," he concluded, pocketing the index cards. He got up and made for the coatrack. "Come. There's a splendid restaurant nearby with the improbable name of Sam and Harry's. The best beef this side of Kōbe. We'll have a good dinner and talk some more."

Moscow, 8:25 A.M.
Friday, January 31, 1992

Viktor Yazov leaned forward to look down through the Plexiglas nose of the boxy Kamov helicopter. Two thousand feet directly below was the Pirogovskoye Reservoir, now covered with a thick crust of dirty ice. Ahead, a bright reflection from the morning sun flashed out from the tree-covered hills.

"That it?"

Beside him, Sergei Fedorovich Okolovich, acting head of Russian intelligence, glanced up from his notes, got his bearings, and nodded.

Several minutes later, the pitch deepened as the rotor blades slapped the heavy winter air. Soon they were coming down in a whirlwind of blowing snow churned up by the helicopter's downdraft. The helicopter bumped and settled into a squatting crouch on the concrete pad. The whine of its turbines died, and the blades windmilled to a slow stop. Just off the pad, a stubby Japanese four-wheel-drive station wagon started up and made for them, its exhaust trailing a white plume in the subzero air.

At the height of the Brezhnev era, Finnish architects, American plumbers, and German construction crews had built the serenely luxurious glass and natural stone building that sprawled comfortably in among the birches and evergreens in the hills just north of Moscow. Inside, the building resembled a cozy Swiss ski lodge. Colorful striped wool rugs covered rich hardwood floors; exposed brick and stone walls supported cathedral ceilings arched with beams of English oak. The Ministry of the Interior listed the building simply as Facility 29.

Aleksandr Solzhenitsyn's *Ivan Denisovich* ripped aside the veil hiding the Gulag Archipelago, the Ministry of the Interior's bone-breaking prison camps strung across the USSR. But the ministry's other archipelago was less known. Facility 29 was one of thousands of luxurious refuges that had been hidden away inside the ramshackle

Soviet national poorhouse. Facility 29 was part of a vast underground network that had cared for the party elite, providing 1 percent of the classless society with a standard of living only dreamed of by the other 99 percent.

Okolovich and Yazov followed a small dark-haired woman dressed in well-cut slacks and a bulky ribbed sweater.

"This is a hospital?"

"A clinic," Okolovich said, not feeling like talking at all. In spite of its determined cheerfulness, the place depressed him. He imagined he could smell the putrefaction of death behind the treated pine-scented air. "He comes here for therapy."

Yazov smirked. "Goat gland injections?"

"Cancer." Okolovich lobbed the word as he might a grenade, taking grim satisfaction in freezing the lascivious smile on Yazov's face.

Yazov slowed, distancing them several paces from their escort. "Yeltsin's chief of staff has cancer?" As he considered this, a perplexed look came across his face. "And he's powerful?"

Okolovich's disdain was evident. "It's *because* of the cancer that Yeltsin trusts him. Yeltsin knows Aristov won't turn on him. Aristov's the most dangerous kind of man—the kind who doesn't have to worry about tomorrow."

There were no opening niceties. Dimitri Petrovich Aristov, a bear of a man, waved Okolovich and Yazov to two straight-backed metal chairs. A word was whispered about Aristov—*sukhar*—dry like a bread crust, no human touch at all. Once a professional soldier, the man's resurrection of a demoralized and battle-torn armor division had been one of the few bright spots in the dismal mess of the Afghan War. Aristov's personal bravery was matched only by his fierce devotion to the welfare of his troops. Dimitri Aristov and his division rolled out of Afghanistan with their heads held high, and thereafter he carried with him like a banner a reputation as a tough, nonideological troubleshooter.

The small suite was at the end of a corridor. Aristov, dressed in gray flannel trousers and a dark green cashmere sweater, sat at a Scandinavian teak desk. Behind him, a window faced out on a distant Moscow. The Kremlin's spires were barely distinguishable under a thick pelt of black coal smog. In the corner, Okolovich saw a large leather chair, an American recliner. Beside it was a metal stand for intravenous drip bottles. His hands went clammy and he fought to keep his eyes off it.

"You said there is a problem," Aristov rumbled.

"There was a defector, a Czech named Miloslav Valek."

"There are many defectors now, Sergei Fedorovich."

Okolovich winced inwardly at this, but plunged on. "This one was working in our central registry. Several weeks ago, Valek didn't show up for work or call in. We sent someone by. He had packed a change of clothes and was off. But he'd been careless. We found this under a chair." Okolovich produced a clear plastic evidence bag from a coat pocket and leaned across the desk to put it in front of Aristov. Inside the bag was a tiny cardboard packet.

Aristov looked at it, but made no effort to pick it up. "This is—"

"A packet for film. For a Minox camera." Okolovich held thumb and index finger about two inches apart. "We give them to our agents to photograph documents."

Aristov absorbed the information. "So he ran away after photographing files. And you tried to find him?"

"He made it to Washington and to the CIA." Okolovich motioned to Yazov. "Colonel Yazov finally caught up with him."

"He's dead?" Aristov looked at Yazov, who nodded, giving a reptilian smile. Aristov looked back to Okolovich. "Then what's the problem?"

"The problem came when we interrogated Josef Broz."

"The Czech?"

Okolovich nodded. "He was a known acquaintance of the defector. We staked him out and observed him meeting with two Americans —CIA. We picked him up." Okolovich detailed the interrogation.

Aristov listened intently, his eyes never leaving Okolovich's face. Minutes later, Aristov sat back in his chair. "And so this man . . ." He paused and looked inquiringly at Okolovich.

"Valek."

"Andropov sent him to Canada to kill the man who supposedly killed King."

Okolovich nodded.

"What do the files tell us?" Aristov prompted.

"Nothing. The entire block of Valek's operational files has been destroyed." Okolovich saw Aristov's eyes widen. "I found a destruction order. It was dated 8 May 1968, and signed by the KGB chairman, Yuri Andropov."

Silence deadened the room for long moments. The muscles along Aristov's jaw pulled his mouth into a tight frown. "Does that mean we killed King and were trying to cover up?"

"It could mean that or—"

"Or . . ."

"Or even if innocent, Andropov believed we had to keep suspicion from centering on us. Remember, America was falling apart. The Vietnam protests were at their peak. Blacks were rioting in all the big cities. President Johnson was being driven out of office. If he and Hoover could have blamed the King killing on us—"

"But Andropov was wrong," Aristov interrupted. "Ray lived, and no one pointed fingers at us—why? And why did Valek fail?"

Okolovich shrugged.

"Well, we aren't going to get any answers from Valek." Aristov looked accusingly at Okolovich, then at Yazov.

"We didn't know about Valek's mission until Broz talked," Okolovich countered. "By that time, Valek was already dead. Besides, if we'd let him live, we still wouldn't have gotten the answers. The Americans would have."

Aristov leaned back in his chair, and Okolovich watched him rub the inside of his left arm with his right hand. Okolovich felt his eyes drawn back to the IV stand. Aristov saw the dread and fascination on the intelligence chief's face.

Okolovich realized Aristov was watching him and he felt his face flush momentarily. He clumsily broached the point that had bothered him since Yazov early that morning had reported on breaking Broz. "After what Broz told the Americans about Valek, they'll be convinced that we did kill King."

"*Proof*, Sergei!" Aristov snapped. "You said it yourself. The Americans can intellectually masturbate about this forever. But without proof . . ." He opened his empty hands in a bowl-like gesture. "And don't overestimate them. Just because some field officer in CIA knows something doesn't mean it's instantly known everywhere in America. We can still contain this. It is an election year in America. No one will want to bring this up."

For the first time, Yazov spoke. "Should we dispose of Broz?"

Aristov looked at Yazov, then Okolovich, who maintained an expressionless face, passing the buck. Irritably, Aristov stood, signaling the end of the discussion. "I *said*," Aristov addressed Okolovich, ignoring Yazov, "we can still contain this."

Minutes later, Aristov stood at the window, smoking a cigarette, one of three he allowed himself each day. The little Japanese station wagon, racing out to the waiting helicopter, was a black insect against the snow.

His earliest childhood desire had been to be a Russian hero; to be read about in schools; to have children taught that, at this time and at this place, Dimitri Petrovich Aristov did something that was so great, so immense, so *magnificent* that the people of Russia would remember him in their prayers forever. It was a dream that had survived the corrosive cynicism of adulthood, of over thirty years of army service.

The chance for immortality had not come in the army, though he had been a good soldier, one of the best. He had taken care of his men and he had been brave. But one didn't stand out because of bravery alone. There had been a lot of brave men in Afghanistan.

The station wagon was now at the pad, and he saw the distance-shrunken figures of Okolovich and the killer, Yazov, clutching their fur hats, long coats whipping around them, walking heads ducked toward the helicopter.

Heroism had eluded him in the army, and it was with typical Russian irony that the opportunity would come now. But the August coup had brought it about, the chance single-handedly to set Russia on a new course. He had devoured books on earlier Russian reformers and had become intrigued by the parallels that had faced Pyotr Stolypin. In 1907, against rising public unrest as the czarist empire crumbled, Stolypin, as prime minister, had ruthlessly rammed through land reform, compulsory education, and economic modernization. Field court martials dealt with his opponents, and the busy gallows had become known as "Stolypin's necktie."

But it was all too late. In 1911, a police agent, probably working for the royal family, assassinated Stolypin, and the next act in Russia's tragedy was foredoomed. The Bolshevik takeover was just around the corner and the beginning of a long night for the Russian people.

The helicopter was now rising, a dark shape within the white, swirling snow.

He would have preferred to ride into history at the head of his troops, he thought, feeling a nostalgic longing for the army. Soldiering was a straightforward business. But the brave lads of Afghanistan couldn't fight this battle. Instead, he needed those who thrived on deception and deceit. The helicopter, nose down like a giant dragonfly, was gathering speed and coming straight toward him.

He couldn't understand why the CIA was pursuing this King matter. He drew deeply on his cigarette, savoring the earthy fullness of the smoke in his lungs. Maybe it was just an American craziness, this obsession with the killing of a long-dead rabble-rousing witch doctor.

After all, he had read only recently about the Americans digging up their former presidents to settle the arguments of some obscure scholar. But the limit to this macabre fun was where it might endanger his legacy to the Russian people and his place in the history books.

Overhead, the helicopter made a muffled beating sound as it carried Okolovich and Yazov back to Moscow. There was a soft knock on his door.

"Come."

Behind him, the nurse, the dark-haired woman in the slacks and bulky sweater, came in and began setting up the IV drip beside his chair.

He turned from the window and began rolling up the left sleeve of his sweater. "After you put that damned needle in, have them bring a telephone," he told the nurse.

She looked questioningly at the telephone on his desk.

Aristov shook his head and ground out his cigarette. "Tell them I want the scrambler."

Washington, D.C., 5:13 A.M.
Friday, January 31, 1992

In a little over two hours, the tempo at Dulles would pick up and the huge airport would begin to resemble the hectic flight deck of an aircraft carrier. DC-10s and 747s would be lining up to race the sun on their long nonstop flights to the West Coast and on to Asia. In the midafternoon, the planes from Europe and the Middle East would begin coming in—Airbuses, an occasional Ilyushin, and today, Friday, there would be a cameo appearance by the aging but beautiful celebrity, the Air France Concorde.

Now, however, Dulles was dark and its taxiways and runways empty. The only movement was a lone snowplow grating against the concrete as it tidied up slots near the midfield terminal. Then, from the northeast corner of the airport, halogen floodlights and the running-up of jet engines pierced the predawn stillness. Moments later, from a private hangar on Page ramp, a sleek sky blue Gulfstream IV taxied to runway one-niner left.

Twenty-five minutes later, the Gulfstream was at 41,000 feet and eastbound at 575 miles an hour. Two hours later, Gander control radioed oceanic clearance as two on-board inertial navigation systems automatically updated position data with a satellite fix; the sleek plane was set for the North Atlantic crossing.

In the left seat of the darkened cockpit, Tom Farmer made his calculations on an old-fashioned circular flight slide rule. Temperature and a fifty-knot tailwind favored the Gulfstream. He jotted down a flight time of nine hours and four minutes. He then punched the same data into the state-of-the-art flight computer. In less than two seconds the computer confirmed Farmer's math: nine hours, three minutes—nonstop from Washington to Moscow. He smiled triumphantly and turned the controls over to the pilot. It was characteristic of Farmer that his first thought was that the computer had made the one-minute error. The fun flying was over for now. He'd take over again when they got into the approach to Sheremet'yevo.

Before he left the cockpit, Farmer sat for a moment, scanning the instruments. He had a passion for flying and flight. A workmanlike ability to fly was easily acquired, and getting easier, what with the advances in avionics and communications. But dexterous, exciting flying was still a rare commodity, and he instinctively homed in on the hard to get.

Being good at flying was like being good at making money. Neither was worth a shit for its own sake. What was important to both was that you were in control. When flying, you controlled the three dimensions and a little bit of time itself. And making money wasn't just piling the stuff up somewhere, or buying things. Making money meant power and thus influence. Controlling business and politics was tougher than flying, but it was a challenge. He was goddamned good at both, he told himself as he turned toward the cabin.

His eyes adjusted quickly to the bright lights. Capable of seating as many as twenty-seven, half the spacious cabin had been outfitted for Farmer's living quarters. There was a complete galley and a full-sized bath and dressing room. Everywhere there was lush carpeting, exotic woods, or butter-soft leather. The other half of the cabin was an equally luxurious communications center. A telex, two fax machines, and three high-speed computers occupied one equipment bank. There were four overhead television monitors and VCRs. A bird's-eye maple conference table ran down the middle of the compartment, and two satellite communications automatic switchboards brought in twelve voice and data-link channels for instant direct-dial anywhere in the world. No matter where he was, Farmer could instantly contact any or all of his thirty-three offices in twenty-eight countries.

Farmer's publicists described him as the latest reincarnation of the Yankee trader, the American business wizard who could march into the jaws of hell and come out grinning, waving a contract like a banner of victory, the rebirth of American entrepreneurship.

An investigative reporter for the *Washington Post* was less generous, featuring Farmer in a series of articles as a Daddy Greenbucks, plowing his way through Washington and fertilizing the landscape with prodigious amounts of money. Farmer gave to Democrats and Republicans alike. His only criterion was utility. And for their part, neither the Democrats nor the Republicans bitched about Farmer's down-and-dirty pragmatism. Farmer's money was too big to demand party loyalty of him.

Farmer had become one of the Kremlin's favorite American businessmen because of the vagaries of Soviet politics. In 1979, he had come to the Soviet Union to put together his first deal, a modest contract for September oats. While the big boys like Dwayne Andreas and Armand Hammer were toasting the aging and decrepit Brezhnev, he had to content himself with sweating through tough negotiations with a smart but unknown young party insider who was the Minister of Agriculture. He and the minister had cut a damn good deal, and in so doing began a long and profitable acquaintance. Six years later and many millions richer, Farmer had laughed at his good fortune as the unremarkable agriculture minister, Mikhail Gorbachev, vaulted into the leadership of the Soviet Union.

Once established, Farmer adroitly built bridges into every faction of Soviet officialdom. He had detected Boris Yeltsin's rise to power before anyone. Within months he had one foot firmly in Yeltsin's camp while keeping the other in Gorbachev's. In Moscow, as in Washington, he knew how to become indispensable, the constructor of deals, the business diplomat.

Hanging his leather flight jacket in a closet and slipping into a cashmere sweater, Farmer checked the array of clocks on a bulkhead. He would arrive in Moscow just after ten o'clock, twelve hours after Aristov had called. Even over the scrambler, Aristov's concern had come through. It sounded like bad news for the Russians.

Perhaps not for Farmer, however. Even while Aristov talked, he had begun to feel a familiar stirring, the sexual thrill of tracking a prey. You couldn't sell where there wasn't a need, and once more, the Russians needed him.

Farmer glanced again at the clocks and sat down at a computer to call up the latest from the Japanese markets. Whatever was bothering the Russians could be handled. And it would bring Tom Farmer more money, more power, and the opportunity to make things happen his way. He knew what other American traders didn't: that the Russians would soon ask for another hundred million bushels of wheat in food aid. That ought to get some action in Chicago. At least a fifteen-cent-a-bushel bump. And he held options on twenty million bushels. He reached for the telephone to make the first of his calls around the world. He had almost seven hours before Moscow to get some work done.

Moscow, 10:23 P.M.
Friday, January 31, 1992

Farmer was back at the controls when they touched down in Russia. Sheremet'yevo tower was uncharacteristically efficient. Taxiway instructions were prompt, almost courteous, and an air force follow-me truck was waiting to lead him to a waiting hangar. As the hangar doors rolled open, Farmer smiled as he recognized the gleaming IL-62 inside; it was Yeltsin's personal aircraft. Parked under the wing of the big Ilyushin was a black Zil limousine. Still taxiing into the hangar, Farmer glanced out the cockpit's side window and saw with satisfaction the pairs of armed guards in a security perimeter around the huge building.

The Gulfstream's engines were still winding down when Farmer threw the levers that opened the side door. He stood for a moment in the doorway, the dry cold of the hangar carrying with it the sleek smell of jet fuel and hydraulic fluid.

The door of the Zil opened and it was Dimitri Aristov who stepped out to meet him, not Boris Yeltsin. Farmer felt a stab of displeasure. He had long imagined that he and Yeltsin had a unique one-on-one relationship. It was a relationship Farmer prized for ego's sake far more than he did for the millions of dollars it brought him. He never understood why Yeltsin increasingly shoved Aristov between them. He resented it, and it caused him to struggle with an unaccustomed sense of intrusion and rivalry, although he would never dare say anything to the mercurial Yeltsin.

When the two men shook hands, Farmer took secret satisfaction that Aristov seemed older and more drawn since they last met in

September. Finishing the brief greeting, Farmer made as if to walk to the Zil.

Aristov, however, put a gloved hand on Farmer's shoulder and steered him toward the yawning open door of the hangar.

"I don't understand." Farmer's confusion and irritability showed on his face. He *had* been called for a meeting with Yeltsin, hadn't he? Tom Farmer didn't get out of bed at oh-dark-thirty and fly halfway around the world to meet with some flunky, no matter how highly placed. He got the sinking feeling that that was just what he had done.

"Forgive my small hospitality," Aristov said in his heavily accented English, "but this meeting will be little. You will want to leave right away."

From the corner of his eye, Farmer saw his pilots and mechanic huddled with a Russian air force ground crew and fuel hoses being snaked toward the Gulfstream.

The two men walked outside into the darkness. It was a rare windless night and the black sky was dusted with unblinking stars. Behind them at a discreet distance, two men with submachine guns followed.

"I've come a long way," Farmer began, intending a rebuke.

"Last month"—Aristov spoke over Farmer, as if he hadn't heard the American—"a senior KGB officer defected to the CIA."

Unlike many big-egoed men, Farmer was a good listener. It was a quality that helped him make his millions. Something in Aristov's somber tone warned him it was time to listen.

They walked along the frost-rimed tarmac, driven close by the cold, their shoulders almost touching. As Aristov worked through the story, Farmer felt a clutching despair, as if he were in a casket and Aristov was hammering home a nail with each revelation. He wanted to shut out Aristov, but the Russian relentlessly soldiered on through Valek and Toronto, the files Andropov had ordered destroyed, and Broz and what he had told the Americans in Prague. At last, Aristov fell silent and turned to face Farmer, waiting for his reaction.

Farmer shook himself, as if that would help him make sense of it. "Couldn't you have stopped it?" he finally asked Aristov.

"We tried." Aristov detailed the killing of Valek.

"You killed—" Farmer got an incredulous look.

Aristov grabbed the American's jacket.

"Don't look at me that way, American," he rumbled ominously. "Great nations come apart." Aristov paused, reaching for the rest of the thought. "Today is our turn. Tomorrow is maybe yours." He tugged at Farmer's jacket, bringing his face close to the American. "We will put it back together because we have guts to do what we have to do. Do you?"

Farmer's hand came up, catching and twisting Aristov's wrist, freeing himself from the Russian's grip. "Don't question *my* guts," he said venomously.

The two men glared at each other, frozen by anger. It was Aristov who broke the standoff. "We tried to stop this by ourselves, but now we need help. Take this." Aristov reached into his heavy coat and came up with a thick, cream-colored envelope, which he thrust at Farmer. "It is the details of this talking of mine. What we know and what we don't. A proof we are earnest." He watched as Farmer took the envelope, examined it briefly, and put it inside his own coat.

Farmer could tell that Aristov was looking for the correct English phrase. Then: "Your CIA. They work hard to blame us for killing King."

Farmer's mouth locked into a tense frown. "Did you?" he asked.

Aristov swung his arms across the front of his body in a warming-up movement. "Perhaps." He shrugged. "But perhaps not."

The offhand response sent Farmer off again. *"Perhaps?"* Farmer's voice rose and cracked and he stared at the Russian in wide-eyed disbelief. "This is like some goddamn Third World soap opera! What am I dealing with here?" Farmer was now shouting. "You fuckers run around shooting up niggers and popes and, for all I know, the Kennedys as well, and then you say you don't know if you did it?"

"Who knows what happened? Who did killing is not the importance," Aristov leveled at Farmer. He drew himself up and measured Farmer with an appraising look. *"Voskreseniye,"* he finally said.

Farmer looked at him, then nodded. The round was over, and they started back toward the hangar.

Voskreseniye. Farmer had first heard the word from Yeltsin. Farmer had pulled out all stops to get an appointment with the Russian leader. Yeltsin had carved fifteen minutes out of a crammed schedule, mostly, Farmer felt, out of politeness. But as Yeltsin had listened, and as the implications of what Farmer was saying had sunk in, Yeltsin became more intent and animated. Yeltsin's appointments went unheeded as he and Farmer talked through the rest of the day and well into the night. When they finished, Yeltsin had enthusiastically pounded a fist on the table and said it: *Voskreseniye*—Resurrection.

What Farmer had proposed was nothing less than lifting a new, free-enterprise Russian economy from the ruin brought about by seventy-five years of Marxist central planning.

Soon known in Washington as well as Moscow as Operation *Voskreseniye,* Farmer's plan involved Farmer hocking and leveraging everything he owned to gain control of Transnational, a merchant bank. Transnational was worth nothing except as an umbrella under which he could put together a monster package of interlocking projects, the whole of which would jump-start a new Russian economy.

The principal players in the Transnational package were the elite of the *Fortune* 500: Chevron, AT&T, Chrysler, General Electric, and Dow Chemical. Chevron would take the lead. The Russian government, through Transnational, would contract with the American oil company to develop the huge oil field of Tengiz in Kazakhstan. With known reserves of over twenty billion barrels, the Chevron venture would be the money machine, cranking out the precious hard currency to build the rest of the manufacturing, transportation, and communications infrastructure that would bring Russia into the world economy.

CIA and State Department analysts missed it, but *Voskreseniye* had been the hidden driving force behind the coup against Yeltsin and Gorbachev. The old guard leftists feared it; it was a rising tide that would wash away their monopoly on power. Failing to stop the project with bureaucratic sabotage, the hard-liners foolishly resorted to the August coup. When that failed, *Voskreseniye's* only potential enemy remained the United States Congress.

"We let this shit go on," Farmer said to Aristov, "you can kiss *Voskreseniye* good-bye."

"Kiss?" Aristov puzzled over Farmer's use of the word.

"*Vpuskaetsa v tyalyete!*" Farmer put it in his pidgin Russian—"It goes down the toilet." He watched Aristov nod his understanding. The Chevron linchpin depended on international financing. And the international bankers insisted on a guarantee from the U.S. government. Working quietly with a handful of Democrats in Congress and a key staffer or two in the White House, Farmer had engineered a precarious fix: the one-billion guarantee would be hidden in an emergency aid bill. With the American economy on shaky ground and unemployment rising, support in Congress was thin enough. But letting it out that the Russians had killed King would not only put everything in the toilet but would also flush it down as well.

The sky blue Gulfstream shimmered under the hangar lights, taking on an almost ethereal glow. Farmer looked at it with aching love. Its flowing sleekness embodied mystery and adventure, power and future. It was more than an airplane; it exemplified everything worth having. From it, Farmer surveyed the world. From it, all things were possible. He imagined it being taken away from him, imagined it belonging to someone else. It was like imagining his own death. He felt a churning, falling sensation, then a raging desire to lash out with his fists, to fight to keep what was by-God his.

Washington, D.C., 6:50 A.M.
Saturday, February 1

The Gulfstream braked to a halt as soon as it nosed onto the Page ramp. Before the engines had begun shutting down, the door opened with a hydraulic sigh and the onboard steps snaked out and angled down to the tarmac. Farmer scrambled down the steps and into the waiting limousine.

Forty-three minutes later, the glistening car rounded the corner onto New Hampshire Avenue, pulling in under the awning at the massive ziggurat of Watergate South. A liveried doorman swung the thick glass door open with deceptive ease. Farmer gave his name, and a plainclothes guard nodded and escorted him down a carpeted hallway to a private elevator.

John Francis Delaney, director of the Federal Bureau of Investigation, was waiting at the elevator entrance in robe and slippers, freshly showered and shaved.

Delaney was a tall man, well over six feet. His sharp, handsome features somewhat softened by age, Delaney, a bachelor, was a sought-after article by Georgetown's hostesses. He was everywhere in Washington—receptions at the Kennedy Center, charity galas, small private dinners with centrist politicians of both parties. Yes, he was everywhere in Washington, but at the same time, he was a man about whom little was known.

In the process of becoming a Washington fixture, Delaney made certain that the Bureau he ran faded into the background. Not that the Bureau wasn't doing its job. Delaney merely took special pains to remove it from the critics' firing line. With Delaney at the helm, there were none of the gaffes of the past that had embarrassed the Bureau and bedeviled the White House. John Delaney could watch the evening news with the assurance that there'd be no surprises.

Network anchors no longer tumesced over the prospect of fucking the Bureau in front of thirty million viewers after Sunday dinner. That was precisely how John Delaney wanted it.

His mastery of the FBI ran far deeper than public relations. His trump card was an exquisitely maintained intelligence operation that spied on everything and everyone of consequence in and around Washington.

In his office Delaney had a walk-in vault to which only he held the combination. A dozen handpicked subordinates kept a steady stream of official and personal dirt flowing into the vault. It was a lesson Delaney had learned from J. Edgar Hoover himself: a prudent man invested in blind-side insurance in Washington.

There was no smile of welcome or extended hand. "I hope it's important, Tom." The voice, which always carried an undertone of menace, was rich with the Bostonian accents and inflections that resonated mystically in a Washington still enthralled with two Kennedys long since gone. Delaney studied Farmer's face for a cold clinical second, then turned and led the way back into the apartment.

Delaney's library overlooked the Potomac and Georgetown's harbor front. He motioned Farmer to a small sofa and took a leather Queen Anne chair opposite. For half an hour, the businessman talked, explaining in detail and with precision the summons from Aristov and the meeting at Sheremet'yevo. Once or twice, Delaney interrupted, but mostly he remained silent, unwaveringly fixed on Farmer. Occasionally, his eyes still on Farmer, Delaney would extend his right hand to a large world globe set into a mahogany pedestal. He would flick it languidly, then let his fingertips glide over the slowly spinning globe. When Farmer finished, Delaney sat thoughtfully, then looked at the globe, giving it another spin. He stopped it abruptly with the palm of his hand.

"Aristov gave me this." Farmer handed over the heavy cream-colored envelope. Arm extended, Delaney took the envelope and for a second held it between thumb and forefinger as if to weigh it. Then, tearing off one end of the envelope, he withdrew a sheaf of papers and two glossy photographs. The photographs, taken by some Russian agent, were of Sims and Houghton, waiting in their car in Prague's Old Town Square. Farmer leaned back in the sofa and massaged his eyelids while Delaney read. At one point, Delaney, obviously cued by something in the document, scrutinized the photographs of Sims and Houghton. Finally he folded the document, held it up, and waggled it at Farmer.

"Why you?"

"Why?" Farmer's expression was of a man insulted. "Shit, John, I've been Mister Fix-it for those assholes for goddamn near twenty years. They know me. They know my connections, especially with Kaiser and the Chiliheads." Farmer paused to judge the effect of his outburst. Delaney was regarding him in grave silence.

Farmer added his cap: "And they know I got my ass and overcoat in the Resurrection project. Goddamnit, John, who do you expect Aristov to call in—some fucking State Department pussy? 'We just killed a defector of ours in a Georgetown clothing store but that didn't do any good and we need your help'?"

Delaney was emotionless, his face and eyes hard and unrelenting. "Are you *certain* that's what it is? Absolutely—"

Farmer leaned forward, as if to reach out to Delaney. "John, I leaned on him. Hard." Farmer's voice took on a rock solid assurance. "He's not that good an actor, John." Farmer recalled Aristov's face before him in the freezing Russian night. "They're scared shitless that they might have killed King."

"Maybe they did, Tom." Delaney's voice was sly and teasing.

Farmer's face turned ashen as he thought about the limousine waiting for him down below, the Gulfstream at Dulles, his worldwide net of offices, his global empire. "Oh shit, no!"

Delaney's smile was razor cruel. "That's right, old friend. Never forget there's a lot more at stake here than your goddamn Resurrection project." Delaney was certain that Farmer knew the stakes. Delaney reveled in the knowledge that Farmer never had a waking moment when he didn't think about the files that he, Delaney, had on him— enough there for a good twenty years for stock fraud and illegal currency manipulations. He passed the photographs and documents back to Farmer. "You might arrange a meeting with Kaiser and get him to put a crimp in the Agency's hose."

Washington, D.C., 8:40 A.M.
Saturday, February 1, 1992

A Mozart flute concerto from a concealed stereo softly accented the vaultlike stillness of Warren Kaiser's walnut-paneled office. A low fire burned in the fireplace and outside a feathery snow was falling, covering the sweep of the White House lawn. Pennsylvania Avenue, normally busy, was deserted. It was one of those occasional Washington winter mornings when even the workaholics chose to stay at home.

Warren Kaiser had been unhappy about being dragged into the office. He usually worked Saturdays as well as an occasional Sunday. But this was a weekend meant to be taken off. It would be the last he'd have for months to come. The 1992 presidential campaign would get under way next week and Congress would be coming back into session. It was his weekend to have the children and he had made all the arrangements for skiing up at Massanutten. Then Farmer had called.

"You haven't eaten."

Kaiser looked down at his plate. His breakfast was untouched, the Canadian bacon now a greasy raft in a sea of congealed egg yolk. He had been hungry, too. Until Farmer had handed over the documents and photographs. He had read them, and as he did so, his apprehension clotted within his throat. The papers and photographs now lay on the polished tabletop almost under Kaiser's right hand, and to Kaiser they held the morbid fascination of Pandora's Box.

Warren Kaiser was the White House chief of staff. A former Texas oil man and three-term congressman from Houston, Kaiser had his eye on 1996. Four years from now, the American electorate would roll the dice again and there would be a free-for-all for the Republican nomination. Warren Kaiser intended to win. Already he was carefully watching his potential challengers and building alliances.

Kaiser's ambition and his restless search for political backing had led to his association with Tom Farmer. At least, that was what Kaiser believed.

Farmer had come to Kaiser to ask his advice. Kaiser, like Yeltsin, had been thunderstruck as Farmer described the Russian project. What he needed, Farmer had said rather innocently, were introductions to Texas oil men who would understand the value of developing the Tengiz fields. And did Kaiser know of any place he could start?

Con schemes work best when the victim has a trace of larceny in his own heart. Kaiser saw the project as a way to set himself up as the Chiliheads' man in the White House, a man they would want to be president in 1996.

It was a con because Farmer didn't need Kaiser as a go-between. Hell, Farmer could go directly to the Chiliheads. What Farmer had in mind was using the Chiliheads to snare Kaiser in order to get an advocate in the White House for *Voskreseniye.*

The Chiliheads made you or broke you in Texas. The eight most powerful men in Texas oil, they saddled up their executive jets to get together on the first Tuesday of each month for bowls of Pedernales Red (onion, oregano, cumin, tomatoes, hot chile peppers, and lean beef chunks—and *no* goddamn beans) washed down with bottles of ice-cold Pearl. It was after such a meeting during the 1990 governor's race that they had decided to abandon the front-running flap-jawed Claytie Williams in favor of underdog Ann Richards. After she became Texas's first woman governor, Richards always made certain the Chiliheads had a place at her deal-cutting table.

Kaiser had made his discreet pilgrimages to Texas, introducing Farmer to taciturn leathery men in Long View, Pecos, and Van Horn, with stops in between at Odessa and, of course, Houston. The Chiliheads had climbed on board the *Voskreseniye* bandwagon. This put Kaiser squarely in a vise, where Farmer wanted him. If *Voskreseniye* succeeded, the Chiliheads would be grateful and Kaiser's presidential prospects would prosper. On the other hand, if Kaiser got blamed for the project's failure, he not only lost his chance at the presidency, he also wouldn't dare show his face in Texas again.

Tom Farmer mopped up the last of the egg yolk with a piece of toast. "Good breakfast, Warren."

"How could you eat?" Kaiser knew Farmer could detect the thin edge of hysteria in his voice, but he didn't give a shit. "If this gets out"—he pointed gingerly at the envelope, as if it might explode—"Congress'll run like a scalded cat."

"That's exactly what I told the Russians, Warren," Farmer said coolly.

Kaiser was having trouble breathing. Farmer's attitude made it worse. "How can you sit there so goddamned casual about this, Tom? Don't you know what the stakes are?"

Farmer put on a slow, calculating smile. "I *always* know what the stakes are, Warren. You do, too. That's why we get along so well. You, me, and our friends in Texas."

Kaiser thought of the Chiliheads and it got even harder to breathe.

Farmer leaned across the breakfast table and swatted the distraught Kaiser on the shoulder. "One thing I learned in the deal-making business, Warren, is to rely on the experts, the specialists." He stood and fetched his coat and hat from a nearby chair. As he buttoned the coat he gave Kaiser another confident smile, and leaning to the table, he nudged the photographs and documents closer to the chief of staff. "You're the specialist on government, Warren, and we have a government problem. I don't want to tell you how to run your business, how to—how do you Texans put it?—suck eggs? I'm sure you'll come up with something."

On his way out the West Wing corridor to his waiting car, Farmer stopped his marine guard escort, who listened, then pointed toward the men's room. Inside, Farmer glanced around, making sure he was alone. Stepping into a stall and bending over a toilet, he vomited, giving in at last to the cramping nerves that had threatened to betray him in Kaiser's office.

Washington, D.C., 7:30 A.M.
Monday, February 3, 1992

When she had finished community college in 1972, Martha Milsworth Hudgins left York, Pennsylvania, for Washington. She had looked forward to the excitement of a well-paying job in government and then, after a few years, to settling down and raising a family. Twenty years later, she was a GS-14 in the White House and resigned to the prospect of being single the rest of her life. An arrangement with an attractive man would be about as close as she'd get to a reasonable substitute for love, marriage, and children. Better that than the alternatives, she often thought, shuddering as she remembered the grim and seemingly endless forays in brass and fern bars with Irish names on the window and condom dispensers in the women's john.

This Monday morning, Martha had awakened and smiled as she lay in bed and heard Tim's noises in her small kitchen as he fixed her coffee before he rushed off to work.

She had met Tim Nicholas at the White House two years before. She had just become Warren Kaiser's special assistant, and he had reported in as the FBI's new liaison to the latest drug task force. He was determinedly single and seven years her junior, so she never deluded herself that it would go anywhere. But he *was* attentive, cute, and a good screw. Now, transferred back to the Bureau, he was still interested in her, and so the relationship had stayed on an even keel. And, Martha thought as she rolled over and waited for Tim and the coffee, that was good enough for today.

Twenty minutes later, Tim Nicholas left. In his attaché case, he carried an audiotape he'd secretly made: a recording of Martha Hudgins describing the emergency Sunday meeting she'd had to set up for Warren Kaiser, a meeting between Kaiser and the CIA director.

Tim was on top of the world. A good fuck for himself and a golden take for the boss. Not a bad start for the week. Not bad at all.

Langley, 8:10 A.M.
Monday, February 3, 1992

Driving to the Agency, parking, walking through North Lot—the routine of going to work—meshed so smoothly it seemed to Sims unreal that he had been in Prague the Monday before, waiting for Janik and all that was to follow. He was still thinking about it as he slipped his badge into a slot at the hallway entry gate and punched in his access code.

The gate refused to swing open, and a flashing panel on the display told him to reenter his access code.

"Bradford Sims?"

The voice came from behind him. Turning, Sims faced two bulky men in civilian clothes whose stance spelled Office of Security. The larger of the two had the questioning look on his face.

Sims motioned to the balky gate. Then, with a small chill, it came to him that the security officer knew his name. The big man had a black plastic name tag fastened to the lapel of his blue blazer. The tag read EDWARDS.

The security officer registered Sims's awareness and increased by a notch or two the professionally condescending, calming tone that told Sims there was a good deal to worry about.

"I'm certain we can straighten it out." Edwards motioned to the uniformed guard and the gate swung open.

"My badge," Sims protested, pointing to the slot in the display panel.

"We'll take care of it," the big man said in his soothing rumble, pointing ahead, down the hall. He moved to Sims's right, the other cop to the left.

They wound through the ground floor corridors without talking. The security officer on his left led slightly while Edwards kept a half pace behind. They were good at it, Sims thought. They soon came to an unmarked door on D corridor, the part of the building Sims knew was allocated to the Office of Security. With a large index finger, Edwards poked at the buttons of a cipher lock. There was an answering click and they entered a suite of offices, went past the secretaries, ending up in a bland, windowless room.

Edwards pulled out a chair for Sims at the scarred gray metal conference table. "Coffee?" He held the chair for Sims with one hand and with the other motioned toward the coffee maker.

"No. What's this?"

The big man cocked his head. "A meeting."

"Meeting with who?" Sims felt his heart racing.

This brought a sunny smile. "They're on their way down now," Edwards said. "Sure you won't have some coffee?"

Sims stood by the chair, saying nothing. Edwards's smile grew even bigger. He went to the coffeemaker and stack of Styrofoam cups. He poured a black coffee, turning to Sims and making a show of sipping it with evident pleasure.

Sims took his seat and waited, elbows on the table, hands loosely clasped. Across the table from him, opposite the door he had come in, was another door. He forced himself to breathe deeply and willed his pulse to slow down. He scanned the room. It seemed totally unremarkable. Edwards was putting the coffeepot back on its burner when the door opposite opened.

"Good morning, Morris," Sims said, wanting to take the initiative.

Cantwell pulled out the chair across from Sims with an awkward jerking motion, then looked up with a defensive expression on his face. Two other men followed Cantwell. The first, a thin angular man with a distracted air, Sims recognized as Browder, the general counsel. Sims couldn't remember the second man's name, a small baldheaded man with hooded eyes, but he knew he was the Agency's inspector general. This was trouble. Behind him, he heard Edwards pull up one of the chairs along the wall.

"What's this, Morris?"

"This is a notification of a personnel action," Browder, the lawyer began. "It does not constitute a legal proceeding in the sense that—"

Sims pointed to Cantwell. "I asked *you,* Morris."

Browder stopped with a petulant look on his face. The room was quiet except for the sound of Edwards, the security man, shifting in the chair behind Sims.

Cantwell looked at Browder. The lawyer nodded reluctantly. Cantwell opened his mouth experimentally, then blurted out, "You have conducted unauthorized operations, you have misappropriated

Agency properties, and you have revealed sensitive information to uncleared persons."

It seemed to Sims that Cantwell was racing to get through his part before he forgot his lines.

Sims forced himself to remain expressionless until Cantwell began to fidget and make his small throat-clearing noises, then: "Moscow sent Valek to kill James Earl Ray. What do you think of that, Morris?"

Sims liked the results. Cantwell blinked, worked his mouth wordlessly again, then turned toward Browder, the lawyer. Browder was off balance, and the IG's eyes narrowed even further.

Cantwell had a trapped, furtive look. "Broz isn't—"

"Mr. Sims!" Browder sprang to life, practically elbowing Cantwell aside. "This is a government agency. It is not a preserve for conspiracy nuts."

Cantwell's panicked expression confirmed Sims's suspicion. The lawyer and the IG were not sufficient witnesses to this meeting. It was being taped, but the Agency didn't want Sims's information on those tapes. The IG frowned and shifted uncomfortably.

"I was running an authorized investigation of a defector's testimony and background."

"It's not for you to say what's authorized," countered Browder.

Sims ignored the lawyer and bent toward Cantwell, forcing the CI chief to look him in the eye. "You're saying the Agency doesn't want to know who killed King, Morris? That you're closing this down?"

Cantwell seemed to have awakened. "Closing down?" He shook his head. "No, I wouldn't say that." He thought for a moment. "We never opened anything up, Brad." He looked back to the lawyer for approval.

"The courts, Mr. Sims, decided long ago who killed Dr. King," Browder added.

Sims kept looking at Cantwell. "What happened to Valek, Morris?" Cantwell recoiled as Sims leaned across the table. "I left him here, alive and well, damnit, and now he's dead. What the hell happened?"

Cantwell got a cornered look and shrank back into his chair.

"Mr. Sims!" Browder's voice was strangled as he looked past Sims. From behind, Sims felt, rather than heard, the big cop shifting in his chair. "Mr. Sims," Browder tried again, more certain of himself, "the Central Intelligence Agency does not have to explain to you the circumstances of Mr. Valek's death."

It had the ring of a rehearsed proclamation. "I suppose Valek never happened," said Sims.

"He's dead." Cantwell said it with smug satisfaction. Browder put a restraining hand on Cantwell's arm. Cantwell, now feeling on top, ignored him. "He died of a heart attack in a clothing store. He's dead. There's nothing more."

Browder nudged Cantwell and slid a single sheet of paper in front of him.

Cantwell held the paper up, as if it were an exhibit. "Except, of course, the matter of the personnel action," he said, still looking at the paper. He began reading with relish: "For the convenience of the service . . ."

9

Edwards, the big security officer, walked Sims to the parking lot. There, two uniformed security guards waited in a mud-splattered sedan. The driver, a surly kid, was smoking. The other guard, older, fatter, was slouched in the passenger's seat, reading a newspaper. As Sims got in his car, the big cop watched intently, as if he would have to report later all the details of how Sims went about it. The sedan followed Sims out of the lot. As he passed through the gate, he glanced in his rearview mirror. The sedan was pulling a U-turn and heading back into the Agency grounds. He felt humiliated and oddly shortchanged by the casual indifference. A firing from the world's greatest intelligence agency ought to involve more than this. People went to more trouble to put out the garbage.

He faced his first decision at the interchange of Chain Bridge Road and the George Washington Parkway. Straight ahead was the Potomac and home. The ramp to his right led down the parkway. He realized dimly that he didn't know what he wanted. He did know what it was he didn't want, and that was to go back and sit in his apartment.

Fifteen minutes later, Sims switched off the engine and got out of his car. Without consciously intending to, he had ended up at Hains Point, parked in the same place where he had asked for Houghton's help on Valek's initial interrogation.

Ignoring the snow working its way down into his shoes, he cut across to the seawall railing facing an inlet of the Anacostia River. He stood at the river's edge for some long moments, staring across the channel at the two-story red brick homes of general's row over at Fort McNair. For the first time in his life, he felt truly lost. He didn't know what he would do tomorrow, much less beyond that.

Sliding his chilled hands into his pockets, he felt the hard corners of his credentials case. He took it out. The dark blue cover was embossed with a gold Agency crest. Flipping open the cover, he studied his photograph. The face's innocence seemed to mock him. He started to sail the credentials out into the channel, then, thinking of the years before Valek, he pocketed them, reluctant to throw them away.

He looked around. He and Houghton had sat in the car just over there, talking about the killing of King. And here, where he now stood, there had been two boys passing a football. It had been a little more than three weeks ago, he realized with disbelief. Twenty-three days.

It was as if part of himself were here, while another part was somewhere else; a detached observer looking down on him standing here. He could switch between the Sims-here and the Sims-there. The detached Sims knew that the other Sims was coming out of the shock, and that the next emotion would be raging anger.

Conventional wisdom suggested getting shit-faced in situations such as this. Go to a bar and get mean, nasty drunk. But as he felt his anger coming on, filling him heavy and hot, like molten lead, he knew he didn't want to dull it or drown it.

The three faces came back to him in gross caricature as he gave in to the bigotry he had always fought and thought he had kept at bay. He wanted to lash out first at Cantwell, that supercilious WASP asshole. And then at Browder, the putty-faced Hymie lawyer. And the goddamn wop IG, too, what's-his-name. Fucking white devil faces! If he'd been an Irishman—some fucking Mick bastard—looking into Jack Kennedy's death, would they have done the same thing to him? He beat his hands on the icy metal rail, not feeling the pain. The stolid impassive forms of the generals' houses across the channel mocked him, reminding him of the white men across the table sitting in smug judgment of him. He clenched a bleeding fist and shook it at the houses.

Sims found an open garage on K Street and made his way toward Riddle's shop a block away. Exhausted from his raging at Hains Point, he had sat in his car and thought of going to his uncle. But to explain where he was now, he'd have to retrace the entire trail and give his uncle a primer on basics like compartmentation, the CIA-FBI rivalry, and defectors. It was too much for now.

There was another reason, too, he realized. Calvin Harris had been against him going into the Agency from the start. Harris wouldn't say anything about it—not today, anyway—but there'd be an undercurrent of I-told-you-so, and Sims didn't want to put up with that.

Houghton would have understood. But it struck a wrong note for some undefinable reason, a reason that hung tantalizingly close to Sim's consciousness but stayed maddeningly out of reach. Riddle answered the door himself rather than buzzing Sims in.

"Riddle—"

"I know."

It seemed to Sims that age had finally caught up with Riddle. The hazel eyes were watery and the skin of his face somehow thin and brittle like old parchment.

"How?"

"Mr. Alberich called." Riddle turned and led Sims into the depths of the shop. "He was quite distraught and angry. Most unlike him. Said he had called your apartment first. I took the liberty of calling Houghton." He pointed to Sims's customary chair. "Coffee?"

It was a short story and Sims told its bare facts in a clipped, unemotional tone. After he finished, Riddle sat impassively, lips pursed in thought.

Sims felt oddly better. The recital had created an island of rationality in a sea of violent emotions.

"Nothing about the circumstances of Valek's death?"

"No."

"Mr. Alberich told me that Valek's remains were cremated." Riddle said it with a sighing reluctance, a professional accusing his profession of malpractice.

"No autopsy?"

"Apparently not. They did it last night."

"A cremation on Sunday," Sims laughed mirthlessly. "They were in a hurry." He watched as Riddle made a note.

"Broz, then"—Riddle looked up from the index card—"you said Cantwell started to say something about Broz—"

"Before the lawyer cut him off."

"But he said Broz *after* you said—"

"After I said Moscow had sent Valek to kill Ray."

Sims's anger was disappearing. Instead, he felt a clutch of excitement in his throat as he saw the question Riddle was driving at. "How did Cantwell know about Broz?"

"Exactly. The Czech service officer—Janik? Perhaps he told Prague station."

Sims shook his head. "Janik knew I was meeting with Broz. But he didn't know what Broz told me."

"Cantwell obviously connected your knowledge about Valek's mission with Broz as the source."

"How did he know?"

Riddle regarded him for a long time. "There's no sense asking that question unless you are willing to find out."

Sims thought about his firing and the anger returned.

Seeing it, Riddle said quietly, "It happened to Houghton."

It was then that Sims felt he knew why he hadn't gone to Houghton.

"Yeah, it did. But the first thing Houghton thought about wasn't the color of his skin."

"And you did?"

It was hard, damn hard, trying to put it back together, how he had felt in that room with Cantwell. Sims felt Riddle patiently waiting and worked more at it. "It hurt me that they were doing this to me. They were saying I was a goddamn failure—or trying to say that—and here I was, sitting there, and the first thought that came wasn't a 'Screw you' to Cantwell but that they were doing it because I was black."

"You were, after all, one black man in a room with three—four—white men."

Sims waved Riddle's attempt away. "Remember, Riddle, when I was in the hospital? When I got the medals? I didn't think that way then. I didn't think I was as good as the citations made out, and I thought headquarters had laid it on a little too thick. But I never thought I was getting the medals because I was black." Sims thought for a moment. "You know, Riddle, it doesn't bother me that my skin's black. But *being* black's more than the color of your skin. It's meeting expectations."

"Expectations?"

"I had a teammate who told me once, 'You're not really black.' I asked him why. You know what he said? 'You're not disadvantaged.' " Sims shook his head, still finding it incredible. "That's what he said."

Riddle listened intently, his face a somber mask.

"Black expectations, too," Sims said, thinking of Congressman Stanley. "Everybody's supposed to *act black*. Be the kind of black my teammate had in mind. And for me that would mean being and doing everything my father spoke out against." He paused reflectively. "It would have bothered him that I thought about being black as an *excuse*. That Cantwell was firing me because I was black. He didn't have any use for excuses." Sims recalled his father's face and felt it important to explain. "He grew up in a sharecropper family near Moultrie, Georgia," Sims recounted in a voice so low that Riddle had to strain to hear. "His father died when he was ten; his mother a year later. He came to Washington as an orphan on the chicken bone express."

"I don't know that term."

"Chicken bone express? It came from the farm blacks who came up from the South. Walking and riding the rails. The only food they had was the cold fried chicken they packed for the trip."

"Washington was still a Southern city then."

"But it was better than Moultrie. Dad lived with an aunt, got a job stoking furnaces at night, and finished high school. Went into the army and after Korea used the GI Bill to get a degree and on with the D.C. police."

"A man used to hard work."

"Sacrifice was a word he used a lot. You worked hard, you got an education, you bought a house, and you took care of your family." Sims was surprised by a tear that broke and ran down his cheek. The memory of his father gripped him more powerfully than it had in years.

"Values," Riddle offered gently.

"He wouldn't have used that word. Those were the things good people just did. And good people went somewhere. It was important that you be going somewhere."

Sims thought for a moment, then raised his hand and turned the back of it to Riddle. "Damnit, Riddle, I want to be judged on *me*, on what I've done."

"And what do you want to do?"

The lost feeling left Sims and was replaced by a calming certainty. He got up and went to the hall tree and shouldered into his coat. "Simple, Riddle," he said, laying on the bravado, not for Riddle, but for himself. "I want to find out what happened."

10

After leaving Riddle, Sims walked several blocks, then called Houghton from a pay phone. Houghton started to launch into a clumsy offering of sympathy, but Sims cut him off, asking if they could meet that afternoon at the National Gallery of Art.

At four, Sims was sitting on a nubby brown sofa watching a thin middle-aged woman in paint-stained jeans and smock at an easel, grimly trying to copy a Cassatt oil. Sims watched the woman at her easel for several minutes and decided Cassatt wasn't in danger of being outdone. He idly studied a brochure about the Impressionists while watching for Houghton. Ten minutes later, the older man showed, wearing his cheap raincoat and carrying the beat-up Irish walking hat.

Sims watched as Houghton made a slow circuit around the room. Just as he was ready to pass through to another gallery, Sims got up and fell in beside him.

Houghton glanced at Sims, not meeting his eyes. "Riddle told me."

"Yeah."

"If it's any consolation—"

"Thanks."

"You need any help?"

"Not yet. I've got some savings. And there's my retirement. There'll be a lump sum settlement, unless Cantwell steals that, too."

"What're you going to do?"

Sims laughed bitterly. "Maybe go into brain surgery?"

They left the gallery and entered the main statuary hall, an Olympian affair of greenish black marble floors and skylights set into high vaulted ceilings. The hall was almost empty, and their footsteps came off the marble in hollow cupping sounds.

Houghton could tell that Sims was preoccupied and waited for a change in subject. A few steps later, Sims told him about Cantwell, how the chief of counterintelligence had known something about Broz. Houghton listened carefully, walking as if stalking, his eyes on the marble floor, hands clasped behind his back. In the rotunda, they stopped at the fountain.

"I've thought about it since Prague," Houghton said in a low voice. "Valek. Why did he lie? Why did he come over if he wasn't going to play by the rules?"

It had never been written anywhere, but over the long years of the cold war, every intelligence officer came to know and accept the rule: If you defect, you don't hold out and you damned sure don't lie. Your only security lay in helping your new masters stay ahead of your old ones. Get caught lying and you'd likely get pitched back into the pond.

Sims looked into the fountain and watched the water reflections play off the marble. "Imagine you're an American who did some work for the KGB a long time ago. Maybe they blackmailed you into it or you did it for ideological reasons. You might have even believed they were the wave of the future. Anyway, fast forward to now. You know your name's in their files—"

"You thought you were safe," Houghton picked up. "The last thing you could imagine was the USSR falling apart."

"Or the KGB disintegrating," Sims finished. "Along comes Valek. Around the corner from retirement and suddenly no more special privileges for the *nomenklatura*. American executives have golden parachutes. Why not old intelligence officers? Reports, payment receipts, photographs and tapes of meetings—enough stuff to blackmail your way to a nice place in Malibu."

"He could have built up quite a stash."

Sims puzzled over something that had bothered him since intercepting Valek in the Rosslyn Metro. "If he was going to defect, why didn't he come over to us in Europe? Walk into a place like Berlin station. Maybe Paris. But he wouldn't have risked coming all the way to Washington without security.

"He came here to go into business." Sims saw it clearly, now. "Somehow they got on to him. He ran to us—to the Agency—not to defect, but for sanctuary. We'd protect him, and when the time was right, he'd jump ship and go out on his own.

"That's why he tried to avoid the King connection. We would've put the clamps on him. He didn't want to appear too valuable. Just enough to keep the hunters away."

Outside, at the Constitution Avenue exit, it was beginning to snow again, and the few pedestrians were bending into a rising west wind. Houghton jammed his floppy Irish walking hat on his head, thrust his hands deep in his pockets, and stood facing Sims.

"What's next?" Houghton asked.

"I want to give this a shot."

"How much of one?"

"I want to get this over and move on. I don't want it haunting me . . ." He trailed off because he had been seeing himself in Houghton twenty-five years from now.

"Yeah." Houghton said it with some bitterness, knowing what Sims was thinking. He dug into his coat, came up with a cigarette, and lit it, shielding his lighter in his hands. Squinting into the wind and smoke, he fixed on Sims. "So we give it a shot. So what's next?"

"The first commandment of counterintelligence?" Sims asked Riddle's trademark question.

Houghton grinned. "Find the connection."

As Houghton said it, it came to Sims how hard it would be. He no longer had the Agency behind him, the support he'd become accustomed to for the past thirteen years. "See if we can track Valek and James Earl Ray. See if Ray did have a buddy named Raoul."

Houghton took this in, then nodded. Sims looked over Houghton's shoulder, slowly focusing on a massive building across Constitution Avenue. At one end of the building, a carousel of slender columns tried without success to create a visual balance against a ponderous stack of white granite blocks and green glass windows at the other end. He smiled at the irony. The building was the Canadian Embassy.

That night the snow turned to a light rain, and by early morning, a thick mist shrouded the path through Rock Creek Park. John Delaney ran lightly and well, only the slightest sounds coming from his rhythmic breathing and the brushing whispers of his nylon jacket. Ahead of him, he saw the back of a man in hat and overcoat. The man was unused to the outdoors and walked with a clumsy gait over the uneven pavement. Delaney was but several paces away, and the man gave no sign he'd heard anything. Delaney slowed to a walk, coming up behind the man. "Hello, Morris," he said.

Startled, Cantwell wheeled about, mouth open, eyes wide.

"Let's just keep walking, Morris. Keep our backs to the traffic." Delaney motioned down the path and then to the morning commuter traffic beginning to fill the one-way road on their left. "You and the Judge met with Kaiser this weekend."

Cantwell wasn't surprised that Delaney knew about the meeting. What registered immediately with Cantwell was that Delaney obviously thought the meeting was important. Why else call *this* meeting?

Falling into pace beside Cantwell, Delaney felt a familiar rise of almost exuberant joy. He had collected toy soldiers as a boy. Platoons, regiments—entire corps of them. He didn't keep them to play war. He would take them out of their boxes and array them on the worn carpet of his attic playroom. He had given each of them names, families, personalities, complete histories. He would stand astride them and, at a whim, reach down and change their little lives. Reward some, destroy others.

Glancing at Cantwell, Delaney thought of the vaulted room in his office back at the Bureau, of the files and the lives those files controlled. He was now even more powerful than the child-colossus. It was a marvel, really, how he had even gone J. Edgar one better. A warm sexual flush, a feeling of silken lasciviousness came over him. He could reach into any folder and . . .

"The topic was Martin Luther King." Delaney's voice carried an unmistakable reproach.

"I would have called if I thought you were interested—"

"*I* decide what I'm interested in, Morris." The tone was barely civil. "Tell me about the meeting."

"It was the Judge and me in Kaiser's office late Sunday morning. He'd been drinking," Cantwell said primly. "Kaiser was *very* upset."

The White House chief of staff had actually screamed, *Goddamnit, Judge, if you want a fucking chance—a* chance!—*at a seat on the Court, and if you, Cantwell, want to take over when the Judge leaves, you two better* fucking *well show you can control that* fucking *place out there!* There had been more, but nothing new except that Kaiser had started interjecting *fucking* between syllables as he continued to wind himself even tighter. It had been what tantrum specialists would call a four-wall day for Warren Kaiser.

"Get on with it, Morris," Delaney ordered.

Cantwell had a drained, reedy-thin feeling, and he knew it showed on his face. It was a one-two punch, having to face Delaney after the vicious tongue-lashing he had gotten at the White House. "He—

Kaiser—wanted to know about an investigation into the King assassination."

"Go on."

"There was an unauthorized activity—"

"What do you mean?"

"One of our case officers was tracking down the *bona fides* of a KGB defector. The case officer got off onto the King killing. The case officer was black," Cantwell added parenthetically, as if that explained it. "Kaiser somehow heard about it and wanted it stopped."

Delaney forced himself to take several steps before he asked: "How far did your man get?"

Concerned with his own wounds from the White House, Cantwell nevertheless detected an anxiety in Delaney. The FBI director had paled and was running his tongue over his lips. Not a good poker player, Cantwell thought, but a dangerous loser. Cantwell shrugged. "It's hard to say. He came back from Prague with a wild tale that his defector, a Czech named Valek, had been sent by the Russians to kill James Earl Ray."

"And the defector's—"

"Dead."

"Oh?"

"We're calling it a heart attack."

"Calling it?"

"We aren't taking it further."

"You've closed the books on King." Delaney began to feel better and was careful to keep his voice even.

"As I told the case officer, we never opened a book on him."

"And the case officer—the nigger?"

Cantwell got a sour look. "Kaiser wanted his ass."

"How did the Judge take that?"

"It bothered him. He liked Sims—the case officer—but Kaiser wanted him gone, and the Judge wasn't ready to take it over Kaiser's head."

"To the president, you mean."

Cantwell nodded.

Delaney thought for a moment. "Send me a copy of his personnel file."

Cantwell looked puzzled.

"The case officer's, Morris," Delaney said with some exasperation.

"I—"

"This afternoon'll do, Morris. The regular courier."

Cantwell gave him a sidelong glance. Delaney's profile was dark and hard against the soft gray mist. Delaney knew everything about him. He knew next to nothing about the FBI chief. The imbalance was intimidating.

Cantwell made a show of dismay. "What are you going to do?"

"Do? Why, *help* you, Morris," Delaney said in an overly solicitous voice. He added, with a smile of disdain, "It's a disappointment, Morris, to find that you're such wimps. What's the matter? In the movies, the Agency's always able to take care of something like this. After all, didn't you guys kill JFK?" Delaney turned on his heel and disappeared into the mist.

Minutes later, Delaney sat in the back of his chauffeur-driven Buick, Kevlar armor and bulletproof glass forming a cocoon that isolated him from the thickening traffic outside. He poised a pen over a yellow legal pad in a rich leather folder. He drew several experimental dashes to get his thoughts started.

God, he had wanted to wring everything out of Cantwell. But it wouldn't do to appear too interested. Cantwell might be light on his feet, but he wasn't stupid.

He made an *o* and then filled it in with ink. Beside the bullet, he neatly printed Toronto. If the Czech Valek had been sent to Toronto, Delaney reasoned, that might mean the Russians knew about Ray's activities *before* the killing. And if the Russians knew *that* . . . He made himself stop thinking along those lines. You do that and you make your enemies ten feet tall and you give up without a fight.

He made a second bullet: Path. Where from here? There was nothing like White House pressure to close down something like this, but it would still be smart to put a tail on Sims. He put a checkmark by the bullet and drew another.

Viktor Yazov. Delaney's people had picked up the Russian coming through Dulles. Outside the Georgetown clothing store, the FBI team tailing Yazov had run into another FBI team, this one covering Valek and his Agency handler. Not much doubt about it. Yazov had come for serious business. Valek hadn't died of a heart attack. In spite of the convention of spooks in and around the store, Cantwell and his Agency goons apparently didn't know that Moscow was actively involved.

With the feeling of comfort that comes from having money in the bank, Delaney drew two heavy lines under Yazov. Comforting, and

perhaps even useful, to know something the Agency didn't, Delaney thought, a small smile crossing his face.

Sims was almost asleep when the telephone rang. It rang again and he buried his head in the pillow. The recorded greeting came on and then the beep tone. Sims heard his uncle: "Bradford." The deep voice spoke authoritatively, as if he knew Sims was listening. Sims swung his feet to the floor. Squaring his shoulders, he punched the disconnect button and picked up the telephone.

"I heard about it, Bradford." The voice was gentle.

Sims waited a moment, breathing deeply. "I was still settling it myself."

"I'm sorry."

The simple genuineness of it disarmed Sims and caused a catch in his throat.

"You never wanted me to join the Agency—"

"No, son," the voice comforted him, "I just wanted something different for you. I guess I wanted something familiar. All that spy business frightened me. It doesn't mean I wasn't—that I'm not— proud of you."

"I wasn't looking forward to telling you," Sims confessed. Then curiosity pricked him. "Who did? Who told you?"

"My old friend Donald Stanley," the voice touched *old friend* with the lightest of irony. "Said he didn't have your number. Wants to see you."

The House Committee on Intelligence locks itself away in a win-dowless warren directly under the huge dome of the Capitol. Sole access is an off-limits elevator one floor below the magnificent ro-tunda. The occasional tourists who ignore the elevator's warning sign find themselves in the custody of a well-armed Capitol Hill policeman when the elevator doors slide open on the fourth floor.

This morning, the policeman checked Sims's driver's license against a roster, wrote down an entry time, then pointed down the hall.

Donald Stanley had none of the photographs here that he kept in his larger office in Rayburn. Instead, around the walls large ceramic plaques displayed the crests of America's intelligence community. There were the well knowns: CIA, DIA, NSA, and the military services. But there were other plaques, too. The committee—Stanley—had oversight of the intelligence budgets of the FBI, Treasury, and Department of Energy, as well as the State Department.

Stanley, in shirtsleeves, tie loosened, was seated in a large leather lounge chair, reading. When he saw Sims, he rose, putting his glasses and a thick typescript document on a side table. Sims saw the document had a red security classification cover.

Stanley gripped Sims's hand, then waved him to a chair. Stanley took his seat.

"I found out two days ago," he began. "I couldn't find your number, so I called Calvin. I hope you don't mind."

Sims shook his head.

Stanley leaned forward, resting his forearms on his knees, and gave Sims a solicitous look. "Why do you think they did this, Bradford?"

"You mean fired me?" Sims said the words he knew Stanley had been dodging. "They didn't like what I did in Europe."

"Europe? Can you—do you care to tell me?"

Sims thought for a moment, then gave Stanley a slightly sanitized version of the events in Czechoslovakia. Prague became a European city, Broz a reliable—but nameless—source. Stanley listened intently, eyes never leaving Sims's face. When, minutes later, Sims finished, the congressman sat back in his chair.

"This man, your 'European source,' you believe him?"

"I don't believe or not believe," Sims said carefully. "It's a story that conflicts with other stories. Valek's mainly."

Stanley shook his head. "This place"—he waved a hand around —"has all the trappings of power. I watch over a thirty-billion-dollar-a-year intelligence budget. I have instant access to the president, secretary of state, CIA, FBI, all that. But they play games with me. They'll answer any question I ask—"

"But you have to ask the right question," Sims finished.

"And the answer is very precise. It fits what I ask, nothing more." Stanley put his feet up on the coffee table and stretched back into the chair, putting his hands behind his head. "So you have a story you neither believe nor disbelieve. What do you do with it?"

"Find out what I should believe."

Stanley regarded him for a long moment. "You got better things to do with your time and talents."

"Oh?" Somehow Sims wasn't surprised.

"Maybe Ray was part of a conspiracy. Maybe the Russians did have something to do with it. Maybe even the FBI and your old friends out at Langley were involved. Let's say they were." Stanley swung his feet off the coffee table and sat up, pointing a finger at Sims. "Let me tell you what's going to happen. You're going to run into a wall of silence, built by the guilt of a racist society. You'll never get behind any of this. I hate to see a man of your ability beating his head against that wall."

Sims considered his words carefully. "I've thought about that."

"I hear a 'but' in there," Stanley said with an I've-tried-my-best smile.

Sims nodded. "I've got to give it a run."

Stanley stood and held out his hand. "I don't agree, Bradford. But I guess I understand." He put a hand on Sims's shoulder as he walked him toward the door. "But keep in touch. I can't do much, but I do have contacts."

11

Late in the afternoon, a week after he'd been fired, Sims took the Metro down escalator at Seventeenth Street. Leaning against a railing, he opened a newspaper and over the top of it watched as one train, then a second, stopped, loaded, and left. Satisfied no one had followed him onto the platform, he pitched the paper and left the subway by the Eighteenth Street exit. When he got to the bookstore Houghton was already there. He was surprised, though not greatly so, to find Alberich there as well.

Riddle swept a hand toward Houghton and Alberich. "I have performed the introductions. It is good to see Mr. Houghton again. It is a cliché, but time does have a way of slipping past one." Riddle pointed to the back of the office, to a small table with chairs, pads of paper, pencils, and a transparency projector. "Mr. Houghton tells us you've had a busy week."

It had been a week of eighteen-hour days, a total immersion in Martin Luther King and James Earl Ray and the way stations in their lives that had led them to the fatal meeting in Memphis. He and Houghton had spent hours hunched into the magnesium glare of microfilm readers, searching newspaper accounts of the killing and its aftermath. They had gone through a thin collection of books, the latest a nonrevealing autobiography by Ray, and tens of thousands of pages of plodding testimony from the hearings of the 1978 congressional hearings of the Select Committee on Assassinations.

Sims felt very pleased with himself and how it had turned out. He had rediscovered his old passion for history and found that he had gotten more adept at fulfilling it. The Agency had, if nothing else, given him the patience for sifting and the discipline to keep to the harder trails and not chase off after every rabbit that ran across his path. He found great satisfaction in taking a scattering of small truths and from them deducing larger ones, much like the forensic pathologist who reconstructs an expressive human face from a fragment of skull. There had been great stretches of time when he forgot the savage emotions of the day they fired him.

Alberich steered to a place at the table as Riddle eased into his chair. Sims thought Riddle needed only a powdered wig and robes to look like an English judge. "So, how do we start?"

"With the case against James Earl Ray," Sims answered. "On the morning of April fourth, Ray rents a room in a flophouse at 418 Main Street, in Memphis. The room faces room 306 of the Lorraine Motel —King's room—about two hundred feet away. Shortly after six that evening, right after the shooting, three people in the flophouse see a man run away from Ray's room. The man carries a bundle.

"Seconds later, a bundle is dropped in the doorway of Canipe's Amusement Company. Canipe's is next door to the flophouse. Mr. Canipe doesn't see the dropper's face. Only that it is a man in a dark suit. The flophouse landlady, Bessie Brewer, later testifies that Ray wore a dark suit when he rented the room from her that morning. Two customers at Canipe's also saw a man in a dark suit walking— not running—past the store. Both customers also saw a white Mustang pull away from the curb after the bundle was dropped.

"The bundle was made up from an old bedspread. In the bundle, the police found a Remington Gamemaster rifle, ammunition, a pair of binoculars, toilet articles, and a portable radio. The radio had an identification number on it—James Earl Ray's inmate number at the Missouri state penitentiary. Ray's fingerprints were found on the rifle and radio." Sims then motioned to Houghton.

Houghton, several transparencies in hand, arose and marched to the projector. He snapped a switch and stood to the side of the silver square flashed onto the screen.

"First, a bare-bones chronology, and then the anomalies," Houghton rasped as he put the first slide on the projector. The entries began with Ray's birth in Alton, Illinois, in 1928 and cascaded through six decades.

Houghton made a circling motion against the screen with the eraser end of a pencil. "In 1959, Ray is sentenced to the Missouri state penitentiary for twenty years."

"For?" asked Riddle.

"Armed robbery. A grocery store. One hundred twenty dollars."

"Not exactly a Willie Sutton." Riddle ventured his small joke.

"Sutton?" asked Alberich. Sims looked equally puzzled.

"It's nothing." Riddle sighed and Houghton smiled. Riddle pointed to the screen. "Go on."

"Ray tries to escape twice. He gets out the third time. In April 1967." Houghton underscored a line on the screen. "The first place he shows up after the escape is Montreal in July '67."

Riddle nodded and turned his attention to the screen.

Houghton tapped his pointer down the chronology. "A month later, Ray's in Birmingham, Alabama. He buys the white Mustang there. He begins to travel: Mexico in October—Los Angeles in November—New Orleans in December. In January, it's back to LA until March '68. This time, he gets a plastic surgery job. He leaves LA and buys a rifle in Birmingham, Alabama, on 29 March."

"The murder weapon?" Riddle guessed.

Houghton nodded. "Next event's the killing. Memphis, 4 April. Two days later, he ditches the Mustang in Atlanta. He shows up in Toronto on 8 April. He leaves Toronto on 6 May."

Alberich, intent on the screen, waved a restraining hand, and looked at the screen for a moment more. "Almost a month in Toronto, a long time," he said to himself in a low voice.

Houghton pointed to another date. "It's not until 19 April that the FBI put out a wanted on Ray."

Riddle was incredulous. "Even with the evidence in the bundle and all?"

Houghton nodded, then returned to the chronology. "Ray was quite the traveler. He gets to London on 7 May, then leaves for Lisbon the next day. He stays in Lisbon for ten days, then returns to London. He's arrested in London on 8 June, trying to catch a flight to Brussels." Houghton turned off the machine. "They deport him to Tennessee. There's no jury trial. He pleads guilty and gets a ninety-nine-year sentence. He's been in prison ever since."

Riddle sat silently, like a great Caucasian Buddha, surveying the screen and occasionally making a note on his index cards. Finally he looked at Houghton, then at Sims. "You said there were anomalies."

"Start with Ray at the flophouse. This is a dingy place full of boozers. Ray has a choice of renting by the day or by the week. He pays in advance for a week. He's dressed in a neat dark suit."

"Rather conspicuous," Alberich offered.

"In that place, he might as well have been wearing a clown costume."

Sims glanced at his notes, then continued. "There are the witnesses: Not one person can place Ray in that flophouse when King was killed. They only saw a man in a dark suit carrying a bundle—"

"And that bundle," Houghton cut in, "if Ray had the white Mustang waiting outside, why didn't he just put the bundle in the car and drive away? He was a small-time crook, but he would have been smart enough not to leave his name and address at the scene."

"Certainly the forensics—" Alberich began.

Houghton laughed disparagingly. "Ray's prints were on the rifle. But there were other prints on the rifle that the FBI didn't identify. None of Ray's prints were found anywhere in the flophouse."

"They struck out on ballistics, too," Sims added. "The bullet that killed King broke into three fragments. They identified the slug as a Peters .30-06, but they couldn't say that the Remington rifle with Ray's fingerprints fired that bullet."

"So another rifle could have fired the shot?" Riddle asked.

Sims nodded and watched Riddle with his blue index cards. The older man searched each card, as if he might find something there between the lines of his notes. At last Riddle tapped the deck of cards on the tabletop. "And no one places Ray at the scene of the crime. The evidence that does so is highly circumstantial."

"There's more." Sims nodded to Houghton.

"There're the aliases Ray used." Houghton flipped on the projector again. Four names flashed on the screen:

ERIC GALT

JOHN WILLARD

PAUL BRIDGEMAN

RAMON GEORGE SNEYD

"These are in the order in which Ray uses them. He uses Galt from July '67 until April 3, the night before the assassination. He rents the flophouse room under the Willard alias. When he gets to Toronto, the first place he moves into, he uses the Bridgeman name. On 18 April, he moves to another Toronto rooming house and becomes Sneyd. He gets a Canadian passport in Sneyd's name."

Sims motioned to the screen. "They were all real men, Riddle. All four lived within five miles of one another in the Scarborough section of Toronto. And Ray had never been in Toronto until after he killed King."

"A phone book pick?" Riddle suggested.

Houghton threw on a new slide. Five men looked out of the screen. "Ray's at top right."

The images reflected in miniature in Riddle's glasses. "My God," he whispered in awe. "The similarity—"

The faces were close enough for a family resemblance. All were brunette with similar hairlines. "Even to the dimples in their chins," said Riddle, still fascinated with the pictures. Sims, Houghton, and Alberich also stared at the screen, captivated by its mystery, their faces highlighted by the glare.

"If Ray had made random picks, he was damned lucky," observed Houghton. "No baldies, blonds, or redheads. None too fat or too thin, too old or too young."

"Statistically impossible," Alberich offered.

"There's something else," Sims said, turning from the screen to Riddle. "Galt was the name Ray used longest. At the start, it was Eric *Starvo* Galt. Starvo's unusual and eye-catching."

"It's the middle name of the real Galt?"

"No, Riddle, the real Galt is Eric *St. Vincent* Galt."

Houghton took over. "But the real Galt used to abbreviate the St. Vincent. He used little *os* instead of periods, so his signature would look something like this." Houghton put a new slide on the projector. The signature was clear and clean, with the Eric and Galt standing out. Between them was the abbreviated St. Vincent—Sto Vo.

"It would be easy to misread that as 'Starvo.' " Houghton paused to emphasize his next point. "If that's what happened, whoever got Galt's name would have had to have seen something that had the real Galt's signature on it."

Riddle had a puzzled look.

"Like records, Riddle," Sims supplied. "The real Eric Galt had a security clearance. There were also government files or licenses on the other three: Bridgeman worked for the Toronto government, Sneyd was a cop, and Willard was an insurance appraiser."

"All the investigating—did they ever turn up anything on the aliases? How Ray got them?"

"No," Sims answered. "Congress—the House Assassinations

Committee—never bothered talking to the real Galt or Sneyd. They said they couldn't locate Bridgeman or Willard." He looked to Houghton, giving him an opening.

"Nobody followed up," Houghton said, draining the last of his coffee. The room was silent except for the cooling fan of the projector. Riddle laced his hands together, the index fingers extended, lightly touching his lips. A steeple, Sims thought, remembering the children's game. Open the doors and here's all the people. Riddle looked up, bringing Houghton, then Sims into focus.

"You have more in your bag of tricks, Mr. Sims?"

Sims reached into his briefcase and pulled out a ragged paperback book with a dark blue cover. "A report of the Royal Commission, an inquiry of the Canadian Parliament—June 27, 1946." He opened it to a marked section. "Even then the Canadians were worried about KGB activities in Toronto. According to this report, the Russians had turned it into a passport mill. The Soviet agent who killed Trotsky in Mexico was traveling on a Canadian passport he had gotten in Toronto."

"Rudolf Abel?" Houghton threw out the name.

Riddle nodded. Abel had been one of the best of the KGB illegals in the United States. He had operated out of New York for several years before the FBI got him. He was later exchanged for Gary Powers, the U-2 pilot shot down in the Eisenhower administration. Abel had spent the remainder of his years in KGB's Directorate S, training other illegals for service in the United States.

Seeing Riddle nod, Houghton finished, "Abel, too, was a phony Canadian, living in Brooklyn on a passport he'd gotten in Toronto."

Sims waited a moment. "This brings us around to Raoul. Ray claims Raoul was his constant companion from just after the escape from prison to King's killing." Sims reached into his briefcase for another book, another paperback, this one with a tan cover. "This is volume one of the Assassinations Committee hearings." He scanned pages marked by paper clips.

"In March 1977, Dan Rather interviewed Ray. The Assassinations Committee printed the transcript. Rather homes in on Raoul here"— he found his place—"page two twenty-six, volume one. Rather puts Ray in Montreal, just after escaping from prison in Missouri.

" 'RATHER: And how did you happen to make contact with Raoul?

" 'JAMES EARL RAY: I originally went down there to attempt to buy or possibly roll a drunk for his . . . merchant seaman papers where I could use them to leave Canada. But it is difficult explaining how you make contact with somebody outside the law. It is just . . . comes natural . . . you learn after a certain length of time. But that is where I made contact originally, in the waterfront area of Montreal . . .

" 'RATHER: And then—uh—it was Raoul, was it or wasn't it, that suggested you go to Birmingham?

" 'JAMES EARL RAY: Yes. He is the only individual I ever had any contact with.' "

Sims thumbed through the pages. "Ray talks about his travels. Claims that Raoul is the tour guide. New Orleans, Mexico, Los Angeles. Ray goes there, always because of some deal Raoul cooked up."

"Where did Ray get the money?" Alberich asked.

"Raoul doled it out a thousand or so at a time. And Raoul was always promising a passport."

"Holding it just out of reach," Riddle guessed.

Sims scanned a page. "Rather picks up where Ray and Raoul meet in Atlanta.

" 'RATHER: And that is when the sequence of events began with his going with—oh—you to Birmingham to buy the weapon?

" 'JAMES EARL RAY: That's correct.

" 'RATHER: The shooting of Dr. King took place at six P.M. April 4, 1968 . . . the night before, this was April 3. At the New Rebel Motel in Memphis . . . that's where you saw the man you call Raoul, at the New Rebel Motel?

" 'JAMES EARL RAY: Yes, that's correct.

" 'RATHER: And, there you gave him the rifle you had purchased in Birmingham?

" 'JAMES EARL RAY: Yes.

" 'RATHER: Then he asked you to meet him the next day at a certain address in Memphis?

" 'JAMES EARL RAY: Yeah . . .

" 'RATHER: But the address turned out to be the now infamous rooming house from where Dr. King was shot?

" 'JAMES EARL RAY: I'm certain that was the address, yes.' "

"Rather questioned Ray in detail about April 4—the day King was killed. Ray said he took the white Mustang to a garage to get a flat tire fixed. The garage couldn't take him. So he went back to the rooming house to meet Raoul. He got back there and the place was swarming with cops," said Sims.

"And Raoul?"

Sims opened the hearings to another page.

" 'RATHER: So, when you came back to the rooming house area and you saw police cars you decided, to use your phrase, [to] high-tail it out of there.

" 'JAMES EARL RAY: Yeah.

" 'RATHER: And then what did you do?

" 'JAMES EARL RAY: . . . I think it was about six-thirty. I heard a report on the radio that . . . of the shooting. . . . they was looking for a white Mustang or two white Mustangs or something. And I went to . . . through Birmingham, Atlanta and left the car somewhere in Atlanta. And I took a bus to Canada.'

"To Toronto," Houghton finished. "And he left Raoul in Memphis."

Sims closed the hearing record and walked to the window. Outside, a cold metallic rain was snarling Washington's traffic. What difference, he thought, did any of this make to those people down there? Why should any of them care? It was unrelievedly depressing, a tale of a long-ago betrayal.

"Raoul was going to leave Ray holding the bag and almost got bagged himself," Sims said, looking again at the rain and the traffic. "Question is, whatever happened to Raoul?"

"But there's no evidence of Raoul," Alberich said.

"FBI didn't think so at the time. Ten years later, the congressional investigators didn't do any better. Even most of the conspiracy nuts don't believe Raoul existed. Ray claims he met with Raoul in all these places." Sims motioned to include Houghton. "We estimate there were twelve to fifteen contacts in a nine-month period. If you believe Ray."

"Where do we go from here?" Riddle asked.

"Toronto," Sims replied, watching Riddle nod and Houghton begin to break out in a smile. "Like you said, Riddle, careless men leave trails."

There was the abrupt high-pitched whine of Alberich's servomotor as he backed his wheelchair away from the table and announced that he had to leave. Sims saw the looks of surprise from Riddle and Houghton. Motioning them to stay seated, Sims followed Alberich through the shop, catching up with him at the door.

Alberich looked up. "What they did to you has a bad smell to it. But I'm still on the Agency's payroll. I believe in loyalty. Not to shits like Cantwell, but to the Agency. I thought I'd better leave before you got into operational details. I wouldn't be much use to you in that kind of stuff, and it's better the fewer who know what you're up to.

I won't pass you any classified information—that's where I draw the line. But if I can help"—Alberich gave a mischievous grin—"without going to jail—"

Sims, moved, opened the door. "They haven't built the jail that could hold you."

12

The journey to Toronto began with Sims's visit to a quick-print shop near Eastern Market. Three hours later, he paid cash for a minimum order of five hundred business cards identifying him as Franklin Morgan, a partner in McKittrick, Gray, and Read, a behemoth law firm with offices several blocks from Riddle's bookstore on K Street.

From the print shop, Sims took a cab to Georgetown University's law library. Presenting his new business card, he was directed to a carrel where he began his search through the birth and obituary notices in the *Baltimore Sun*. Within an hour, he found a notice that met his needs. Jamal Settles, born April 23, 1961, had died in a fire in East Baltimore two years later. Checking the metropolitan sections of the *Sun,* Sims found the account of the fire. Settles was the only victim. Sims recognized the neighborhood as a black slum.

An hour and a half later, Sims gave a winning smile and his business card to a motherly clerk at the Maryland Bureau of Vital Statistics in Annapolis. His law firm represented a major real estate developer, and his boss was squeezing him hard, Sims explained. He had had to drive to Baltimore, then over here to Annapolis on a cold day to see if any residual legal claims existed against the owners of an apartment in which a child had reportedly died in a tragic fire.

This was his last stop, Sims explained wearily. He had everything he needed, he said, except proof that Jamal Settles had, indeed, existed and was now dead.

The older woman nodded sympathetically, glanced at Sims, then at his business card. Sims gave the dates of birth and death. For a

143

few dollars, Sims ended the day with certified copies of Settles's birth and death certificates.

The next morning, he drove to Baltimore. Paying cash, he rented a box from a private mail-forwarding service that provided subscribers with a street address rather than a post office box. Then, with the birth certificate, he registered to vote, giving the mail-forwarding service's street address as Jamal Settles's legal address.

That afternoon, he met Houghton at the waterfront aquarium. Houghton drove him to the Department of Motor Vehicles, where Sims applied for a driver's license. He told the curious clerk that he had only recently left military service and this was his first civilian license. He worked quickly through the multiple-choice exam, had his eyes checked, and took the driving test in Houghton's old BMW. Jamal Settles now had a valid driver's license.

In Washington, Sims negotiated a one-month rental of an office with a shared secretary and answering service in the National Press Building. Sims celebrated the birth of Media Research Associates with a beer and hamburger around the corner at the Occidental Grill.

A visit to yet another print shop resulted in business cards and a dozen blank three-color Media Research Associates "press pass" blanks. Two of these he filled out with identifying data and photographs of Houghton and himself. The rest he pitched into a back alley dumpster. At a nearby photo shop, he had the passes laminated under heavy plastic, and at a discount luggage store bought two good-quality imitation leather credentials cases.

Just after eight, Sims began looking for his father's longtime police partner, Rollo Moss. His first stop was the VFW Post at Capitol Heights. By eleven, he had traversed Rollo's country—the bars, pool halls, and restaurants of New York Avenue, Benning Road, and Anacostia. He asked a question, got a head shake, left a message, and moved on. At midnight, he was finishing his first beer at Tunnicliff's, sitting at a back table where he could watch the door.

As he signaled to the waiter for another round, a thin young black man who had been sitting at the bar when Sims came in got up and left. Five minutes later, the thin man came back and walked directly to Sims. He stood back from Sims's table, just out of reach, hands hanging loosely at his sides, balanced lightly on the balls of his feet.

"Mr. Moss is outside."

Sims looked blankly at the man. "Moss?"

"You been looking for him all over town."

"I said we'd meet here."

"He's outside. It was you who said you wanted to see him." The man's eyes were unblinking and hard. "He's waiting."

Sims got his coat, then went to the bar to pay for his beer. He sensed the thin man standing several paces behind him and off to his right. Pushing change back across the bar as a tip, Sims glanced out the window. A dark Chrysler idled at the curb. He couldn't see inside.

The thin man stood back from the door as Sims opened it. Suddenly, Sims ducked through the doorway onto the narrow sidewalk, slamming the door between himself and the thin man. Sims, flattened against the outside wall, grabbed and twisted the thin man's wrist as the man burst through the doorway. The man stopped, as if he had run into a wall. Sims brought the wrist up higher and the man rose up to tiptoe. Sims pushed him against the car and with his free hand slipped a 9mm Glock from the man's shoulder holster.

The Chrysler's rear door opened. From the depths of the car came a familiar heavy voice that sounded like tumbling boulders. "Let him go, Bradford. He ain't much, but good help's hard to find."

Seconds later, Sims and Rollo Moss were in the backseat of the Chrysler, headed up Pennsylvania Avenue. To their front, the illuminated Capitol dome glowed like a white sugar loaf against the night sky.

Rollo Moss filled his side of the car, a huge man inside a voluminous fur coat and honest-to-God homburg hat. He had a round face, and a four-carat diamond ring set off the little finger of his right hand. Sims's early and enduring memories of Rollo Moss were of a big man in uniform who once a week came home with Sims's father for dinner.

The looter who killed Sims's father had also wounded Rollo, and Sims always suspected some hidden guilt, some imagined sin of omission, had driven Rollo off the force after his partner's funeral. At any rate, soon after turning in his badge, Rollo had set up his first "enterprise," providing protection for Washington's growing black Mafia. Ignoring the frowns of Sims's mother and Uncle Harris, Rollo made it a point to be at the graduations, football games, and other landmark events of Sims's growing-up.

Calvin Harris had at first refused Rollo Moss's contributions to a scholarship fund set up in Sims's father's name, but Rollo persisted and Harris finally gave in. When Sims tweaked him about it, Harris laughed good-naturedly. "Rollo's helping the Lord's work, Bradford. And I like to believe the sinners need me more than the righteous. I don't approve of him, but I think I understand him."

"Been a long time, Bradford. Last time you're back in Washington, I was in jail."

Sims ran his hand appreciatively over the rich leather upholstery. "Looks like you're doing OK."

"My enterprises are flourishing, Bradford. Absolutely flourishing." Rollo waved a hand and the diamond sprayed blue-white splinters inside the car. "Total quality management, Bradford—TQM. TQM and lawyers. That's where I fucked up before. A businessman like myself has to hire lawyers. Hell, lawyers is why the CEO of AT&T's not in jail." Rollo laughed at his joke. "You want me again, Bradford, you don't have to drive all over East Jesus. Just call my office." Rollo gave a number.

Sims memorized the number, then: "I need a couple of guns."

Rollo showed no surprise. "You're to the point."

Sims looked steadily at Rollo without saying anything.

"I thought you Feds could get hydrogen bombs."

"I'm not a Fed anymore."

Rollo brought his face close to Sims, giving him a look of parental scrutiny. "You in any kind a trouble?"

"We had a disagreement."

Rollo continued to search the younger man's face. Not finding any answers, he fell back into his corner of the car and wormed himself deeper into his fur coat. He said unhappily, "They got twenty-four-hour gun shops over in Virginia."

"You still have to register."

Rollo's face was now lost in the shadows of the corner of the car, the homburg hat, and the collars of the fur coat. "You planning something?"

Sims detected a tone of worry and disapproval. "I need some insurance. It's just temporary."

Rollo finally nodded. "What do you want?"

The following morning, Sims drove down Rock Creek Parkway and across Memorial Bridge. Finding a parking garage, he set out on foot through the sterile canyons of Rosslyn toward Key Bridge. Approaching the Potomac, the buildings gave way and the north wind, coming down the river, caused him to pull his overcoat closer about him.

Suddenly, he doubled back, as if having missed an address. Casually searching the crowd, he detected no abrupt moves. Even so, he burrowed into a pack of office workers sweeping into a building. Getting off an elevator on the third floor, he found the skyway walk to an adjoining building and from there, an elevator to the ground and an exit facing another street.

A block from Key Bridge, he stopped to stare wistfully at the gray majesty of the spires of Georgetown University. It was a scene out of a fantasy, a blend of Renaissance Europe and a fairy tale. "Look, Toto," he whispered to himself with nostalgia, "it's Oz."

At the bridge, he turned right onto a paved path. The path soon took him to a pedestrian bridge crossing the traffic-packed George Washington Parkway and then to Theodore Roosevelt Island. There, a parking lot, just a narrow strip of asphalt, paralleled the channel for several hundred yards.

As Sims walked the length of the lot, a dark gray van pulled in off the parkway and backed into a slot down near the bridge to the island. He checked his watch. Not bad, considering the vagaries of Washington's rush-hour traffic. Near the van, Sims saw through the passenger's window that a dashboard coffee cup holder was empty. Glancing around, he approached the van, opened the passenger door, and got in.

"Bitch of a morning," Alberich complained, "and it's supposed to sleet later today." He lightly bounced a hand off the special steering levers. "Bonzo's not the best on ice, even with four-wheel drive." The van had no driver's seat; Alberich would drive his wheelchair up the ramp into the van and lock it into place behind the steering controls. It gave him mobility, but he still hadn't worked out the challenges of valet parking.

"I hope it wasn't too much of a rush."

"It's back there." Alberich pointed over his shoulder.

Sims twisted in his seat and picked up a notebook computer and a slightly battered attaché case.

"Turn it on," Alberich said.

Sims balanced the computer on his knees, opened it, and turned it on. Following Alberich's brief instructions, he found himself in an ordinary-looking word processing program.

"You type out your message," Alberich explained. "It shows on the screen in plain text. But when you hook this to a telephone line, a chip inside enciphers everything before sending it."

Sims touched another key combination and the screen showed eight telephone numbers, the area codes indicating numbers in D.C. and suburban Maryland and Virginia.

"Trouble numbers. I'm certain they're clean, but use the scrambler or the computer anyway."

The attaché case looked like an electronics salesman's sample kit, full of multicolored wire coils, alligator clips, and instruments with display windows, antennas, and red-green-yellow indicator lights. Most Sims recognized—a telephone pager, a portable scrambler, wire- and radio-tap detectors, and a small cigarette pack-size broadband receiver to intercept radio bugs. Sims held up an ordinary-looking pocket dictaphone, turning it around curiously.

"Audio jammer," Alberich explained, taking the device, and, holding it up, he pressed a button. A tiny green lamp glowed. "Closest thing to a cone of silence. Screws up the magnetic field around you. Microphones just overload."

Sims took the jammer back and put it into its niche in the case. "Neat." He looked inquiringly at Alberich. "This stuff's—"

"Mine. I made it all, courtesy of Radio Shack. None of it's Agency."

"I owe you."

Alberich looked away, straight through the windshield, past the rushing traffic on the parkway. "I saw you run, once."

"Run?" Sims asked, puzzled.

"Your senior year. My first year at Langley. Riddle took me."

Sims remembered. "Davidson."

Alberich nodded. "Third quarter, seventy-three yards, all the way down to Davidson's six."

"We didn't score."

Alberich nodded again. "But you *ran*—my God, you ran." He twisted to face Sims. "I see things through this filter"—he slapped his wheelchair lightly—"through what I am, and maybe I make too much of it." He turned back to look out the windshield. "But the way you ran was something special," he said wistfully. "There was a certain cleanness to it."

Sims was relieved when Alberich broke the silence by starting the van. Then Alberich looked at Sims and smiled. "You owe me, all right. Keep running."

The message light on Sims's answering machine was blinking when he came back from meeting Alberich. Following the instructions on the machine, he parked two hours later at the Washington Sailing

Marina. Engine off, he sat for a moment, trying to memorize the other cars in the near empty lot. At precisely 11:30, he got out and started walking north along the path bordering the Potomac. At the first-mile marker, he checked his watch, then glanced behind him. It was 11:40 and no one was in sight in either direction. He frowned and checked his watch again. The sullen voice on the machine, he was certain, had been that of Rollo Moss's skinny bodyguard.

Sims continued north for a few more minutes, then, with growing irritation, gave up and walked back to the marina. Looking into his car while fumbling in his pocket for his keys, he saw the package on the passenger's seat. He turned and checked the lot. The same cars were there. He walked slowly around his car—there were no scratches or jimmy marks, no footprints or strange trash in the frozen slush. The car alarm light glowed steadily, unaware that it had been violated. Sims whistled softly in admiration. The thin man might not be the best at walking through doors, but he had some impressive tricks of his own.

Sims drove north along the parkway a mile to another parking lot just off the end of National Airport's main runway. Every three or four minutes, a jet thundered overhead, sending shivering vibrations through his car. He reached for the package. Though not more than three inches thick and perhaps eighteen inches on a side, it resisted him with a leaden inertia. With a penknife, he cut the heavy cord and tore away the stiff brown paper.

He smiled appreciatively, as if meeting an old friend. The weapon was a Mark 2 Uzi, an ugly little beast: eight pounds of plastic and stamped metal. So small it could have been a child's toy, the Israeli submachine gun could put ten 9mm slugs into a playing card at fifty yards in less than five seconds. Sims slanted the box, and the winter light played along the metal surfaces. No fingerprints marred the rainbow oil film. Beside the Uzi were three long box magazines, each carrying forty cartridges. Two Browning 9mm pistols filled the rest of the box, separated by plastic bubble wrap. Sims was certain that they, too, had no fingerprints and that the serial numbers had long ago disappeared into limbo if, indeed, they had ever been recorded in the first place.

Three hours later, after vainly checking one camera store after another, he found what he wanted in a pawn shop in North Arlington. That night in his apartment, he worked with snippers and soldering iron. Soon, he had eviscerated the large commercial video camera. Its guts—the electronics, drives, and tape cartridge assembly—lay to the side on a towel spread over his dining room table. Fieldstripping the Uzi and Brownings, he spent the next hour with sponge rubber and tape, wedging their barrels, springs, bolts and other assorted parts into the empty camera body, which he had lined with lead foil. Finally he latched the camera shut and sat back, looking at it with satisfaction. It wouldn't pass a thorough inspection, but in a small crate with a Media Research mailing label, it shouldn't stand out in the veritable river of Express Mail that poured daily into Toronto from the States.

The following morning, he took the box to Riddle to keep until he, Sims, got to Toronto and set up a receipt address. That afternoon, the mail-forwarding service yielded up a card certifying that Jamal Settles was a registered voter in the State of Maryland. On the same day, Houghton's final documents came in from Virginia, under the Meyers cover name. Meyers, according to the legend, was a public relations consultant for Media Research Associates. That evening, Sims took a United flight from Dulles International. At the same time, Houghton was boarding an American flight at National. They would arrive in Toronto within minutes of each other.

It was just past eight in the evening, and political gossip, black ties and bare backs, and the soft strains of a string quartet filled Buffy Tolenz's elegant Kalorama manor. The occasion was a private dinner for those who had pledged $100,000 or more to the Democratic party.

"Russian aid?" The senior senator from Rhode Island and chairman of the Foreign Relations Committee dropped his eyes to his scotch and rocks, swirled the squat glass, and, with a cornered expression on his blade-thin face, finally looked back at Tom Farmer. "Russian aid?" he repeated, obviously hoping he'd heard Farmer wrong.

Farmer nodded, ready to wait out his quarry when Buffy Tolenz herself materialized at his elbow, whispering that he could take the telephone call in the library.

Thirty minutes later, Farmer sat in John Delaney's FBI office, a tennis-court-size expanse of rosewood paneling, Federal period antiques, and lush carpeting. He leafed through pages of a thick black three-ring binder. Delaney, behind Hoover's old desk, watched patiently, Pennsylvania Avenue and the Capitol dome a backdrop through the huge window behind him. Farmer turned a page and an eight-by-ten glossy caught Bradford Sims and Edward Houghton in midstride, outside, against a white stone background.

"Our boys coming out of the National Archives. We got the call numbers of their requests—King. Same shit over at the Library of Congress. They left tonight for Toronto."

Farmer casually scanned through several more pages of closely typed surveillance reports, then closed the notebook. "They're still after it."

Delaney, settled back in his chair, stared into the space above Farmer's head.

"It could be the Agency." Delaney spoke in a soft, deferential tone Farmer knew wasn't meant for him. "They might not have fired the nigger." The FBI director gathered momentum. "It could be some convoluted plot by the Judge. They've always been after us, you know." Delaney nodded, a small smile on his lips. "Yes, of course you'd know." He fell silent, and then his eyes refocused and met Farmer's.

Farmer waited a moment, then broke the silence. "You going to have them followed up there?"

Delaney again got the distant look and asked himself what he'd come to think of as his guiding light question: How would Hoover have worked this? He listened to the cautionary voice. He shook his head.

"No," he told Farmer. "Too high a profile. Too much paperwork and too many chances of crossing wires with the Mounties."

"I could send some of my people."

Delaney cocked his head for a moment, then: "No. We'll watch from this side of the border." He paused. "You staying in Washington?"

"I've got a meeting in Singapore day after tomorrow."

"If it doesn't cost you a billion or two, cancel it. You might want to stay near the next couple of days." Delaney glanced at the clock on his desk. "You've got plenty of time to get back to Buffy Tolenz's and give some more money away."

"Where's your camera?"

The door opened against the chain lock. Fella Szpakowski squinted at Sims, then behind him at Houghton.

Sims waggled the false press pass. "We're doing the research, ma'am. Questions. The cameras come later."

"It *is* television?" she asked suspiciously.

"We go back to the studio," Sims explained. "We write up what we've found. The producer decides whether to send the camera crews. It depends"—Sims dangled the bait before her—"on what we hear. Who talks to us."

The thin woman looked Sims and Houghton over again. She closed the door. Sims heard the rattling of the chain and the door swung wide. "Living room is over there," she said, pointing. "I'll fetch some coffee."

Houghton set up the portable recorder, fussing over hooking up the small microphones. Sims, consulting a wire-bound notebook, went over the basics. Fella Szpakowski's rooming house on Ossington Street was James Earl Ray's first stop in Toronto. Ray had arrived on April eighth, four days after the Memphis killing. As Paul Bridgeman, Ray had stayed eleven days.

During the time, Fella Szpakowski recounted, Ray had received but one phone call. "My daughter, Lidia, answered it. Mr. Ray wasn't here."

"How old was your daughter?" Sims asked.

"Then? Oh . . . eight, yes, eight."

"Did you see Ray with anyone?"

Fella Szpakowski frowned. "I've answered all this before."

"For television?" Sims made it enticing.

Still frowning, Fella Szpakowski gave in. "A man came one day. But Mr. Ray wasn't here."

"What did he look like?"

"He was blond. Or light haired. He was short, for a man. And thin."

Sims nodded encouragingly. "Did he come in?"

"No." She shook her head. "He stayed out on the stoop."

"You talked with him."

"Not at first. First he held up an envelope. Didn't say nothing. Just held up the envelope."

"An envelope?"

"Yes. A long white envelope. It had 'Bridgeman' typed on it."

"Just stood there, holding up the envelope?"

"Yes. I told him Bridgeman—Mr. Ray—wasn't here no more. And—"

"When was this? What date?"

"After. A week after Mr. Ray moved out."

"You told him Ray wasn't here. Did he say anything then?"

Fella Szpakowski thought. "No. Well, maybe. I think he may have said thank you. Something like that. But he turned and went away."

"You'd never seen him before? Or since?"

"No. Never again."

Sims took an envelope from his inner coat pocket. He had given the photograph to Alberich two days before, explaining what he needed. Alberich had studied the photograph, and nodded. That night, Alberich had used the Crays to rearrange millions of microscopic pixels. Wrinkles disappeared. Hair thickened. Muscles took on new tone and definition. Sims handed over the new photograph.

Fella Szpakowski's eyes narrowed, examining a Miloslav Valek as he would have looked twenty-five years before. She looked at Sims, then down to the photograph, and up yet again. "It's him." She nodded her head emphatically. "This is him."

Minutes later, in the car, Houghton turned to Sims. "Broz was right."

"Valek was looking for Ray," Sims conceded. "Chasing him down from behind."

"And he knew Ray's Bridgeman alias." Houghton pulled the car away from the curb. He drove silently through the streets of the working-class neighborhood. A thought hit him and he turned to Sims. "When did the Bureau figure out that Galt was an alias? That they were looking for Ray?"

Sims checked his notebook. "April nineteenth."

"And when was it that he moved out of the Polack broad's house?" Houghton's voice had a slight tremor. "The one we were just at?"

Sims still had the book open. The answer came quickly. "Same day. April nineteenth. He moved into Mrs. Loo's under the name of Sneyd."

"Cute," Houghton said with a trace of irony. "Ray was running one week ahead of the KGB and two aliases ahead of the Bureau. Pretty good work for a fuck-up, wouldn't you say?"

Sims grunted an acknowledgment. Then, because he'd caught a look on Houghton's face back at the house: "Something was going on with you."

"Me?" Houghton asked, warily.

"Yeah, who else?"

They drove for a while in silence. Houghton finally spoke. "It was exciting. It was like I think I would have felt . . ."

"If you'd been talking to that woman twenty-five years ago?"

Houghton laughed. It was hollow and entirely too loud, as if he were trying to slough off what Sims had said. "Yeah. Maybe. Something like that." He looked over to Sims. "You got the map. How do we get to the Chinese lady's house?"

Yee Sun Loo's house was on Dundas Street, in one of Toronto's Asian neighborhoods. It was a rambling three-story Victorian place, red brick and not without a certain tattered grace. Next to it was a blocky sand brick building with a yellow door and sign. The sign, in Vietnamese and Chinese, proclaimed it to be the Tai Bay Buddhist Temple of Toronto.

Mrs. Loo was fifty-seven, but looked younger. Her shining black hair pulled into a bun at the nape of her neck showed no sign of gray. Her face was a delicate saffron with a touch of blush in the cheeks. She accepted Sims's cover story without question and soon the three were in the front parlor. Sims and Houghton sat on a sagging sofa. Mrs. Loo sat opposite them in a wicker chair. Between them, Houghton set up his recorder on a small lacquer table. A wizened Asian woman, obviously a servant, brought three cups and a teapot in a quilted cozy.

"That is correct. Ray came here on the eighteenth of April and moved in the next day." She said it with the confidence of an often-told tale. Ray had stayed eighteen days, paying rent by the week. "He would come into the kitchen, pay his rent, then disappear. He was pleasant, but he never said anything."

"Did anyone call him?" Houghton asked. "The telephone?"

"Once. I answered the telephone and a voice—a man's voice—said, 'Get Sneyd.' I went to his room"—she pointed to the floor above—"but he—Ray—wasn't in."

"What did the caller say when you told him?"

"Nothing. I tell him. He hang up. Click. Like that."

Houghton went back. "When you answered, he said, 'Get Sneyd.' Like that?"

"Yes."

"Like he knew Ray—Sneyd—was staying here?"

Mrs. Loo nodded.

As Houghton scribbled in his notebook, Sims took up the questioning. "Mrs. Loo, the papers said that someone came here and met with Ray."

"Yes." She nodded, still the assured near-professional witness. It was on May second at noon. Mrs. Loo had just diapered her son and had put him in his high chair for lunch. "I heard three raps on the front door," she recalled. "A man asked, 'Is Mr. Sneyd in?' Like that," she repeated, " 'Is Mr. Sneyd in?' "

"He knew Sneyd lived here," Sims encouraged her.

"Yes." She nodded and continued, "I went upstairs. Mr. Sneyd—Ray—was in his room. I told him a man was here to see him. Ray, he came down those stairs"—she pointed toward the dark walnut

154

stairs—"and went out there." She pointed to the front door. "It was warm. The inside door stayed open. I saw them talk outside."

"Did you hear anything?"

She shook her head. "No. I saw the man hand Ray something. Ray put it in his inside coat pocket." She mimed the gesture.

"Something?" Houghton asked. "Like a box, something big?"

"No. It was folded. Like papers, maybe."

"The visitor," Sims asked. "What did he look like?"

Again, the recital smoothed from many tellings. A tall Caucasian. Fat. Perhaps forty with dark hair. She lapsed into silence and looked expectantly at Sims and Houghton.

"His voice," Sims asked. "Was there an accent?"

The woman thought. She opened her mouth several times, as if to speak, then stopped, as if held up by yet another thought. "I have more English now than I did then. It used to be it all sounded the same. So foreign." She paused and thought again. "The man . . . he seemed . . ." She trailed off, again lost in thought.

Sims waited, hoping he was concealing his impatience.

Mrs. Loo finally nodded, as if everything was now satisfactorily in place. "Yes," she said precisely. "He was American."

"American?" Houghton asked.

Mrs. Loo frowned at Houghton's interruption. "And there was more." She nodded in agreement with herself. "He had a list."

"List?"

"Yes. Thhh"—she mimicked a sputtering *s*—"his lip must have made it that way."

"How so?" Sims asked softly, gently reaching for a thread, hoping it would not snap.

Mrs. Loo touched her index finger to the center of her upper lip, just below the nostrils. "Here. Scar. A big scar. It probably made him talk that way. List?" She made a question with her eyes. "That is correct? List?"

Sims nodded and glanced at Houghton. He had the same glittering bingo look he'd had at Fella Szpakowski's. The lisp was something new. Nothing in their research had mentioned Ray meeting a man with a lisp.

"Going back to the visitor," Houghton bore in. "You say you went to Ray's room, told him there was someone waiting for him. That Ray nodded and went downstairs?"

Mrs. Loo looked at Sims, as if for reassurance, then to Houghton. "Yes," she said in an apprehensive whisper.

"Mrs. Loo," Houghton asked softly, "he didn't ask you what this guy looked like?"

A head shake. Mrs. Loo reached for her cup of tea, now cold, and held it before her, a porcelain shield.

"Mrs. Loo," Sims began cautiously, as if he were stalking a skittish prey that might suddenly bolt, "it was a long time ago, I know. But did you get the impression that Ray was expecting this visitor?"

The woman stared first at the ceiling, then at the floor. Tentatively, she nodded her head. "Yes." She nodded again, this time with more certainty. "Yes. He was expecting the fat man."

The servant hobbled in, inspected the teapot, and looked inquiringly at Mrs. Loo, who shook her head. With that, Sims, then Houghton stood.

Sims ventured a last question. "And no one else came here to meet with Ray?"

Mrs. Loo shook her head.

"After? Did anyone come looking for him?"

"Of course. The police. The reporters. I had no time for anything else."

"A single man. One person."

Mrs. Loo thought, then stopped in the act of shaking her head. "Yes. There was one. The first after Mr. Ray left. That same week. Friday, I think it was. That's the day rents were due. He didn't give a name. Just asked if Mr. Sneyd was still here."

Sims showed her Valek's photograph.

The woman studied it carefully, cocking her head. Then she looked up at Sims. "No."

"No? You're certain?"

"No. I mean, yes, I'm certain. It is not him. The man who came was not as handsome as this. His hair was thicker. And his nose—" She pushed the side of her nose with her index finger. "It had been broken. It was an ugly nose."

Ba Tuyen carried herself with the serenity of those who have lost the fear of death. After all, at sixty-one she'd been the oldest in her escape group. She made the jolting night journey from Saigon (those who lived there refused to call it Ho Chi Minh City) to the coastal town of Vung Tau. And then survived the horror of the boat: the heat and thirst that had driven younger ones to madness, suicide, and cannibalism. She endured Thai pirates and the refugee camps. As gamely, she took up a new life and language in Toronto, taking comfort in her extended family and her position as Madame Loo's personal servant.

She'd learned to wait unobtrusively when Madame Loo had visitors. To know when to serve tea, when to collect the cups. And so she had listened to the conversation from the hallway just outside the parlor. It was an unusual event, the Americans. For that reason, she forced the words into her memory—in particular, the names. Oh, yes, and the description of the Americans. That evening, she would relate all this to her nephew, Khai. They would sit over cups of *cà-phê dên,* and Khai would listen politely as she told him about the Americans. He would ask a gentle question or two. And he would take down everything in the small leather notebook, writing with a beautiful golden pen.

13

The Silver Dollar Tavern was two blocks from Mrs. Loo's boarding-house. Sims and Houghton parked across the street and reviewed their notes.

FBI, congressional investigators, and the Canadian Mounties agreed that between 30 April and 3 May 1968, James Earl Ray spent two or three consecutive nights at the Silver Dollar.

Sims had uncovered the testimony of one of the dancers, a woman named Patti Stanford. Ray had sat at a table next to the dancers' runway, paying for his beers with American twenty-dollar bills. Stanford claimed that Ray was with a friend each night. Sims studied the description and idly wondered where Patti Stanford was now. Ray's companion, she had remembered, was fair complexioned and heavy-set. Two waiters had corroborated the dancer's statement.

Sims and Houghton entered the Silver Dollar, an unabashed drinking place, a basic no-frills saloon. Booths lined the left wall. The long bar, complete with brass foot rail, ran the length of the right wall. It was early in the evening. As yet, the yeasty smell of beer had not won out over the sharpness of the pine-scented detergent. A single customer standing in the darkness at the back surveyed the two Americans.

They pulled up stools near the front of the bar. The bartender, a few feet away, was busy at a sink washing glasses. He did it with an easy two-handed efficiency. He was a burly black man, with tight silver ringlets over a large round head. Massive sausage-sized fingers wrapped completely around two glasses he'd pulled from the soapy water. He glanced up and saw them. Eyes fixed on Sims and Houghton, he sloshed the glasses through the rinse sink, then onto the drying rack. He straightened up from the sink and came toward them, wiping his hands on the short white apron at his waist.

"Yeah?" The eyes were permanently red-streaked.

"The owner, Isidore Gibbs?" Sims asked.

The bartender's eyes narrowed, first studying Sims, then Houghton. Slowly, menacingly, the bartender nodded just once, then waited. Sims heard the dripping of water into the sink and, from outside, the sound of evening traffic noises.

"If he's here, we'd like to see him." Sims pushed his business card across the bar.

The bartender regarded the card unhappily. People who came into bars and handed out business cards were trouble. Reluctantly, he picked it up. He turned and walked toward the back, holding the card at waist level, studying it as he walked. He got to the end, raised a hinged segment of the bar, and disappeared around a corner.

Sims heard the muttering of a radio commercial, then, after several moments, the lifting of the hinged bar section and the heavy tread down the duckboards. The bartender stopped at the sink and looked at Sims. "He'll be here in a minute."

The bartender plunged back into the sink, attacking glasses and picking up the same rhythm he'd had before being interrupted. He worked in silence, then: "You here about Ray?"

Sims was startled as much by the bartender's timing as the question itself. "How . . . ?"

The bartender laughed disparagingly. "You think you're the first? Shit! If I had a dollar for every reporter that came in here I wouldn't be doin' this shit." He nodded to the sink of soapy greasy water. He removed and rinsed two glasses, held them up to the light. They passed inspection, and he stacked them upside down in the drying rack. Straightening up, he wiped his hands on the apron and studied Sims. "Lots of reporters. You're the first black."

Sims gave the bartender a blank look.

"Well," the big man asked sarcastically, "you *are* black, ain't you?"

Sims looked steadily at the man and did not answer.

"What's *your* angle?" taunted the bartender. "Everybody's had a try at it. Tryin' to prove the FBI did it? Or the CIA? Or maybe the Black Panthers or them little green men off the flyin' saucers?"

"You here in '68?" Houghton asked.

The bartender looked at him scornfully. "No, Mister Reporter, I wasn't here in '68," he said sarcastically, as if enjoying a secret bitter joke. "Not here in '68," he repeated. He turned back to Sims: "Tell me, brother, what's the angle?"

"Angle?" Sims asked back with irritation. At that moment, there was the sound of the bar hinging open and of creaking footsteps on the duckboards.

Isidore Gibbs was a paunchy man of medium height. He had the sickly pallor of night people, accentuated by the greenish glare of the neon lights from the street. His artful arrangement of thinning strands of black hair only called attention to his baldness, and his thick lips had the sagging pout of an aging whore.

The bartender went back to his work. "Shee-it," he muttered into the sink. "Everybody's got an angle."

Sims introduced himself and Houghton, using their aliases, Settles and Meyers. Gibbs gave a slight nod and stood well away from them. He listened woodenly as Sims worked the cover story, his eyes darting between Sims and Houghton and occasionally to his hand, which held Sims's card.

"I told everthin' to tha' Mounties," he said as Sims finished, leaving no doubt that he wanted the conversation over.

"Just a few questions," Sims persisted. He pulled out the picture of Valek and shoved it across the bar. "This man might have been involved. He could have come in here looking for Ray. Maybe a foreign accent."

Gibbs took the picture and studied it, turning so the light from the street would fall on the photograph.

"He got a name?"

"No," Sims answered. "You ever seen him?"

"What do you want him for?"

"You ever seen him?"

After a long moment, Gibbs lay the picture on the bar. "Never seen him," he said with a trace of a bully's defiance.

Houghton reached for the picture and handed it to Sims. "There was another man," Houghton said. "The papers called him the fat man."

Gibbs sneered. "Yah. Fat man. Lotsa those."

"This one had a thick scar here." Sims ran his index finger down the center of his upper lip. "Talked with a lisp."

Gibbs's eyes blanked momentarily, then refocused. "Naw," he said gruffly and a little too quickly. "No fat harelips, either. Now"—he gave a mocking deferential bow of his head—"if you gentlemen don't mind, I gotta bidness to run."

Back in the car, Houghton turned to Sims. "That prick knows something. Gibbs has seen our friend Valek before. And we rang his chimes on the fat man, too."

Sims started the car. He felt the elation he'd seen earlier in Houghton. He'd caught Gibbs's expression, too. Gibbs knew the fat man. And probably much more.

Across Toronto, a man gripped a telephone, his eyes widening as he listened. Leroy Rose was what they called a banty in his native South: compact, wiry, intense. He was the kind of man who as a boy had the choice of either submitting to the bigger boys or enduring endless beatings. Leroy fought. After a while, he learned how to win. Sometimes it took a blade or a kick in the balls, but winning any way was still winning. A cigarette burned dangerously close to his lips, the smoke wreathing his head. "Don't say no more," he warned, "I'll meet you. By the racetrack. Half hour."

The telephone crashed into its receiver.

"What'd he want, boss?"

"Shut up, Elton. Let me think." Leroy crossed the Vegas-garish office and jerked open the built-in refrigerator. The faggot decorator had said it was the latest thing. Bleached English oak? It had cost a goddamn fortune. He pulled out a Molson, twisted off the top, and swigged greedily from the bottle.

The harelip—nobody else had come up with that. He drank against a rising desperation. His very worst sweat-soaking nightmare now gathered around him like a threatening storm: THE NIGGERS WERE LOOKING FOR HIM! He'd watched it happen over the years, the frightening changes, the rise of the deadly-eyed men with their militant discipline, their quick looks, the short hair. Leroy drank again. This could be bad. And they were on to Gibbs! Gibbs would fold like a cheap suitcase the minute one of those bow-tied bucks started working him over.

He drained the beer, slammed the bottle on the polished mahogany desk, and kicked Elton's feet off the sofa. "Get the car."

"Where we goin'?"

"Never fuckin' mind, Elton. Get the fuckin' car."

Gibbs happily wheeled his big Buick along Lakeshore. From the corner of his eye he saw with satisfaction that Leroy Rose was pulling on the cigar he had given him. Leroy would recognize quality. Thirty years ago, Leroy had been a gofer, hanging out at the Silver Dollar.

Leroy had fought his way to the top of Toronto's underworld while Gibbs had stayed at the Silver Dollar, making a small-time buck or two on the side.

"Real Havana, Leroy."

"Umh." Leroy exhaled. The rich spice-and-leather smell of the tobacco filled the car.

Gibbs smiled into the night. Here they were, just the two of them, almost like equals. Two wise guys talking business. This thing with the nigger wasn't the best way to get back into Leroy's life again, but it was an opportunity. And Izzy Gibbs was just the guy to make lemonade out of lemons. After the nigger, he'd get Leroy to cut him in on a small piece of the action, maybe a slice of working the harbor. Gibbs smiled to himself, imagining a flashing rise to sit at Leroy's right hand, and—who knows—maybe, if Leroy got careless, to take over. He'd have the money, the cunts, everything.

"There was two niggers?"

"Huh?" Gibbs was still in his fantasy.

"Two niggers askin' about me?"

"Uh, no. One. One nigger. One white guy. Older."

Leroy weighed this for a moment. "They maybe working for Torricelli?"

"Nah." Gibbs rolled the cigar around in his mouth. Leroy was worried about his competition. "Don't think Dominic's ever hired any niggers."

"What'd they look like?"

Leroy listened as Gibbs described Sims and Houghton. He puffed occasionally on the cigar and glanced in the sideview mirror to make certain Elton was following just behind. We'll ride in your car, Izzy, he'd told Gibbs. I don't want Elton in on our business. He'd almost laughed as the bar owner had puffed up with self-importance.

"Who did the talking?"

"The nigger." He waited for a second. "He had a picture of the foreigner."

"The one who came after—lookin' for Ray?"

"Yeah."

"He didn't give no clue, you know, who it mighta been?"

"No."

"You didn't tell the nigger, did you? That you seen this guy, the foreigner?"

Gibbs gave a goodfella laugh. "Hey-y-y, Leroy. I'm a stand-up guy, you know that. I always been a stand-up guy."

"Yeah, Izzy, I shoulda known better," Leroy said contritely, as if giving himself a rap on the knuckles, "ever'body knows that about you. A real stand-up guy."

Gibbs laughed softly again.

"You said something about J.J. They know about him—that he had a harelip?"

The evening traffic was thinning out and the snow was beginning to fall. To the left of the boulevard, the winter winds were whipping whitecaps up on Lake Ontario. Inside the car was a snug haven of warmth, cigar smoke, and the glow of dashboard lights.

"Yeah. The nigger asked about a fat man. That was nothin new. That was in all the papers. In books, too. I read in one a them that—"

"The harelip, Izzy. What'd the nigger ask about the harelip?"

Gibbs shifted his grip on the wheel and took a drag off his own cigar. "He pointed to his lip and said the fat guy had a scar. Talked with a lisp. That was new. Nobody ever asked that. That's why I called you."

"Did he know J.J.? I mean, did the nigger use his name?"

"No. He just called him the fat man."

"Did he know about me?"

The hard edge in Leroy's voice alarmed Gibbs. His hands suddenly felt slippery on the steering wheel.

"No, Leroy. I swear! There was nothin'. Nothin' at all. Don't worry. That nigger doesn't know anything about you and J.J. Just knows about a fat man and a harelip. That's all." He looked over to Leroy and felt it necessary to repeat himself. "That's all."

Leroy gestured through the windshield. "Up ahead, take that left. We gotta talk more later, but I gotta get back to the office."

Gibbs felt relief, followed by a warm trickle of excitement. He turned off the boulevard. Across the harbor, you could see the red and green lights of the island airport. It was going to be a good new year—you could just feel it.

They pulled to a stop. Elton, following behind in Leroy's car, pulled alongside on the left.

"Another thing, Izzy. The nigger. Was he the law?"

Gibbs shook his head. "No. I don't know what he was, but he wasn't the law. I gotta feelin' about those things." He gave Leroy his best nobody-bullshits-me look. He was gratified to see Leroy's broad grin.

Leroy was silent for a long time, thinking. Then he asked, "You know how to get in touch with him?"

"The nigger?" Gibbs remembered Sims's card in his pocket. "Yeah." Then more quickly, "Yeah, sure, Leroy. If you want me to."

Leroy made gathering-together motions, tightening his scarf, and buttoning his overcoat. "Maybe, Izzy, maybe I ought to talk with him. You set it up?"

Leroy got out and came around between the two cars. He rapped on Gibbs's window. When Gibbs rolled the window down, Leroy reached in and squeezed Gibbs's shoulder. "I'm lucky to have friends like you, Izzy."

Back at the hotel, a message light glowed on Sims's telephone. Five minutes later, he knocked on Houghton's door and motioned him out into the hall. "Tomorrow night," he whispered, "we have a meet. It's the bartender from the Silver Dollar."

Sims parked the car on a backstreet. He checked his watch; five minutes to wait. He turned off the engine and sat, trying not to think, listening instead to the pinging metal sounds of the cooling car. He glanced at his watch again. Time to go.

Walk the north side of Adelaide, the bartender had said, between Portland and Spadina. Sims rounded the corner onto Adelaide. Houghton had been at work for the past hour, watching the street, on guard against opposition surveillance. Sims saw him across the street, walking on the south side, an unremarkable figure in the cheap overcoat and the floppy Irish hat. Houghton continued down the street in the opposite direction—the all-clear signal.

Ten minutes later, Sims was ready to call it quits. There was only so much strolling one could do in Toronto in the winter.

A figure fell into step beside him. "Nice coat," the bartender offered.

"Not for this weather," Sims groused.

The bartender laughed. He wore a short leather jacket, a colorful muffler, and a brightly knitted tam. He didn't apologize for being late.

Sims punched the button on the cigarette lighter in his pocket and was rewarded with two confirming vibrations from the small box strapped under his right arm.

They walked together in an easy, natural cadence. They passed a park, a school, and shops still open for evening shoppers.

"Where's the white man?" the bartender asked. "The one that was with you yesterday?"

"Home," Sims lied. "You wanted to talk with me."

"The white man," the bartender persisted, "he work for you?"

Sims felt a flash of irritation. "I don't see what dif—"

"You in charge?"

Sims sensed the up or down nature of the question. He looked directly at the man. "Yes," he said emphatically, "I'm in charge."

They walked several more steps. "Settles your real name?"

Sims looked at him and, not wanting to answer, offered his hand. "Yours?"

"Brewster." His hand swallowed Sims's.

They dropped hands and took up walking again. "After you left," Brewster began, "Gibbs got on the phone. He—"

"The one by the cash register?"

"Yeah. Two calls. First to Leroy Rose. Somebody else answered and wouldn't put Gibbs through. Gibbs got pissed and started yellin'. Buncha shit about Leroy and him goin' back a long way. The guy on the other end must'a gave in. Anyway, Gibbs puts on his ass-kissin' voice. 'Leroy,'" Brewster mimicked, "'a hard-lookin' nigger was here.'" The bartender cocked his head, giving Sims an appraising look. "Hard-lookin' nigger. That's what he called you. That what you are?" he asked in a provocative, challenging way.

"Rose?" Sims forced himself to say it quietly. He asked Brewster to spell the name. "Who is he?"

Brewster scowled. "Big fucker around town. Stops in the bar once in a while. Gibbs sucks up to him."

"What's the rest of it? You recall exactly what he said?"

Brewster thought, frowning in concentration. "The nigger asked all the questions," he recounted, no longer imitating Gibbs's voice. "He wanted to know about Ray and J.J."

"Who?" Sims asked sharply.

"Jay-Jay," Brewster repeated, slowly, emphatically. "That's what he said."

"Did J.J. have a last name?"

Brewster shook his head no.

"Do you know any J.J.'s?"

Another head shake.

"And then?"

Brewster shrugged. "That was about it. Gibbs doesn't like to talk on the phone."

"The second call?"

"It was different, but the same."

"How?"

"Gibbs dials another number. Doesn't ask for anybody. Just gives his name. Then says that a black and a white were askin' questions about Ray and the fat man, that the black man had a picture of a foreigner who was lookin' for Ray. Gave whoever it was the stuff off your card. Description of you and the honky with you. That was it." Brewster thought for a moment, then nodded his head. "Yes," he repeated, having checked his memory, "that was it."

"Nothing in the second call about J.J.? Just called him 'the fat man?' "

Brewster nodded.

They'd gotten to the end of the block. Sims motioned to the other side of the street and they stopped at the corner for the light to change. Sims watched the passing cars: people going home, knowing what was for dinner, what they'd be doing tomorrow. Ordered lives, no world-conquering ambitions, maybe at most a secret dream of winning the lottery and telling the boss to fuck off. Their days and nights lay ahead, days and nights they could count on.

"Why did you call me?" Sims asked.

Brewster considered this. "You—you comin' here. I heard all that talk about conspiracies. Used to think it was shit." He shook his head. "There's somethin' real about this."

They walked in silence, and then Brewster finished his answer. "Like I said at the bar, I seen a lot of people come in askin' questions, but you're the first black man."

"It's not about blacks," Sims said.

Brewster's reaction was explosive. "Hell it's not!" He jammed a gloved index finger in Sims's chest. "You're black! I'm black! King was black!" His voice dropped as he added ominously, "And the muthafucka that killed him was white." He paused, winded from the emotional struggle.

Brewster's anger vanished, leaving him looking tired, older. "Your honky friend asked me if I was here in '68." His haunted eyes focused on Sims. "You know where I was? Fuckin' hospital in Hawaii—Tripler Army. Damn near got my ass shot off in Hue." He drew himself up in pride. "Did *my* time in Nam. Time while the fuckin' Harvards came up here to sly by the draft." He remembered the sickening hospital smells of sharp alcohol and sweetly rotting flesh. The shifting groaning sounds of the living and dying. "Lay there, watching shit drip into my veins, hearin' about them killin' King in Memphis."

Brewster wound up his bitter recital. "No, Mister Settles, don't tell me this shit isn't about blacks." They had reached a major thoroughfare. Evening shoppers milled about them. Brewster took a few steps, then turned to Sims. "You can't fool me. I hope you're not fooling yourself."

While Sims and Willie Brewster were meeting in Toronto, a dilapidated Renault nosed its way through the bicycle- and *cyclo*-jammed streets of Hanoi eight thousand miles away. The tiny car stopped at a barbed-wire barricade just off the street the French named the Street of Needles. A sentry in dark olive green inspected papers, nodded to yet another sentry. The pole gate lifted and the Renault passed on to stop half a block later.

Feeling a twinge in his hip, Pham Ngo Thach followed slowly as the young lieutenant sprang up the steps. The old French *lycée* was as he remembered it: cracked dirty yellow stucco, red tile roof, peeling dark green trim. Inside, a creaking grate-doored elevator took them to the third floor. The lieutenant motioned down the hallway. Thach followed, his sandals making soft slide-slapping sounds on the terra cotta tile floor.

The lieutenant had come for him. Thach had been in his small garden picking *trai vu sua*. He would save the best of the sweet fruit for his grandchildren. The rest he would take to the market. They would bring a much-needed supplement to his monthly pension. Thach was fretting over the prospect of the fruit spoiling when the lieutenant stopped and rapped softly at a closed door.

The office showed its origins as a classroom. A simple desk faced a handful of folding metal chairs scattered in the depth of the room. Slate chalkboards lined the walls. Overhead, lazy fans stirred the thick air.

A slender man at the desk stood and extended an arm in greeting, swinging it to point to the chair nearest the desk. He wore *ba-ba dên*. Even Vietnamese peasants rarely wore the black pajamalike shirt and trousers anymore. It was an affectation, Thach thought. Like the pictures he had seen of aging American veterans who still wore their battle dress uniforms.

"*Chao*. Little has changed since you were here, *dai-tuong*."

"General?" Thach made a mock show of protest. "You forget, Phuong, I am merely a poor pensioner." Thach approached the chair. "I see you've maintained a proper revolutionary frugality. Or at least," he added heavily, "the appearance of it." Thach stood, his hand resting on the cool metal chair back. Phuong smiled and settled himself behind the desk. He picked up the telephone and held it against his chest. "Tea?" He looked inquiringly at the older man.

Thach ignored the offer. "Why did you send for me?" he asked stonily.

Phuong's smile went away and he put the telephone back on its cradle. From a drawer he pulled a pack of French cigarettes. He extended the pack to Thach, who waved it away. Shaking a cigarette out, Phuong lit it with a worn Zippo lighter.

Thach remembered the lighter. In 1964, he and Phuong had been on a mission into Saigon. Phuong had stopped and bought it from a street vendor in front of one of those garish Tu Do bars frequented by American GIs. The next night, they had blown up the bar. Thach occasionally wondered what had happened to the little man who'd sold Phuong the lighter.

"We need you."

"I am an old man."

"You are only sixty-five."

The little man had probably gone up with the bar. The bombings were that way. You always ended up killing more Vietnamese than Americans. You wrote them off as the cost of revolution, sacrifices to the righteous struggle, the end justifying the shattered corpses. "Give me a cigarette," he demanded.

Reflexively, Phuong jumped up, collecting the cigarettes with one hand and diving with the other into a lower pocket of the *ba-ba dên* shirt. He handed Thach a cigarette and carefully lit it, holding the Zippo with both hands in an almost supplicating gesture.

Thach inhaled, coughing slightly from the rough tobacco.

"There is the manner of my leaving," he said dryly. "As I recall, the words *disgrace* and *dishonorable* were used."

Phuong made a contemptuous motion with his hand, as though he had had nothing to do with Thach's downfall. "It was a matter of expediency. Someone had to be found and you were available. No —*convenient*. That is a better word."

Thach took another drag, this time fully enjoying the taste and feeling slightly light-headed. It would be nice to be able to afford to smoke again. Or to have an occasional beer, perhaps even with ice. "You still haven't told me why I'm here."

"We learned several weeks ago of a defection."

"Go on."

"From the Russian service. Someone you knew. A Czech . . ."

"Valek. Miloslav Valek."

Phuong's eyes widened in surprise. "Yes. How did—"

"A guess. He was the type." Thach gestured with his cigarette to Phuong. "Do the Russians think it serious?"

"They say not, but our man in Moscow believes otherwise."

"Where is Valek now?"

"Dead. But before that, he was in the hands of our friends at Langley."

"Did they kill him?"

"Who knows?" Phuong shrugged. He opened a dirty green folder, pulled out a message flimsy, and extended it to Thach. "Valek alone would not have been enough to get you here. But here, read this."

Thach's face tightened and he cocked his head forward, into the message. The message from Toronto recounted Ba Tuyen's account of Sims' and Houghton's visit to Madame Loo's boardinghouse, their descriptions, and the questions the two men had asked. He glanced up, then read the message again. Finally, he looked up at Phuong. "The Americans are on the trail." His voice quavered slightly.

"It would seem," Phuong laughed nervously. "Twenty-five years late. Now that we no longer need it." He leaned forward on his elbows, a look of deep concern on his face. "This could have certain consequences with which we are ill-prepared to deal. You, of all people, should appreciate the sensitivities of this."

"I have some understanding," Thach said warily. Hanoi was flat on its back. The war in Cambodia—Vietnam's own Vietnam—had to be paid for. Ho Chi Minh's revolutionaries were good fighters but miserable economists. The revolution was bankrupt. Perhaps the Americans might be enticed to come back to Vietnam, this time to help. That is, unless . . . Thach fully understood what was at stake. "What do you want?"

"Your help. You set all this in motion." Excitement crept into Phuong's voice. They had been great days. At Thach's side, he had played in the world's most dangerous game, going against the might of America. "Because you conceived Operation Le Loi. You know its intricacies. And you know the man—"

"And because, having lost everything, I have nothing else to lose," Thach finished with a bitter edge in his voice. He looked around the office, noticing for the first time the Japanese stereo, the American refrigerator. "I failed once, why should I not fail again?"

"You are too hard on yourself." Phuong put the message from Toronto back into the dirty green folder. He adopted a professional tone. "We have all the files, but Le Loi was your plan. We need your understanding."

"Understanding? To do what?"

Phuong shrugged and spread his hands to show uncertainty. "For now, to follow the Americans. To keep them in sight."

"And later?"

Phuong shrugged again. "To make sure that the sacred sword of Le Loi doesn't get shoved up the backsides of our esteemed leaders on the politburo."

14

Early afternoon the following day, Sims retrieved an Express Mail packet at the post office. Inside was the information Riddle had assembled on Leroy Rose. Sims called the hotel for Houghton. By prearrangement they met half an hour later on Yonge Street, in a back booth at Shopsy's.

They ordered and after the waitress left Sims handed over the envelope. "Shit," Houghton exclaimed in amazement, shuffling quickly through the packet of index cards and handing them back to Sims. "Where does he get this stuff?"

Sims shrugged and pulled a card. "Leroy Rose is a prime badass. America's contribution to Canada."

"American?" Houghton asked.

"Was. Might still be," Sims said, the envelope in his lap. He worked through the packet of index cards. "Came up through the rackets," he summarized, reading off a card. "Extortion, gambling, prostitution. Then added drugs. That's when things started heating up."

"How?"

"There's been a war on since Leroy started trespassing on Dominic Torricelli's turf. Dominic's the godfather of the family that used to have Toronto all to itself." He scanned the remaining cards. "Says here"—he nodded toward a card—"that Rose came to Toronto in '66. So he was here when Ray and Valek came through." Sims snapped a rubber band around the cards and put them back into the envelope.

From a smaller envelope, Sims took Leroy Rose's mug shots. The police photographer had captured a sly cunning and a streak of cruelty. It was a face that, once seen, was unlikely to be forgotten.

171

Sims stared at the picture, willing it to talk. "And you know the fat man," Sims said to Leroy Rose's picture. "You know a fat man named J. J."

Two hours later, Sims's telephone buzzed. The desk announced a call holding for Jamal Settles. Sims checked the portable recorder, then answered the telephone.

It was Isidore Gibbs. The Silver Dollar owner's reedy voice came over the speaker.

"Can we meet?"

"Sure," Sims replied, wishing he had a trace working on the call. "What about?"

"You asked about a guy with a foreign accent."

"Yes?"

"I remember some stuff."

"So?" Sims glanced over. Houghton was listening intently, rolling a pencil in his fingers.

"Not on the phone."

"Why not?" Sims asked, in a slow, friendly manner. "I've got plenty of time."

"Not on the phone." Gibbs was insistent.

"OK. Not on the phone. Where?"

"The end of Polson Street. Tonight at ten. I'll be driving a gray Buick."

"How about your place?"

"I don't wanta talk here. Don't want nobody to see us."

"All right. Polson Street at ten. And Gibbs—"

"Yeah?"

"I drive up and blink my lights twice. You get out—"

"Hey, goddamnit, I ain't—"

"—and we meet in the open."

"It's *snowing,* for chrissakes," Gibbs whined, "an' I—"

Houghton saw Sims's jaw tighten and his body tense forward as he leaned into the telephone.

"In the open, Gibbs. You and me. Just you and me. Take it or leave it."

Gibbs was silent. Then, sullenly, "You got it. Ten o'clock." Gibbs hung up.

Sims unfolded a Toronto street map. Polson Street dead-ended at the harbor in one of Toronto's industrial and warehouse districts. "Not the best place for a meet."

Houghton came around and looked over Sims's shoulder. He looked at the map and shrugged. "Didn't expect him to pick a church, did you?"

A gusting north wind rocked their car and wrapped it in thick swirling eddies of snow. The wipers slapped noisily, barely clearing the windshield enough to see the headlights of oncoming cars.

"Why does the spy business have to be so goddamn miserable?" groused Houghton as he fiddled with the heater controls. It was from espionage's common catechism of complaints.

"Weeds out those who're only in it for glory." Sims gave the formula response a lightness he didn't feel. Polson Street was but two miles away.

A sharp edge dug into Sims's side. He shifted in his seat and felt the submachine gun's thick nylon strap tug on his neck and shoulder. The Uzi's pressure was reassuring and disquieting. It reminded him that things could go bad very quickly.

Minutes later, Houghton turned onto Polson. As he did so, a lull in the snowstorm revealed warehouses down both sides of the street. At the end were the docks. Fingers of cargo-loading booms reached into the night sky and, across the harbor, Sims made out the lights of the CN Tower, its spire lost in the low, scudding clouds.

"There he is." Houghton gestured to the car in the shadows at the end of the street. Some fifty yards away, the dark car sat, inanimate and dimly menacing. Though the car's roof was hidden by a thin layer of snow, a splintered reflection of light glinted from a cleared arc of windshield.

Sims reached under the seat and came up with a pair of bulky night vision binoculars. He scanned the car, the warehouses, then came back to the car. Polson Street stood out in sharp relief, etched in tones of black and celery green. Nothing but the warehouses and the car and, just beyond, the harbor.

Passing the binoculars to Houghton, Sims worked the submachine gun out from under his coat. He unlatched its magazine and slid the long narrow box from the pistol grip of the gun. Placing a thumb over the top bullet, he pressed down, testing the ease of play of the spring follower. Moving a hand to the operating knob on top of the weapon, he jacked the bolt back and forth several times. Satisfied, he inserted the magazine, slapping it on the bottom to make certain he had fully seated it. The snicking metallic sounds punctuated the silence in the car.

"You're sure you want to do this?"

Sims eyed the distance to the dark car. A good runningback could cover it in—in what?—six, seven seconds? Oddly, he remembered the long-ago Delaware game and the defensive end who'd given him the half-moon scar on his cheek. What was that Delaware end doing tonight? He slammed the submachine gun's bolt back into the firing position, then let the cocking handle slide forward. "Give him the lights. Twice."

They waited. "He's out of the car," Houghton rasped. "Can't tell who it is."

Sims waited until he, too, could see the figure at the end of the street, slowly making its way through the snow toward him. Gibbs— if that's who it was—took several steps away from his car and stopped just inside a pool of light by the nearest warehouse.

Sims opened his door. At that moment, the snowstorm began picking up. A cold sooty wind clawed at his coat. "Luck," he heard Houghton say.

Footsteps crunching in the newly fallen snow, Sims strained to make out the face of the figure before him. With each step, he felt the submachine gun brush his left side. He kept to the right of the street to give Houghton a clear view.

"That you, Settles?"

Relief washed over Sims as he recognized Gibbs's voice.

Sims's answer was interrupted by a blast behind him. He heard the chutting sound of a high-velocity slug, and inches to his right, the street exploded in a shower of ice and asphalt chips.

Gibbs, frozen in surprise for an instant, wheeled and began running in a clumsy lock-kneed gait. Sims struggled to keep his feet beneath him as he sprinted after the fleeing Gibbs.

Gibbs was almost to his car when Sims took him. The American's momentum carried both of them into the snow. Another blast and again ice and asphalt sprayed the two men.

"Goddamnit!" Gibbs shrieked and flailed at Sims. "Lemme go!"

Adrenaline surging, Sims tightened his grip on Gibbs and rolled them both to shelter closer to the side of Gibbs's car. A third shot shattered the car's headlight. The slug bored into the car's body, cutting through sheet metal and drilling through the heavy frame members with a staccato hammering sound.

Sims crawled forward to peer past the front of Gibbs's car. It had to be the warehouse just to his left front. As if in confirmation, a fourth shot crashed into the car.

Gibbs was now shrieking in uncontrolled terror, huddling close to Sims for protection. The sulfurous stench of Gibbs's emptied bowels mingled with the sharp, clean odor of gasoline from a torn fuel line.

The submachine gun was under him and tangled in the lining of his coat. Struggling to free his weapon without exposing himself, Sims heard another shot, a popping noise far different from the booming rifle shots. He chanced a look around the front of the car. A dark form, rifle still in hand, tumbled from the roof of the nearby warehouse. The man hit the ground in such a way that Sims knew he wouldn't get up again.

Sims imagined Houghton, slipping out of the car and working his way to the warehouse roof.

Suddenly he heard the roar of an engine.

A car, lights off, screeched out of the alley to his right. Fishtailing slightly in the snow, the car slid to a stop some twenty feet away. The back door swung open.

"Leroy!" Gibbs scrambled to his feet before Sims could move. Gibbs was up and running, jerky and fear-fumbling, arms spread, as if to embrace the refuge of the open car.

In a freeze-frame, Sims recognized Leroy Rose from his mug shots. The man was framed in the open car door, a shotgun braced across his lap, a wild, manic smile on his face.

"Leroy!" Gibbs screamed again, almost to safety.

Struggling to one knee, Sims finally freed his submachine gun.

"Hurry, Izzy." Leroy smiled his encouragement to the running man.

Leroy was still smiling as he deliberately shifted the shotgun and shot Gibbs squarely in the stomach. Running, Gibbs literally exploded. A red torrent of blood and flesh sprayed Sims and the snow around him.

As Gibbs was going down, Leroy fired again. Several of the heavy double-aught lead shot ricocheted off the pavement in front of Sims. Others splattered Gibbs's car. A tire exploded with a pneumatic gust. Sims felt a violent tearing in his left arm, then a tingling numbness.

Stunned, Sims watched as Leroy pumped another shell into the shotgun. At the same time, he saw that the driver, pistol in hand, was opening his door. In a second, he would be facing two guns, but as if in a dream, it seemed to him that he had all the time in the world to act.

"Sims!" Houghton's shout sliced into the injured man's reverie.

Sims fired first at Leroy: a short burst of three shots. Fire low, he

175

told himself. Then he swung the stubby submachine gun in a small arc toward the driver. His next burst was longer, slightly higher.

It was done in less than two, maybe three seconds. For all the violent excitement of aiming, firing, aiming and firing again, the act itself was curiously distant; remote, as if it had all taken place years before, or he were a bystander, watching someone else doing it.

Sims's sense of detachment vanished, replaced by a chilling panic. He'd missed completely. The driver and Leroy were untouched. It carried Sims back into his childhood nightmares of unslayable monsters coming at him, unslowed by his lame efforts to stop them.

In the next instant, Sims, transfixed, watched as the driver, a dark hole now visible over his left eye, disappeared back into the car. Leroy's menacing leer jerked into a look of surprise. Then, still in his seated position, he slowly pitched forward, out of the car. As he crumpled into the snow, one leg twisted grotesquely beneath him.

"You OK?" came Houghton's voice as if over a great distance.

"Yeah," Sims grated, trying to catch his breath. The submachine gun was the weight of death around his neck, and he fought to keep his knees from buckling. A dark stain was spreading through his coat sleeve. He flexed his left hand and moved his arm. At least there were no broken bones. He wiped his face. His hand came away stained with the bar owner's blood.

Gripping the submachine gun tightly, Sims cautiously approached Rose's car. The driver stared with flat sightless eyes at the car's bloody interior. All the same, Sims reached in, found the revolver, and flung it out into the harbor. Several feet away, Leroy Rose groaned in the snow. Sims walked over and kicked the shotgun underneath the car. Placing a toe under Rose's chest, he rolled the man onto his back.

"Damn." Rose winced in pain, eyes darting from Sims's face to the submachine gun pointing at him, then back to Sims's face. "You gotta do somethin'. I'm dyin'."

Sims regarded the man for a moment, recalling Rose's face over the shotgun and how he'd laughed as he'd killed Gibbs. He looked over the top of the car and saw Houghton, pistol in hand, eyes sweeping the nearby warehouses. Sims turned back to Rose.

"You got a choice, Leroy."

Rose's eyes had a trapped animal glitter to them.

"I can call the ambulance," Sims offered, "or I can call Dominic Torricelli." Sims could tell that one of his rounds had ripped into Rose's knee. No more dancing, Leroy, he thought with some satisfaction. Then he noticed another dark spot ominously spreading through Rose's trousers just below the belt buckle.

"Oh my God." The animal eyes widened. "What the fuck you gonna call Dominic for?"

Houghton was warily making his way over to the warehouse to check out the shooter he'd taken off the roof. The north wind was blowing fresh snow in off the harbor.

"I'm going to call Dominic unless you talk to me. He'd like to eliminate his competition."

"Talk?"

Sims nodded. "You talk to me. If I like what you say, I'll call the ambulance. And maybe you won't die."

"I'm bleeding." Rose's voice rose in a sobbing cry.

"Me too, Leroy. We'll both stop bleeding as soon as you talk."

"OK, OK, talk. For God's sake, hurry."

"Who was J. J.?"

"Fuckin' Izzy told you." Anger and outrage crossed Rose's face.

"Who was J. J.?"

"Goddamn Izzy. Cheatin' cocksucker—I was right to kill the fucker," Rose cursed. A wave of pain twisted somewhere deep in his guts. He gasped. "Oh God, I need a—"

"J. J. Who was he?"

Rose's mouth worked soundlessly. "Barrineau. St. Louis."

"How did you know him?"

"St. Louis . . . he was St. Louis . . ."

"St. Louis? What was St. Louis?"

"The organization. I . . ."

"What organization?" Sims knelt close to Rose. The man was going into shock. "Name? What was the name of the organization?"

Rose shook his head back and forth, struggling with the fear of talking and the fear of dying. He looked at Sims. The nigger would let him die, no doubt about it. "Southern—Southern States Council," he said in a choked, weakening voice.

"When?" Sims was now on his knees, face close to Rose. "When did they call you?"

"Eight . . . '68."

"When?" Sims's voice took on an urgent tone. "Before or after King was killed?"

Rose's lips curled in a punk's pride. "Before. Week . . . March."

"Did J. J. call you?"

Rose nodded, teeth clenched.

"What did he want you to do?"

"Help J. J."

"What did you do?"

"Passport. Picked up pictures." Rose was passing deeper into shock. Sims tugged the man's coat around him. "Arcade Studio. Took application. Made pickup."

"Did you see Ray?"

"Yeah. Silver Dollar with J. J. Gave him passport."

"Did J. J. give Ray money, too?"

Rose's eyes blanked for a long moment. Sims was about to repeat the question when Rose answered. "J. J. gave money, lot of money."

"A lot of money?"

Rose smiled remembering it. He coughed, and the laugh was a liquid gurgle in his throat. He was feeling better now. Everything would be better. The pain was leaving him. "J. J. . . . J. J. made . . . joke."

"Joke? How, Leroy?" Sims asked, trying to hide his desperation. "How did J. J. joke about it?"

Rose gurgled again. "Said it was Russian money. Russians paid to kill a nigger Commie."

Stunned, Sims felt a rippling convulsion that had nothing to do with the cold.

"The Russians killed King?"

Rose's eyes again lost their focus. Sims put his mouth near the dying man's ear. "Where's J. J.?"

Sirens cut into the north wind.

The sound revived Rose. He found Sims and gave him a defiant look.

"J. J., where is he?"

Rose twisted his head a fraction of an inch, spit into Sims's face, then died.

15

Sims floated up toward light and consciousness as if freed from the depths of a dark well. First came the off-white ceiling, the pale green walls, and next the smells of antiseptic and alcohol. Then there was Houghton leaning over him, his face blurred and voice fuzzy and far away. There was a sense of warmth and safety. Lingering remnants of the anesthetic reclaimed him and he closed his eyes. Before he drifted off, he saw kaleidoscopic images of their escape from Toronto.

They had gotten away from Polson Street scant seconds ahead of the police. Houghton had found an all-night pharmacy in North York. In a parking lot, he had tended to Sims's wound as best he could with a stinging antiseptic and bandages. At a nearby convenience store, he had bought several six-packs of beer and Sims drank one bottle after another, washing down massive doses of aspirin. The beer and aspirin didn't do much good, and within an hour, the pain in his arm had become a throbbing creature with a life of its own.

The worst had been the wait near the border at Niagara. Fearing a closer immigration inspection during a night crossing, Sims had insisted on waiting until daylight. East of the town of Grimsby, Houghton had driven deep into the woods to wait to join the morning traffic into the States.

"You OK? Hungry?" Houghton had opened a package of doughnuts.

Sims shook his head and turned to stare out into the blackness of the night.

"Bothers you, doesn't it?"

Another look out the window, then back to Houghton. At first, he hadn't wanted to talk about it, but suddenly he wanted to very much. "Yes, yes it does."

"You can't let it get to you."

"Sure. Killing's just a day's work. That it?"

"Leroy wasn't Mother Teresa."

Sims saw Gibbs's blood as it sprayed the white snow. With startling clarity, he remembered a vivid scrap from childhood play. Small brown hands with an old toothbrush dipped in red watercolor, and —flick—a spatter of red dots onto white construction paper. The tiny drops, no two alike. "It was in Rose's face, how he enjoyed it."

"But it bothers you that you killed him?"

"I didn't want to—" Sims began, then realized he was saying what he felt he *ought* to say. "No, I *did* want to."

"That's what's working on you?"

"I don't like being drafted to be executioner." In frustration, Sims raised a hand in supplication, then dropped it into his lap. "The book was closed on King. We—*I've* opened it up again. Now there're four dead men."

"That too high a price?"

"Is one too many? A hundred? I don't know. What's it worth?" Sims regretted it immediately. It sounded weepy and melodramatic.

"Depends, I suppose." Houghton shrugged. "On the market. Who's selling. Who's buying."

Sims had felt a clarifying swell of pain build and radiate outward from his arm. He had taken more aspirin with beer and had finally fallen asleep, staring out into the night.

There had followed an eternity in the car. Houghton driving. Houghton fiddling with the radio and drinking endless cups of coffee. And always the pain—growing, swelling, then retreating, only to return again. He remembered calling Rollo Moss from a roadside pay phone in Maryland; Houghton taking the phone, getting directions, and bringing him here, where he now lay on a gurney. He opened his eyes again and this time Rollo was bending over him. Houghton stood to one side and the thin black bodyguard on the other. Sims tried to talk, but the effort was too much, and he drifted off to sleep once more.

Leonid Mikhalin was the Russian *rezident* for Toronto. It was the evening after Sims's encounter with Leroy Rose, and Mikhalin was lighting his ninth cigarette since dinner as he went over his report yet again. Most traffic he sent from his Toronto *rezidentura* was low-level stuff. Not this. He slugged the cable straight to Okolovich.

He was certain it was the pair of Americans Okolovich was looking for. There had been the telephone call from Gibbs: a black with a white companion asking questions about Ray. Then the shootings on Polson Street. Mikhalin's source reported that the Mounties, convinced it was a gangland killing, were putting the heat on Dominic Torricelli. Given Moscow's interest and the call from Gibbs, Mikhalin suspected the Americans. Shocking lack of finesse, Mikhalin mused, but for Langley, a surprising show of balls.

He looked at his clock. It was dawn in Moscow. They'd digest his report and send back follow-up questions. He'd also asked for photographs of the Americans and the defector Valek. He'd get a couple of hours' sleep at the most. Wearily, he pushed back from his desk and walked down the short hallway to communications.

"The Odd Couple in Toronto," John Delaney said to himself, dropping the document on his desk and walking to the window to stare at the Capitol.

Like so many of the FBI's institutions, the Director's Daily Bulletin had been started by J. Edgar Hoover. The DDB was a top-secret two-page index of significant worldwide events in law enforcement and counterespionage. Whatever subsequent directors' work habits, the DDB always arrived on their desks each morning at six-thirty. That was when Hoover had begun *his* day.

Delaney treated the DDB with respect. It was a thread of continuity that wove its way back through Bureau history. Its pages had chronicled the many secrets of the American century. Delaney frequently imagined Hoover at his shoulder, reading, advising, making precise tic marks with a sharpened yellow government pencil.

A construction crane was swinging into action on the Capitol's west lawn, and morning traffic toward the Hill had already begun to clog Pennsylvania Avenue.

The entry in the report that had caught Delaney's eye was on page two.

> Toronto liaison reports shooting death of ROSE, Leroy.
> (File 79J-MO; COINTELPRO).

"I queried Toronto liaison," Delaney said, still imagining Hoover there beside him. "The Mounties are looking for one of his competitors. But I think the nigger and his friend did it." Delaney stood quietly in thought for a moment, looking at the Capitol. "They could have gotten everything and they could have gotten nothing."

There are times to know things, Hoover was telling him. *Wait,* said the voice at his shoulder. *Wait and watch.*

Delaney paused, then his mind was made up. "We'll pick up surveillance. If the nigger got something up there, he won't be sitting still."

Five blocks from where John Delaney was communing with the spirit of J. Edgar Hoover, Bradford Sims stirred restlessly, shifted in his bed, and then settled back into a deep sleep. It was a sterile, comfortable room that could have been in any Marriott or Hyatt across America. Thick curtains shut out the morning winter sun, and a nurse sat quietly in a corner chair, reading a newspaper by the light of a dimmed floor lamp.

"Some infection, the doc said," Rollo Moss explained to Houghton. The two men stood at the foot of Sims's bed. "Double-aught's bad shit. Doc said it carried a lot a shit in with it—dirt, pieces of his coat. Lucky it didn't hit bone."

Houghton gestured around the room. "How long?"

"Doc says two days, three at most. Had to take lotta stitches, and they shootin' him up for the pain."

The two men stood for a moment, then walked to the door. Houghton stopped and turned back to Sims, sleeping in the darkened room.

"He oughta pack it in," Rollo said.

Houghton nodded, still looking into the room. "You think he would?"

Rollo shook his head.

Mikhalin checked the address once more. Moscow had sent the photographs in record time, along with a long list of very specific questions. That's the way it is in the business, Mikhalin grumbled to himself. You're either bored or they're working you to death. He knocked.

Fella Szpakowski cracked the door open. Mikhalin saw the chain stretch across the opening. He reached inside his coat pocket and came up with the official-looking credential case with its heavy gold badge.

"Toronto police, Mrs. Szpakowski."

"I didn't think they was television," the Polish woman told Mikhalin over coffee minutes later. "They didn't have no camera . . ."

Mikhalin interrupted her, showing her the pictures, first of Sims, then of Houghton.

"That's them. They took up my day with all them questions about Mr. Ray."

"I'd like to talk about the questions they asked you, Mrs. Szpakowski." Mikhalin produced a small wire-bound pocket pad and ballpoint pen. He smiled reassuringly at her. "For the official record."

Ryan McCullah, registry clerk, Royal Canadian Mounted Police, had uncles, cousins, and a married older brother in Northern Ireland. It did not particularly surprise him, therefore, when he had been approached seven years ago by a gentleman from Enniskillen. Ryan, said the gentleman, could serve the cause without betraying his trust to the Mounties. After several meetings, Ryan agreed, took the republican oath, and, in the following years, served with distinction. Ryan McCullah was a spy, a soldier in the Fermanagh Brigade of the *Oglaigh na Heireann*—the Irish Republican Army. Or so he thought.

Ryan took the shuttle elevator down to the third parking level. He was the last one out of his office. The traffic was sparse, even on College Street. It was Friday evening; much of Toronto was already at home, in restaurants, or at the theater.

Shifting his worn attaché case to his left hand, he groped in a trouser pocket with his right. For a heart-stopping moment, he couldn't find it, then his fingers closed around the small hard cylinder, not much larger than a pencil eraser. Press hard with the edge of a fingernail—he mentally rehearsed the instructions—and the capsule's interior wall would rupture, releasing the acid that would destroy the contents. They would know, of course, that he'd been up to something. But they couldn't prove it in court. He'd lose his job, no doubt. But the IRA would take care of him.

Coming off the elevator, Ryan glanced around the nearly empty garage. His car, a blue Toyota, was parked against a far wall. As he approached his car, he slowed, looked down, then stopped. He set the attaché case next to a concrete support column and stopped to tie his shoelace. A second later, he was again walking toward his car.

Ryan eased his attaché case onto the car's roof, taking care not to scratch the glossy finish. Fishing in his pockets, he came up with his keys, unlocked the door, and retrieved the attaché case, ducking into the car to put it on the front passenger seat. He scanned the garage. No sign of life. Shouldering out of his heavy winter coat, he pitched the coat into the car on top of the attaché case, got into the car, and started its engine. While the engine warmed up, Ryan adjusted his seat belt. Safety pays, he told himself.

Minutes later, he pulled into a curbside parking space just off St. Clair Avenue, found a pay phone, and dialed a number. He let it ring seven times, hung up, and again dialed the number. It rang three times. Someone on the other end picked up, said nothing, and hung up. Ryan breathed deeply, obviously relieved. Another mission accomplished. He had a date tonight. He was looking forward to a few drinks, a bit of dancing, and some good screwing.

As Ryan McCullah got back in his car, a man left a phone booth in the lobby of the Sheraton Centre Hotel. He entered a car waiting outside. Four minutes later, he and his companion pulled onto the third level of the parking garage on College Street.

Driving slowly, the car's headlights picked up the mark Ryan had chalked on the concrete column while tying his shoelace. The small gray film cassette was in place—a crack in the wall just opposite where Ryan had swung open his car door. The Mounties could have let Ryan chalk the "drop is loaded" sign and load the drop, then arrest him and lie in wait to bag whoever came to service the drop. The telephone call had been an extra precaution. And, like Ryan McCullah, Mikhalin believed that safety pays.

Just after midnight, Ryan McCullah's film arrived at Sheremet'yevo. Watched by a pair of surly couriers from Okolovich's office, the duty consular affairs officer opened the diplomatic pouch and handed over a small fiberglass box that Mikhalin had sealed in Toronto.

The couriers delivered the box to a tightly guarded complex southeast of Moscow at Yasenevo, half a mile off the ring road. Within two hours, technical services had developed the film, made a duplicate for registry, and delivered the prints to a waiting Sergei Okolovich. Four hours later, Okolovich sat down in Dimitri Aristov's Kremlin conference room.

"The Americans are still chasing down this King killing." Okolovich slid the photographs of Sims and Houghton across the table to Dimitri Aristov. "These are the two who interrogated Broz in Prague. They showed up in Toronto several days ago. They questioned a tavern owner named Gibbs about James Earl Ray. Gibbs was a low-level agent we had recruited several years ago as an underworld informant. Gibbs notified our *rezident.*"

Aristov's face clouded.

"It gets worse, Dimitri. Two nights later, Gibbs was killed in what the Canadians believe to be a gangland dispute."

"I suppose it wasn't." Aristov said it with the air of a man who knows none of the breaks are going to go his way.

Okolovich shook his head. "We got a copy of the police report. In addition to Gibbs, a man named Leroy Rose was also killed."

"And he was?"

"A major figure in the Toronto criminal class." Okolovich slid Rose's personal history card across the table. The photograph, over twenty years old, captured a ratlike cunning in the tight, unlined face. "He showed up in our computer search as an agent of influence."

Agent of influence. Not a spy, but someone on the rolls for his or her ability to exert influence.

"I thought all the files had been destroyed."

"Everything with an apparent connection with King. These had no such connection."

"At the time," Aristov corrected.

"Yes."

"And now there is a connection."

"Years ago in the United States, Rose belonged to something called the Southern States Council."

"What does that have to do with the shooting in Toronto?"

"The Southern States Council," Okolovich explained, "was a militant white racial association in the sixties. It mounted secret attacks against American blacks."

"How do we know this?" Aristov probed, his stomach suddenly greasy and cramping.

"Because we assisted the council."

"Why?" In frustration and despair, Aristov wondered if there were any limits to the KGB's storehouse of past stupidity.

"Perhaps to enable it to make war on the blacks. Divide America."

Aristov felt a rising foreboding. "What was Rose's place in this council?"

"A wealthy American named Barrineau founded the council in the city of St. Louis. A man with delusions of grandeur. Apparently he wanted to extend the reach of his organization. He sent Rose to

Toronto in 1966. Toronto had—still has—a large colony of Southern American whites. Industrial workers, that kind of scum. Rose was a rabble-rouser and recruiter."

"Our money went to Rose?"

"No. We dealt only with Barrineau." Okolovich pulled another personal history card. The yellowing black-and-white photograph showed a chubby grinning man with light hair. "We believe he is still alive—somewhere."

"And these?" Aristov pushed the photos of Sims and Houghton back toward Okolovich.

"Our Toronto *rezident* traced portions of Ray's known trail. He found a woman who rented a room to Ray. She said that these men"—Okolovich pointed to the photographs of Sims and Houghton—"had just been there. They also showed her a picture of defector Valek."

"Yes?"

"She identified Valek as the man who came looking for Ray." Okolovich watched for Aristov's reaction. He didn't have to wait long.

"So now," Aristov said, picking up the photographs of Sims and Houghton, "we know for certain that these two have connected us with the killing of King." He looked at the photographs for a moment, then raised his eyes to Okolovich. "And Barrineau is the only link to us?"

Okolovich nodded. "The only living link."

A half hour later, Aristov's operators made radio contact with Tom Farmer at the controls of his Gulfstream IV during his approach to Jakarta's Soekarno Hatta International Airport. By the time Farmer had taxied the sleek blue jet off the runway, a car from the Russian embassy was waiting at the ramp. In another fifteen minutes, Farmer was in the embassy's communications room, on the scrambler to Aristov.

Farmer's face drained in dismay as Aristov recounted the events in Toronto. In the past several weeks, the scale of human suffering in the former Soviet Union had swung substantial American sentiment toward a massive aid program. With it, the prospects improved for Farmer's joint venture, Resurrection. But with gloomy economic times in the States, that American sentiment was fragile. Farmer shuddered at the thought of headlines screaming that Moscow had killed Martin Luther King.

Farmer had to have Congressional approval for the loan guarantees soon or the massive project would fall apart. Daily, more battalions of German, French, and Japanese businessmen stormed Moscow's gates, eager to make their own deals with the Russian government.

His thoughts flashed to the ramp where the blue Gulfstream was now being serviced and provisioned for his next giant leap across his worldwide empire. If Resurrection failed, it would take the international bankers, those goddamn sharks, less than a day to destroy what he'd spent a lifetime building.

The conversation was soon over, and seconds later, the details Aristov had promised were coming in over the fax. Farmer looked at the bank of clocks on the communications room wall. It was just after nine in the evening on the East Coast. Fifteen minutes later, he was back aboard the Gulfstream, dialing a number in Washington. Cursing silently at recorded messages about satellite ground station delays, he repeatedly redialed the number. Finally the circuits cleared and Farmer pressed the telephone hard into his ear, as if it would bring John Delaney closer to him.

"John, this line secure?"

Delaney pressed a button in the base of his telephone. A blinking green light and an echoing halo around Farmer's voice told him that the scrambler was working. By now, Farmer's tone was familiar, Delaney thought sourly. It's how he begins when he has bad news from the Russians.

Delaney rummaged in a bedside table and came up with a pen and a yellow legal pad. The beginning of the bad news was unsurprising. Sims and Houghton were definitely backtracking on Ray. They had a witness who could place Valek in Toronto and they knew that a fat man had come looking for Ray. From Ray's rooming house, they had obviously gone to the Silver Dollar and from there, somehow, made the connection with Leroy Rose.

Delaney's hand trembled slightly when Farmer got to the Southern States Council. The KGB had been feeding money to Barrineau! And Sims and Houghton were well on their way to building a solid case against the Russians. Farmer read more of Aristov's report, but Delaney wasn't listening.

Delaney had written "Yazov" on the legal pad and was underlining it repeatedly in bold black strokes. He interrupted Farmer.

"Bring it all back here, Tom." Delaney hesitated, listening to the silence. "Bring it all back here," he repeated pensively, thinking it was time for some international cooperation. He underlined Yazov's name yet again.

Pham Ngo Thach left Hanoi on the morning flight to Hong Kong. A brush contact in a Kowloon alley, and he had the passport and personal papers of a retired Chinese printer. It was under this cover that he cleared customs at Paris's De Gaulle Airport thirty hours later.

At a dead drop in the Bois de Boulogne, Thach shed his Chinese identity and emerged from the park a French citizen of Vietnamese extraction, one Ma Son Nhan, an emigré from France's vanished colonial empire.

Weary, Thach passed through American customs in San Francisco. At an airport hotel, he carefully pried open the hidden panel in his otherwise unremarkable luggage. There, sealed in plastic wrap, were fifty thousand dollars and the naturalization papers, driver's license, and Social Security card of Le Van Hoan.

It was as Hoan that he flew the next day to Atlanta, Georgia. There he rented an unobtrusive apartment on the fringes of that city's small Vietnamese colony. He would soon be getting help. Four of his watchers would come to Atlanta from the Mexico City embassy, another two from New York. Those two would have the more difficult time; the Americans watched the Vietnamese mission to the UN very closely. Together, the seven of them would throw a surveillance net around the bait, Arthur Barrineau. Thach switched on the television and opened a cold beer. A comfortable place, he thought, for watching a trail.

16

"Where's this?"

Rollo went to the window and opened the drapes. It was gray and it looked like morning. "My doctor's. You been here three days."

Sims looked at his bandaged arm, then raised it. It hurt like hell, but nothing like it had before.

"The stitches come out in a week, ten days."

Sims threw back the covers, swung his feet around, and sat up on the edge of the bed. A fleeting dizzy spell caused him to stop and shake his head. When everything cleared, he stood up. "Clothes?"

Rollo pointed to a closet. "Your white friend got some clean stuff from your place." Rollo watched as Sims, naked, made for the closet. "Your friend isn't much for talkin'."

Sims concentrated on getting his clothes and a small overnight bag out of the closet. He pulled on boxer shorts, then his slacks. When he turned, he found to his disappointment that Rollo was still waiting for an answer.

"Damnit, Bradford, I get you guns. My doctor fixes you up after— after what, I don't know. But I don't need one a my damn lawyers to tell me that that makes me an accomplice to something. And I want to know what it is."

Sims stood for a moment, shirt in hand, looking at Rollo. It came to him that inside the Agency you had far fewer decisions on who to tell what. The system, imperfect as it had been, had taken care of that. He forced himself to look clinically at Rollo, to weigh how Rollo might be used to advantage and how Rollo might become a liability.

189

Sims worked the shirtsleeve over his bandaged arm, then over his good one, and sat on the corner of the bed facing Rollo. "It has to do with King, Rollo."

Rollo squinted. "Martin *Luther* King?"

Sims nodded. "If Ray killed him, he didn't do it by himself. I—"

"*If* Ray killed him?" Rollo, looking like he'd seen a snake, cut him off, waving his hand violently. "That's enough, Bradford!"

"I'm willing to tell you—"

Rollo shook his head violently. "I don't *want* to know any more. I can see why the CIA didn't want you messin' in that."

"One man at CIA didn't."

Rollo was on his feet now, an expression of rebuke on his face, as if correcting a child. "Shit, Bradford, a lot of people wouldn't."

"You?"

Rollo softened around the mouth and eyes. "All I ever wanted to be was a good cop. That night when your daddy was killed . . ." He fell silent, then his face turned murderously hard again. "Sum'bitch who killed Martin King *stole* from us. Stole your daddy, my friend, stole me bein' a cop." Then Rollo shrugged, and the killer look left his face. A leering smile twisted his mouth. "Still, I'm doin' good, and when your business is good, you don't go out lookin' for trouble."

Sims regarded the big man for a moment, then, evidently disappointed, got up and went to the closet for a nylon parka. "I understand, Rollo," he said in a cool voice.

He put on the parka, picked up the overnight bag, and was at the door when Rollo called his name.

He stopped and Rollo came up to him, a begging look on his face. Rollo cupped Sims's shoulder in a big, kneading hand. "I'm a businessman now, Bradford. I can't change the past. I worked hard for what I got and I'm not about to piss it away."

"I said I understand, Rollo." Sims made as if to turn and was stopped as Rollo's grip tightened.

"Goddamnit, Bradford, you think you got some kinda call on me because a your daddy?" Anger mixed with pain in Rollo's voice.

"Do I, Rollo?" Sims asked, looking steadily at the big man.

Rollo froze, a man cornered. Finally he dropped his eyes, turned, lumbered back across the room, and picked his coat and hat off a chair. He stood for a moment, coat over one arm, head bowed, studying the hat brim as he turned it in his hands. Finally he looked up to Sims. "I'm a businessman," he said, throwing it up once again as a shield. He brusquely waved his hat toward the door. "Come on. Your white friend's waitin'."

Once outside, Houghton lit a cigarette and offered to take Sims's overnight bag. Shaking his head, Sims glanced around to get his bearings. They were at Fourteenth and H, where offices for lawyers and lobbyists were crowding out the first wave of prostitutes, the ones who had worked the streets. The cold air felt good to Sims, and he breathed deeply to clear his lungs of the medicinal staleness of Rollo's backstairs clinic.

"We got about a block," Houghton said, motioning up H Street. Waiting at the parking garage for an attendant to bring down his old BMW, Houghton lit another cigarette. He had gone to Riddle after leaving Sims with Rollo Moss. Riddle had come up with a trace on Barrineau.

In the lobby of his building, Sims emptied his stuffed mailbox into his overnight bag and took the elevator to his apartment. Making a fresh pot of coffee, he stripped and showered, holding his wounded arm away from the spray. Shaved, and with coffee at hand, he sat down to go through his mail. At six that evening, he walked a block from his apartment building to hail a cab to K Street and Tabard Books.

"James Joseph Barrineau," Riddle intoned in his plummy English magistrate's voice. "Born July 27, 1938, Covington, St. Tammany Parish, the state of Louisiana. Parents: Effie Ascension Barrineau and Jules Lacombe Barrineau. The birth certificate tells us both were white."

Sims and Houghton sat at the table in Riddle's loft office. *Punch* engravings and bookcases filled with rare folios and quartos vied for wall space, and a deep red and very costly Azerbaijani carpet covered the dark wood floor. Riddle strode back and forth as if pacing a stage, reading from his blue index cards.

"Parish public schools. Two years at Louisiana State University. Army service 1958 through 1960. Finance corps." Riddle recited from another card. "President and chief executive officer, Pickens and Company, cotton brokers, St. Louis, Missouri, 1961 through 1968." Riddle placed the card neatly over the first.

"Then?"

"Then, young man?" Riddle looked inquiringly at Sims. "Then *nothing*," he answered dramatically. "Both the Social Security Administration and the Internal Revenue Service list 1968 as the last year in which they received payments from Barrineau. To be precise, Barrineau did not file a return for his 1968 taxes. The IRS was idly curious as to his whereabouts, but, like the Social Security, carries him as presumed deceased." Riddle stopped in midstride and stood, head cocked in inquiry.

Houghton made a note in a spiral notebook. "Relatives?"

Riddle gave a small approving smile and produced another index card. "In the army, Barrineau completed a Department of Defense Form 398 for a secret clearance. It lists a sister and two brothers. One we've already located: Arthur Delcambre Barrineau, in 1958, a student. Arthur went on to graduate from Tulane law school. Alumni records show him in practice in Atlanta, Georgia."

"The Southern States Council?" Sims asked.

Riddle dug into a pocket and came up with two more cards. "We must—" The big man paused to frown at his slip, then began again. "*I* must continue research. There are, however, numerous accounts of the organization in St. Louis newspapers. J. J. Barrineau is reported as the council's president. There are no further mentions of Mr. Barrineau in the media after April 1968."

Sims thought he saw the hint of yet another secret in Riddle's smugness. "But there's something else, isn't there, Riddle?"

Yet another blue card materialized at Riddle's fingertips. "On Thursday, May 16, 1968, a Portuguese bank got an order to attach Pickens and Company's accounts."

"Portuguese?"

"The Banco de Bragança in Lisbon. It seems that Pickens and Company, using its St. Louis accounts as collateral, borrowed a sum from the Banco de Bragança. The sum was then transferred to a bank in Beirut, with the intent to buy Egyptian cotton. The Portuguese bank received a copy of the bill of lading showing that the cotton was in a bonded warehouse in Marseilles."

Sims followed the transaction, frowning in concentration. "And?"

"And it came apart when the Egyptian broker pressed a claim against the Portuguese for full payment. It turned out that the Pickens representative had paid the Egyptians only a deposit for the cotton. By the time the Portuguese sorted all this out, months had passed."

"The Beirut account?" Houghton asked, already knowing the answer.

"Cleaned out Tuesday afternoon, May 7, 1968. Down to the last farthing." Riddle had a mischievous, triumphant smile.

"The day after Ray left Toronto. How much was it?"

Riddle clucked his tongue in admiration. It was, after all, a very smooth operation. "Five and a half million dollars. A tidy getawa sum."

"The brother, Arthur—"

"Yes," Riddle agreed before Houghton could finish. "That is th place to start."

Sims began a question: "Have you—"

"Why of course, young man." Riddle put on an act of indignity. took two notebooks from a dispatch case and pushed one across table to Sims, the other to Houghton.

"This is Arthur Barrineau as seen from the perspectives of creditors, his doctors, his colleagues, and his government. Just ab anyone who keeps records of any sort. I know you will underst that these books cannot leave here." Riddle pointed to a ceramic holding a quiver of sharpened pencils and a stack of yellow pads. "Feel free to make as many notes as you wish. I shall s fresh coffee."

Houghton stared reflectively at the door through which Riddl disappeared. He and Sims then set to work, surveying Riddle search.

Diagrams summarized telephone calls over the past twenty bar charts and line graphs showed destination and frequency of Annexes listed each number called and the names behind numbers. Riddle provided the same meticulous detail for cred purchases. Business records. Bank and stock accounts. Med surance claims. To whom Arthur Barrineau spoke, where an he ate, the size and seller of his suits, where he vacationed. S Annuities. Voting registration. Automobile mileages. The pa pieces of a modern man's life, trapped forever in electronic available for a modern archaeologist such as Riddle.

In the final section of the notebook, Riddle had pieced these bits of Barrineau's life into a day-by-day chronology. Th read, on April 4, 1968, the day King was killed, Barrineau phoned an attorney in Spartanburg, South Carolina (10:37 A.M A.M. EST). Later, he had lunched at a small grill on Peachtre ican Express charge). In the afternoon and evening, he h four more calls, all in-state (LaGrange, Savannah, Brunsv Augusta).

"Damn." Houghton's voice cut through Sims's absorption. "Do you realize the sources Riddle must have to come up"—he pointed with awe to his notebook—"to come up with this?"

"We know more about Arthur Delcambre Barrineau than he knows about himself." Sims smoothed the papers in front of him, ironing them out with the palm of his hand. "Now we find out if he knows anything about his brother."

The next morning, Sims took Delta flight 989 from Washington National. Arriving at Atlanta's Hartsfield airport just after 9:15, he found the Avis counter and did the necessary paperwork for a car. Contract and keys in hand, he took the airport subway to the United gates, where Houghton would be arriving. The morning rush hour had slackened, and fifteen minutes later, they were on I-75/85, speeding into downtown Atlanta to meet Arthur Barrineau.

Standing squarely in the center of his law office, Barrineau was waiting for Sims and Houghton. The first impression was of a starched-for-Sunday Presbyterian elder. Rail thin and bald, Barrineau's long, narrow face was accented by rimless glasses with gold wire stems. Arthur Barrineau was a man for dark blue suits, and he wore his today complete with a vest and a conservative burgundy pin-dot tie knotted small and pulled snugly against a snow-white collar.

Barrineau's grip was surprisingly firm and he directed Sims and Houghton to the chairs facing his desk. He took his seat in a leather-upholstered high-back armchair. He interlocked his fingers and clasped his joined hands in his lap, elbows on the arms of his chair. Sims noticed that Barrineau wore a wedding band. Riddle's notebook had said he was a widower. At ease, Barrineau gave them a welcoming smile that was also a question.

He motioned to the secretary who was closing the door. "Nancy said you were on government business." He kept his smile as Sims slid his old credentials across the desk.

"I didn't know that the Central Intelligence Agency gave its people credentials," Barrineau said pleasantly. "It somehow doesn't fit the image I had."

Sims tried, but couldn't detect the slightest animosity. "We wanted you to know who we are."

Barrineau took a second look at the credentials in the cocked-head way of lawyers, then returned them.

"How may I help?"

"We're looking for your brother," Sims said.

Barrineau didn't change expression, but a veil seemed to slip over his eyes. "Why?" The question was carefully neutral.

Sims's reply was as carefully crafted. "Because we believe he might have information relevant to national security."

A small smile played at the corners of Barrineau's mouth. "National security," he echoed softly, as if to himself. "What makes you believe I know anything about my brother?"

The prying knowledge from Riddle's notebooks caused Sims a passing flush of guilt. "You have maintained close ties with your family. Your mother and father required long hospitalization." Sims did not say, "before they died," but he saw Barrineau's mouth tighten. "You paid back-breaking medical bills."

"And you no doubt can prove that I didn't have the income to do so at the time," Barrineau said with a quiet, knifelike precision.

Houghton cut in. "You reported as a partner in this firm that you transferred over five million dollars into an Austrian bank—"

"Which you should know, as I'm sure you do, operate under stricter privacy laws than do the Swiss," Barrineau interjected.

Sims ignored him. "That transfer was on 8 May 1968, the day after your brother emptied an account in Beirut of that same amount."

Barrineau studied them both, his face long and mournful. His shoulders gave way into a slump of resignation. "The Central Intelligence Agency, I believe, has no powers of arrest."

Sims forced himself to remain calm despite a sudden exultant hammering of his pulse. "We're not after an arrest, Mr. Barrineau. We're seeking information from your brother." Then, as he saw Barrineau about to speak, he added, "But I do want to warn you: while we can't arrest your brother, I can't offer him immunity, either."

A sad, ironic smile crossed Barrineau's face, making him look even more like a churchman. "Immunity? I believe James has all the immunity he needs." The lawyer consulted a pocket watch he drew from his vest. He scribbled on a slip of paper and pushed it toward Sims. "My address. If you will be so kind as to pick me up this evening after supper, I shall take you to talk with James."

17

Sims drove and Arthur Barrineau sat beside him, speaking only to give directions. Houghton was a quiet presence in back. They left the northbound interstate fifteen minutes out of Atlanta and turned west toward Marietta. After half an hour on winding back roads, Arthur pointed toward an entrance onto a private drive.

Huge pecan trees lined the drive, their branches laced together against the night sky. Beyond the trees, Sims made out an expensive white fence. When you spent fortunes on horses, you didn't put well-bred animals inside cheap fencing.

Abruptly, they crested a low hill, breaking out of the trees.

"Damn," came Houghton's awed whisper from the back.

Half a mile away on another low hill, white columns and woodwork trim gleamed spectrally against the darkness of the huge brick main house. Flowing around it like a frozen river, the gravel drive glowed in the pale moonlight. In a month or so, the magnolias bordering the broad walk would soften the house's hulking menace. Now, however, their thick trunks and leafless branches reached like talons out of the cold earth.

"It survived Sherman and the war," Arthur said. "It has been James's love."

Sims imagined the house's history. A place of hell, an antebellum principality built on the bloody labor of those born to die as slaves. He had heard Jews talk about places like Auschwitz, Belsen, Treblinka. They talked about their visits: how, decades later, they ran their fingers over the clawed brick of the gas chambers. They said they could *feel* the screams of those who had died there.

Sims had listened and doubted. After all, these were Jews who'd spent the Holocaust in safety. Some hadn't even been born at the time. Even so, they talked of the killing camps with such an immediacy it was as if they themselves were fresh from the delousing sheds, the chambers, and the ovens. They talked as if the Germans had injected a virus into the vast cultural bloodstream that then infected the souls of those whose arms had never been tattooed. Now, seeing this house, Sims understood.

Arthur pointed to a parking place at the edge of the drive. "There's fine."

Sims and Houghton followed the lawyer toward the door. Their footsteps ground in the gravel and their breath frost was a feathery white in the frigid air.

The massive door swung open smoothly, quietly before Arthur could knock.

Arthur motioned to Sims and Houghton. "These are the men I called about, Otis."

WPA photographers had captured men like Otis in the Depression South. Men who sat beneath Nehi signs at country stores and chewed and spit. Men with seamed faces and tight, sunken mouths. Men whose eyes had taken on a vicious, calculating menace from malnutrition and childhood pellagra. Mean, hating men who wore cheap straw hats and whose scrawny buttocks swam lost in faded overalls.

Otis stared past Arthur to Sims. "You dint say nothin' about a nigger." He wore a cheap wrinkled wool sport coat without a tie. The coat failed to conceal the straps and webbing of a shoulder holster.

Sims felt a wash of primal fear and anger. He instinctively sought a talisman to ward off this personification of evil. An image crossed his mind of thrusting a crucifix into the face of the devil.

Arthur stepped forward. "These men, Otis, are here to see Mr. Barrineau." Grudgingly, Otis stepped aside.

A single dim lamp lit the foyer. Oils of hunting scenes and men in uniforms hung in ornate gilded frames. The dark wood floor was waxed and polished, bearing proudly the scars of almost two centuries of spurred boots. To the right, a wide staircase swept upward in a walnut spiral.

"He's up there." Arthur started toward the stairs. Ignored, Otis stood expressionless, his back to the closed door.

"All we need is Scarlett O'Hara," Houghton muttered, following Sims and Arthur.

The stairway brought them to a hallway overlooking the foyer.

Arthur stopped before the second door on his right. Sims looked down into the foyer. Otis had vanished. Arthur stopped, his right hand on the doorknob.

"It is cancer of the bladder," he said quietly in the clinical tone people take up to shield themselves from the horrors inflicted on a loved one. "It has metastasized. He wanted to die here rather than a hospital. He will die of uremic poisoning." Arthur made a small apologetic smile. "The poisoning affects his mind, you see. Sometimes he is very clear. Other times . . ." He made a helpless gesture and opened the door without knocking.

It was as if Arthur had opened the door to a furnace. An oppressive wave of heat battered Sims. Then he smelled—and almost felt—the putrefying sickroom stench of medicine, urine, and disinfectant. A small lamp cast a yellowish glow over a man looking shrunken and doll-size in a huge canopy bed. To the side, in a small chintz-covered chair, a nurse dozed, her spectacles hung on the end of her nose.

The nurse woke with a start. Before she could start on an excuse, Arthur waved her out of the room. As the door shut, Arthur took her chair and waved to Sims and Houghton. "Those straight chairs over there. Pull them up."

Arthur turned to the figure in the bed. "James?" He spoke loudly, as if summoning a spirit from the beyond.

"I *hear* you, Arthur," complained a dry, rusted voice. "No goddamn need to shout." There was a slight but unmistakable lisp, the lisp Ray's Chinese landlady had described. Barrineau opened his eyes, as if granting a favor. He had been a big man, but now his flesh draped loosely over his face. A pallid ribbon of old scar began just below his nose, ran over his lip and into his mouth. He looked questioningly past his brother to Sims, who was still standing.

"He wants to talk with you, James."

Barrineau pinned Sims with a long, silent scrutiny. The bedridden man's dark eyes were a pair of glistening parasites, restless tenants in a rotting and dying host. Finishing their survey, they fixed on Sims's face.

"You here to carry away my sins, boy?"

Sims regarded Barrineau for a moment, then moved a chair close to the bed, putting himself between Arthur and his brother. At the same time, he flicked the switch to start the small recorder under his right arm.

Sims leaned forward, bringing his face inches from Barrineau. "They bother you—your sins?"

Barrineau's cracked lips pulled into a grimace of profane amusement. "Bother? Hell no. No, they don't. Man's sins are his only treasure!" He gave an insane, high-pitched cackle. "Sins the only things a man carries into the hereafter. I have *big* sins. *Big* sins. Nothin' picayune."

Barrineau fell silent to stare off into the distance, taking stock. "Enjoyed them once. But now—" Perceptibly, his eyes dulled, and the grin became a pout. "Now I'm tired of them. They don't have any . . ." He stopped and looked at Sims as if to enlist his sympathy. "They don't have any *sparkle* left."

"Sparkle?"

"No sparkle now." Barrineau sulked. The eyes turned suspicious. "What do you want here?" he demanded belligerently.

"I want to talk to you about the Southern States Council."

"Oh?" Barrineau grinned crazily.

Behind him, Sims heard Houghton mutter to himself in exasperation. Sims tried again. "A man in Toronto said he knew you: Leroy Rose?"

"Ah, *that.*" It was a flat statement. Barrineau seemed to find Sims's question unremarkable.

Sims struggled to keep the surging mixture of excitement and revulsion from his voice. "Rose said you laughed about the Russians paying to have King killed."

Barrineau seemed to gather strength. His eyes glittered, remembering, enjoying the time again. "Yes."

"Did you know for certain it was Russian money?"

"Certain?" he asked querulously. He went off in a world, talking to himself. Sims strained to hear. It was gibberish. Sims heard a movement behind him. Houghton reached around to hand him the Valek photograph. Sims held it in front of Barrineau. "You ever see this man?"

Barrineau's eyes wandered, then focused. He stared at the photograph intently, then nodded. "That's him. My Russian. He was a foreigner . . . on account of the accent."

"He have a name?"

"Wouldn't give one. I just called him Mike."

"When did you start getting the money?"

"Couple weeks later."

"How much?"

"Eight, maybe ten thousand a month."

Sims heard Houghton give a low whistle. Center wasn't known for its generosity. They were doing well by the Southern States Council. Or maybe it was the other way around.

"How did Mike's money come in?"

"Drafts. Islands Refractories Limited—the Caymans."

"Good memory." Sims's tone was skeptical.

"*Mem*-o-ree?" Barrineau taunted in a singsong lilt. "I've got a good *mem-o-ree,* but I got more than that."

"Oh," Sims challenged, "what more do you have?"

"James!" It came as a warning softly spoken, the warning of a legal counsel.

"Quiet, Arthur!" a suddenly stronger Barrineau snapped at his brother. "This boy ain't about to drag my ass off to no jail." Confiding to Sims, he said, "Arthur's the *law*-yer." And then back to Arthur: "Always been that way, haven't you, Arthur?" Barrineau asked affectionately but laced with the undertone strychnine of brotherly resentment.

Sims waited patiently. Barrineau closed his eyes, resting for a moment, then opened them. Slowly his hand crawled across the blanket to a push button on the nightstand.

Sims heard nothing, but within seconds, the door to the hallway swung open. Otis came in to stand beside the bed.

Barrineau smiled and wagged his hand in greeting. "O-tis." As if switching to a different dialect for the natives, Barrineau took on a deeper drawl. "The vault in the li-berry—fetch everythin' in the bottom drawuh. Give 'em to tha boy heah." He pointed to Sims.

Otis looked at Sims with venom.

"Go on, O-tis," Barrineau coaxed.

Otis hesitated the merest fraction of a second. His lips curled into a beginning snarl, then he was gone.

"I was a money man," Barrineau resumed. "I handled a lot of money."

"A bank in Lisbon would like to know about some of that money," Sims offered.

Puzzlement, then comprehension, then triumph animated Barrineau's face, an injection of instant vigor. "Goddamn Portuguese," he sniggered contemptuously.

"How did you end up in Toronto with Ray?"

"Called. Said he needed help."

"You met Ray at the Silver Dollar?"

"No." Barrineau shook his head. "Before."

"When?"

"March '68."

"Not in Toronto?"

Barrineau closed his eyes and kept them closed until Sims feared he had drifted off to sleep. Then the eyes opened again and bored in on Sims. The eyes were brutal and demanding. "Put another log on the fire, boy."

Sims was looking deep into the eyes, feeling their insistent pull.

"I sed a log, boy."

Sims sat motionless and unhearing. Houghton made a move toward the fireplace.

"I didn't tell *you*, mister," came the rasping voice. "I told the nigger."

Sims sat without moving. Barrineau's eyes were hard and glittering, anticipating victory. "You gonna do it, boy," he hissed, " 'cause you want to know more'n I want to tell you."

Still Sims didn't move. Behind him Houghton was making tiny uncomfortable throat-clearing sounds. In the fireplace, an ember popped, sending a small flash across the room. Sims suddenly stood, Houghton rising with him.

Slowly, Sims bent over the bed toward Barrineau. "Fuck you." He spit the words at the eyes.

A silence followed, and still leaning over Barrineau, Sims whispered to him, "You got it wrong, you miserable bastard. You *want* to tell it, because you've kept it a secret and you want to let it out before you die. You can tell Otis. You can even tell Arthur, here. But it won't mean anything. It won't mean as much as telling me. And you know something else—you know this's your only chance to tell it."

With that, Sims got up and walked toward the door.

Barrineau's eyes widened at the prospect of losing Sims and he looked first at his brother, then at Houghton in supplication.

"March . . . ," Barrineau finally called out to Sims in a hoarse, desperate whisper. Sims turned, paused, then quietly took his seat. Subdued, Barrineau's strength had gone. He was noticeably weaker, more feeble.

"March?" Sims prompted.

"In March," Barrineau continued, "this fella came to see me."

"Ray?"

Barrineau slowly waved his hand, barely clearing the fingers from the sheet. "No. 'Nother fella. Offered to kill King. Wanted money."

Every fiber of Sims's being screamed in protest. He wanted to run from the house, run from the stench of corruption that washed over him. He forced himself to ask, "A contract on King?"

"Sixty thousand." Barrineau coughed, wincing with a pain hidden deep within. He fell silent, his eyes beginning a nervous circuit of the room. "Cold. Colder'n hell in here." He looked at Sims in pleading urgency. "Cold." It came out almost a child's whimper. The dying man's face was vacant; life seemed to be draining away, even from the restless eyes.

Sims got up. "I'll put another log on the fire." He pulled the screen aside and laid two logs on the fire. Standing there, he watched the flames flare up and imagined they were cleaning the poisons from the air around him. Reluctantly, he returned to Barrineau's bedside. As he did so, Otis reappeared, handed a large accountant's case to Houghton, and left.

"The man who took the contract," Sims continued. "What did he have to do with Ray?"

"Next time I saw him, a week later, Ray was with him. Like they'd been traveling together." Between long silences, Barrineau told his story. Barrineau met the two in a bar in South St. Louis. Ray and his partner wanted an advance on the contract. Barrineau had just gotten a payment from the Caymans. He gave them an advance of five thousand dollars from the Russian money.

"Tell me about Ray."

"Wasn't much. Didn't say hardly anything."

"Did he talk about the contract?"

Barrineau thought about the meeting. "No. But he knew about it, I'm just certain he knew. I didn't stay long. Just took him and his partner the money."

"That was your only time with Ray in St. Louis?" He watched as Barrineau nodded weakly. "But then you went to Toronto?"

"Moved him. To a Chink place. He had papers for a new name."

"Papers? Where'd he get them?"

Barrineau's face was blank.

"You gave him money?"

Barrineau nodded.

"But no papers?"

Barrineau nodded again.

"Did Ray say anything about the killing?"

"Just called it the 'jam' in Memphis."

"His buddy. Did you see him in Toronto?"

"I asked him—Ray—and he didn't say much. I asked him, where's your partner? He never gave me a good answer. Just said they got separated in Memphis." Barrineau shook his head. "Wasn't much interested in seeing Raoul again."

Stunned, Sims leaned closer to Barrineau. "Raoul?" Raoul! The man the Bureau and Congress had said didn't exist.

Barrineau didn't answer. His eyes were closed and his breath came in shallow uneven gasps.

"Raoul?" Sims repeated loudly. He recalled the Chinese landlady's description. "Did he have a broken nose?"

Barrineau's eyelids fluttered, then opened reluctantly, as if against a great weight. He nodded. "Spik . . . jail. Had to get out . . . jail."

"Jail? Where?"

Barrineau didn't respond. His eyes rolled loosely, tracking the flight of invisible beasts around the room. The eyes passed by Sims, then flicked back to lock on him, as if seeing him for the first time. Barrineau's eyes began a panicked race, flicking from right to left, right to left, as if suddenly realizing they had stayed too long in their host and now couldn't escape. The slide from sanity was terrifying. The eyes took on a wild, demented look.

Sims was now a black avenging angel, towering over his bed. The paper-thin skin over Barrineau's face and hands flushed with a mottled greenish undertone.

Barrineau reached a hand toward his brother. "Arthur, I been *trying*." He ran his tongue across his lips. "House—everything—goes to niggers, doesn't it?"

Arthur took the withered hand. "Yes, James."

"In the will, ain't it?" Barrineau looked anxiously from his brother to Sims and back again. He wanted Sims to hear it.

Arthur sighed. "Yes, James. It's in the will."

Barrineau looked hopefully at Sims, then into the darkness at the end of the room. The horror on Barrineau's face cut to Sims's very core. It came to Sims that the evil heritage of this house, the sickness of master and slave, was the other malignancy eating at Barrineau, and was prowling just beyond the firelight, waiting for Barrineau. Sims had a moment of fear when he was afraid it was waiting for him too. Barrineau looked beseechingly at Sims.

"You think I'll see him, boy? When my time comes?" His voice high and clutching. "What you think? Will I see him when my time comes?"

"God?"

"Not Him. King." A pause. "You think I'll see King, boy?"

Sims looked into the darkness, then back toward the dying man. "I hope you do see him, J. J.," he said softly, "I honestly do."

18

Otis stood on the veranda and watched the nigger drive away. The taillights seemed to flicker, but it was just the car passing behind the row of pecan trees. Had me a rifle, Otis thought wistfully, if I just had me a rifle . . . He sighed as the car gained the top of the hill. *Mister J. J. wouldna given them the books and stuff if he hadn't been sick. No excuse for Mister Arthur, though*. The taillights finally disappeared from sight.

Otis, puzzling over Arthur Barrineau's inexplicable behavior, went inside and closed and bolted the heavy door. He was still thinking about it as he opened the small closet off the foyer. Banks of green lights gleamed. As he reached for the main switch, a blinking red light caught his eye. That would be the door off the kitchen.

Goddamn help! Tell 'em and tell 'em. They still go out and forget to lock the door.

He'd have to reset the sensors. He grumbled as he made his way toward the kitchen, so familiar with the huge place that he didn't bother to turn on the lights.

Arthur Barrineau's large Georgian house sat back from the street, its high hedges separating it from equally large homes on either side. In another month, the lawn would be a crisp green palette splashed with clumps of daffodils and crocuses. Then the flowering dogwoods and azaleas would turn it into a riot of color.

"I ought to sell it," Arthur said, looking out the car window. The house was lighted but seemed obviously empty. "But the children still come home for the holidays."

Like a sad mechanical toy, Arthur wound down. For a long time he sat motionless, studying his hands and twisting his gold wedding band, first in one direction, then another. Then, greatly distraught, he turned to Sims. "It was an ugly story, wasn't it?"

Sims nodded.

"I didn't know it. Not what we heard tonight."

Sims started an obligatory assurance, but Arthur cut him off.

"I knew James was involved in—in *that.* But I never knew exactly what he was up to. He never said anything direct. He—I think he would have told me. If I had ever asked. I sometimes think he was waiting to see if I *would* ask. I guess I didn't want to know."

"It's called denial. We all do it."

Arthur Barrineau continued to ignore Sims. "I didn't just turn my back to it. I encouraged him in it."

"How?"

Barrineau blinked behind his glasses as he focused on Sims. "I gave J. J. all kinds of little hints that, whatever he was doing, we appreciated it."

"Appreciated it?"

Barrineau waved his hand to take in the neighborhood of handsome homes and manicured lawns. "We—the pillars of Atlanta *society.*" He gave *society* an ironic emphasis. "Oh, we'd make a simpering denouncement in church once in a while. Or maybe even an editorial in the *Constitution.* But that was just playacting." Barrineau opened his door. The dome light cast deep shadows over his eyes.

"The real message came in the winks and nudges we gave to J. J. and Otis and all the rest." He got out of the car.

He ducked his head to peer through the open door and extended his hand to Sims.

"I'm glad you came, sir," he said, like a man who had finally decided to get on with setting things in order. And with that, he turned and walked toward the house. Sims watched. A man should never have to be that alone, he thought.

Houghton moved up to the front seat and Sims pulled away, driving slowly through the unfamiliar neighborhood. Houghton slumped wearily into his seat and massaged his eyelids with his thumb and forefinger. "Broz, Rose, J. J.—now there's a Raoul. A real one."

"Conspiracy." Sims said it slowly and deliberately.

Saying the word, that particular word, was itself a revelation. It struck Sims as odd that, given all that had happened, *conspiracy* had up to now been an out-of-bounds word. He hadn't used it, nor had Houghton.

It had to do with the human tendency to let things lie. James Earl Ray was a tidy, if pathetic, package. Everything began and ended within that sad sack of shit. He did the killing. They found him guilty. They locked him away at Brushy Mountain. That wrapped *that* up—no loose ends, no comebacks.

But Houghton said it: Now there's Raoul. Raoul, who had come to Barrineau and planted the idea of killing King. And Raoul had to be only a part of it. It meant others had had a hand in the killing. Who were they? And where were they now?

"What?"

"Light's green," Houghton repeated.

Ahead, Sims saw the neon lights of an all-night restaurant. He pulled into the parking lot and shut off the engine. The red and green lights cast a grotesque carnival glow into the car.

"What'd J. J. give us?"

Houghton bent over the case and unsnapped two latches. He pulled out three heavy cloth-bound books. With them came the mildewed smell of old paper.

"Ledgers of some sort," Houghton said, riffling through the pages of one. He handed the book to Sims.

The entries were printed in black ink in a neat hand. Sims scanned several pages. Work for an entire green-eyeshade brigade, he thought with distaste. Turning the pages, he heard Houghton mutter an exasperated curse.

Houghton, finished looking through a second book, was trying without success to jam it back into the leather case. Tilting the case into the light, he peered inside. He reached in and pulled out a heavy cardboard box, perhaps half an inch thick and six inches on a side. He lifted off the top. It was a large reel of recording tape.

Houghton examined both sides of the reel, then the box itself. "No label. Nothing."

Sims reached for the key to start the car and his hand froze there.

"Tomorrow," Houghton suggested without much enthusiasm, "he might be better."

Sims still hesitated, thinking about the dying man, his evil house, and Otis. Then he nodded to Houghton and started the car. Beside him, Houghton gathered the books and the tape and fit them back into the leather case. Maybe Houghton was right. Maybe tomorrow in the light everything would be better.

* * *

From a hilltop overlooking the plantation house, Pham Ngo Thach had watched as Sims drove away. There was a certain comic aspect to this, the old Vietnamese thought. The Russians had followed the Americans out here, and he and Nguyen had followed the Russians. He recalled a cartoon in which a fish swam, unaware that it was almost in the jaws of a larger fish. The second fish, in turn, was about to be eaten by a third and even bigger fish.

The Georgia night was cold and Thach was thankful for the heavy down jacket and gloves. He poured tea from a thermos. His watchers had made it safely to Atlanta. Five of them were patroling the foot of the hill, providing a loose security cordon for him and Nguyen. Several meters away, Nguyen had anchored the tripod and was absorbed in adjusting the laser. The instrument's invisible beam, Nguyen had explained, would bounce off a window in the house below, returning to be captured by Nguyen's receiver. The reflected beam would carry with it any conversation inside the house that caused the window to vibrate. Thach marveled at Nguyen, how the young accepted as a matter of course technology that would have been sorcery thirty years ago. The wind picked up, and Thach found himself hoping that the Russians would make quick work of it.

Sims awoke reluctantly and by degrees. Opening his eyes only long enough to find the TV remote, he waved the device in the general direction of the foot of the bed, then burrowed deeper under the blankets. A CNN weather report gradually intruded, predicting snow flurries from the Piedmont to Maine. He opened his eyes again. Through the partially drawn curtain, as if confirming the weather report, scudding gray clouds pressed down from a darkening sky.

Just after seven, he and Houghton stopped at a convenience store for coffee and danish. They stood shoulder to shoulder, sipping the scalding coffee and looking out the plate glass window at the intermittent snow and sleet.

"There's a small medieval town south of Florence," Houghton said dreamily, closing in on an old memory. "San Gimignano. Peaceful. No cars. Just walls, towers, hills, grapes." He looked reproachfully at the leaden sky through the fly-specked window. "And sun," he added wistfully.

"A good place to be." It was a small-talk response.

Houghton went on, as if talking to someone other than Sims, seeing in the distance Tuscany's light and warmth. "Helen and I stayed there for a year. A small stone house just off the Piazza della Cisterna."

She must have been the wife, Sims thought, hearing the name for the first time and filing it away for later. "Vacation?" he asked, knowing it wasn't.

Houghton lost the dream and in a quick motion drained the last of his cup. "A place to pull in for repairs," he said dismissively. He crushed the cup and pitched it into a waste receptacle. He settled his coat around him and buttoned it. "You still want to go out there?"

"Not really." What he wanted to do, Sims thought, was to drive to the airport, turn in the car, and fly back to Washington. Nevertheless, he dug into his pocket for change and called Arthur Barrineau's home from a pay phone. He listened to the phone ring ten times, then hung up. He made a second call. No one answered at Barrineau's law firm.

Houghton motioned to the door. "Probably in the shower and it's too early for anybody at the office. Let's go if we're going to go." Fifteen minutes later, they pulled into Arthur Barrineau's drive.

"You took care of the book bag?"

Sims nodded. "Fed Ex." The bonded courier had shown up within an hour of Sims's call. He hadn't wanted to leave J. J.'s ledgers at the hotel this morning. And he damned sure wasn't going to carry them back out to the plantation and put them within Otis's reach again.

Twenty minutes later, they parked in Arthur Barrineau's drive. Sims checked the dashboard clock. Seven-forty. "Let's get him." He opened his door. If anything, the temperature had dropped since daybreak. Sims reached into his coat pocket for his gloves.

Sims motioned to Barrineau's home and the other baronial houses on the block. "Might as well keep the neighbors from getting on edge."

At the door, Sims pushed the doorbell and heard the faint ring of chimes inside. He looked around. Down the street, a dark green Cadillac backed out of a drive. The car slowed as it passed Sims and he saw the pasty white face inside giving him a suspicious once-over. He turned and gave the doorbell another jab.

Houghton stepped back to scan the second-story windows, then shook his head.

Sims waited, then rang again. The chimes sounded louder, and he felt edginess prickling the backs of his arms and legs. Houghton was watching him expectantly. He tried to peer through the curtained glass panels on either side of the door. Another glance around and he gripped the heavy brass handle, pressed the latch, and pushed. The door opened smoothly.

"Not good," muttered Houghton suddenly behind him. Sims felt it, too. He rolled his shoulder to loosen the pistol in the holster under his left arm. Leaning through the open doorway, he called for Arthur Barrineau, then cocked his head to listen. Nothing except the reedy whispering of the wind.

Houghton came in behind him and closed the door. To the right was the living room. Ahead, a hallway and stairs to the second floor. He called again for Barrineau, and again: no response. He and Houghton went into the living room.

The house had a hushed, suspended quality about it; a pendulum stopped in midswing. A faint scent of rose and lavender hung in the warm air. Striped wallpapers, floral upholstery and drapes spoke of a genteel brightness of an Atlanta decades gone.

Sims saw the portrait over the fireplace of a thin attractive blond in an azure strapless dress. This was the woman who had put this house in order. She was gone, but Arthur Barrineau was keeping it for her, carefully tended to, faded and fragile like a pressed flower. Above them came a single, muffled thump.

Sims caught Houghton's look. At the Farm, they train you to clear a building from the top down. Going up a flight of stairs into some-body's gun got you a failing grade in the course. But this wasn't one of the Farm's exquisitely choreographed training exercises complete with grappling hooks and rope ladders. He saw from Houghton's expression that he didn't like the idea either.

Crossing the living room, Sims pulled the Browning from his holster and thumbed off the safety. He heard Houghton do the same.

Sims looked up the stairs and saw nothing. He heard only the drumming pulse of his own blood in his throat. You don't go up slowly, he warned himself.

Houghton was caught by surprise. Before he could react, Sims was sprinting up the stairs.

Sims felt his legs driving him in giant bounds. Now just four steps to the top. It would happen this way: a dark figure would spring from one of the rooms and aim with two-handed combat grip down the stairs. He remembered the Uzh and Toronto. He would feel the slam-ming shock of the bullet hit centuries before the sound of the pistol registered. He fought against the locked muscles of his chest, forcing himself to breathe.

Stumbling onto the second-floor hallway, he threw himself against the wall and listened. The second door down was partially open. He heard the most minimal of sounds, the slightest movement of air, then a slight clicking scratch on wood.

Keeping his back to the wall, he crabbed sideways to the doorway. The door was partially ajar. Through the narrow opening, he saw a large mirror on the facing wall. The reflection showed a large canopy bed, its feather comforter tossed aside. Again, this time closer, lower, the scratch-click noise.

He looked down, swinging the pistol to follow his eyes. From around the corner of the doorway, a large buff-colored cat gravely surveyed him. Dismissing Sims as irrelevant, the cat walked by, tail high, and proceeded down the stairs, ignoring Houghton altogether.

"Shit." Houghton exhaled a long-held breath.

Sims's legs were watery, and he wondered if Houghton knew how frightened he had been. He waved his pistol down the hallway. "I'll check up here."

Houghton nodded and went down to work the first floor and basement.

Only one person had been in Barrineau's bed. And the cat, Sims added, looking at the smaller indentation in one of the pillows. He began moving around the room, searching one small imaginary square, then another. Twenty minutes later, Sims was downstairs, standing before the hallway closet. Houghton came into the hall from somewhere in the back of the house.

"The suit and shoes he wore last night are upstairs," Sims said, still taking inventory of the closet. "But I don't see the overcoat. You'd think—"

"Come on back," Houghton interrupted, motioning down the hall.

They stood in the kitchen. Houghton had swung the back door open. "See?" He tapped the dead-bolt lock with a ballpoint pen. Sims leaned closer. A spray of tiny scratches, bright in the brass, illuminated the key slot. A sloppy pick job, Sims thought. He straightened up. "And"—Houghton pointed to the garage—"his car's there."

With first light, the wind brought snow. Flurries of hard white pellets scoured the hilltop where Thach and Nguyen kept their watch. Thach, bundled against the cold, sipped tea from the thermos and, with his binoculars, periodically scanned the plantation house below. Nguyen, headset covering his ears, monitored the portable display panel and digital recorder. Just clearing the top of the brush, the laser trained its invisible beam onto a window.

Thach and Nguyen had no way of knowing that the room the laser focused upon was J. J.'s library. They couldn't see the paneled walls draped with Confederate battle banners and crossed cavalry sabers. They only knew that this was the room in which Viktor Yazov, the Russian, along with Dominguez, the Cuban interrogation specialist, had, with the aid of persuasion, threats, torture, and drugs, worked thoroughly and methodically through the night on Arthur Barrineau and Otis.

"Dominguez." Yazov roughly shook the dozing Cuban by the shoulder.

Slumped in a recliner chair, Dominguez jerked awake, his startled eyes registering on the room, then Yazov. He, Sebastian de Tomás Dominguez, had seen much evil done in the name of the revolution, but this man Yazov—he put down the urge to cross himself—put the devil to shame.

Dominguez looked at the two men before him. The sick one upstairs had been of no use at all. The other two were healthy. Or had been, he amended. He glanced at Arthur Barrineau, slumped against the heavy nylon constraints, still in his pajamas and overcoat. That's the one who had the story. Dominguez stood and stretched the stiffness from his back and shoulders.

"You want me to bring them around again?" he asked Yazov, motioning to the unconscious men in the chairs.

Yazov shook his head at the little Cuban. It was getting late. All they could get from here on would be repetition, shadings. He was confident he knew what they had told the black. Except for the damned books, he thought, the damned books. Dominguez was standing there with the hypodermic kit in hand. "No. We have to leave."

"Shall I kill them?" Dominguez asked in a soft, considerate voice.

Yazov shook his head. "They are unconscious—for how much longer?"

The Cuban shrugged. "An hour."

"At most," Yazov asked impatiently, "or at least?"

"At least."

Yazov made certain he had the interrogation tapes securely locked in his attaché case. He looked at the two men strapped in their chairs.

211

"Unstrap them and leave them sitting in their chairs." Yazov turned to leave the library.

"Where are you going?"

"To check on the one upstairs and to get the others. Don't worry, Dominguez, we won't leave you here."

On the hillside, Nguyen looked up from his portable monitor. "They are leaving."

From habit, Thach looked at his watch. Almost eight o'clock. The Russians were cutting it close.

Sims stopped the car at the top of the hill.

"Son of a bitch," Houghton muttered in awe. Before them was the other hill, the one dominated by J. J. Barrineau's plantation house. The wind beat the smoke close to the earth, and the fire had already brought down the roof. Two yellow pumper trucks, their feed hoses sucking water from a nearby pond, played streams on the walls. The fire paid no attention, and went about finishing off the rest of the house.

They're all dead, Sims knew with certainty, hypnotized by the scene before him. He remembered Arthur Barrineau's anguished face in the car and the man's lonely walk to his empty house. Sims felt a cold darkness inside his chest. He eased the car forward, toward the sparkling light show of the red and blue strobes of the ambulances, fire trucks, and sheriff's cars.

Some two hundred yards from the burning house, a fluttering yellow and black police tape stretched across the road. Sims stopped the car short of the tape, and he and Houghton got out. Seeing them, a young deputy separated himself from a knot of firemen and ambulance attendants and walked over. The deputy studied Sims's Media Research credentials, then Sims and Houghton. Muttering a "Wait here," he walked back to the cluster of men. Something inside the house flared and flames licked out two side windows. There was a murmur of exclamation from the cluster of men watching and the fire hoses swung slowly to the area. Sims couldn't see that the hoses were doing any good.

Sims saw the deputy pointing them out to a shorter, heavier man, also in uniform. The man made his way over to them with the hip-rolling walk of men used to wearing heavy pistol belts. There was another squinting scrutiny of identification and studying of Sims and Houghton. He handed the press credentials back. Sims read the name Collins on the sheriff's shiny metal name tag.

Collins said nothing and stood, hands on hips, waiting. He looked first at Houghton, then at Sims.

Sims nodded and put on an ingratiating smile. "Can you tell us what happened?"

Collins raised his jaw a fraction. "If you'n tell me why you give a shit."

From the corner of his eye, Sims saw Houghton shift uneasily. "We've been talking with an Atlanta attorney," Sims said evenly, taking care to speak slowly. "We came here to meet him to do a story."

Collins pursed his lips considering that. "To do a story." It came as a derisive echo—real men didn't do stories. "He got a name, this Atlanta lawyer?" He took a small wire-bound notebook from his breast pocket. His ballpoint pen had a Colonel Sanders logo.

"Arthur Barrineau." Sims saw the sheriff's pen hesitate, and so he spelled the name. Anticipating Collins, he handed over a Media Research business card. "Any questions come up later, give me a call."

Collins examined the card, turning it over, then tucked it in the notebook. "Nine-one-one call came about an hour ago." He consulted his notebook. "Eight-fifteen."

"Any idea," Houghton asked, "what caused it?"

Collins looked meaningfully at Houghton, then at Sims. "*I* don't." He waited expectantly, rocking back and forth slightly on the balls of his feet.

Sims said nothing. Collins was putting on the intimidation act. He knew it and he knew Sims knew it, but it was something you just did.

Collins waited another second or two, then turned and stumped off toward the house and the emergency vehicles. Without looking back, he waved Sims and Houghton to join him. "Come on. If you want to see what's left."

Collins led them to the lee side of an ambulance. On the ground were two folding gurneys, each covered with a coarse green sheet. Sims caught a trace of the putrefying sweetness of burned flesh. You don't want to see this, he told himself, but he stood there as Collins bent down and took a corner of the sheet on the nearest gurney. The sheet seemed to lift in slow motion.

A blackened claw of a hand was raised, as if to ward off the flames. There was the oddly clean glint of gold. This had been Arthur Barrineau, Sims told himself, the widower who still wore his wedding band. The fire had burned away Arthur's lips. The seared jaw muscles had drawn the mouth open, freezing a scream on the charred noseless face. Sims felt his mouth go suddenly wet and his stomach begin contracting, and he threw his shoulders back and sucked desperately at the cold air.

The sheriff dropped the sheet. He gestured toward the other gurney. "Looks like another man." His rasping voice was subdued. "We'll have them ID'd today. Afternoon, maybe."

A gust of wind wrapped them in a streamer of gritty black smoke. There was the soapy smell of wet ashes. Sims rubbed his stinging eyes. "Two?"

Collins nodded, then, turning away from the gurneys, spit on the ground. "Just these. On the first floor. Firemen got them out before the roof came in. Couldn't get upstairs." He hitched his pants and pistol belt up onto his belly and made a minute adjustment to his wide-brimmed hat. "Well, if there's nothing else, I'll be over there" —he jerked his head toward his car—"tending to some paperwork." When Sims and Houghton said nothing, he pursed his lips again in thought, hesitated, then turned on his heel and left.

"J. J. must've been in his room," Sims heard Houghton say as both of them watched Collins walk away.

"He probably wasn't much use to them." Sims stared into the fire and the house.

"You've got to figure that they got everything Arthur had: what he heard and all."

Houghton saw that Sims wasn't listening. He followed Sims's gaze. The two pumper trucks were still playing their arches of dirty water on the house. Without warning, a section of the second floor wall crumbled, the falling bricks sending up a huge swirl of sparks and ashes.

Sims imagined lying helpless in the bed in the dark room. First feeling the heat, then hearing the roar of the fire, and finally seeing the wood-paneled walls burst into flame. Waiting for hell to come get you. He put his bare hand out and clutched at the cold metal of the ambulance for reassurance. Had J. J. known what was happening—there at the last? And had he seen anything in the flames?

Near the small town of Braswell, Sims pulled into a Texaco station. Two open lubrication bays adjoined a small office housing a Coke machine, racks of wormy peanut butter crackers, and a kerosene heater that cooked away on the verge of exploding.

"Something the matter?" Houghton asked.

"Something I thought of," Sims said, a brittle edge in his voice. He paid the attendant five dollars for use of the lube rack, saying he wanted to check out a noise. The attendant showed Sims the hydraulic controls, then shuffled back to the stifling office to smoke more cigarettes and watch the morning cartoon show.

Beneath the car, Sims systematically worked from front toward the rear, running his hands into every recess in the car's underbody.

He found it under the chassis crossmember behind the rear bumper. His fingers explored it, an object about the size of a deck of cards. He lifted and the magnets gave way with a sticky reluctance.

"Homing device," Houghton said, looking at the black matte box.

Sims caught himself before he could hurl the box against the grease-stained concrete floor. That's why there'd been no one behind them; no headlights on the dark back roads to J. J.'s home. It wasn't necessary. This fucking black box just beeped every few seconds. A Kosmos satellite picked it up, downlinked it to someplace like Semipalitinsk, where they ran it through the computers. And a few minutes later in Moscow—and Atlanta—there it was: J. J.'s plantation, pinpointed down to the nearest ten meters.

Sims looked at the black box, and it seemed to mock him. They had set up at J. J.'s, Sims guessed, then gone back into Atlanta and brought Arthur out. He remembered Arthur Barrineau's clawlike hand with the wedding band.

"Shit," Sims said to himself in angry self-recrimination. He wrapped the homing device in a handkerchief and stuffed it in his overcoat pocket.

Houghton's hand was on his shoulder. "I didn't think of it either."

Sims lowered the lube rack. Through the thin partition to the office, he heard the prattle of the television cartoon show. The attendant was lighting another cigarette and drinking another Coke.

Walking outside, Sims found a pay phone in one of those open-cabinet affairs on the wall by the rest rooms. He bent forward, sheltering himself from the sleet and hiding the scrambler he connected to the phone. Houghton, filling the car at a self-serve pump, covered Sims's back, one hand on the hose, the other wrapped around the Browning in his coat pocket.

Riddle answered on the first ring.

Uneasy in spite of the scrambler, Sims didn't identify himself. "The brothers are dead. We think our old friends did it. Can you check previous associations?" Sims felt the silence at the other end of the line and imagined Riddle's grave hazel eyes measuring him.

215

"I shall get on it," Riddle replied, his voice flat over the scrambler. "You should know that the friend you recently made in Prague has died."

"Causes?"

"They say natural."

"They *say?*"

"They say." The disbelief was evident in Riddle's voice.

There was another silence, this one had an expectant quality to it, like the silence after Riddle had moved a piece on the chessboard.

"They're after us, Riddle."

The silence continued for a beat, then Riddle's voice came, the tone of cool appraisal unsuccessfully covering his apprehension. "Take care, young man."

There was the metal sound of Houghton jamming the gas hose back into the pump receptacle. He walked over to Houghton, the fear settling around him in layers as the implications of Riddle's message took hold. He stood for a moment, feeling the cold cut through him. "Riddle says Broz's dead. He thinks they're after us, too."

Houghton rubbed his hands against the cold, then pulled on his gloves, all the while squinting at Sims. "Surprise you?"

"No," Sims admitted. If they had been bagged along with Arthur, he and Houghton would have been lying under those sheets back there. What did surprise him, however, was how exposed it made him feel. The danger wasn't new. But in the Agency, he'd had protection. No matter how bad it got between CIA and the KGB, the cardinal rule was no personal vendettas. You, as an individual, were as faceless to them as they were to you.

Now someone was looking for *him.* He was no longer Agency. But he would always be Bradford Sims, and that was who they were after.

He took off his heavy coat, threw it in the backseat, and got behind the wheel. He and Houghton reached quick agreement. To avoid airport surveillance, they would drive the rental car back to Washington. As they headed north, Sims got a chilling feeling that he would soon learn how Ray had felt on the run after Memphis.

In Moscow several hours later, Sergei Okolovich sat motionless at his desk, listening to Yazov's report over a scrambler. His knuckles whitened around the telephone as Yazov detailed Barrineau's interrogation. Yazov took his time with the bad news, each revelation worse than the preceding, an excruciating water torture. The money. The Cayman Islands. Okolovich wanted to rip the telephone from his desk and hurl it against the wall. Finally, Yazov finished. Okolovich hesitated for a moment, attempting to calm himself. He only partially succeeded.

"Listen, Yazov," he grated, "you stop this. You and your friends do whatever you must, but stop it."

He heard Yazov begin an excuse.

"Yazov," he interrupted menacingly, "you or the nigger." Okolovich slammed the phone down. It was only then that he ripped the instrument from his desk and hurled it against the wall.

19

The CNN weather report that morning had been accurate. All day, Sims and Houghton ran into increasingly heavy snow as a major storm blew down from Canada. By midnight, they were just south of Richmond on Interstate 95. Sims, driving, was concentrating on fighting fatigue and the dull ache in his left arm.

North of Richmond, the road signs picked up on the mileage to Washington. The capital had always meant sanctuary, the shelter of familiar people and places. Now it was as dangerous as precoup Moscow. There'd be no going back to his apartment, to the Occidental for a beer. At a truck stop, Sims shaved his mustache and bought a cheap pair of Terminator dark glasses. At 2:00 A.M., they paid cash for rooms in an Econo-Lodge in the Ballston section of Arlington, several miles west of Washington. The next morning, they ate at a crowded diner on Columbia Pike. Afterward, Sims used the scrambler in an outside phone booth and called one of the trouble numbers Alberich had given him.

Sims listened to a stuttering of relays, then Alberich answered. His voice was curiously flat.

"You OK?" Sims asked.

"Keep it short. Somebody's got me covered. Riddle too."

"Riddle tell you about Atlanta?"

"Yes."

He was suddenly worried that the ledgers and the tape had disappeared. "And the stuff arrived?"

"Yeah. But I need some help. King is on the tape. But there's a

218

voice I don't recognize—maybe somebody near King. And the conversations are somewhat cryptic—" Alberich let his problem hang in midair.

Sims thought for a moment and came up with an answer. "Is there someplace you and Riddle can meet us today?" Sims looked at his watch. It was just after eight. "Around four this afternoon?"

"Call me on another number." The line went dead. Ten minutes later, Sims called one of Alberich's alternate numbers from another pay phone. Alberich described the meeting place. From yet another phone, Sims called his uncle in Sandston. Harris answered on the first ring.

An hour later at National Airport, Sims let Houghton out at the Metro stop. Then, after making his way through the morning traffic, he dropped the car off at Hertz, and caught a cab into Alexandria. There, he rented another car, this time from Avis. At the same time, Houghton was signing a contract for his car from yet another agency in Rockville, Maryland.

Sims called Rollo Moss's doctor and in a cramped office in Anacostia had the stitches removed from his arm. From there he drove to the beltway and to the gargantuan mall at Tyson's Corner, had lunch at a fast-food creperie, then bought a ticket at the multiplex cinema and sat through Warren Beatty working off his hostilities in a gangster movie.

The movie over, Sims strolled through the mall, and at 3:15 he entered the B. Dalton bookstore, browsed among the new releases, then made his way back to the biographies. Calvin Harris, huge in his shooting jacket, looked up from an open book. His smile became an uncertain frown.

"You look different," Harris said, unable to put his finger on it.

Sims touched his upper lip. "Shaved it off. You're parked outside?" Getting a nod from Harris, he motioned toward the front of the store. "We'll take my car. I'll drop you back here when we're through."

"Through with what, Bradford?" Harris closed the book and put it back on the shelf.

In the car, Harris turned to Sims. "Rollo Moss called me when you were hurt. It's something to do with Martin, isn't it?"

Sims nodded. He started the car and, once on the beltway, headed south toward I-95. As he drove, he took his uncle through the events in Prague, Toronto, and Atlanta, ending with J. J. Barrineau's confession and subsequent death.

"Barrineau belonged to something called the Southern States Council. You know about it?"

"There were so many of them." Harris worked at remembering. "Yes, I recollect talk about it. Birmingham?" He shook his head. "No, it was St. Louis, wasn't it?"

Sims nodded. "Did you have anyone who kept track of the white hate groups?"

"You mean, like an intelligence officer?" Harris asked with a trace of gentle irony. "No. Not really. When we learned about a new group, we'd report it to the Justice Department, but that was all. You've got to remember"—he seemed still amazed to have survived the times—"we didn't have any trouble finding out who our enemies were."

"There were some you overlooked. There was a Russian connection," Sims said, taking his eyes off the road to watch for his uncle's reaction. "We think the KGB was helping the whites go after King."

Shoulders slumping as if under a heavy weight, Harris winced.

"It gets worse. At the same time, the Russians were feeding money to somebody near King."

"To do what?"

"It was enough that somebody took the money. The Russians did it so Hoover could see Russian money going to—"

"To us." The enormity of it struck Harris. "Oh my God." He looked questioningly at Sims. "How do you know this?"

"Three weeks ago in Prague, from the man who was head of Czech intelligence." Sims felt remorse at the stricken look on his uncle's face. He handed over a clipping. "It was a KGB standard, setting up a money trail. A lot of people were on Moscow's sucker list."

Revelations from the Communist Files

U.S. Party Said Funded by Kremlin

By Michael Dobbs
Washington Post Foreign Service

MOSCOW—Couriers for the Soviet KGB intelligence service delivered suitcases packed with dollar bills to U.S. Communist Party leader Gus Hall over a period of more than three decades, according to a Russian prosecutor who said signed receipts are now in the possession of Russian investigators.

. . . Russian deputy prosecutor-general Yevgeny Lisov said that "The Politburo would instruct the KGB to arrange the transfers. They were usually delivered in cash through the diplomatic pouch. A KGB agent under diplomatic cover would then hand the money to the local [U.S.] party leader, who would sign a receipt. We found receipts signed by Hall in the party archives."

Documents revealing clandestine Kremlin funding of dozens of left-wing political parties around the world are contained in the mountain of evidence collected by Soviet prosecutors examining the failed summer coup. A separate inquiry is now under way into the financing operation which was approved and supervised at the highest levels of the Soviet Communist Party.

Harris looked up defiantly. "Martin *did not know*," he said, each word metered with conviction. "Because if he had learned of it, he *never* would have allowed it." Harris shook his head. "Even in the hardest times, he wouldn't have taken their money. He knew what the Russians were like."

"There *were* Communists near King," Sims said simply.

"We knew who they were. If they wanted to help—"

"They used you," Sims interrupted, remembering Prague and Broz and how the Czech had described the operation of the Afro-Asian Solidarity Committee. "If you couldn't see it then, how about now?"

Harris sighed. "Look," he said patiently, "the Communists—they were losers then and now. Now they've finally lost. Only a nation of fools would want to be like the Russians. Everybody knows that."

"Not everybody knew it then, uncle," Sims countered quietly. Minutes later, Sims turned off I-95 at the Fort Belvoir-Newington exit. He spotted the tank farm in Alberich's instructions, then the road off to the right leading into a small industrial park. Rows of drab one-story prefab buildings with garage-door fronts housed a catchall of start-up businesses from computer repair to furniture refinishing and carpet sales.

Sims found Hunting Tree Lane, a barren asphalt strip between the second and third rows of buildings. He turned left and pulled up in front of unit thirty-seven. There was another rental car, probably Houghton's, parked two doors down.

Riddle answered the door. His surprise was fleeting and instantly covered by a welcoming smile. "You are Calvin Harris," he said, extending a hand. "I am—"

"You are Riddle," Harris finished. The good chemistry was instant.

Harris took Riddle's hand in both of his, and as he did so, it occurred to Sims that the two men, though vastly different, were also in many ways alike.

The room was simply a large box: raw concrete floors and walls lighted by fluorescent lamps suspended from industrial ceiling beams. The warm air smelled of the scorched metal of electric heating. Alberich had driven his van in through the overhead garage door and was supervising Houghton, who was setting up a large reel-to-reel Teac tape deck.

Sims made brief introductions, then he and Harris took seats with Riddle around an unfinished wood table. Uncorking a large red thermos, he poured three Styrofoam cups of coffee. Soon, Alberich and Houghton were finished with the tape deck.

"We've made some progress on the activities and ledgers of the Southern States Council," Riddle announced. "But first, the tape."

Sims nodded to his uncle. "We need to know what we're listening to."

"There're three recordings on this reel," Alberich began. "The first is a telephone tap. It's between somebody named David and Dr. King." Alberich pushed a button on the console at his right shoulder. The large reels jerked, took up the slack in the tape, and the first sound that came through the speakers was a telephone in midring. It rang twice more before a deep resonant voice filled the small room.

This's David, Martin. You got to come down here.

Sims made a cut motion and Alberich stopped the reels. Riddle looked questioningly at Harris.

"Ralph *David* Abernathy," Harris explained. "King always used Abernathy's middle name." Riddle nodded and Alberich started the tape deck again.

Come on, David. Can't you talk to them? Won't they listen to you?

Martin, this's going to be on television. The networks are lined up waiting for you. These people want you, not me.

Sims quickly lost the sensation of eavesdropping and became absorbed in the humanity of the conversation. Here was King, not giving the grand speeches, but talking with an old and trusted friend, working out the trivia of logistics that history ignores in its pursuit of the great events.

OK, I'll come.

Sims saw his uncle's eyes widening in comprehension.

Martin, don't you fool me, now. You'll come?

David, did I ever tell you I'd do something and then not come through?

When will you be here?

As soon as the limousine can get me there.

The tape deck was silent except for the whisper of the turning reels. Alberich pushed a pause button and all eyes turned to Harris. "It was Wednesday, April 3. We were in Memphis," he said. The memory had been brought back to life. Once-faded colors were now fresh again. "Martin was supporting the city sanitation workers' strike. We had had a disastrous march there just days before. That afternoon, the U.S. district court had issued an injunction against another march. Martin was determined to challenge it, but it was a depressing development. It got worse as the day wore on. He was supposed to address a rally at the Mason Temple. But there was a huge storm. He was afraid there would be only a small crowd, that his enemies would say he was losing support. So Abernathy went to the temple instead."

"And you?" Riddle asked softly, as if not wanting to intrude.

"I stayed with Martin at the motel. It was just the two of us. Jesse Jackson, Don Stanley, Andy Young—they all went with Abernathy." Harris slipped back in time again. "They got to the temple and there were thousands of people. And all the network television cameras. They didn't want to hear anybody but Martin. So David—Abernathy —he called Martin." Harris gestured toward the tape deck. "And there was that."

"You're certain?" Houghton asked.

Harris nodded. "It was about eight-thirty. I was in the room with Martin at the time." He took a deep breath. Sims could see that it was clearly hard going for him. "When Martin said those words, I was there."

"That puts this next recording in context," Alberich said. "It's the speech itself." Harris nodded and Alberich started the tape deck.

Transfixed, the five men listened to King, with thunder and heavy rain in the background, speaking to the multitudes in the temple. King told the world why he had come to Memphis, why he was thankful to have lived to see the advance of civil rights, why he was grateful to have been able to tell America of his dream. Sims's throat caught as King's voice, with voices from the audience in the background, picked up the heartbeat cadence that closed his last speech.

Now, it doesn't matter.

(Go ahead! Go ahead!)

It really doesn't matter what happens now. We've got some difficult days ahead.

(Yeah! oh yes!)

But it really doesn't matter with me, now.

(Oh yes!)

I've been to the mountaintop!

[Cries and applause]

Like anybody, I would like to live a long life. Longevity has its place. But I'm not concerned about that now. I just want to do God's will. And He's allowed me to go up to the mountain.

(Go ahead!)

And I've looked over.

(Yes, doctor!)

And I've seen the Promised Land!

(Yes, sir, go ahead!)

And I may not get there with you.

(Yes, sir, go ahead!)

But I want you to know tonight that we as a people will get to the Promised Land.

([Applause, cries] Go ahead, GO AHEAD!)

So I'm happy tonight. I'm not worried about anything. I'm not fearing any man. Mine eyes have seen the glory of the coming of the Lord!

[Cries, applause]

By now, Sims was there in Memphis, feeling a thundering tide of raw emotion. King reached out to him and carried him to the mountaintop and spread before him his vision of America:

We will be able to achieve this new day, when
all of God's children
—black men and white men,
> *Jews and Gentiles,*
>> *Protestants and Catholics—*
will be able to join hands and sing with the Negroes
in the spiritual of old,
"Free at last! Free at last! Thank God almighty
we are free at last!"

The room was frozen in the silence that blankets a forest after the felling of a giant tree. Shaking himself as he returned from Memphis, Sims slowly registered the expression of loss etched on Houghton's face.

Houghton exchanged a private look with Sims. Amen, he mouthed silently. Harris was staring at the tape deck, tears streaming down his strong face.

Alberich shifted his chair slightly, the electric whine of its servomotors breaking King's spell. "The third recording is like the first—a telephone tap."

The tape deck was silent, its large reels turning, then a hissing second of static, then hoarse muffled voices.

Yes?

All day tomorrow in the motel.

All day?

They have meetings scheduled after lunch.

In 306?

No. Downstairs conference room.

So all day in the motel.

He's going out to dinner.

Where?

Reverend Kyles's house. They're leaving here at six.

How's he going?

Driver's a man named Jones. Solomon Jones. Borrowed limousine from funeral home.

They're leaving at six?

I told you that! I've got to go.

"Again," Harris ordered, his voice surprisingly harsh, carrying with it an undertone of hidden wrath. And again the voices, then silence. Harris finally spoke.

"We got back from the temple. Must have been eleven, eleven-thirty or so." Harris was tentative, working at putting that night together again. "It was a joyous time. Martin had broken his earlier despair. We didn't have the next day's schedule all worked out until—maybe just after midnight."

"That call was probably made that night," Sims said. "Who would have known those details then?"

"Judas," Harris said in his Judgment Day voice. Then he shook his head. "Bradford, Bradford," he exclaimed, bedeviled and frustrated, "I don't *know!* It was so *long* ago!" He buried his head in both hands, resting his elbows on the table. "It's there, then it's gone before I can put a hand on it."

"Sounds like they were trying to hide their voices," Houghton suggested.

Alberich touched a button and the tape began to rewind. "Can't hide from the voiceprint, though."

"You can make an ID from that?" Sims asked.

"We could if I had a comparison on file."

"And you don't," guessed Riddle.

"And if they aren't in our files . . ." Alberich shrugged.

Riddle stretched his arms and clasped his hands behind his head, leaning back in his chair. "Which brings us to forensic analysis."

"First, the taps themselves," Alberich began, referring briefly to his notes on his wheelchair's small computer screen. "They were induction taps." Seeing Harris's puzzled expression, he explained: "Induction means never having to connect physically to the telephone lines. You just slap the pickup device near a phone, switchboard, or cabling. Anyway, most of the induction taps they had in the sixties picked up harmonics—reflections—from nearby alternating current sources—power lines, that kind of thing. These taps didn't. They were state of the art for 1968.

"Then, there's the tape itself. It's a professional quality quarter-inch, ferrous oxide acetate tape, Scotch brand, catalog number one ninety. 3M dropped it from the inventory in 1972.

"This tape is the original. It doesn't have any of the physical distortion and stretching that is characteristic of duplicate tapes. I can get a lot more off the tape, but the most important thing is that the recorder was a Nagra 4.2. It's a beautiful instrument, even for 1968. Very precise and compact. Voice activated, it can record for twelve hours on its internal batteries. Built by Kudelski SA, Lausanne, Switzerland."

Harris was intrigued. "You got *that* from listening to the tape?"

"Flutter analysis," Alberich said, enjoying an audience. "Even the best tape recorders can't record all tones accurately. Tonal distortion results because any mechanically rotating part in the recorder that's slightly off center will cause—"

"Flutter," Harris guessed.

Alberich smiled. "The amount of flutter is proportional to the diameter of the rotating part and the distance the rotating part is off center. In this case, the rotating part is the tape drive motor. Different recorders use different drive motors. Each motor has a signature—a fingerprint, if you will."

"So this's a Nagra." Houghton shrugged. "So?"

"So," Alberich said with precision, "the Nagra 4.2 is an expensive, hand-built machine, the Rolls-Royce of recorders. It came on the market in mid-1967. For 1967 and 1968, they sold a total of only forty-three in the U.S. Of those, just seven were retail sales." Alberich paused, as if to enjoy his bombshell. "The FBI bought the remaining thirty-six."

"No surprise," Harris rumbled heatedly. "They were bugging us, tapping our phones—the *bastards!*"

In the silence following Harris's outburst, Sims got up, walked to the tape deck, and picked up the square box that the tape had come in. He looked at it for a moment, turning it in his hands.

"I know your question," Riddle said. Sims raised his eyes. "If the FBI did that"—Riddle pointed toward the box in Sims's hand—"then how did J. J. Barrineau get it?"

"I don't see what difference it makes," Houghton cut in. "We pretty much have these bastards cold. The KGB was funding Barrineau's white-sheet outfit and it let a contract to Ray to kill King."

"Perhaps we should go public with it, then," Riddle suggested.

Sims detected a test. He shook his head.

"Why not?"

"There're still too many unanswered questions."

"There will always be questions. Don't you think you have enough to go to the *Post* or the *Times?*"

Houghton joined in. "It's circumstantial. The only place it'd get printed would be in one of those supermarket rags. Next to an article about UFO aliens helping Winston Churchill win the war. It'd last all of a weekend."

"I agree." Riddle smiled. "Now what?"

"The Southern States Council. We must connect them to Raoul, Ray, and the KGB." Sims was obviously set to battle on. Houghton nodded.

"I believe I hear my cue," Riddle announced in a Charles Laughton voice. He left his chair and walked to the tape deck, fishing in his coat pockets with both hands. Turning to face the table, he brought out a packet of blue index cards, then found a pair of reading glasses that he propped over the end of his nose.

"The ledgers of the Southern States Council are a gold mine," he noted. "And like a mine, we are still working them." He peered at Sims over the top of his glasses. "J. J. Barrineau, Mr. Sims, was accurate, even in his final dementia. The claim of a payment from the Cayman Islands Refractories is correct. That was ten thousand dollars per month, a princely sum for the KGB. This was by no means the SSC's only income. We are still tracing the other sources."

Riddle slid a new card to the top of the deck. "Among the regular disbursements were monthly payments to the Ontario Democracy Project. These amounted to several thousand dollars, beginning in March 1966. I suspect that date will coincide with the late Leroy Rose's arrival in Toronto."

Sims noticed his uncle had the rapt expression of discovery.

In his schoolmaster fashion, Riddle raised his voice slightly to recapture Sims's attention. "I beg your indulgence for what may seem to be a digression.

"In 1964, after the killing of three civil rights workers in Mississippi, the FBI declared war on what they called white hate groups.

"Following long-established procedures, the Bureau relied heavily on local authorities. In Missouri, this was the Missouri State Police 'Red Squad,' formed in 1956 by a secret act of the Missouri legislature.

"The Red Squad was an undercover organization. Its original purpose was to search out Communists. Like any bureaucracy with generous funding, the Red Squad grew. Soon it had more investigators than Missouri had Communists. And so it eagerly lent its talents to the FBI, if only to justify its appropriations. The Red Squad also sent report copies to Langley because of possible foreign involvement.

"The St. Louis Red Squad was meticulous. Langley received thousands of pages on the Klan, the Minutemen, the Birchers, the American Nazi Party—apparently any meeting of two or more bigots anywhere in Missouri—" Riddle stopped abruptly, a genial storyteller, his eyes alight with anticipation. He waited a beat. Sims found himself holding his breath. "But nothing on the Southern States Council."

"Shit!" It was a quiet exclamation, and Houghton passed an apologetic look toward Harris, then turned his astonishment to Riddle and Sims. "The SSC's got a cash flow of hundreds of thousands of dollars. It's running a front in Canada. It's putting out contracts on people. And a long-established undercover police outfit that's penetrated the Klan doesn't say crap about it?"

"The hound that didn't bark," said Alberich.

"Well?" Sims gave Houghton a questioning look.

Houghton looked back for a moment or two. "The KGB got to them?" he suggested.

Riddle walked to Sims and made him a present of one of the blue index cards.

"Sam Niles?" Sims read from the card.

"Head of the Red Squad until the governor disbanded it in 1973. His current address and telephone number are on the back. He's still alive."

Sims turned the card over to the St. Louis address and phone number, then passed the card to Houghton.

It was dark as Sims drove his uncle back to the mall to pick up his car. Coming toward them, the headlights of an endless convoy of commuters escaping Washington burned Sims's eyes and fed his weariness.

Sims and Harris were quiet for a long time, lost in their thoughts.

Finally, Harris shifted in his seat and made a tentative clearing noise in his throat.

"That's the kind of work you did for the CIA?"

Sims was immediately on the defensive. "Something like that."

Harris was silent for a moment. "Except getting shot at, I think it would be interesting."

Sims found this surprisingly reassuring. "That tape bothered you?"

Harris nodded, a troubled look on his face. "Some of what I thought was . . . wasn't. I thought *I* was in the real world. That tape made me realize I was only an actor on a stage. The real action was going on behind the sets. I didn't have a clue about that."

"You were real. King, too."

Yet another silence, then, sadly: "He came alive again in there. I realized how much I had papered over what happened in Memphis. That tape took me back, reminded me just what we lost. It was Martin and a lot more." Harris sighed. "But that's my worry. How about you? You having second thoughts about this?"

"Every day." Sims found Harris's battered Ford in the emptying mall parking lot. "Russia's falling apart. If we pin this on them, it won't help. Bad timing."

Harris opened the door, got out, and came around to Sims's side. He ducked down toward the window. "Don't you bother about timing. We used to get that everywhere we went. 'Wait,' they'd tell us. 'Not just now,' they'd say." Harris stood up and pointed a finger at Sims. "You keep on as long as you think you're right, Bradford. And remember: there's never a convenient time for the truth."

20

U.S. 50 took Sims and Houghton as far as Clarksburg, West Virginia. There they swung south through Charleston, then Huntington, spending the night in a motel outside Lexington, Kentucky. The next morning, with Houghton at the wheel, Sims reviewed the file Riddle had compiled on Sam Niles.

In all likelihood, his fellow cops admired Sam Niles's equanimity even as it mystified them. In 1973, Missouri's new governor, an ACLU liberal, disbanded Sam's Red Squad and, for good measure, threw Sam off the force as well. The common thinking was that the governor had just fucked up. After all, Sam had established a hotshot reputation for skilled investigation against the backdrop of the state's dismal record of inept police work. Head of the Red Squad for all of its seventeen years, Sam had built one of the nation's best police undercover operations, one adept at deception operations, surreptitious entry, exotic surveillance techniques, and agent recruitment, training, and management. Unusual skills for a police unit in the American Midwest, but then, pursuing Communists was unlike tracking down S&L embezzlers, ax murderers, and serial rapists.

Everyone was certain that if Sam had exerted a little squeeze, a place would have been found for him. But Sam cheerfully accepted the imitation parchment scroll of appreciation and settled down in St. Louis to make his fortune.

The fact is, Sam Niles secretly welcomed the end of the Red Squad. Shortly after he had gotten his crew into shape, it had occurred to him that its talents could find a richer market outside the chaffing restrictions imposed by limp-dicked liberal governors.

After a two-month hunting vacation in Alaska, Niles returned to St. Louis and founded Pyramid Protective Services. His first employees were former Red Squad guys. As Pyramid grew, the hiring pattern continued to favor former cops from the highway patrol and the big city departments of St. Louis and Kansas City. Pyramid's ex-cops kept their fraternity status—and access—even after turning in their badges. Their buddies and ex-partners still on active duty came to appreciate Pyramid. It was an alternative employer, a haven against the day you had to retire and sit around the house with the old lady. It paid to stay close to Sam Niles, to help him along from time to time with small favors.

On Pyramid's logo, the Great Pyramid stood on one bank of a river—the Nile? Sims wondered—while the Sphinx sat on the other. It was bad geography, but accurate symbolism, for Pyramid worked both sides of the law.

From the start, Niles had recognized the commercial and illegal potential of the Red Squad. Smokestack industries were out, electronics were in. The competitive edge in electronics went to the company that could get to the leading edge of technology first. Getting there first, Sam's logic ran, depended on keeping their research secret from their rivals. The Midwest's biggest high-tech companies reasoned the same way and flocked to Pyramid for the latest in industrial security.

On the other hand, Sam reasoned, companies back in the pack appreciated the value of information as much as the more complacent big boys. Moreover, some of the little guys were desperate. For them, survival, not just bonuses, depended on clawing out an advantage, no matter how thin, no matter how illegal. And so Sam Niles became the man to go to. Sam described that kind of work as "discreet investigations." The law, however, wasn't so kind, calling it industrial espionage.

Sam Niles also prospered from spin-offs from Pyramid's main endeavors. His files bulged with personal information on businessmen, politicians, media personalities, sports figures, and just about anyone else whose access or bank accounts were worth tapping. And occasionally, even America's major law enforcement agencies needed help in areas declared off-limits by the courts. So while they suspected Pyramid of working on the other side of the line, they found Pyramid's pro bono work valuable enough that they filed such suspicions in the bottoms of neglected desk drawers.

Sims closed the file and sat for a long time staring at the passing scenery. "I can't imagine Niles is just going to sit there and open up to us."

Houghton flexed one arm, then the other, to shake off the stiffness from driving. "You've got to ask nicely first. Hell, he might even say yes."

"Bet?"

"No," Houghton said, working on his arms some more.

They got to St. Louis just after four in the afternoon and checked into a Days Inn near the towering Gateway Arch and within walking distance of Sam Niles's Pyramid offices on Olive Street. The following morning, Sims and Houghton pushed through etched-glass revolving doors and found themselves in the immense rose marble lobby of an office building that couldn't have been more than a year old.

Sims marched toward a receptionist behind a marble counter while Houghton lagged behind, studying a building directory. The receptionist, a heavyset woman in a tailored and too-tight blue suit, controlled entry to the elevators to her rear. At her side, a uniformed security officer worked through a communications test, punching buttons and observing lights on a control panel that looked to Sims like something from a space shuttle.

Sims passed the woman one of his business cards. She gave him a suspicious look and carefully ran a pencil down a printout until she came to the Media Research Associates appointment. Frowning, as if disappointed that she had found it, she touched a hidden button and buzzed him and Houghton through the gate to her right. The elevator was all plush carpeting and heavy bronze. Sims pressed a button for the thirtieth floor, a muted chime sounded, and the car began a smooth, surging ascent.

"Pyramid's got the top two floors," Houghton reported in a low voice. "Pretty classy."

Sims looked around the car. There were also metal detectors in the receptionist's gate to the elevators, he thought, but didn't want to say it here.

The elevator opened to another reception area of soft buff, trimmed with Chinese blue crown moldings and chair rails. Another overstuffed receptionist, a gentler twin of the one in the lobby, sat behind an antique partner's desk. Sims gave up another business card, and the receptionist waved them to a waiting area of Chippendale reproduction chairs and sofa. A side table by Sims's chair held the most recent issues of *Architectural Digest,* and he saw Houghton pick up and thumb though a blue-jacketed *Foreign Affairs Quarterly*. Through the double glass doors behind the receptionist, Sims could see down a long carpeted hallway, lit by brass hall lanterns.

As Sims and Houghton waited to see Sam Niles, Special Agent Loren McAlister, parked in a gray Pontiac Grand Prix across Olive Street from Niles's building, radioed his report to Tim Nicholas. Nicholas was manning the surveillance center set up in two adjoining rooms of St. Louis's downtown Hyatt. He passed McAlister's terse message on to John Delaney in Washington. The FBI director listened, then hung up without so much as a well done or thank you. Faintly disappointed, Nicholas stood for a moment looking at the dead phone in his hand. He had expected some sign of praise, a little excitement at his having successfully tracked their quarry. After all, he had rushed out here to set up the stakeouts, and Sims had walked into one of them within the first twenty-four hours. That might not be a record, but it was a damned good average.

Halfway through the second *Architectural Digest*, the receptionist signaled, pointing through the glass doors. Sam Niles's office was at the end of the long corridor.

It was, Sims concluded, a typical executive suite. As he and Houghton made their way soundlessly down the hall, polished brass nameplates announced the offices of vice presidents of administration, operations, finance, and information systems.

At Pyramid's founder's door, the nameplate simply said NILES. Through the door, they found themselves in a small tastefully furnished secretarial office. A tall immaculately dressed silver-haired woman waited, her hand on the knob to an interior door. With a smiling "He's waiting," she opened the door, gesturing Sims and Houghton through.

Sims involuntarily caught his breath as he recoiled to keep from falling. For a second, he thought he was on an outside ledge of the building, four hundred feet above the cold streets below. Through a nearly invisible glass wall immediately in front of him, stretched a vast panorama of the Mississippi, framed by the colossal silver span of the Gateway Arch.

"Helluva view, ain't it?"

Still transfixed, Sims slowly turned toward the voice. The glass wall continued to his left, the narrow corridor in which he stood opening up into a huge office. The office was divided in half, Niles's portion

234

being elevated six inches or so over the guest area occupied by a sofa and upholstered chairs. Behind a massive dark wooden desk Niles himself sat in pouting majesty like some huge toad, all bald head and heavy belly. Sims smelled an undertrace of cigar smoke in the synthetic filtered air. Behind Niles, a glass interior wall looked out on a computer room on the floor below. The room stretched out of sight, and Sims guessed it took up much of the twenty-ninth floor.

Niles waved a hand toward the arch and the Mississippi. "Had a time with that fucking glass. Stuff would blow out all of a sudden. First time, hit some asshole waitin' for a cab." Niles sat back and looked at the view with a small smile of mastery. "Got it fixed, though."

"What about the guy waiting for the cab?" Sims asked.

Niles looked puzzled for a moment. "Killed him." Niles shrugged dismissively. "But insurance took care of it." He waved Sims and Houghton to the chairs in front of and below the massive desk. Selecting a cigar from a carved ivory humidor, he clipped the end and thrust the entire cigar into his mouth. He then discharged it slowly through his thick, liver-colored lips. Rolling it in his fingers, he rubbed a string of saliva into the tobacco wrapper. A large wooden kitchen match exploded into a blue cloud of sulfur and flame, and Niles puffed the cigar to life with wet sucking sounds.

Finally satisfied with the cigar, Niles turned his attention to Sims. He looked as if he were focusing Sims's image on a camera behind his eyes. Done with that, Niles swiveled to an extended arm of his desk, tapped on a keyboard, and watched the answer come up on a computer screen. He swiveled back to Sims and Houghton, regarding them through heavy-lidded eyes.

"Wonderful gizmos, computers."

Sims said nothing, knowing it was a preamble.

Niles drew on the cigar and sailed a cloud of smoke toward Sims and Houghton. "That thing"—he nodded toward the computer screen—"tells me Media fucking Research is a zero." He thrust his head forward, lizardlike, eyes black and deadly. "A flat, fucking zero," he added for emphasis, eyes still fixed on Sims and Houghton. "You said you wanted to do business. You assholes can't afford five god-damn minutes of my time."

"We're researching a media project," Sims said, watching for Niles's reaction.

"Media?" Niles said with a note of caution.

"A program about subversives in the sixties, and police red

squads." Sims saw Niles's lips play with a small gloating smile of reminiscence.

"Why me?" It was a test question.

"You ran the Missouri Red Squad."

"Special investigations task force," Niles corrected.

"You also helped the FBI with white hate groups."

"Yeah?" he said, squinting suspiciously through a cloud of cigar smoke.

"There was the Klan, of course," Sims said, "and the White Citizens' Councils." Niles barely nodded. Sims made a show of consulting a small notebook he pulled from his coat pocket. He raised his eyes to Niles. "How about a man named Barrineau? J. J. Barrineau—"

"You're wasting my time—" A screen passed over Niles's reptile eyes.

"And his Southern States Council?"

Niles took a deep drag on the cigar, leaned back in his chair, and tilted his chin up so he looked down on Sims and Houghton. "You're a fucking zero," he rasped contemptuously.

Sims was turning to Houghton when the door opened. Four uniformed guards materialized with leather-creaking quickness beside Niles's desk. Niles waved his cigar toward Sims and Houghton. "Get these fucking *zeros* outta here."

Niles's guards silently escorted Sims and Houghton down the elevators and to the street. Looking behind, Sims saw them standing stolidly on the sidewalk, blocking the building entrance. Wordlessly, Sims and Houghton walked the several blocks to the arch and the Days Inn.

Business travelers and salesmen filled the lobby, checking in and out, lugging large carry-on bags they would stuff in economy-class overhead luggage compartments so they could fly to other cities and stay in other cheap hotels. At the elevators, Houghton glanced around to be sure they were alone.

"We've got some new friends."

Sims didn't take his eyes off the elevator panel, where lights blinked up and down. He had spotted the couple following him and Houghton several blocks back. "Yeah. Man in dark green overcoat, woman in camel hair?"

Houghton nodded. The elevator doors opened, and they had the car to themselves.

"What now?" Houghton asked.

"We leave. Shake the tail."

"Then?"

"Figure out how we get to Niles."

A half hour later, Sims checked his rearview mirror as they left the motel. Behind them, on Market Street, a blue Buick pulled away from the curb.

"They there?"

Sims nodded. "The woman's driving."

In light midday traffic, Sims drove east, crossing the Mississippi into Illinois, then heading northeast on I-55. The blue Buick clung to them, obvious, but at a respectful distance.

Houghton pulled down his visor and glanced in the mirror. "Not very subtle."

"Better than tar and feathers."

For the next several miles, Houghton fiddled with the radio, finally gave up, and left it tuned to a ranting evangelist. He looked in his visor mirror again.

"Damn. How long're they going to stay there?"

As if to answer, the blue Buick began to fall back. A mile later, the car took the exit at Fairmont City. Houghton laughed and flipped up his visor. "Goddamn woman driving waved at us."

Sims didn't answer, busy as he was replaying the scene in Niles's office. Each time something seemed to whisper for his attention. Each time it eluded him when he backtracked to find it. Then, several miles farther, he was suddenly smiling and vaguely optimistic. He swung south on I-255.

"I think we got him by the balls," he announced to Houghton. Two hours later, they were in the southern fringes of St. Louis. Twenty minutes after that, Sims was connecting the scrambler to a pay phone, dialing Alberich.

Weiss Airport is a small field twelve miles southwest of St. Louis. With a single 3,000-foot runway, it is used mostly by private aircraft owners and flying clubs. VFR, or visual flying rules, shut Weiss down in bad weather or darkness. Both were closing in the following afternoon as Sims and Houghton parked by a low wooden building that passed as flight operations.

Inside, a magazine rack with dog-eared magazines and a sofa with rusted chrome-tube legs and split maroon Naugahyde marked a waiting room of sorts. On their right, a glass counter displayed a dusty collection of pilot's logbooks, Ray-Ban glasses, and other cockpit accessories. In an alcove behind the counter, a middle-aged man sat at a small metal desk, working over a set of books. He looked up with bored disinterest.

"Got somebody coming in." Sims motioned toward the flight line. The man with the books nodded and Sims and Houghton stepped out onto a covered porch that ran the length of the building.

Houghton stood downwind and lit a cigarette. "Going to be dark soon." The late afternoon sun was already behind the flat gray winter clouds, and the wind was beginning to rise.

Sims paced the length of the porch several times before he heard the faint high-pitched moan of turboprop engines. The sound disappeared in the wind, then returned. Sims searched the horizon.

"That's him."

The darker speck against a dark sky quickly took definition. Nothing about the small plane was graceful. It looked like a child's first model with its square twin tails and a slab-sided box of a body slung under ruler-straight wings. In another minute, Sims could make out the two engines stuck onto the wing, the fixed landing gear, and the old-fashioned wing braces.

In minutes, the Shorts Skyvan was swinging around in front of the porch, aiming the ramp of its cargo compartment directly toward Sims and Houghton. With turboprop engines idling, the ramp dropped. Inside the black cave of the cargo compartment, two lights flashed on, bright, then dim. A crewman in orange flight overalls bounded down the ramp and turned to face into the lights. With a circling hand signal, a motor started. The crewman, now semaphoring with both arms, waved Alberich's van down the ramp and onto the hardstand.

Minutes later, Sims sat in the van with Alberich, watching the clumsy airplane waddle out to take off. It bore the insignia of Southern Air Cargo, a charter outfit he knew to be one of the Agency's proprietary companies. In earlier incarnations, Sims speculated—and under different logos—the Skyvan had probably hauled guns in Nicaragua or Stingers out of Peshawar to the *mujaheddin.*

"VIP treatment. Impressive."

Alberich shrugged. "Airops owes me favors," he explained, referring to the Agency's secret air arm. "They need a little after-hours computer work, I need a little transportation." He gunned the engine and pulled around the flight operations building to fall in behind Houghton, who had already backed the rental car out and was heading toward I-44.

* * *

Shortly after nine that evening, a small mechanical beast Alberich had christened Punch quietly worked its way through a maze of smooth sheet metal. The climb to the thirtieth floor had been the most strenuous part of its journey. Once there, however, the horizontal ductwork posed no obstacles. Quickly, it found the first opening into Pyramid Protective Services.

In the back of Alberich's van parked in the underground garage of the same building, Sims studied the layout of the Pyramid offices that he had sketched onto a glass status board. The tracer light that followed Punch's progress began a series of insistent flashes. "What now?"

Alberich touched a keypad. "He's at a grate. Now we take a look at Mr. Niles's office."

Punch's receiver registered the command. Just below its infrared sensor, a panel flicked open and a spaghetti-thin probe wormed its way through the grate opening.

To Alberich's right, a television monitor bloomed. Sam Niles's desktop filled the screen.

"How's this work?" asked Houghton.

"Fiber optics," Alberich replied. "We'll get pictures of every square inch of brother Niles's office and the computer room." Alberich pushed a button and from the corner of his eye Sims saw a video recorder come to life.

An hour and a half later, Alberich was satisfied. Videotapes captured both floors of Pyramid Protective Services. Working the joystick and keypad, he brought Punch to the vertical shaft of the heating system. There, Punch extended four arms until they pressed firmly against opposite sides of the shaft. Minute servomotors began driving the small rubber treads on the end of the arms. Slowly, Punch edged down the shaft to the garage and Alberich's van. Later, Alberich would see to adding a small decal to Punch's side; another mission, another outline of a tiny footprint.

By 1:00 A.M., Sims and Houghton had shifted racks of equipment from Alberich's van into Sims's room. A special 100 MHz AST 686 computer was powered up and connected to three massive optical storage drives. Another cable ran through a data encryption standard module and the motel's telephone system to communications systems and data bases throughout the world. His face reflecting the electric blue glow of a huge NEC monitor, Alberich settled himself in his chair to launch his assault on Pyramid Protective Services.

For an hour, he went over Punch's tapes, fast-forwarding, rewinding, fast-forwarding again. Finally, he flicked off the video player and turned to Sims and Houghton. "It's not going to be easy," he announced worriedly. "Niles runs a tight ship. We couldn't find the usual carelessness. No scrap notes left lying about, no passwords taped to monitors."

He worked a joystick, and a small white circle two inches in diameter appeared on the screen. He drew another larger circle around it, and a still larger circle around them both. A handful of lines extended outward like rays from the largest circle.

"This's the problem," he announced, thinking aloud. His eyes were fixed on the concentric circles, like a marksman taking aim at a target. "The circles represent Pyramid's computer system." A chrome yellow cross skittered across the three circles.

"The Pyramid system's connected to a number of national data bases through these outside telephone lines." The cross pinged the rays from the largest circle. "From Punch's tapes, I know that Pyramid is using a Unix system and is a subscriber to Tymnet, a service that connects computers all over North America."

"Why not Ma Bell?" Sims asked.

"Tymnet is noise immune, Ma isn't." Alberich's eyes went back to the screen. "Now, all I have to do is enter Tymnet with my number and ask for Pyramid." Alberich fingered his keyboard and the cross moved in toward the largest circle along one of the lines.

"I can connect to the Pyramid computer"—the cross entered the outer ring of the target—"but without a password, I can't get into the working files that Niles and his people use." The cross hit the second circle and skidded around along it, unable to cross the barrier.

"Let's say we capture a password somehow and get inside the second circle." The cross moved toward the third, inner circle. The bull's-eye.

"The password won't get me into the core—what I call the protected systems area." Alberich looked around and saw the puzzled expression on Houghton's face. "Put it this way: The protected systems area contains the basic software programs that make Pyramid's computer work. It's like the heating and electrical control rooms for an office building. Those rooms aren't open to the renters. Only the keepers —the custodians—have special keys to the protected systems area."

Houghton nodded slowly. "How will you get in?"

Alberich smiled. "Hell, I don't know." Sims saw he was clearly excited. Alberich turned toward the screen again. "First, we get us a password." He worked his keyboard. Instantly, the screen responded.

WELCOME TO PYRAMID PROTECTIVE SERVICES

DO YOU WANT TO:

LEAVE A MESSAGE
ACCESS FILES

Alberich fingered A to access files. A second screen flashed and another message came up.

PYRAMID PROTECTIVE SERVICES

LOG IN NOW
ENTER YOUR PASSWORD:

Alberich made an entry. "Recording the log-in message," he explained to Sims and Houghton, who sat on either side of him, their faces reflecting the bluish glow of the monitor. To Sims, the log-in message was demanding and laden with menace.

"What now?" Houghton asked, whispering, as if Pyramid and Sam Niles might hear.

"It's common practice to let each worker choose his or her own password. I'm betting that some will have picked something common. You'd be surprised how many people use their names, their kid's or pet's names, or even words like 'open.' " Alberich danced his fingers along his keyboard. The AST computer displays flickered in a staccato rhythm as the drive responded to Alberich's commands. "This program is sending twenty thousand of the most common passwords to Pyramid. If just one of them works . . ."

The monitor suddenly flared an angry red. At the same time, a caterwauling tone pierced the room, rising and falling with the screeching intensity of some wounded beast. Instrument lights on Alberich's AST computer flashed wildly in an electronic panic.

Houghton, startled, came out of his chair. "What the hell—"

"Damn," Alberich muttered, tapping the keyboard.

The caterwauling stopped and the monitor's red screen returned to blue. The Pyramid log-in message had disappeared.

"What happened?"

Alberich made a head-clearing motion. "Bastard had a hacker-blaster program. It detected our probe." He worked the keyboard and a window opened filled with numbers. Alberich whistled. "Remember those old movies about castle sieges? Where the people on the walls poured melted lead and crap on the guys trying to climb up ladders? That's what Niles just did. Dumped over fifty megabytes of random binary input—tried to bury us in meaningless numbers," he explained. "We took a heavy hit, but shunted most of his garbage off to the optical storage drives." He pointed toward the boxy devices. "Computer trash compactors."

"So he shut us out," Houghton said.

"Worse than that. We've got some decisions to make. Somewhere in the protected systems area—the control room—for Pyramid, a light's flashing. When the system operator comes on later this morning, he or she'll find out that somebody tried to break in."

"And?" Sims asked.

"The least they'd do is cut off all outside connections. They'd shut down Tymnet. We couldn't get in. They'd change all passwords, maybe put in a challenge-response program. Make it a real bitch to get back in without a massive effort."

Sims nodded. "So we have to work fast."

"There's more to it than that." Alberich had a worried look. "If I were running Pyramid, I'd build a tracer program into the hacker-blaster."

"Tracer?" Sims asked.

"Unh-huh." Alberich operated the joystick and a squiggle line snaked across the monitor's blue screen. "I'd fix it so my computer would follow the trail of the hacker."

"You mean Niles could come knocking on our door?" Houghton asked.

"Exactly. We could move. But that'd mean we would lose time. By the time we'd get set up again, Pyramid—"

"Would have cut all connections and we couldn't get in," Sims finished. He exchanged looks with Houghton, then Alberich. "If we stay here, how long will it take?"

Alberich shrugged. "Maybe ten minutes. Maybe an hour. Maybe never."

"But you have something in mind?"

"Of course." Alberich had an offended tone in his voice.

Sims looked at Houghton, who nodded. Sims opened a dresser

drawer and took out the Uzi and two magazines and laid them on the bed. "Shit, let's go for it."

Alberich grinned and turned to the monitor. With a few keystrokes, he called Pyramid's log-in message back to his screen. He studied it for long moments, then muttered, *Yes, yes,* to himself. Another keystroke and the screen was blank and waiting for Alberich. He made the first entries.

```
ECHO -N "PYRAMID PROTECTIVE SERVICES"
ECHO -N "LOG IN NOW"
ECHO -N "LOG IN:"
SET ACCOUNT __ NAME
ECHO -N "ENTER YOUR PASSWORD:"
SET PASSWORD; \
```

Alberich's face became set in concentration, eyes fastened on the screen. The first taps on the keyboard were tentative and hesitant. The fingers then moved more quickly, then flew, as if Alberich were racing to capture the symphony only he could hear. He was no longer bound to a wheelchair but soaring somewhere among the spires of his intellect. Sims watched, fascinated, as Alberich fell under the spell of his own creation.

An hour and a half later, he was finished.

It took several seconds before Sims realized Alberich had stopped. Houghton, dozing in his chair, jerked awake and blinked his eyes open.

Alberich scrolled through the program on the screen, the cabalistic signs and computer language a blur. "That's it."

"Now what?"

Alberich again dialed the Pyramid number through Tymnet. The welcoming logo came on. Alberich stared at it for a moment, shrugged, and hit his enter key, sending his creation—his program—winging into the synapses of Sam Niles's computer.

"Now," Alberich answered, "we wait and pray."

Sidney Pollit was the unlikely answer to Alberich's prayers. Pollit gave new meaning to definitions of computer nerds. He never quite got over the wonder of Pyramid *paying* him to work. Not when the work meant access to Pyramid's computer system, known throughout the St. Louis computer cognoscenti as the most advanced in the Midwest.

Pollit came to work early and left late. Single, he lived only for his hours with the Pyramid Unix and would have happily set up house in his cramped cubicle if Pyramid would let him.

This morning, because of a slight cold, Pollit had slept in. This meant he didn't get to Pyramid until 5:00 A.M. Parking his car in the underground garage, he stopped by the all-night coffee shop off the lobby. Armed with two bagels and a Styrofoam cup of coffee (two sugars, two creams), Pollit flicked on his monitor, then his desktop computer.

WELCOME TO PYRAMID PROTECTIVE SERVICES

DO YOU WANT TO:

LEAVE A MESSAGE
ACCESS FILES

Pollit typed A. As he expected, the log-in message came on.

PYRAMID PROTECTIVE SERVICES

LOG IN NOW
ENTER YOUR PASSWORD:

Pollit entered his password, and, through reflex, started to call up the file he had been working on the night before. To his consternation, the screen was blank, save for what was to Pollit an accusatory rebuke:

SORRY! TRY AGAIN

Pollit's reaction was one of shock and alarm. This had never happened before. It wasn't in Pollit's nature to suspect that he *hadn't* entered the wrong password. He knew Unix was infallible. He re-entered his password, hoping against hope that Unix wouldn't hold his mistake against him.

When Sidney Pollit reentered his password, Alberich's virtuoso program caused two things to happen. First, Pollit's first password had been entered correctly. Alberich's program had snapped shut, trapping it, and had then sent it back out of the Pyramid system and along the Tymnet lines. Second, Alberich's program then erased itself,

244

leaving no trace within the Pyramid Unix. Just before disappearing, it charitably let the distraught Sidney Pollit log on and get to work on his precious files.

At 5:43 A.M., Alberich's computer chirped. Sims started at the sound, coming out of his chair. He'd been dozing, he realized, feeling foggy, with a bad taste in his mouth from too much coffee and greasy fast food. He stood behind Alberich. A single word leaped from the screen.

SEXYMAN

Sidney Pollit's personal password.

At the same time Sidney Pollit's fantasy password was showing up on Alberich's screen, Frank Silverio unlocked his office on the twenty-ninth floor of Pyramid's office building. Silverio, Sam Niles's computer systems director, saw the alarm light flashing. His own directives called for an immediate disconnect from all external lines, but there had been false alarms before. The workday would begin shortly, and reestablishing contact would mean lost time, and lost time meant lost dollars. He paused before his screen, balancing the trade-offs of immediate disconnect against an internal systems audit. He decided on the audit. He'd track the intruder down himself.

Now inside the oblivious Sidney Pollit's account, Alberich explored the barriers protecting the Unix operating systems. It was a painstaking process. Sims watched as Alberich tried one command after another, exploring directories and subdirectories, plotting the pathways, dead ends, and looping circuits that made up the electronic maze.

Silverio leaned into his screen with a trill of excitement. The audit showed that the hacker, whoever he was, was in the system *now!* He began scanning the working accounts. It was now later in the morning, and more accounts were opening up. A window on his screen arrayed eleven open accounts in alphabetical order. He punched a command and started his search in Maria Hoffmann's account. Four lines below Hoffmann was Sidney Pollit.

Alberich's monitor showed the diagram he had built of Pyramid's Unix system. Outside, the roar of traffic on the interstate was growing louder and the sky was turning from indigo to orange.

245

"Pyramid uses a rather elegant editing program created by a West Coast computer guru named Stallman," Alberich said, eyes fixed on the diagram as he moved his chrome-yellow cross up one branch of the diagram. He stopped at the inner circle that marked the Holy of Holies, the inner sanctum that was Pyramid's corporate brain. "Stallman even put in a mail system. Our boy, SEXYMAN, can send mail anywhere inside the Pyramid boundaries. The question is, can he send it into the protected systems area?"

"I thought nobody could get in," said Houghton.

Alberich nodded. "Most defenses are configured to keep people from altering programs. And to keep someone from getting in and taking something out."

"But maybe you can get in and leave something?" Sims asked.

"That's what we're going to find out." Alberich typed in the mail command. The screen asked for destination. Alberich filled in the Pyramid designator for the protected systems area. The wait seemed an eternity. Sims heard Alberich's breathing and Houghton nervously clearing his throat. Then the screen asked:

MESSAGE?

"Gotcha," Alberich whispered triumphantly. In the query for message, he typed out the file in his own AST that he had built after Sims's first phone call. Pressing the enter key, Alberich's subversive file flickered through the Tymnet communications lines and into Pyramid's protected systems area just as Frank Silverio began his inspection of Sidney Pollit's working files.

Sam Niles smashed his cigar into the lead crystal ashtray. "Frozen! What the fuck you mean it's frozen?"

Silverio, standing before Niles's desk, could only make a helpless gesture with his hands.

"Somebody was in the system. I was getting close"—Silverio's voice cracked—"but then he shut everything down."

"Goddamnit!" Niles screamed. "You mean you can't get into our own fucking computer?" Even as he raged, part of Niles calmly assessed the damage. It was bad now and would get worse with each passing hour. Everything that was Pyramid was in that computer. There were files so sensitive that he didn't even trust Silverio with the password. And, Niles remembered, he hadn't allowed them to be backed up.

Silverio shook his head. "I tried, Sam. The bastard who wrote the program did a number on us. Every try I make erases a chunk of our files. The first ones were just housekeeping files. But I suspect they were warnings. We try more and we really start to lose the good stuff."

Niles's face flushed a deep purplish red. He pointed to the door. "Get the fuck outta here, Silverio. And keep your fucking hands off that computer." He stood watching his computer director leave. He found himself breathing heavily, as if he had been under great exertion. Scrabbling in his humidor for another cigar, he stuck it in his mouth and bit off the end. He spit the tobacco onto his desk and punched the enter key on his keyboard. Sims's doggerel message flickered on to mock him.

SAM NILES:
PYRAMID'S A FUCKING ZERO TOO.
DON'T CALL US.
WE'LL CALL YOU – ☺

21

Pacing his office, Sam Niles looked down on the work floor below. Workers sat idly at their blank monitors, gossiping, reading magazines, or doing crosswords. Nobody could communicate, gather or send information, or bill hours. It was almost noon, and Pyramid had lost damn near fifty thousand dollars.

The sight put him on an emotional roller coaster. Thinking of the money drove him into a fist-hammering rage. The rage would crest. Then he'd realize his helplessness, and that dropped him into the depths of an immobilizing depression.

The console set into his antique desk gave a soft chirp. Simultaneously, a soft yellow display light flickered on. Still scowling at the work area, Niles walked over and punched a button.

"He says it's Zero," came the voice, tentative and at the same time curious.

"Put him on." Niles felt his heart hammer in his throat. His finger was already on the trace button when he remembered that communications security was also handled by the paralyzed Unix. He started the up cycle of his roller coaster again, savagely jabbing the useless trace button, as if to punish it.

Had it been working, the trace wouldn't have done anything for Sam Niles. Sims was calling from a phone booth and his message was short.

"*Walk?* Goddamnit, it's cold—" The voice ignored Niles's protest and he had to scribble furiously not to miss anything. The phone went dead and he stood there, looking balefully at the note. All his life, frustration and helplessness called up an urge to lash out. Reach-

248

ing into a bottom desk drawer, he came up with the snub-nosed Smith & Wesson .38 he had carried during his police years. He thumbed back the locking latch and snapped the pistol with a rolling wrist motion. The cylinder flipped open on its oiled hinge. He inspected the primers of the five cartridges for discoloration, and, satisfied, with a reverse motion, locked the cylinder back into the frame.

For an instant, his finger coiled around the trigger, and he imagined squeezing round after round into the face of the man who *dared* to do this to him. Pulling his coat open, he jammed the stubby pistol into the waistband of his trousers over his left hip.

It was five cold blocks to the Cervantes Convention Center, and Niles was still smoldering as he pushed through the Delmar Boulevard entrance. The third pay phone on the right near the rest rooms bore a hand-lettered out-of-order sign. He sneered in contempt. The sign reassured him; Zero had fucked up. He touched the grip of the .38 under his coat and again imagined dropping the hammer on the black man and his white partner.

He was walking away when a phone rang. Niles stood motionless for a moment, then turned and stared at the out-of-order phone, willing it not to ring again. But it did. His hand trembled as he answered. There were more instructions.

Thirty-five minutes later, Niles paid off a cabby and stepped into a spitting rain at Lambert International. Another point for the nigger, he glumly reflected; he damn sure couldn't take his pistol through security to the gates. Slipping the Smith & Wesson from his trousers, he palmed the little pistol into his overcoat pocket. Inside the terminal, he found the rental lockers and stored his overcoat. He didn't notice Houghton, who had watched the transfer from a pedestal table at a nearby fast-food concession. As Niles made his way toward the security check and its metal detectors, Houghton walked over to the rental lockers.

At United's VIP lounge, Niles made an inquiry, and the receptionist handed over a note. Gate C8, said the note; the other end of the terminal. Niles recognized the drill. The long walk to the convention center, the cab to the airport, the desk at the goddamn lounge, and now the walk back to the gate. It gave them a chance to watch him, to see if he had brought along any help.

Behind a newspaper in the corner of the lounge at Gate C4, Sims saw Niles stump by. Sims waited five more minutes, trying to follow an account of last night's Caps-Blues match, then joined the stream of travelers in the corridor. Through the crowd, he saw Houghton hunched over a phone in a booth opposite C8. Houghton looked up and gave him the all clear.

As instructed, Niles sat facing the plate glass window. Outside in the rain, ground crews in orange storm suits unloaded luggage from a DC-10, and a catering truck had elevated its cargo van on scissored supports to mate it to the side of the huge plane.

Sims sat down beside Niles. Niles turned angrily toward him.

"You son of a bitch," he seethed.

"You'll go a long way, Sam," Sims said smoothly, taking pleasure in provoking the ugly man, "always busting your ass to win new friends."

"My fucking business is—"

"Is going to be just fine after we talk." Sims pointed a finger at Niles's chest. "Or, rather, after *you* talk," he amended. Niles started to say something, but Sims held up a hand. "A minute, Sam. Let me tell you how it is." Sims glanced around to make certain no one had moved within earshot. "Just so you'll work a little harder for the truth.

"You've probably heard about computer viruses, Sam," Sims said, seeing pure hate in Niles's eyes, "but do you know anything about trapdoors?"

Niles scowled, a man unused to being forced to listen to others.

"A trapdoor, Sam, is a covert way of getting into a computer. Hidden files, secret programs, unbreakable passwords. Even a smart guy like your man Silverio could never find it. We left a trapdoor in your system, Sam. After you talk, we'll take out the virus. But the trapdoor stays."

"You fucking—"

"We can open it anytime with a phone call and stick in another virus. Maybe the next time one that will eat all your files. Or maybe, Sam, send all your files to the local newspapers. I imagine *that* would make you a lot of friends in St. Louis."

Niles felt suffocated. He inhaled deeply, then again. "What do you want?" he said in a strangled voice.

"Let's start with you and J. J. Barrineau."

Niles rolled his head, still struggling with himself, then gave in.

"J. J. had big ideas. A real political operator. Good on the details. Raised a helluva lot of dough, always met the payroll. Yeah, a real operator, J. J.," Niles mused. He looked innocently at Sims. "Whatever became a him?"

"I'm asking the questions."

Sims slipped the picture of Valek from an envelope, the one that showed him as he might have looked in 1968. Lips pursed, Niles examined it, twisting it to get a look from different angles. He shook his head and handed it back to Sims.

"Never saw him. Not that I remember. Lots a mug shots of lots a assholes."

"Ray and J. J.—did you ever make that connection?"

"Oh, yeah. Early." Niles exhaled through his mouth, his lips making blubbery sounds.

"Before King was killed?"

Niles nodded. "Ray had a sister . . . Carol, I think. Anyway, she had a bar here in St. Louis. Down on the south side." He paused, trying to remember. "Grape Vine Tavern. Ray's brother John was bartender and manager."

"You knew them before the King killing?"

"Sure." Niles nodded. "St. Louis PD had the place staked out after James Earl escaped from the pen at Jeff City." He looked owl-eyed at Sims. "Remember George Wallace? Runnin' for president then? Well, his campaign headquarters was across the street and his staff all hung out at the Grape Vine. J. J. was a big Wallace man. Paid the salary for Wallace's state chairman. All the Wallace people sucked up to him. J. J. was in the Grape Vine two, maybe three times a week, playin' wheeler-dealer."

Sims thought about this, then asked the question Houghton had first raised. "The St. Louis cops were watching the tavern Ray's sister owned. You knew Barrineau. Why weren't you reporting on the SSC?"

Niles's alarm bell was now deafening. He had always equated knowledge to power. And this black, whoever he was, knew things like where the reports had gone. You didn't know these things unless you were connected.

Niles looked over his shoulder. Waiting passengers had filled the row behind them. He made a jerking motion with his head, and with Sims following, he got up and walked to the huge plate glass window. Outside, the catering truck had finished loading the DC-10 and was lowering its cargo van. Niles spoke in a low whisper, his shuttered eyes on the plane. Sims saw Niles's face reflected in the glass of the window, distorted and lined by the gray winter light, a sketch in corruption.

"The Bureau put Barrineau off limits."

"Why?"

"Just told me to stay away. I didn't argue. You didn't back then. You didn't fuck with Hoover. He'd cut your dick off." Niles drew his shoulders in.

"Guess, Sam. Make me a guess."

Niles scratched the side of his nose. "Suppose it was because they didn't need me. They was watching it themselves. Had it all wrapped up."

"How do you know?"

"A new guy shows up in town. Special agent in charge of the St. Louis office. Right after that, I start hearin' rumors about the Bureau undercover boys—the COINTELPRO outfit—and how they're workin the SSC and J. J. Then there's talk about a contract—"

"Contract?" Sims flashed back on J. J. Barrineau's ravaged face and the smell of the sickroom. "Did the Bureau put out a contract on King?"

Niles twisted his mouth in a contemptuous smile. "Not directly. Didn't have to. They had J. J. as a front."

"But you knew about a contract?" He watched Niles nod. "How much?"

"Fifty-sixty thousand, somethin' like that."

"You never heard anything about the Russians and the contract?"

"Russians?" Niles got an incredulous look. "*Russians?* Shit, no. Just the Bureau. I figured the Bureau had somethin' goin and didn't want me crossin' wires with them." Niles shook his head. "Never understood how they pulled it off. When King got whacked, I thought for sure the shit'd hit the fan."

"Raoul," Sims threw out. "Did that name ever come up?"

"Sure. He was the guy Ray says did it."

"No, I mean, before."

Niles shook his head. Sims continued to look at him. Niles shook his head again.

It was a thought that almost never made it into Sims's consciousness. "Barrineau had to bail somebody out of jail sometime in March '68. In St. Louis. I want the rap sheet, booking documents, print card."

He saw Niles's protest coming and cut it off. "That shouldn't be hard for you, Sam. You can get it this afternoon," he said, adding, "once your computer gets well." He jotted one of Alberich's accommodation addresses on a scrap of notepaper and watched as the man looked at it, then stowed it in his shirt pocket. "Express Mail."

"When's my computer fixed?"

"When I make a phone call. But, Sam, don't forget that trapdoor stays. Insurance."

"That it?" Niles asked, wanting to be gone.

Sims held up a restraining hand. "The Bureau guy—he have a name?"

"Fred. Frederick Isom."

"What happened to him?"

"Retired. I heard down in Sainte Genevieve."

Minutes later, Niles hurried down the corridor with a sense of relief mixed with humiliation. Through security, he found his rental locker. His confidence was returning, and he dared to think about revenge. As he shrugged the coat onto his shoulders, he heard a dull metallic sound. He thrust his hand into the pocket where he had stowed the .38. A warning like a razor sliced through him as his fingertips touched it. The gun was there, but strangely light. Then his fingers found the bullets floating loose in the pocket. He rolled one after another into his palm, counting. He did it again. There should have been five. There were only four.

He stood for long seconds, staring in dismay into the passing crowds. The blank faces infuriated and frightened him. Danger lurked behind those faces, taking advantage of their indifference. Didn't they understand how vulnerable he, Sam Niles, now was? Hell no! Nobody gave a shit! He wanted to scream against the unfairness of it all, but instead he huddled himself inside his coat and walked quickly to the cab stand, a cold stream of fear running through his innards.

Two hours later, Niles waited in the Muddy Waters Saloon on North First. Francisco Latimer, a short, fidgeting man with thinning black hair, showed up a few minutes later. Not giving any sign of recognition, he took a stool some distance away and ordered a draft. Still in his overcoat, he sipped the beer, then made his way to the back.

Niles casually glanced around the nearly empty bar, then followed Francisco. It was a two-urinal, one-stall head that smelled of strawberry disinfectant. Francisco was combing his hair at the sink. Niles bent over to look under the stall door to make sure it was empty.

"Well?"

Francisco, who was an SG-11 files clerk in the St. Louis PD registry, fished around inside his overcoat. "Only one." He handed a thick brown envelope over to the man he hoped would one day take him into a better paying job at Pyramid.

Taking a quick, shielded look into the envelope, Niles recognized the paperwork, and J. J. Barrineau's name and signature. If that's all there was, that's all there was. The nigger said Barrineau had posted bail in March '68 and this was it. He made a mental note to slip a little something extra to Francisco this month.

At the post office, Niles paid for an Express Mail pouch, addressed it, and shoved it back across the counter to the clerk. Good fucking riddance, he told himself, impatient to get back to see if the nigger had kept his word.

22

Sims telephoned Riddle and summarized his meet with Niles. Two hours later, Riddle called back: Frederick Isom lived in the village of Ste. Genevieve, sixty miles south of St. Louis. A faxed biography would be on the line within minutes.

"Beautiful place. Restful." Houghton peered through the windshield. The car had stopped in front of a three-story white frame farmhouse. Two huge sycamores towered over the house, and on the steeply pitched roof, lightning rods stood picket duty against the summer storms that would come booming in off the Great Plains.

"It looks familiar," said Sims.

"*American Gothic,*" Houghton said. "All's you need is Ma and Pa and a pitchfork."

From the low hill, the Mississippi, sun-dappled with highlights of hammered silver, lay half a mile away just beyond a stand of cottonwoods. To the south, the hill dipped gently into Ste. Genevieve, first settled by the French over two hundred years before and reminiscent of the neatly kept villages of the Sologne, with their step-gabled brick and timber houses.

Sims nodded, enjoying the view and the house. During the early afternoon, a westerly wind had carried the rain away and the sky was a clean-scoured coppery blue. He imagined how it would have been a hundred years ago to spend the afternoon in one of the high-backed rockers on the large wraparound porch, watching the riverboats plow the Mississippi from New Orleans to Moline.

Sims had scanned Riddle's faxed report during the drive. Frederick

Baines Isom was born December 10, 1930. He had attended Pittsburgh public schools, then got a degree in accounting at the University of Pennsylvania. An infantry platoon leader in Korea, he had garnered a Silver Star and Purple Heart. Law school at the University of Maryland on the GI Bill, and from there, straight into the Bureau. His specialty was counterintelligence. After assignments in Manhattan—watching the United Nations, Sims guessed—he was overseas liaison to MI-5, then back to the Bureau's field offices in Birmingham, Charlotte, and finally, St. Louis. Turning down a promotion and a move to Washington, Isom retired in May 1968, claiming a medical disability from wounds in Korea. He and his wife had stayed in Missouri, buying the sprawling old house on the hill from its original owners, floating a mortgage of $97,000. By 1984, Isom had established himself as a sculptor of some note and was featured in exhibits up and down the Mississippi Valley.

A woman answered the door. Slender and attractively graying, she wore faded jeans and a man's plaid wool shirt. Sims introduced Houghton and himself, handing her a Media Research business card. He saw her eyes narrow when he explained they were doing a story on King's assassination.

The woman regarded the two men on her front porch with a long, grave look. "He doesn't like to talk to the media." She talked loudly through the thin glass on the closed storm door.

"It's just research," Sims replied, a friendly yet plaintive note in his voice. "We drove down from St. Louis. We would have called, but you weren't listed."

Her face softened. "Just a minute," she said, then closed the main door. Sims saw his breath frost and at the same time felt the chill of the wind coming down the valley.

A moment or two later, the door opened again and the woman motioned to her left. "Around back. The barn's where he's working."

Rough-hewn four-by-fours supported a galvanized roof over the bricked walk connecting the house and the red-painted barn. Sims lifted a latchkey to a small door set into the larger sliding door of the barn. As he did so, he heard a high-pitched cutting sound taper off.

Fred Isom's studio blocked off the northeast corner of the barn. Sims's first impression was of light and stone. The studio interior was painted a soft peach and the top half of the north wall was a vast window. Stone was everywhere: chips ground underfoot, great marble boulders were strewn about the floor, and rough-cut blocks perched

Sims listened intently, knowing what he would hear and not wanting to hear it.

"Somebody—I don't know if it was Hoover himself—came up with the idea of harnessing a white outfit to disrupt and harass black organizations like King's SCLC or that guy Stokely Carmichael's—"

"SNCC." Sims gave the initials. Student Nonviolent Coordinating Committee.

Isom nodded. "Yeah. Slick and snick."

"You—"

"I met with Barrineau. Passed him information, advised him, gave him money. Helped him expand." Isom said it in self-reproach.

"Did Barrineau know you were Bureau?" Houghton asked.

Isom shook his head. "I never said anything, but I'm sure he had a pretty good idea."

"What did you have him do?"

"Just goon stuff at first: heckling, disrupting rallies, hate mail, that kind of thing."

"At first?"

Isom studied the backs of his hands as they rested on his knees. "It got more serious in January."

" '68?"

"Yes. Up till then, Attorney General Ramsey Clark, like Bobby Kennedy before him, had been routinely approving Hoover's requests to bug King—tap his phones. For some reason, in January Clark got cold feet and wouldn't sign any more approvals. Hoover tried, but couldn't get him off the dime."

Suddenly, Sims saw it. How J. J. Barrineau had gotten the tape of the night of April 3. "So you put the Southern States Council to work, didn't you?"

Isom rewarded Sims with a rueful smile. Seeing Houghton's searching look, he explained, "I ran training sessions for basic tradecraft, surreptitious entry, bugging, telephone taps, the works."

"Even bought them the equipment," Houghton said, now understanding, "like Nagra 4.2's?"

"And Barrineau fed you the tapes—"

Isom shook his head. "I got cut out when the taping started. It was too sensitive for me to be connected with it. Everybody in St. Louis knew my face. Washington sent an undercover from COINTELPRO. The undercover guy took over. They ordered me to break with Barrineau and the SSC altogether."

"And the undercover man?" Sims asked.

"I never saw him. He ran the operation with Barrineau. He'd pass me the tapes by mail or a dead drop."

"He have a name?"

"I only knew his code name: Jigtime."

"Jigtime?" Sims felt his face flush. "Ever talk with him?"

"Three or four times we had a phone conversation with a scrambler and voice warbler."

"About?"

"Minor stuff. Logistics, that kind of thing. He was getting his policy direction straight from Washington."

"The phone conversations—was it the same person each time?" Sims asked.

"I think so." Isom nodded.

"Barrineau hung out in the Grape Vine Tavern." Houghton picked it up. "James Earl Ray's sister owned it. Did Ray himself ever show up there?"

Moments passed and Isom seemed frozen on the stool. From the waist up, he began an almost imperceptible rocking motion. "Saturday, March thirtieth. There had been a meeting of the Wallace campaign committee across the street. I got a report from an informant of mine. Said Ray was in the tavern and was with Barrineau."

"And you—?"

"I reported it. Ray was an escaped felon." Isom opened his hands in a helpless gesture. "I got a telex telling me not to get involved, that Jigtime was handling everything. I made the connection, of course, when Ray showed up in the papers."

"How about Raoul?"

Isom smiled derisively. "Ray's mythical fellow traveler? That's all bullshit." He looked at Houghton, then Sims, then back to Houghton again. "It is, isn't it?"

Houghton didn't answer. He waited to let the silence build the tension. "Tell me about the contract."

Isom got a look as if poleaxed. "Oh, God!" It came as a lament with years of pent-up anguish behind it. Isom's eyes dropped to the floor, then up again. His lips had become a tight line and nearly invisible in his beard.

Houghton pressed. "You knew about the contract, didn't you?"

Isom stared into the distance for a long time. "Yes."

"Did Jigtime tell you?"

"No."

"Then how'd you know?"

"I got it from one of my informants. That was the morning of April second, two days before the killing." Isom leaned forward from his perch on the stool, resting his elbows on his thighs and wringing his hands together between his knees. He looked up with an expression of deep-cutting pain. "I *thought* I had it stopped." His head went down again, chin to his chest. "God, I thought I had it stopped."

"What did you do?" Houghton asked softly.

For a moment, there was no answer. "I disobeyed orders and went to Barrineau." The words came slowly, being dragged through years of agony. "He denied it, of course. Then I reported it."

"What happened?"

A tear ran down Isom's cheek and into his beard. "I got a call. Washington said that Jigtime had taken care of it."

"Yeah," Sims said bitterly.

Isom sank his face into his hands. "I *thought* he had. I didn't have any way of checking." He dropped the hands and interlocked the fingers in his lap.

"And the night of April fourth?"

"I found Barrineau," Isom said, now massaging the knuckles of his right hand with the fingers of his left. Sims noticed for the first time the largeness of the sculptor's hands. "He still denied everything."

"Jigtime?"

"Gone." Isom shook his head. "The telephone numbers, the telex address. They were gone, as if they'd never existed. The next day, Barrineau disappeared. All I had was a guilty conscience and a handful of smoke."

"Then you left the Bureau," Houghton said sympathetically.

"I tried to put it all away." Isom looked around the studio. "But I've lived with it every day," he said plaintively. "Somehow, I set up King for Memphis."

Sims held out Valek's photograph. Isom studied it, shook his head, and started to hand it back. "Who's he?"

"A Russian. KGB."

Isom looked at the picture again, somewhat longer, but in the end handed it back to Sims. "Never saw him. There's a Russian connection?"

"We think the Russians did it," Houghton said, surprising himself by saying it.

"Oh." Isom said it blankly, and sat for a moment on the stool, as if finding a new piece to a puzzle he thought he had solved long ago.

Sims watched Isom drop deeply into thought, trying to work that out. Isom slid off the stool, walked to the loft's railing, and looked down on the floor. Then he turned to face Sims and Houghton.

"When King was killed, I thought we had done it. I've lived with that. Now two . . ." Isom looked at Sims and Houghton with curiosity. "Two strangers come here and tell me it could have been the goddamn Russians." Isom turned away and looked down on the work floor again. "What the hell do I believe now?"

Sims's and Houghton's eyes met in mutual agreement. "We'll be going," Houghton said to Isom. The man didn't seem to hear, but stood, clutching the railing.

Finally, Isom sighed and squared his shoulders. "I'll see you out."

On the work floor, Houghton paused by the easel where Isom had been working when they came in. It was a marble slab about a foot by two feet. Toward one end, Isom had sculpted a bas relief.

"Pro bono work. There's a paupers' cemetery downriver at Belgique," Isom explained. "State doesn't provide markers, just a grave." He looked at his work, running a hand over the smooth white stone. "We adults leave a life behind us, our own markers, but the children deserve something."

"The innocents," Houghton murmured, seeing the small animal Isom had lovingly carved, remembering from somewhere that the lamb was the symbol of redemption.

Sims drove back toward St. Louis along a winding secondary road that connected old river towns with names like Danby, Festus, and Herculaneum, towns of the time of Mark Twain. Missouri had raised the possibility that the Bureau, not the KGB, had killed King. He wanted proof, not more possibilities. He was frustrated and impatient. He realized he wanted this over, one way or another. Tomorrow was the long drive back to Washington. The only lead left was the money. He wasn't looking forward to the tedious tracing of the trail from the SSC to the Cayman Islands and from there to who knows where?

Houghton cracked his window and lit a cigarette. "Tells us why the Bureau didn't want Niles poking around in the SSC," he said, exhaling toward the open window.

"And why Hoover stopped you." Sims kept his eyes on the road. "I always thought that guy was nuts, but that's absolutely goddamn crazy."

"They look like crazy times now, but then it was all serious."

"God, think of what it must have been like. Working a Kluxer like Barrineau. Getting a report on Ray. Hearing about a contract. Passing it on. Thinking you had put a stopper in the bottle, then . . ." Sims searched Houghton's face. "You think it could have been the Bureau? Maybe not Isom, but somebody else?"

"Like Jigtime?"

Sims nodded. The code name still pissed him off.

Houghton wearily shook his head. "Hoover wanted King gone. Whether he wanted it bad enough to kill him . . ." He let it trail off, taking another drag off his cigarette. "There's another angle. In an outfit like the Bureau in the sixties, Hoover wouldn't have had to give a direct order. Just a hint. A wink and a nudge. 'Will no one rid me of this turbulent priest?' " Houghton flicked the cigarette out the window, then slouched down in the seat and closed his eyes. "Shit," he muttered to himself, "just when you think you got this bastard nailed down, something else pops up at you."

As Sims and Houghton drove toward St. Louis, Sam Niles was at his desk. In the clearing sky, the setting sun cast a luxuriant glow into his office. Settling back in his chair, he reassured himself with yet another look at the work floor below. The screens were darkening as men and women began closing up for the day. The computer had come back up at noon, shortly after he had left Lambert Airport, and Pyramid was again making money. He smiled down at the work floor. No more goddamn crosswords or bullshit sessions. As if touching a totem, he tapped the keyboard, and the Pyramid logo reassuringly popped up on his screen. Niles grunted with satisfaction, eyes still on his screen. He reached into the humidor for a cigar and began the process of fondling and finally lighting it. Settling back in his chair, he treated himself to the rich taste of the tobacco on his tongue.

Then, like some worm wiggling unpleasantly into his consciousness, he remembered the trapdoor. It was a chink in his armor and, goddamnit, you weren't powerful if you were vulnerable. He exhaled, following the blue smoke swirls with his eyes until they disappeared in the soft eddies of conditioned air. He damn sure didn't want those bastards—whoever they were—getting back into his computers again. He reached for the phone. Silverio could goddamn well earn his pay and track that thing down.

His hand was on the phone when a discordant movement in the distance distracted him. Puzzled, he searched the roof of the building across the street. There it was —the trace of a swift, crouched figure.

Window washers, he thought reflexively. Then he realized it was too late in the day for window washers.

Niles's hand stayed frozen on the phone as he watched. There were four men, moving toward him in coordinated purpose. Cigar clamped in the corner of his mouth, he levered forward in his chair, trying to see more clearly.

Then he imagined their view from across the street. He saw himself through the glass wall, sitting at his antique desk on the well-lighted dais.

Target! the voice inside him shrieked. *Target!*

In panic, Niles sprang from his chair, twisting an ankle while crashing to the floor. Scrambling clumsily to his feet, he began a nightmarish slogging run for the door.

On the rooftop, one of the men knelt, hoisting what appeared to be a stove-pipe tube onto his shoulder. He fit his face to the contours of the cold aluminum cheek rest and, making a final adjustment for wind, sighted in on Sam Niles.

Niles was now in the narrow passageway leading to the door. The left wall, the glass wall, was but inches from his shoulder. From the corner of his eye, he caught a momentary bright flash, like the hard blue fire of a welder's rod. His hand closed on the doorknob to the outer office and safety.

Traveling at just over three hundred miles an hour, the dense antitank projectile punched a neat hole through the window, then exploded a fraction of a second later in the narrow passageway.

Niles felt a massive gust of superheated gases in the confined space, a giant fist slamming him backward. As he flew through the still splintering window, a heavy shard of glass dropped like a guillotine blade. It cut my leg off, Niles thought, amazed at his own detachment. Now plunging to the ground thirty floors below, he rapidly picked up speed. With the same detachment, he watched fascinated as the air rushing by him atomized his spurting blood, transforming it into a spray scarlet against the darkening sky above him. At the fifteenth floor, his speed and the missing leg caused him to tilt head down. He saw the street below spin and twist as it rushed up to meet him. Sam Niles's velocity was such that he had just enough blood left to keep him conscious all the way into the pavement.

23

Police and emergency rescue records set Sam Niles's time of death at 5:32 P.M., too late to make the 6:00 local news. It took three more hours for arson and homicide investigators to agree that an explosion of unknown origin had caused Niles's spectacular death plunge.

Unaware of any of this, Sims and Houghton had dinner at a riverside restaurant in the small town of Arnold, south of St. Louis.

Over second and third cups of coffee, Sims stared glumly out the window at the Mississippi and the lights pinpricking the blackness of the Illinois shoreline. He was locked in a dark room. The only way out was to find the answers. And the answers kept brushing against him, tantalizing, teasing. Whenever he grabbed one, it disappeared. How had Isom put it—a handful of smoke?

Sims twisted in his chair to look for the waiter. As he did so, he saw Sam Niles looking out from the muted television over the bar. He dashed to the bar, his chair crashing to the floor behind him.

"What the hell?" asked the bartender.

"Turn it up," Sims ordered. By now, a long shot of Niles's office building had replaced his face. Superimposed dashes arched from the top floor to the street.

Houghton had come up and was standing at Sims's shoulder. He said nothing for a moment. "Isom," he rasped. "Oh my God, Isom."

Except for the blackness of the night, it was Atlanta all over: the lightning blues, reds, and yellows of the fire engines, police cars, and ambulances, the glare of floodlights of men working in the night, the smell of fire and ashes.

"The bastard likes fire," Houghton said in bitter anger, looking through the windshield as he had the first time that afternoon in Ste. Genevieve. But now, Frederick Isom's house on the hill with the wraparound porch was ashes. Sims had made an anonymous 911 call from a pay phone in Arnold, then they had sped back to Ste. Genevieve.

A handful of smoke. For a second time, Isom's words haunted Sims, and he remembered Isom's tear-stained face.

"Where're you going?" Houghton asked as Sims opened his door.

Sims got a funny look. The answer was obvious. "To see—"

Houghton put a restraining hand on Sims's forearm. "It won't do any good. He's dead. Wife probably, too."

"But—"

Houghton's grip tightened. "*Think* about it!" His voice pitch raised. "What if it wasn't the Russians. What if it *was* the Bureau? We go up there . . ." He pointed to the men in uniform and plainclothes around the gathered police cars. "They got Valek and Broz and Barrineau. Now Niles and . . ." He waved his hand at the house. "Who's left?" Houghton paused and answered his own question. "You and me."

Sims started the car. "And Raoul," he added.

Five minutes later, they were on the interstate headed north.

"What now?"

Sims glanced again in the rearview mirror. "See if that guy's following us."

Houghton made a minute adjustment to the mirror on his door to bring up the lights of the car behind them.

"How long's he been there?"

"Just after Isom's." Sims reached under his seat, pulled out the Uzi, and laid it across his lap.

The lights stayed with them, about half a mile back. A minute or two later, Sims slowed and took the exit toward Goldman. Houghton watched the interstate, craning over his shoulder as they reversed track on the curving exit ramp.

"He went on." Houghton shifted in his seat to keep up with the disappearing car. "But I think he has a friend." A new set of headlights had left the interstate and was following them down the exit ramp. Sims grimaced. Whoever it was had manpower.

They were still in open country south of St. Louis. There were no crossroads, no traffic, no built-up areas, no way to lose the tail.

Thirty minutes later, they were in downtown St. Louis. Their tail had switched cars twice, but was still with them.

Sims checked his mirror. Dodging a shadow was easier in a car than on foot. He could speed up, round a corner, douse his lights and park. Run up a one-way street the wrong way. Make a sudden U-turn. But if he lost his tail, he wouldn't know who it was.

Signaling, Sims pulled over toward the curb. True to form, his tail passed. A green Ford Taurus. The Taurus's partner was probably a block over, running parallel to them and would be in place in seconds. Houghton had already switched the interior dome light off. Sims slowed, and Houghton was out the door, sprinting down a darkened alley. Sims pulled away from the curb. Behind him, half a block away, a pair of headlights rounded the corner.

Fifteen minutes later, Sims wheeled into the Avis return lot near Lambert International, noting with satisfaction that the tail, now a maroon Chrysler, pulled to the curb a half a block away from the exit.

The Uzi slung under his coat, Sims entered the deserted office area. Brightly lit, he knew he stood out clearly to anyone watching from the darkness outside. A red-vested clerk behind the counter looked up over coffee and a cigarette. Sims waved his contract and walked toward the automated check-in booth. Time stamping the contract and scribbling the mileage in the blanks, he dropped the papers into a rubber-mouthed slot.

"Rest room?"

The clerk, Styrofoam cup at his lips, pointed down a hallway. The men's room, as Sims hoped, had a window. It was high and small, and was cracked open to let the winter air cut the swampy smell of the urinals. Pulling himself up over the sill, he pushed the window wider and squeezed through the narrow opening. He felt his overcoat snag and tear on the rough concrete sill.

Knees flexed, he dropped to the ground. He looked quickly around. To his front, an eight-foot chain-link fence with a topping of three strands of barbed wire. The mercury lights in the front cast a pool of inky shadow along the back of the building. Crouching to keep in the shadows, he edged toward the chain-link fence and its barbed-wire armor.

Ten minutes later, the man in the maroon Chrysler lowered his binoculars and checked his watch for the third time. He had guessed from the dumb show that Sims had asked for directions to the bathroom. A veteran of years of surveillance, the man had a sense about things, and his sense was telling him something had gone wrong.

He pushed open the glass doors. "A friend. Black guy," he queried the Avis clerk, who was now reading yesterday's *USA Today.* The clerk pointed down the hallway. It took less than a second for the man to take in the empty rest room and the open window. Dashing out of the office, he left the clerk staring in dull surprise over the top of the sports section.

The overcoat caught the man's eye as he rounded the corner of the building. It hung over the barbed-wire topping, and the slight breeze caused the dangling belt buckle to brush against the chain-link fence. He imagined Sims scrambling over the fence just seconds before. He ran to the fence, searched the darkness beyond, and cursed. Perhaps there was something in the coat . . .

He never heard the slight movement behind him as Sims sprang from the shadows. Swinging with all his strength, Sims smashed the blade-edge of his hand into the vulnerable junction of the man's neck and shoulder. The blow momentarily crushed the carotid artery and the surrounding nerve branches. As if suddenly boneless, the man crumpled face first to the ground. Sims stepped warily back, then, satisfied, dragged the unconscious man into the darkest of the shadows, just along the side of the building, directly under the open rest room window. Retrieving his coat, Sims set out on foot.

Fifteen minutes later, he entered the terminal. Clean-up crews were mopping and buffing the airport's expanse of floors, and here and there, scattered ticket agents were booking the occasional passenger. Sims bought a newspaper and found a bench where he could unobtrusively watch the pickup lane outside.

He was finishing the paper when a dark blue Dodge pulled up and blinked the lights. He recognized Houghton at the wheel.

After Sims had dropped him in St. Louis, Houghton had found a cab and, in turn, an open Hertz office. "Went OK?"

Sims twisted in his seat. Behind them the airport terminal was disappearing in the distance. No cars followed. He told Houghton about the tail and the rest room and the baited overcoat over the fence.

"I shook him down," Sims finished.

"And?" Houghton asked it, keeping his eyes fixed on the road.

"He was Bureau," Sims said, opening up the credentials case for Houghton to see. "A guy named Nicholas."

Houghton glanced over, then focused on the road again, thinking about Isom. "Oh shit."

*   *   *

Riddle sat at a long Sheraton library table. He had pulled the heavy curtains against the early morning sun, casting the shop in darkness. In the center of a cone of light thrown by a green-shaded banker's lamp, he regarded an overnight express pouch. He carefully examined the address label. From a sterile address in St. Louis to an equally sterile address in Washington. He nodded in satisfaction and took a sip of coffee. Cup down, he turned the pouch over. It wasn't that he expected to find anything. It was more a matter of what he'd never admit to—of getting a *feeling* of the contents.

He nudged the pouch with a delicate finger and then deftly slit the bottom with a razor-sharp opener made from an antique Damascus dagger. With precise, economical moves, he extracted a large plain manila envelope, pinched open the metal clasp, and slid a gray file folder onto the table.

"Mr. Niles's contribution."

"His last." Alberich's voice came from outside the cone of light. Servomotors whined as he maneuvered his wheelchair closer to the table.

Riddle opened the file. Metal prongs fastened the papers at the top of the folder. He freed the thin sheaf, gave half to Alberich, and began going over the remainder, jotting precise notes on the inevitable blue index cards.

Half an hour later, Riddle pushed back from the table. "An ordinary enough incident on Saturday night, March 30, 1968. A minor traffic accident in St. Louis. A blue Ford Fairlane, following too closely, crashes into the rear of a black Oldsmobile. Robert Jackson, the driver of the offending vehicle, offers a cash settlement on the spot. The Oldsmobile owner, however, declines, insisting on calling the police. Jackson then attempts to start his car and drive off. The Oldsmobile driver tries to stop him. There is a fight. Jackson beats the Oldsmobile driver senseless. At this point, the St. Louis police intervene. They arrest Jackson."

"Barrineau posts bail the next day, Sunday," Alberich said, picking it up. "Jackson never shows up in court. A warrant is sworn out, and—end of case."

Riddle reassembled the file: the report of the arresting officers, statements of witnesses, Jackson's receipt for his personal belongings, the results of a blood-alcohol test (negative), the bureaucratic residue of crime and punishment. "This"—he handed a stiff white card back to Alberich—"we should track down."

Alberich looked at the fingerprint card. Clipped to it was a mug shot of Jackson, a white man with light hair, unremarkable except for a badly set nose. Alberich looked back at the face in the photograph. First stop would be the National Crime Information Center. Organized in 1967, NCIC was the central clearinghouse for American crime, containing more than twenty-three million computerized criminal records. Still, it wouldn't be easy. Most of those twenty-three million records included arrests only after July 1, 1974, and tens of millions of files before that date had not yet been put on the computer. Alberich mentally added another point to the degree of difficulty: Missouri had not joined the NCIC until 1986.

He waved the card at Riddle. "This'll take some time."

Riddle nodded. "While you start that, I shall forward copies of this to Mr. Sims."

Tim Nicholas stood apprehensively before Delaney's desk. Behind the FBI director, the Capitol glistened in the afternoon sun. Delaney ignored the younger man, leaving him to shift from foot to foot while Delaney signed documents he took from a red folder. For long seconds, the only sound in the huge office was the scratching of Delaney's fountain pen. Finished, he stacked the papers, tapped the sheaf on the edge of his desktop, then returned them to the folder. He sat back in his chair, appraising Nicholas.

"What the hell." He cut up the words, his jaw clenched.

Nicholas made a helpless gesture with his hands. "They—he—"

"*You!*" Delaney exploded. "You fucked up. You lost them. I give you carte blanche on resources to track these bastards and you let them disappear on you." Delaney glowered at the younger man, who was now hanging his head. "All you had to do was track them. Nothing more. You not only screw that up, but they get away with your credentials."

Nicholas started to say something but Delaney cut him off.

"I'll find them myself," the FBI director said coldly. "All you'll have to do is keep from losing them this time. I'll take care of the rest."

"This is it." Houghton pointed through the car window to Leisure Acres, a cluster of beaten-down red brick garden apartments.

Sims drove past, then circled the block slowly, checking the traffic in his rearview mirror. He slipped his right hand under his coat and made a small tugging adjustment to his shoulder holster. Swinging back onto Locust, he turned into a drive guarded by a weathered sign warning: PARKING FOR TENANTS ONLY.

Out of the car, Sims stood in the cold morning mist and surveyed 301 Locust Street. This was the address on Robert Jackson's arrest report. The same address came through when Alberich checked the plates on Jackson's car. The lot was largely empty except for several cannibalized cars. Nearby a battered pickup perched on blocks, a cheap red plastic drip pan forgotten under its engine.

The manager's office was just off the basement landing. Beyond it, a long hallway stretched into darkness. Sims pushed a yellowed button over a card penciled MR. TUCKER.

The door opened and a subterranean wave of sour overheated air erupted into the chilled hallway. Joe Tucker was a short, nasty-looking man with springy red hair and a belly that strained at the buttons of his red wool underwear top. He rolled a dirty toothpick to the corner of his mouth and squinted suspiciously at Sims through blond, piglike eyelashes.

"Yeah?"

"You the manager?"

"Whatcha want?"

"Some information about a tenant."

"Don't talk about tenants." The door started to close, Tucker looking balefully at Sims. The door's motion froze. Sims held a folded ten cheek high.

"It's somebody who left." Sims moved the ten and watched as the piggy eyes followed. "This is just for looking. There might be more if you find something."

Another moment of indecision, then the door opened. Tucker pointed a thumb over his shoulder. "In there." The living room was filled with an assortment of cheap and cast-off furniture. One corner was taken up with a desk surrounded by mismatched bookcases. Rows of record books filled the shelves, thick black binders with plastic label windows on the spine. The neat white labels struck an incongruous note against the general sloppiness of the rest of the apartment.

Sims gave him the name Robert Jackson and the dates: January to April 1968.

Tucker listened, then held out his hand. At first puzzled, Sims stood motionless. Tucker rubbed the ball of his thumb back and forth across his fingertips. Sims handed over the ten. Tucker stuffed the bill in one pants pocket and from the other pulled a pair of reading glasses. Sims noticed that a safety pin replaced a missing hinge screw. Settling the glasses on his nose, Tucker searched the bookcases, found a binder, and took his chair at the desk.

Tucker worked through January, examining each record sheet, running a finger under the name entries with the slow precision of the barely literate. Minutes later, he stopped and stared at one page for a long time. Sims moved to look over his shoulder. Tucker closed the notebook, keeping an index finger in to mark his place. He gave Sims a greasy smile.

"You paid me to look. I looked." He stuck his hand out and made the gimme gesture again. Sims produced another ten and Tucker opened the book and slid it to the side of the desk so Sims could read the mimeographed rental agreement.

On February twelfth, Robert Jackson agreed to rent apartment 297. The agreement noted that he paid one month's rent in advance— $200—with an additional $200, also in cash, as a deposit for breakage and cleaning. The handwriting fascinated Sims. It was the first tangible trace of the man named Raoul. In the block marked previous residence, Raoul had printed a San Francisco address.

"How long did he stay?"

Tucker turned to the next page, an occupancy and rent payment record. He ran his finger along a penciled line, then looked to the top of the page for the calendar scale. He gave a grunt of contempt. "Guy just up and left." He tapped the page with a thick-knuckled finger. "Shows here they waited two weeks after rent was due, then went in. That'd be April fifteenth."

"Forfeited the deposits?" Houghton asked.

Tucker brought his face closer to the book, then looked up. "Looks like." A paper clip at the top of the page glinted in the dim light. Tucker turned the page. The clip fastened a stamped envelope to the back of the page. It was addressed to the Jackson alias at the San Francisco address. Tucker unfolded a single sheet from the envelope.

"Notice to enter," he explained, showing the form letter to Sims, then Houghton. "Have to send it 'fore you go in. Legal, you know."

Sims looked at the envelope. A post office stamp declared "No Such Address," and a purple finger pointed to the Leisure Acres Apartments return address.

"Assholes just up and leave," Tucker said in his threadbare voice.

"Do it all the time." He closed the book, took off his reading glasses and put them back in his pants pocket. Sims and Houghton rose to leave.

A moment later, and out in the hall, Sims pushed open the door to the outside. The morning mist had turned to a spitting rain and drops streaked down the grimy panes of the door.

"Damn," he said to himself and Houghton, "I guess that's the end." Behind him, a door banged open.

"Mister!"

He turned to see Tucker puffing up the steps, the black notebook under his arm.

"I was lookin' again," he started in explanation. Propping the book on the banister railing, he opened it and pointed to a penciled notation. "People leave and leave their shit in the place, we store it." He tapped the notation with a dirty fingernail. "We got lockers in the luggage room." He looked up expectantly at Sims.

"OK." Sims nodded. "How about showing us?"

Tucker put on another greasy smile, closed the notebook, and held out his hand.

"Shit." Houghton sat on a packing crate and looked at Sims in frustration. Tucker's luggage room was little more than a raw dark space among the foundations of the apartment building, a place of rats and spiders, of the dead smells of damp concrete dust and mildewed clothing. Overhead, the anemic glow of forty-watt bulbs did little to cut the shadowy gloom. Cardboard boxes lined one wall, with whitewashed notations on the floor serving as some sort of cataloging indicators. Tucker had searched until he found a flattened medium-size box, then left it to Sims and Houghton to wrestle it out from the bottom of a teetering stack.

It had taken only a few minutes to go through the box. There were clothes of the sixties: a pair of buckle-over dress shoes, two cheap wide-lapeled suits, one tan, one dark blue, three biblike psychedelic ties, and several dress shirts with long point collars. All pockets were empty. Raoul *had* left in a hurry: a smaller carton surrendered his underwear, socks, and toilet articles. Whoever packed the box had pitched in everything, including Raoul's razor, toothbrush, and a now stonelike tube of Crest.

Sims went over a large envelope filled with the usual lay-about dresser-top things: a penknife, a parking lot stub, a restaurant business card, several paperback detective novels, and a folding travel clock that had wound down at 4:10. No photographs, no personal letters, no correspondence of any kind. Nothing to show where Raoul had come from or where he'd gone.

"Shit," Houghton repeated, and began tossing the clothes back into the box. "He damn sure wasn't into material things."

Something about the slender inventory intrigued Sims. "How much for the lot?" He asked Tucker.

Five minutes later, Houghton was at the wheel, heading east on Delmar toward the river and Illinois. Raoul's box was in the backseat, and Sims sat in the passenger seat with the envelope of belongings in his lap. He was going through the paperback books, carefully turning each page, looking for anything Raoul might have jotted down or slipped into a book twenty-four years before.

"Hundred bucks for that shit," Houghton groused.

"Alberich might be able to find something. Laundry marks, something like that."

"My guess's that he never came back to the apartment after he was busted by the cops."

Sims nodded. The arrest would have been catastrophic for Raoul. He would have assumed the Jackson cover was totally shredded. Tradecraft called for a shift into yet another identity. "Robert Jackson probably vanished off the face of the earth the minute Barrineau bailed him out." He put the book back in the envelope and picked up the parking lot stub. Turning it over to look at the time in and out, he held the stub to the light.

"Where're the booking papers?"

Houghton pointed a thumb over his shoulder to the backseat, to a Lands' End canvas briefcase. Unzipping the case, Sims pulled out the fax of the St. Louis PD event report. Scanning through the police jargon, he found the passage describing Raoul's car, then looked at the parking lot stub.

"Different license number," Sims said, again examining the parking lot stub. "In the report, Raoul's car had a Missouri plate—KLB-546. The parking lot stub gives DBI-480. Stub's dated March twenty-ninth, the day before the accident."

Houghton glanced at Sims, then turned onto a side street.

"Where're you going?"

"Find another goddamn motel," Houghton replied. "We have to track that plate number, we might as well be comfortable."

* * *

Alberich called back four hours later. Houghton answered, sitting at a rickety motel desk, making notes and smoking, cradling the telephone between his ear and shoulder. He hung up and turned to face Sims.

"DBI-480 was issued to a Matthew Paul Carey on April 23, '67."

"Sixty-*seven?*" Sims asked, wanting to make certain he'd heard the date right.

Houghton nodded and went on. "The car was a '65 Chrysler. Alberich checked through the feds' motor vehicle registration files. Carey—or Raoul—bought it at a Kansas City lot on April 9, same year. Paid cash."

Houghton stubbed out his cigarette and ticked his pen under his notes. "Get this: the car turned up on a back street in Chicago in June '68. Stripped. There was never any report of a stolen vehicle. Missouri DMV says the owner didn't answer their plate renewal notices."

"Where was he living?"

"Here in St. Louis. Howard Street—2304 Howard." Houghton looked at his notes. "Alberich says the tax records show the owner as Frances Helen Wish. She's owned it since 1937."

Howard Street was old St. Louis, a quiet street of venerable red brick row houses, green lawns, and wrought-iron fences. Tall oaks lined the sidewalks and reached out to meet over the street, successors to the mighty elms that had fallen to the blight almost a hundred years before.

A long flight of white granite steps led to the front entrance of 2304 Howard. A large, arching alcove sheltered a family of stacked oriental pots that would be planted and set out down the steps in the spring. To the right of the massive oak front door was an antique brass umbrella stand. Houghton pushed the doorbell beside the door and chimes rang somewhere deep within the house.

Sims's first impression of Frances Helen Wish was one of a woman never quite at rest. Even before the door opened, he heard the sound of feet hurrying across hardwood floors. Small, silver-haired, and in her seventies, she flung open the heavy front door, took the briefest of glances, and said in a precise, declarative voice, "You're the lawyers."

Houghton, taken aback by her abruptness, took a second to collect himself, then nodded. He had called her an hour before. Matthew

Paul Carey? he had asked. Perhaps she had known him? He had rented from her, she answered, and what, she had asked, business was it of his? There had been a death and a rather substantial estate to be divided, Houghton explained in dry lawyer's tones. Could they drop by?

Frances Wish studied them briefly, then made a welcoming gesture into the house. The old house was bright in spite of the gloomy weather. High ceilings and tall windows captured the best of the winter light, and colorful prints, predominately of soft blues and roses, hung on chrome-white plastered walls.

"In here," Frances Wish directed, leading them into a sun porch on the south side of the house. "I've made tea." She searched Houghton's, then Sims's face. "You *do* drink tea?"

It was as much an assertion as a question. Both men nodded. She directed them to a floral print sofa. She took a white rattan chair opposite and saw to the puttering with tea and sugar and lemon and cream. She held her cup to her lips with two hands and sipped, her bright bird's eyes watching Sims and Houghton over the rim of her cup.

"Mr. Carey," she prompted, settling the cup just so in its saucer.

"Records show this address," Houghton started off.

Frances Wish gave a small smile. "Well, not exactly." At Houghton's puzzled look, she pointed to the back of the house. "In the back—we have what they now like to call a carriage house. Two bedrooms, kitchen, bath. Everything. Was for servants. But now the servants don't like to be called that. Servants, that is," she explained, picking up steam. "And the realtors certainly couldn't rent something called servants' quarters, and so I guess that's why they call it a carriage house, even though we—my late husband, Gerald, and I—never had a carriage." Her eyes were dancing now, focused on a distant time, and there was a flush to her cheeks as she raced toward winged flight. "Why, there's no place for a horse anyway, not for a proper carriage house—"

"The carriage house." Sims said it in a loud, friendly voice. "That's where Matthew Carey lived?"

A sad perplexity, then awareness crossed Frances Wish's face. She made a wry smile of apology. "I'm sorry. I do go on. The older I get, the more there is to chew on. Matthew Carey?"

"How long did he live in the carriage house?"

"He came in March 1967. It was the second week in March." She saw Sims's eyes narrow slightly. "I remember because my birthday is March ninth. He came the next day."

Sims handed her the mug shot. Alberich had enlarged Robert Jackson's full-face mug shot and airbrushed out the ID plate and the height lines in the background. Frances Wish took a look at the picture and nodded. "Yes," she said without hesitating, "that is Matthew Carey."

"How long did he live here?"

"He left a year later. It would have been—yes." Frances Wish nodded. "Late March. It was a disappointment," she said, cocking her head. "He was such a nice man."

"He left suddenly."

Yes, Frances Wish answered Sims. No, no forwarding address, no subsequent contact. Houghton took over the questioning. The woman's answers were concise. Matthew Carey had been a good tenant, paying his rent promptly and in cash. He'd been quiet and had helped her with occasional heavy jobs around the house. He was in sales, she replied, machine tool products. Traveled a lot. Always well dressed. No, she didn't know where he had come from *specifically*, but she got the impression he was from Wisconsin.

At the front door, Sims offered a law firm business card. The phone number was an answering service Alberich had under contract. "If you think of anything that might help us find Mr. Carey . . ." About to leave, a question struck Sims. "Did Mr. Carey have any visitors? Friends?"

Frances Wish shook her head. "No *friends*." The way she said *friends* made Sims look questioningly at her. She got a conspiratorial matchmaker's smile. "There was a sweetheart, though."

"Oh?"

Frances Wish's cheeks colored. "I had been ill. The doctors said a herniated disk"—she delicately touched the small of her back—"and they wanted to operate. I wasn't much for operations—I'm still not—but the doctors, they wanted to cut."

Sims kept his face a mask of innocent interest. He heard Houghton, standing behind him, shift impatiently. Frances Wish, perhaps sensing this, too, stopped.

"The doctors wanted to cut," Sims prompted.

Frances Wish gathered herself and gave him the wry apologetic smile again. "I didn't want the operation, so another doctor recommended physical therapy treatments. I agreed. Anything to keep them from . . . Well, anyway, my new doctor sent me his nurse. She came twice a week. Massages, exercises"—she waved a hand—"that kind of thing. About the third week, I guess it was, Matthew came into the house for something. I forget what. But the two of them met . . ." Frances Wish got a warm smile and nodded to herself. "And I *knew* . . ."

"How long did they—"

"Until he left. That would have been seven or eight months later."

"What did she say after he left?"

Frances Wish shook her head. "I don't know. You see, my back had gotten better months before he left. She stopped coming to see me, but they were—what do they say?—an issue?"

"An item," Sims supplied. "What was her name?"

"Margaret," Frances Wish replied with certainty. "Margaret Hampton. Missouri girl. Lived around here all her life."

"You never saw her after Mr. Carey left?"

A shake of the head.

"The doctor?"

"Purvis, James Purvis." The old woman shrugged. "But he was as old as me and he's dead now." She chuckled. "Always heard about outliving your doctors. Now I'm doing it." She became serious. "Not much satisfaction in it, though."

"Raoul," Houghton intoned. "Robert Jackson. Matthew Paul Carey. Whoever he was, he was a professional."

Sims grunted in agreement. You didn't backstop identities like that without help and money. Raoul had the discipline and smarts to keep Jackson and Carey scrupulously apart. The parking lot stub? A screw-up, but those happened. No cover was ever perfect. Stumbling onto the parking lot ticket had been luck more than anything else.

"Whoever built those identities for Raoul probably got the Canadian aliases for Ray."

Houghton looked at the dashboard clock. "Now we have Margaret Hampton."

Tracing Margaret Hampton took just over two days. Finding no Margaret Hampton in the St. Louis directories or on the city's tax rolls, Sims and Houghton had driven to Jeff City, where the State Board of Nursing confirmed that a Margaret Wilkins Hampton had indeed been a duly registered nurse. A photostat of her application, taken from a microfiche file, showed that she had been born in Cape

Girardeau on October 22, 1937, and had graduated in 1958 from Washington University's school of medicine and nursing in St. Louis. Margaret Hampton's last license renewal was in 1969. Thereafter, nothing.

Back in St. Louis, Washington University records described a B+ student with high recommendations from her professors and supervising physicians. Margaret Hampton had also worked at a part-time secretarial job in the registrar's office. Sims made certain he copied the Social Security number correctly.

At Langley the next morning, Alberich dropped by to see his old friend, Al Srnka. Srnka was a career intelligence officer with the Treasury Department and in his fifth year as Treasury's liaison to the Agency. Srnka never considered asking Alberich for a written request. Government worked better in informal channels. Srnka simply picked up a scrambler phone and called one of *his* old friends at IRS. Just over two hours later, Margaret Lofton's latest 1040 form squirmed out of the encrypted fax in Srnka's office.

Sims and Houghton sat opposite each other over a small table in the motel. Notes and papers from Alberich's Fed Ex package covered the table. Houghton leaned back, cocking his straight chair onto its back legs.

"Well," he said, tired of going through the years of taxes, "at least the arithmetic's good."

Sims had covered his legal pad with notes. He looked back at Margaret Hampton's first return as Margaret Lofton. A joint return for 1970. Spouse: Harold Lofton. Residence: Rural Route #4, Kirksville, Missouri. Occupation: Hers, nurse. His, farmer.

Calvin Harris had finished supper and was clearing the kitchen table to the clattering accompaniment of dishes and silverware. Dora, at the sink, hands in the hot sudsy water, heard it first.

"Calvin. The door."

"Door?"

"Someone's knocking."

Harris listened and heard it too. Going to the door, he swung a wide detour into the living room. He wanted to see the road outside without anyone out there seeing him. As he did so, it struck him that he never would have thought about doing this *before*.

A large dark car shone in the moonlight. Its parking lights were on, and an exhaust plume rose into the cold night air. A dark silhouette sat in the driver's seat. The knock came again.

Harris opened the door, keeping on the heavy chain lock.

"Good evening, Calvin. I am sorry if I disturbed you, but I didn't want to call." Donald Stanley stood on the porch, tall and handsome, a white silk scarf luminous against his dark overcoat.

Overcoming his surprise, Harris momentarily closed the door to slip off the chain, then invited Stanley in. The congressman brushed aside Harris's offer to bring in Stanley's driver. "The car's warm and I won't be long."

Harris led Stanley back to the kitchen. Dora, still at the sink, froze in surprise, a dish in one hand, towel in the other. Stanley gallantly went through the pleasantries required in a meeting after many years. Dora, reading her husband's eyes, finished the dish and put it away. Pleading some reading to do, she set the table with two large glasses of iced tea and a plate of cookies, then left the two men alone.

Stanley, still in his overcoat and scarf, took a chair and sat, hands folded in his lap.

Harris sat opposite, wrapped one hand around his glass of tea, and rested both elbows on the table. "You didn't want to call?" he asked.

Stanley's urgency cut through his studied calm. "I've *got* to see your nephew," he said.

Fifteen minutes later, Harris left home with Stanley, directing the congressman's driver to a service station several miles away. Leaving Stanley in the car, he closed himself into a pay booth. He had dutifully memorized the telephone numbers because Bradford had said they were important. Bradford had called them trouble numbers. Harris had hoped he never would have to use them.

24

Alberich took Calvin Harris's call. A hurried consultation with Riddle had followed, then a scrambler call to Sims and Houghton. While Donald Stanley drove back to Washington, a commercial messenger slipped an envelope with instructions into the mail slot of the congressman's Capitol Hill home.

The following morning, Stanley flew to Chicago, a routine stop on the way back to his home district. But no staffer met him at O'Hare. Instead, at a United service counter, he picked up an envelope with tickets to St. Louis. The tickets bore the name of Francis Burgess.

Stanley's plane touched down at Lambert just before noon. Twenty minutes later, he paid off a cab in the University City section of St. Louis and walked several blocks to the zoo grounds. By one o'clock, he was in the reptile house, reading with pretended interest the plaque by the Komodo dragon's cage.

"Afternoon."

Stanley had heard no approaching footsteps. It was as if Sims had simply materialized at his elbow. Startled, he searched for the beginning words.

Sims gave a cautionary shake of his head. "Not here. Rain's stopped. Let's walk."

The rain dripping from the bare branches of the huge water oaks kept Sims and Stanley on the middle of the wide gravel path leading into the depths of the zoo grounds.

"You took a chance coming here yourself," Sims said at last, when they were well away from the reptile house.

Stanley glanced around. "I worry about passing information through others. I have sources to protect. With any intermediary, there's always a chance of inadvertent compromise." Stanley dropped his voice. "The Bureau's looking for you. A man named Nicholas. He had Niles and Isom staked out. Apparently, they had been part of the Bureau's operation in Missouri during the sixties."

"I know." Sims told Stanley about the man behind the car rental office.

Stanley listened intently. When Sims finished, the congressman added, "He reports directly to Delaney. Whatever else you've done, you've got the Bureau's attention."

Stanley reached into an inner coat pocket and came out with a small manila envelope. "Nicholas is also connected with the Russians in some way."

Sims slid out a surveillance photograph. He saw crowds, luggage, and the sweeping glass and cantilevered concrete roof, the signature of Dulles International. In the center of the photograph, a man walked straight toward the camera.

"His name's Yazov. Viktor Yazov, former KGB, a deputy to Okolovich."

Sims studied the face. A wide receiver, he thought, automatically registering the cant of the Russian's athletic body in the act of walking. The camera captured the black pitiless eyes and the hard set of the mouth.

"Niles and Isom—do you think the Bureau killed them?" Stanley asked.

Sims stared a second longer at Yazov, then put the photograph back into the envelope. "They could have," he answered. "The Bureau's up to its ass in this."

"King?" Stanley asked, his voice hushed.

"Maybe. They had motive and access. But maybe the Russians."

"Who knows?"

"Raoul."

"He's real?"

"He was once."

"Now?"

Sims slipped the envelope with Yazov's picture into his coat pocket. "Now all we have is the name of a woman who knew him."

"Oh?"

"Yes."

"That's not much." Stanley seemed to be waiting for more.

"We've never had very much."

Somewhat abruptly, Stanley checked his watch, then looked at Sims. "Time to go. Are you certain you want to keep on with this?"

Sims smiled somberly and shook hands with Stanley. "I don't think I have a choice. I guess I never did."

Stanley made a waving salute and walked away. Sims stood watching thoughtfully, his eyes following the congressman down the pathway until it twisted out of sight.

From the lobby, Sims called Houghton's room, opening with a meaningless code word to indicate he was not under duress. He detected an edge of excitement in Houghton's voice, and he had barely knocked at the door before it swung open.

"Stanley—"

Houghton cut him off with an impatient wave. "Alberich called." He hurried to the desk, fetched a legal pad, and flipped back through pages covered with his looping scrawl. "He's made the prints!"

"Prints?"

"Prints!" Houghton's voice crackled and he had a wild manic look in his eyes. "The fingerprint card for Jackson-Raoul. It was in the booking papers Niles got. NCIC didn't have a record, but the Army did."

"The Army?" Sims was having a hard time catching up.

Houghton nodded rapidly. "Robert Jackson—Matthew Carey—*Raoul*—is really George Alden Sanchez."

"OK," Sims said slowly, "so Raoul's George Sanchez." He still couldn't figure out why Houghton was so wired.

Houghton got a knowing look. "The Army says George Sanchez died in 1950."

Stunned, Sims sat heavily on the edge of the bed. "Shit." Every time you put your foot down, the ground moved.

"Born 11 August 1932 in Reinersville, Ohio," Houghton read off his notes. "Year and a half at Ohio State. Joins the army in December '49. Basic at Fort Benning, Georgia, then assigned to K Company, 3/34th Infantry Regiment, 24th Infantry Division, Kyushu, Japan. The 24th was one of the first units MacArthur shipped to Korea when the war broke out."

Houghton looked up, as if to make certain Sims was taking everything in, then ducked into his notes again. "The North Koreans couldn't be stopped. They overran K Company on July 8, 1950, near the town of Chonan, sixty miles south of Seoul. Army records show the outfit simply disappeared."

"And Raoul with it."

Houghton nodded. "The North Koreans put most of their POWs into camps inside China. A lot never came back."

"No accounting?"

"Not even now." Houghton shook his head. "Everybody knows about the GIs still missing in Vietnam. Hardly anybody realizes we have over eight thousand unaccounted for from Korea. Eight thousand men just vanished."

Houghton searched the legal pad and found a notation: "Two American POWs who came back say they saw Raoul in a Chinese camp near Qingdao in 1952. At the truce talks in 1953, the North Koreans handed over their list of POWs."

"But he wasn't on the lists."

Houghton nodded. "The army carried him as missing in action until August 1954, then declared him dead."

"Then his fingerprints show up in St. Louis in 1968 under the name of Robert Jackson."

Houghton folded the sheets of the legal pad back into place and cocked his head at Sims. "Something else from Alberich. This guy Harold Lofton—Margaret Hampton's husband? IRS says that 1970, when he filed with Margaret, was the first year Harold Lofton ever filed a return."

The following morning at first light, a hundred and sixty miles northwest of St. Louis, Sims and Houghton parked their car on a twisting farm road. Parting the barbed-wire strands of a fence, they crossed a pasture and made their way up a low hill. The sky was a dark monochrome of grays, and the north wind was kicking up snow swirls that raced across the land below.

They had left St. Louis the day before, just after Sims's meeting with Donald Stanley. Driving west on I-70, they had turned north at Columbia onto a state road that took them into the rolling hills of northern Missouri. Margaret Lofton's home of Kirksville, according to the road atlas, was Missouri's largest town along the Iowa border, the home of a state university and, the atlas said, America's first osteopathic medicine teaching hospital. They had found a small motel south of Kirksville, and after a dinner at a Chinese restaurant, bought cold-weather work clothes at a surplus store near the university.

Nearing the top of the hill, Sims and Houghton dropped to the ground and crawled the last several yards to peer over the crest.

"There it is."

Below them, the Lofton farm's barn, silo, main house, and out-buildings spread over an acre of fenced land. At a greater distance, a stream cut through the valley floor. The snow had been cleared from the blacktop drive that circled the house and ran down to the main road and a stand of mailboxes. Sims smelled wood smoke from the chimney.

They had barely gotten into place when a figure bundled in a dark green parka left the back door of the house and tramped through the snow toward a red pickup.

Houghton squinted into the binoculars. "Can't tell if it's a man or a woman." With a broom, the figure worked over the pickup, sweeping snow from the windows and doors, then bent across the windshield. The brittle sounds of an ice scraper came to them on the wind.

Houghton lowered the binoculars and offered them to Sims. Sims shook his head. "We better get down there before they leave."

Houghton put the binoculars away but continued to stare at the farmhouse, the only sign of humanity in the bleak whiteness of the rolling hills. "Funny place for it to end," he said as much to himself as to Sims. "You always think something big would finish up some-place like the White House or the Kremlin."

Sims nudged him. "It's not over."

Half an hour later, Sims had worked his way to the outbuildings and was crouched against the leeward side of the barn. From his position, he could cover the pickup and the back of the house. He judged the distance to be about seventy or eighty yards. He slipped off his right glove and, reaching inside his down jacket, wrapped his hand around the cold steel and plastic grip of the Uzi.

Margaret Lofton peered through the curtains at the front door. A middle-aged man in a plaid mackinaw stood on the porch, blowing into his hands. He wore a hunter's billed cap, with the flaps dropped down over his ears. Down the hill, on the main road, a dark car was stopped, its hood raised and emergency lights blinking. She opened the door.

"Harley Strothers, ma'am," Houghton said. "Made the wrong turn coming from Milan." He jerked a thumb over his shoulder. "Then my car went on me. Use your phone?"

Margaret Lofton caught her breath and forced a cautious smile. "A

minute," she said. "Let me get my husband." Closing the door carefully, she forced herself to walk slowly toward the kitchen. Once in
the long hallway, however, she broke into a run.

"Harold!" she whisper-shouted. "Harold!"

Her husband appeared in the kitchen doorway. A slender, weathered man, he caught his distraught wife's elbow in a strong grip. She
motioned to the front door with her free hand.

"Man out there with a new hat and coat. Says he came from Milan,"
she said, giving it Houghton's European pronunciation: me-LAHN.
Her husband began a smile. Missouri wasn't picky about pronunci-
ations. Natives called Versailles, a small town in the center of the
state, vur-SALES, and Milan, a few miles away, was MY-lun.

Margaret Lofton shook her head, eyes now desperate. "He pointed
to his car. When he lifted his arm, I saw under his coat. He's carrying
a gun."

Sims stepped out from the barn when the man virtually exploded
out the back door of the house. Before Sims realized what was happening, Raoul was almost to the pickup. On seeing Sims, Raoul swung
his rifle toward him.

Sims flattened himself against a wall just as Raoul fired. The heavy
slug tore through the barn siding high above Sims, and after it, the
shot's crashing echo rolled into the hills.

Freeing the Uzi from his jacket, Sims heard the roar of the pickup
engine and the grating of gears. He made a rolling dive from the
shelter of the barn. On his belly in the snow and frozen mud, he saw
the truck disappearing around the corner of the house. An instant
later he heard the measured pop-pop-pop of what he hoped was
Houghton's pistol.

On his feet and sprinting around the side of the house, he saw the
red pickup take out a mailbox as it fishtailed into a right turn onto
the main road.

"I think I got a tire," Houghton shouted. He jumped from the porch
and ran toward Sims, pistol still in hand, face flushed from the cold
and excitement.

Sims drove, the car sliding on the icy farm road. Rounding a turn,
they saw the red pickup several hundred yards ahead, tilted head-on
into a drainage ditch. Sims stopped as Houghton swept the area with
the binoculars.

"Nothing." Houghton shook his head and motioned toward the
truck.

Houghton had gotten a tire and a brake line as well, judging from the sharp smell of leaking fluid. Footprints led out of the ditch and onto the banks of a frozen stream. From there, the tracks headed north into a valley formed by low, thinly wooded hills. Sims took the magazine from the Uzi, pressed down on the stubby brass cartridges, watching them spring back into place, then slid the magazine back into the submachine gun.

The valley was quiet, almost expectant. At a distance, two hawks wheeled above the hills, waiting for the rabbit or field mouse careless enough to show itself against the snow.

"Godforsaken place," Houghton muttered, wiping his nose on the back of a glove.

"He lived here for over twenty years," Sims thought out loud. "Probably wondered every day when somebody'd show up."

Houghton eyed the trail of tracks into the woods. "Heading for his stash?" It was a basic tenet of tradecraft. Wherever you were, whoever you pretended to be, you always put something aside for a time like today. A hiding place with money, alternate identity papers, a weapon. Was Raoul headed for that or was he simply running scared?

Without a word, Sims started off, Houghton falling in and following some distance behind. The ground rose steadily as the two men worked their way upstream and into the woods.

Behind him, Sims heard Houghton's breathing becoming heavy and rasping. Sims himself felt the exertion of their pace through the snow. The cold air was burning his throat and lungs, his cheeks and nose starting to numb. Still, he pressed on, straining at the same time to hear any sign of Raoul ahead of them.

Raoul was staying to the stream. On Sims's left, loggers had slashed a lane that ran up a low hill almost to its crest, the stumps in the snow looking like blackened teeth. Raoul had to know they'd follow, Sims was thinking. And he had to know this land, the roads, the course of the stream. Sims wondered what he would do if he were Raoul.

"Sims!"

Sims swung the Uzi to his left, ready to fire. He saw Houghton almost on top of him. Red and black pain flashed behind his eyes as Houghton hit him and his head struck the ground. At the same time, he heard the shot.

Instantly, Sims knew what had happened. Raoul had doubled back on his trail. He had climbed the hill and he had watched them tracking him along the stream below.

Houghton weighed heavily on him and Sims realized his own face was wet with blood.

Later Sims would wonder what it was that had put Houghton on to Raoul. Had it been a stray glint on the lens of the rifle scope? Or perhaps a snicking mechanical sound? A quick motion against the stillness of the hilltop?

He heard the second shot and he felt a thumping jolt throughout Houghton's body.

Clutching the Uzi, Sims wrapped his free arm around Houghton and rolled into the frozen streambed. The ice groaned but held, and the overhanging embankment gave them precious inches of shelter from the killing hilltop.

He rolled off Houghton. The older man lay on his back, face turned toward Sims. Blood bubbles painted his mouth and Sims frantically searched under Houghton's jacket for the chest wound he knew he would find. Houghton's eyes screamed silently in disbelief, begging Sims for an answer.

"Fucker . . . the fucker . . ." Houghton gasped for breath, unable to make his collapsed lungs work. Sims found the wound—one of them—high up under Houghton's left arm. He had taken a lateral shot through the chest, probably when pushing Sims to the ground.

"Don't talk," Sims whispered, imploring.

"Fucker . . ." Houghton tried again, his face now drained of all color except for more of the orangeish blood froth that now ran onto the snow and ice of the streambed.

Sims stripped off a glove and tried to hold it against the wound. He felt the wound sucking with each of Houghton's weakening attempts to breath.

"Oh God." Sims, now crying, hugged Houghton to him, willing his own life into the man in his arms. Houghton's body seemed to diminish, as if somehow vaporizing. He heard a gurgling sound and loosened Houghton and looked into his face.

Houghton read the meaning of the sagging finality in Sims's eyes. Weightless, as if from a height, he looked down on the streambed and the two men lying there. A wave of comforting warmth swept him and he sensed, rather than saw, a silver radiance. It was the source of the warmth beckoning him. He rose higher, and as he did so, he saw a man on the hilltop with a rifle.

With a wrenching effort, Houghton resisted the tugging pull of the silver brightness and flew back, holding on to his body for precious seconds. Sims's face was before him with razor clarity: the pores of his skin, the crescent-shaped scar on his cheek, the even white teeth. Houghton smiled his conspiratorial smile.

"Free at last," he whispered, then he died.

Raoul rolled to his left side, reloaded the rifle magazine, then worked the oiled bolt to chamber a cartridge. He knew he had one hit. He might have gotten both. He saw no movement. He waited a second, then stood up to go down and finish off the two men below.

Raoul was still on the crest of the hill when Sims sprang from the streambed.

Sims saw the man on the hill drop to one knee and cock his head behind the rifle scope. For an instant, the haunting fear from Czechoslovakia paralyzed him. Then his uncle's voice came to him, describing the battle at New Market Heights, and his blood pounded in his chest and became a drum.

Cutting abruptly right, he fired a short burst from the Uzi to keep Raoul off balance. The last thing he wanted now was to kill the man. The beat of the drum inside him quickened and he charged the hill, dodging the stumps and fallen trees. The earth felt as if it were quaking beneath him.

Raoul lost the figure in the narrow peephole that was his rifle scope. He cursed, pulling away from the eyepiece to gain a wider field of vision. The man was almost up the hill, weaving, cutting right, then left. Raoul ducked his head to the scope. The man momentarily flashed through the crosshairs. The instant Raoul fired, he knew he had jerked the trigger and missed.

Sims heard the chill air crack overhead and he realized his fear was gone. With the bullet's passage, he had crossed a threshold. Dreamlike, he was invulnerable. The hill, the snow, the stumps, the man trying to kill him—none of it meant anything. The only thing that mattered was the running, the gaining of strength with each leaping step and the roaring of his blood that filled his throat with a savage war cry.

Unnerved, Raoul gasped for breath, his hand panicky and fumbling with the rifle bolt. Working too quickly, he slammed the bolt forward to chamber a new round without letting the spent cartridge eject. The empty brass casing jammed itself between the bolt face and the breech, sticking out from the rifle like an amputated finger.

Cursing desperately, Raoul jerked back to clear the bolt. He looked up. The black man was almost on top of him.

Raoul sprang to his feet, swinging the useless rifle by its barrel, aiming it with a horizontal smash to Sims's head. Running full speed, Sims dipped his left shoulder and moved inside the arc of the swinging rifle. His knee drove high into Raoul's groin. His upper body still in motion, he twisted so the point of his shoulder slammed into Raoul's upper ribs, causing him to drop the rifle. With both hands, Sims locked the man's right wrist and twisted back, wrenching him to the ground. Rage-blinded, Sims raised himself over the man, grabbing him by the collar of his coat, and smashed his head repeatedly against the frozen ground. From deep within himself, a voice warned he was close to killing. Fighting off insanity, Sims fell exhausted to the snow.

Beside him, an unconscious Raoul curled in on himself, clutching his crotch. After moments, Sims managed to get to his feet, staggered a few paces, scooped up a handful of clean snow, and scrubbed his face with it. The gleam of metal caught his eye, and he stooped to pick up Raoul's rifle. A Winchester, he noted. The scope, an Unertl, was gouged, the bluing worn away to show bare metal, and its front lens cracked.

"Drop it." It was a man's accented voice. It came from behind him, from the nearby woods that ran to the crest of the hill.

Sims stood motionless, the damaged rifle in his hands.

"Drop it."

Sims did, keeping his hands away from his body, telling himself to stand very still. He heard footsteps in the snow. As the sound came closer, he was able to distinguish two sets of footsteps. They stopped.

"Hands behind you." The second voice was American New England. Boston, Sims guessed. Sims heard a single set of footsteps come close. Hands jerked his arms roughly as handcuffs snapped tightly around his wrists. The footsteps backed off. "Very well. Slowly turn around."

He turned. Raoul lay in the snow between him and the two men. Both men were armed. The younger, thinner one carried an Armalite rifle. Sims recognized him as the Russian Yazov in Stanley's photograph. Yazov, the Russian killer. The older man waggled his revolver, never letting it leave Sims's midsection.

"I'm—"

"You're John Delaney," Sims said.

Delaney gave a smiling acknowledgment.

"How did you know where we were?"

"*Know?*" Delaney's smile was golden and godlike. "I knew you were here because I *wanted* to know, Bradford Sims, ex-CIA. Georgetown University jock Bradford Sims. Talent-for-languages Bradford Sims. Nephew of civil rights stalwart Calvin Harris Bradford Sims. I know all your faces, Bradford Sims." Delaney's voice rose in excitement, the rich assurance of his power lifting him, drawing him up above all the little people who were files in his vault to be manipulated, to be jerked this way and that; people who, driven by their hormones or unseeing greed, were so stupid as to have given him the weapons he could use against them. Delaney thrust his head back arrogantly. "If I want to know, Sims, I *will* know. It's as simple as that."

"You knew about Isom, didn't you?" Sims asked, deliberately feeding Delaney's megalomania.

Delaney shook his head in mock sympathy. "His death, a pity."

"No, I mean earlier. You knew him in '68, didn't you?" Sims watched as Delaney got a smirk. Yazov followed the conversation with quick movements of his eyes.

"You were Jigtime, weren't you?" Sims asked.

"Ah." Delaney's face wreathed in a smile. "A splendid little ethnic double entendre, hunh?" He waited for Sims's answer. His eyes clouded angrily when Sims didn't answer. "Hunh?" he asked again. Then the eyes cleared as somewhere within him the voice gave him the answer he wanted. He nodded, enjoying himself. "I imagine you immediately jumped to the conclusion that I meant it to be disparaging of those of your color?" Delaney examined Sims's face and imagined his answer there. He nodded victoriously. "Actually, I chose it because of my own Irish heritage."

"And your friend, here?" Sims asked quickly, to keep Delaney going. The rifleman smiled unpleasantly.

"Ah, yes, Viktor Petrovich Yazov. Colonel-General, Russian Foreign Intelligence Service." Delaney paused, and on cue Yazov gave a slight mocking bow. "My own contribution toward a closer working relationship between Washington and Moscow. We joined forces after the unfortunate fire in Atlanta. We realized we had a mutual interest in tracking you down." Delaney pointed to the unconscious man. "At last, my long-lost friend Raoul."

Sims saw the look in Yazov's eye, the way the Russian kept shifting his hands on the Armalite rifle, and desperately sought some way to play for time.

"When he showed up and proposed killing King, you saw a way to win all the way around, didn't you?"

Delaney's momentarily puzzled look was replaced by a sly smile. "Go on," he said, relaxing ever so slightly, as if in anticipation of a moment's enjoyment.

Sims watched Delaney take a step forward and remeasured the distance between the two of them. With the cuffs binding his arms behind him, the calculating part of him worked on how he could somehow get Delaney between himself and the goddamn Russian. At the same time he struggled to bottle up the fear that screamed about the uselessness of it all.

"Yes, you were going to win all the way around, weren't you?" Sims repeated, taking a small step toward Delaney, as if to talk more easily. The Russian didn't move, but the Armalite's muzzle seemed to have dropped a degree or two and Sims was certain the Russian was distracted by the conversation.

"Tell me how," Delaney teased.

"It must have occurred to you when Isom warned Washington that Barrineau had let a contract on King. You told Washington you'd stopped it, but you let it go ahead."

"Why would I do that?"

"Officially, the Bureau couldn't countenance killing King. But unofficially you knew Hoover wanted King gone. And you could hang the killing on Barrineau so you'd get credit for hunting down King's redneck killers." Sims watched as Delaney's smile grew wider. "And," he finished, "your stock with Hoover would go up for putting the whole package together."

"Very good, Sims." Delaney said it with an arrogant lordly tone.

"But it didn't work out that way."

Delaney made a dismissing gesture with the pistol, taking it off Sims. "It worked well enough."

"It left loose ends," Sims taunted. "Ray—"

"He was too stupid to see what was going on."

"He gave you a pretty good run."

"Luck," Delaney countered.

"But then there was Barrineau. Since you weren't able to get rid of him, that left him with a hold over you. What'd you do?" Sims guessed. "Get him a new identity? Put him in the witness protection program?"

"Are you finished?" Delaney asked, his voice jittery with anticipation.

Sims saw the Russian bring the rifle up. Sims nodded toward Raoul, lying in the snow. "You know he just wasn't some goof-ball friend of Ray's who offered to do a job for sixty thousand."

"Oh?" Delaney's eyebrows rose. Sims stepped closer as he nodded again at Raoul. Delaney was now partially hiding the Russian with the Armalite.

"His real name's Sanchez. He's had more names than Liz Taylor had husbands," Sims said. "He's a professional. The army thinks he died in Korea forty years ago." Sims shuffled another fraction of an inch. Delaney was now squarely between him and the Russian.

Delaney stood considering Raoul, head cocked. It seemed to Sims as if the FBI director was listening to some inner voice. Sims tensed, coiling his leg muscles. Butt Delaney. Jump over him. Give the Russian a groin kick or shoulder under the chin. Sprint for the woods and hope he could outrun the Armalite.

Just then Delaney looked to Yazov. "We must be going." He stepped aside, back out of Sims's range and clearing a shot for the Russian. Delaney pointed to the still unconscious Raoul. "We shall take him with us."

Sims knew that Delaney had decided it was over. His chest tightened and he had to fight the temptation to gasp deeply. "There'll be questions."

"Questions?" Delaney raised his eyebrows in mock surprise. "Why, *certainly* there'll be questions." He giggled dementedly and put on his superior smirk. "You should know about *questions,* Mr. Sims. Those who really count in this world aren't going to answer." He shrugged, disdain on his face. "And as long as that's so, little people can ask all they want." He turned to the Russian. "Viktor—"

Yazov's eyes glistened, then, with the sound of a ripe melon smashing, the top of his head vaporized in a red spray. Delaney spun around as Yazov crumpled to the ground. The FBI director's body spasmed violently, doubled over by an invisible fist. He staggered, then jerked upright. One wobbly leg twisted, throwing him toward Sims. It was a disjointed movement, and Delaney became a marionette whose strings had suddenly been cut. He opened his mouth to shout, but no sound came. There was another smacking sound and Delaney was hit again, this time in the back. He lurched crazily forward, arms outstretched, falling face first into the snow.

Handcuffed, Sims stood facing into the silent woods. To his left and downhill was the frozen stream and Houghton. Yazov and Delaney lay side by side immediately in front of him, their blood darkening the snow around them. Off to his right, Raoul moaned, unable to do anything except lie in the snow and clutch himself.

"Well, Raoul," Sims said, watching four men coming toward them out of the treeline a hundred yards away. "There's more company."

The leading three moved easily, spaced around the fourth in an infantry patrol's diamond formation. Sims saw they carried rifles. The fourth man appeared unarmed, and picked his way through the snow slowly, with some difficulty.

Ten yards away, the men stopped. The point man advanced, and Sims saw that he carried an army carbine with a folding stock, a low-power scope, and an elongated silencer. The man circled behind Sims, coming close enough for Sims to see the smooth Asian face.

Sims felt hands checking his handcuffs, then jerking him back into a squatting position. Off balance, he tumbled butt-first onto the snow. He looked around. The Asian was prodding Raoul, digging his toe into the moaning man's ribs. Soon Raoul was sitting up.

The other two riflemen joined with the point man to encircle Sims and Raoul. The fourth man, the one who had moved so slowly, came directly to Sims. Closer, Sims saw that the man was much older than the other three. The man squatted in front of Sims. His eyes were serious and liquid black and he wore a Cossack-style fur hat. The black eyes examined Sims's face.

"I am Pham Ngo Thach," he announced. He stood, and bent over to take Sims's elbow in a surprisingly strong grip. Sims struggled to get his feet beneath him.

"*Cứu tôi vó'i*," Thach ordered, and the nearest rifleman rushed over to help Sims to his feet. Motioning for Sims to follow, Thach walked several yards away from Raoul and his guards.

Thach perched on a stump, pointing to another nearby. "Sit down."

Sims sat. The Vietnamese seemed to be waiting for him to say something, so Sims said the first thing that came to his mind.

"They were going to kill me."

Thach reached into his heavy jacket and came up with a pack of Salems. He offered and Sims shook his head. Thach lit his cigarette. He inhaled deeply, then exhaled, savoring the medicinal smoke. His eyes followed the smoke into the sky, then turned toward Sims. "They would kill the wrong one."

Sims tried to make sense of it, but couldn't. "Why are you here?"

"The same in a way as these." Thach pointed to Yazov and Delaney. "To stop you."

"That only leads to another why."

Thach inhaled again, looking over at Raoul, then back to Sims. "I don't suppose it matters anymore," he said to the wind. He leaned forward, resting his elbows on his knees. "In 1966, I was chief of operations of the Central Research Bureau."

Sims nodded his understanding. The Central Research Bureau was Hanoi's KGB.

"American troops were pouring into South Vietnam. The tide of the war was turning against us. We developed a plan to drive the Americans out. I knew we couldn't defeat the Americans in set-piece battles. They were too strong. So the plan would have to rely on massive psychological pressures to cause the Americans to abandon the effort.

"At first, nothing went well. But then we found the key in Prague. The KGB had a front organization—"

"The Afro-Asian Solidarity Committee," Sims supplied.

"Yes." Thach nodded. "We had representatives in it. We learned that your FBI had embarked on an extensive program to harass the civil rights activists such as Dr. King. On this information, we built a plan we called Le Loi."

"Lee—" Sims frowned.

"Le Loi was a Vietnamese folk hero who drove out vastly superior Chinese invaders in the fifteenth century. The Le Loi plan was built on two hammer blows. The first was to discredit your Pentagon and its claims of military progress, to make the war seem unwinnable. That hammer blow was the Tet Offensive."

Tet. February 1968. The Vietnamese lunar new year festival when the North Vietnamese army swarmed out of the jungles to overrun American strongholds and Vietnam's largest cities. The shock had crushed America's political will. Having proclaimed that there was a light at the end of the tunnel, having told America's mothers and fathers that fifty thousand of their sons had died for freedom on nameless hills and in forgotten valleys of South Vietnam, having said all these things, the generals could not explain why suddenly they were fighting rearguard actions in the streets of Saigon, Hue, and Danang.

"And the second of your hammer blows?" Sims asked, knowing what it would be.

"To ignite a race war inside America." Thach took a last drag on his cigarette, squinting at Sims through the smoke. "To tear at America from within, we killed Dr. King."

Sims felt a molten wave of pain and anger. "You bastards," he cursed.

Thach ignored him. "We aimed for nothing less than all-out armed warfare between blacks and whites."

Armed warfare it had been, Sims thought. But his father had been killed, and Rollo Moss, his father's partner, wounded, not by the guns of whites, but of blacks. "That didn't happen."

"But there were—dividends?—yes, dividends. We forced your president, Lyndon Johnson, out of office. We convinced television actors like your Cronkite that the war was futile. And we ultimately drove you out of Vietnam. We would have gotten you out faster if the rest of Le Loi had worked."

"Which was?"

Thach motioned to Raoul. "Our friend Raoul was a key actor. He had been taken prisoner in Korea. In China, he—how do you say it?—turned coats?" Thach looked inquiringly at Sims. Seeing Sims nod, Thach continued. "Yes. He offered to work for the Chinese. After suitable training and indoctrination, our Chinese friends used him on missions requiring a Caucasian. He performed admirably. When we needed a Caucasian for Le Loi, Peking offered us his services."

"Services?" Sims saw Raoul lying listening, his eyes open, his face flat and stonelike.

"Yes. He found a suitable subject—James Earl Ray—and began building a trail of evidence."

"Barrineau said Raoul came up with the idea to kill King. It was all a setup to frame the FBI for King's death, wasn't it?"

"As you've seen, it wasn't that difficult. We only had to take advantage of what they were already doing. The FBI was conducting all manner of illegal activities. They had written letters threatening King's life. They had tapped his telephones and bugged his conversations. A killing would be quite plausible, don't you think? And don't you think that if the FBI had been caught red-handed it would have caused a racial war in America?"

It damn sure could have, Sims admitted to himself. "What went wrong?"

"Raoul was to have killed King. Then he was to have staged an accidental death for Ray, leaving evidence that implicated Ray. From Ray the trail would have led straight to St. Louis to Barrineau and to his relationship with the FBI through Delaney and the other man, Isom. That trail was interrupted."

"Because you lost Ray. You weren't able to kill him."

"Yes. We had furnished him the Toronto identities. But Raoul wasn't supposed to let Ray get out of Memphis alive to use them. So when

Raoul lost him in Memphis, we surmised he'd go to Toronto. But Raoul was unable to find him. It was only later that we learned Barrineau had moved Ray to another rooming house."

"But the Russians also wanted to kill Ray."

"They were concerned, like your FBI, that a detailed investigation might blame them for the killing, since they, too, had been stirring the pot."

Sims saw it clearly now, chillingly so. "We all contributed to it. Everybody set up King for you. All you had to do was pull the trigger, step back, and let the investigation follow your trail back."

Thach nodded. "Oddly enough, the fool Ray came closest to the truth."

Sims saw that Thach was looking at Raoul. "So after Raoul lost Ray, Raoul became part of the problem," Sims guessed.

Thach nodded. "Yes. He ran. It was too difficult for us to find him in America."

"Until I led you to him."

"Yes."

"You knew were Raoul had been, all the places he'd lived, all the people he'd gotten to know. You watched a place on the trail he'd laid twenty years ago."

"And you and your friend came looking for him and we followed you."

"Where'd you pick us up?"

"At the old woman's house in St. Louis."

Thach looked at his watch. "Our time is going away." He got up from his seat on the stump. At this, two of the riflemen hoisted Raoul to his feet. The man with the silenced carbine waved it menacingly at Sims. Walking to within arm's reach of Raoul, Thach reached into his jacket and came out with a small snub-nosed revolver.

Raoul was worn down from years of watching, fearing, running. He looked at Sims with a dispirited weariness.

"No," he muttered, flat and without hope. It was the only word Sims had heard him speak. Then Thach shot him through the head.

Sims closed his eyes and saw the videotape of the Saigon police chief summarily executing a captured terrorist; the head jolting, the eyes involuntary flinching, the eruption of bone, blood, and brains. Here in northern Missouri he had witnessed the last shot of the Vietnam War.

Thach said something in Vietnamese and one of the riflemen began searching Delaney's body. Finding the key, the rifleman squatted behind Sims and unlocked the handcuffs. Sims stood, rubbing the blood back into his stinging wrists and hands.

Thach pointed down the hill to the stream, then toward the north. "We are leaving this way to avoid Delaney's men." It was an invitation.

"You're letting me live?"

Thach shrugged. "There is no reason for more killing. You have no proofs, no nothing, Ông Sims. You have only a story. And many people tell stories. There is a Vietnamese saying that the tongue, having no bones, may be twisted in any direction."

Sims stood for a moment. Raoul's rifle caught his eye. For a reason he would never be able to explain to himself, he picked it up and slung it over his shoulder.

At the foot of the hill, the Vietnamese waited while Sims scrambled down the embankment of the frozen stream.

Houghton's body lay sprawled on the ice, even more lifeless than when Sims had left him, and it came back to Sims—the unreality that constantly circled back on itself, gathering momentum and renewing its ability to shock—Houghton was dead.

A cold vacantness enfolded Sims when he thought about the cosmic injustice of it, that Houghton had come this far without finding out what had set him up so long ago so that he would die here in this fucking place. Sims looked up into the empty gray sky, wanting to shake his fist at God.

He picked up Houghton and carried him to the bank and propped the body against a tree where it would be found. He took Houghton's wallet with its false identity documentation. Tearing a sheet from his pocket notebook, he wrote EDWARD CAMERON HOUGHTON in block letters, and beneath it, CIA, Washington, D.C., 20505. He tucked the notebook page down the front of Houghton's shirt. Still kneeling, he brushed Houghton's tousled hair with his hand, then leaned forward and kissed the dead man's forehead. The Vietnamese were now dark figures at the fringe of the forest.

"Come, Ông Sims." Thach's voice floated back to him. "It is time to move on."

"Yes," Sims said to Houghton, then got up, and, the rifle over his shoulder, followed the men into the forest.

EPILOGUE

Washington, D.C.
Thursday, March 12, 1992

Sims walked slowly down the hill, keeping to the side of a narrow asphalt roadway that led away from Houghton's grave. Behind him, he heard voices, the whine of Alberich's wheelchair, and the chunking sounds of car doors shutting. Everything was muffled, like all sounds in cemeteries. The cold mist shrouded Arlington Ridge, softening the angles and lines of the Lincoln Memorial and the Washington Monument across the river. With quick, angular efficiency, the honor guard had folded Houghton's flag into a tricorn, and the tall young captain in charge had presented it to Sims. Sims now carried the flag in the crook of his arm, clutching the last of Houghton close to his chest.

The first limousine passed slowly by, and inside he saw the raised hand of the Judge, skin shaded yellow-green by the armor plate glass. The Judge had arranged for the burial at Arlington and for the Intelligence Cross that had accompanied Houghton beneath the red Virginia clay. As Sims rounded a curve, the southeast slope of the cemetery spread out before him, even ranks of white military headstones marking time for eternity.

The second limousine stopped. Calvin Harris got out and waved the car on and stood waiting beside the road, great in his overcoat and soft-brimmed hat. As Sims passed, Harris wordlessly fell into step beside him. They walked in silence for perhaps half a mile in the dying afternoon, stopping as if by mutual agreement at a stone pathway. To their left and somewhat above them the Kennedy gravesite bore its burden, lit by its eternal flame. On their right the Potomac and a soldierly file of the Lincoln Memorial, Washington

299

Monument, and Capitol dome. The light in the dome was on. Congress was still in session.

Harris looked out over the city, then shook his head. "Hard to believe they could cover it up." Yesterday's news: FBI director found dead in his Watergate apartment. The *Post* had carried a sidebar that described the tearful reaction of Special Agent Timothy Nicholas, who had found Delaney.

Sims made a cynical grimace. "A middle-aged man with a bad heart. I imagine Raoul's obituary said something about a tragic hunting accident." Sims watched the low clouds drop to hide the top of the Washington Monument. Yazov? They'd probably dumped the body on the embassy steps to let the Russian ambassador take care of it. He turned to his uncle. "You going down to Sandston now?"

Harris shook his head. "Not just yet. Got a few chores to see to while I'm up here," he said, using his preacher's patriarch voice.

Sims continued to stare at the city. I could just as well stand here forever, he was thinking, not wanting just then to get on with things. Down below, he saw the Judge's black limousine wheel slowly out of Arlington's gates. Harris followed Sims's gaze and saw the limousine, too.

"And the Judge," Harris said softly. "A man on the road to Damascus."

Riddle had read Houghton's citation as the Judge stood by the casket. And after, the Judge had led Sims a few steps away, and they had stood together on the damp gray-green grass, heads bowed toward each other in private conversation. Cantwell was gone, the Judge said, having left for the good of the service. There's always a place for you, the Judge murmured, letting the offer hang. Sims had made appropriate appreciative sounds, but nothing committal. The Judge seemed vaguely disappointed, and then the two men shook hands, clumsy and self-conscious because they knew the others were watching.

"You think you'll go back?"

"No." Sims watched the Judge's car. It was now on the Memorial Bridge, heading straight toward the Lincoln Memorial. "Not now, anyway. I still have some money. I'm going to travel." He pulled his coat closer against the damp. "I think to Italy."

The guard rapped softly on the door, then opened it in response to the muffled voice inside.

Dimitri Aristov reclined in the leather lounge chair, the IV bottle hooked to his right arm. He held a cigarette in his left hand and the smoke of it made a wreath around his head.

He waved Sergei Okolovich in and motioned to the guard. "Leave us."

"But—"

"And close the door."

Okolovich stood just inside the door, uncertain whether to be fearful or angry. His silver hair was still carefully combed into its impressively thick mane, but the ill-fitting prison jacket and trousers diminished him and drew attention to the impending frailty of age.

"I don't understand, Dimitri."

Aristov gestured to the desk. "I have finished the reading." A three-ring binder lay open to the first of perhaps a hundred pages, some of which had been marked by paper clips. A pair of army issue reading glasses on the desk stared emptily, catching the images of the windows and turning them upside down.

Okolovich had to sidle past Aristov to get to the desk. He took particular care to avoid brushing the IV stand with its tubing and glass bottle, involuntarily tightening his body, as if the slightest touch might infect him.

Standing behind the desk, Okolovich took in the ornate title page. Red, blue, and white flags framed the latest coat of arms of the Commonwealth of Independent States. Eyes only, proclaimed the grandiose Cyrillic calligraphy, For the Chief of Staff of the Office of the President of Russia.

"Impressive, isn't it?" Aristov said, closing his eyes and feeling the slight stinging of the needle in his arm. "How the ferrets pretty up such things. Looks like one of those illuminated proclamations a czar would read."

Okolovich turned the page, the stiff paper making a dry fluttering sound.

"It's an auditor's report, Sergei," Aristov explained in a tired, captured voice, his eyes still closed.

Okolovich saw the dated columns, the entries beginning in 1965. He had a sensation of dematerializing as he began to understand the meaning of the numbers.

"A long trail of money." Aristov's voice took on a hollow tone. "From Moscow to the Cayman Islands and from there to our friends in America."

Okolovich turned the pages. He had thought the watertight compartments he had built would last forever, at the least all his lifetime.

Now all the walls were down and any spindly accountant could fit the pieces together.

"You did quite well for yourself over the years, Sergei. As Center paymaster you took special pains to make certain that the Afro-Asian Solidarity Committee was well funded, and after that, the activities of your friend Broz in Prague. Your enthusiasm for financial operations got you to the top of the KGB. It also got you a number of very plump accounts in Vienna and Lucerne." Aristov dragged deeply on his cigarette and exhaled, watching the smoke drift toward the ceiling.

Okolovich started to protest, then gave it up. He had only done what others before him had done. He had been a good Communist. But those days were over.

Aristov pressed a small buzzer by the arm of his chair. The guard opened the door. Aristov looked at Okolovich with pitying contempt.

"Good-bye, Sergei."

Donald Stanley unlocked the two dead bolts, then punched his combination into the alarm system keypad just inside his front door. Though just behind the Library of Congress, Stanley's block had increasingly become a preserve of derelicts, panhandlers, and thieves. Only the week before, a congressional staffer had been held up by two men and a woman. One of the robbers, after taking the man's billfold and watch, then jammed the barrel of a pistol to his victim's head and pulled the trigger. Stanley started to bolt the door.

"Come on in, Donald. And leave off the lights."

Stanley felt as if a massive hand had clutched his heart and plunged it into ice water.

"I seem to think better in the dark, Donald."

Though paralyzed by fear, a small corner of Stanley's brain nonetheless worked on recognizing the voice. "Calvin? Calvin Harris?" Stanley's eyes, now adjusting to the dark, made out a bulking shadow in the armchair by the fireplace.

"Take a chair, Donald. I want to try out my thinking on you."

"How'd you get in?" Stanley asked, relief giving way to growing anger.

Harris ignored him. "One thing I've been thinking about, Donald, is my nephew Bradford. How he got followed to that hilltop in Missouri."

"Calvin!" Stanley tried and failed to make it a command.

"He thought he was running free," Harris went on, as if telling an innocent story, "but somehow Delaney got back onto his trail."

"Delaney? He died of a heart attack."

Harris laughed contemptuously, and the laugh chilled Stanley. "Come *on*, Donald. You know better." Harris returned to his story-telling voice. "Anyway, imagine this, Donald: Delaney *did* lose Bradford, but he picked him up again when *you* called for that meeting." Harris paused. "You set Bradford up, Donald."

"Why would I do that?"

"Because, Donald, Delaney told you to. He told you and you did it. Delaney had you like he had others. Like we all used to say that Hoover had people."

"No!" Stanley protested, his voice dry and cracked.

"Remember the old days, Donald?" Harris said with a touch of nostalgia. "You were our bright young theoretician, the firebrand with the international connections to the world's oppressed. Connections in Algiers, Kinshasa, Hanoi. Always preaching the revolution. The 'revo,' didn't you call it?

"Yes," Harris answered himself. "The revo. Always pushing against Martin, laughing at nonviolence."

"Please, Calvin, it's not—"

"Let me finish, Donald. So the KGB was looking for somebody close to Martin to give their dirty money to." Harris paused. "And they found you, didn't they, Donald?"

"You can't prove—"

Harris rolled inexorably over Stanley. "And then, to incite Hoover, the KGB let the FBI know." The voice became a thundering accusation. "Your little Marxist revo friends betrayed you, Donald. They turned you over to the man! That's how Delaney got his hooks into you."

"No-no-no-no," Stanley voice climbed the register.

"Shut up, Donald, I'm not finished. Even you don't know the worst of what you did. There was a tape . . ." Harris described the tape, the voices, the schedule. "Bradford's friend identified Delaney's voice from the tape. But he couldn't identify the other one. But I know who it was, Donald. It was you."

Harris sat quietly in the darkness. The room was still, and the only sound was a distant siren.

"You see, Donald, the voice on the tape said a man named Solomon Jones would drive Martin that next night. It was a long time ago, Donald. And my memory . . . It took me a time to work it out. But it came out like this: You were the person who made the arrangements. You were the only person that night who knew about Solomon Jones."

303

Harris drew a deep breath and pronounced sentence. "You gave Delaney Martin's schedule. The Kluxers got it and passed it to the man who killed Martin."

Stanley laughed mockingly. "That's all bullshit, Calvin. You got nothing. Nobody's going to believe you."

"I believe it," Harris said.

"So do I," came a voice from a deeper shadow in the corner opposite Harris.

Harris rose from his chair and the light from the shuttered window cast slotted shadows across his face. He nodded to the shadow in the corner. "Donald Stanley, meet Rollo Moss." Harris walked past Stanley, who was still sitting in his chair. He opened the front door and looked back into the dark room. "Good night, Donald," he said, closing the door.

Gander, Newfoundland
Thursday, March 12, 1992

At 41,000 feet over the North Atlantic, Tom Farmer estimated his time of arrival in Moscow, then checked it against the Gulfstream's computers. The times matched within seconds. Farmer smiled, then made his way from the cockpit back to his cabin.

In seconds, he was deep in the butter-soft leather folds of his lounge chair, savoring a Danish beer. Farmer pressed a button, and a television monitor obediently replayed his latest victory.

One member of Congress after another came up to the floor microphone, each making excuses for bouncing hundreds of checks drawn on the House bank. Finally, the Speaker of the House gaveled an end to the spectacle and grandly announced that the Congress would permit the American taxpayers to know the names of the miscreants.

Farmer enjoyed the scene. Congress had been so worried about voters' reaction to the check-bouncing scandal that the Russian aid bill had sailed stealthily through with no debate and almost no opposition.

Farmer drank deeply, enjoying the clean coldness of the beer. Things had worked out very well. He could breathe easier, now that Delaney was gone. It had always been an uneasy partnership, each fearing exposure by the other. And Warren Kaiser was another relieved man tonight. Farmer raised his mug in a mock toast to the White